Well of Bones

Well of Bones

Revealing Hidden Secrets

K.A. Hudson

Arrowsmith Publishing

 A catalogue record for this book is available from the National Library of Australia

ISBN: 978-0-6452708-2-2 (Paperback)
ISBN: 978-0-6452718-3-9 (Ebook)

Printed & Channel Distribution: Lightning Source | Ingram (USA/UK/EUROPE/AUS)
Cover Designed—Laila Savolainen, Pickawoowoo Publishing Group
Editing—Eddie Albrecht, Pickawoowoo Publishing Group
Publishing Consultants/Interior Design—Pickawoowoo Publishing Group
Arrowsmith Publishing: www.arrowsmithpublishing.com.au
About the author: https://kerriehudsonauthor.wixsite.com/website-1
For enquiries, write to: rights and permissions via publisher.

Dedicated to my wonderful family,
Dreams are free – the rewarding part is
making them reality.
Thank you for your love and support in
making my dreams a reality.

PROLOGUE

Kelly Creek Roadhouse was dry, dusty and hot. As far as Annalisa was concerned it had only two redeeming features: a cool, shady veranda, and a clean public toilet. Both were perfect for her needs as she waited for the next ride to come along. She sat perched on a hard-plastic chair with her sore, tired feet propped up on top of a well-travelled backpack and wondered how many more hours she'd be stuck in this uninspiring backwater. Who knew such places even existed. Nothing in her urban German upbringing had prepared her for the experience of the harsh and arid Australian Outback. And the dirt! Bull dust they called it. Its powdery red texture resembled talcum powder and clung to everything. The lightest footstep or the softest breeze was enough to create cloying dust swirls that settled on the moisture of her body and left her feeling grimy. Her sneakers with their white laces and silver Nike tick had taken on the colour of the surrounding landscape, rusty iron red.

Annalisa sighed. Hitchhiking was always a game of patience, even for a young, good looking woman like herself. The people she'd encountered in Australia were happy-go-lucky and friendly, and even though she was travelling alone, she'd felt safe. Until last night, that is. That had been a little different from her usual experiences. On the outskirts of Broome in Western Australia's Kimberley region, she'd encountered Harold, a sweaty, middle-aged man who carried a layer of fat around his middle that he jokingly called his spare tyre. He seemed a friendly man, full of wit and interesting tit-bits about the region. As they rattled along in his Suzuki utility with its double cab and alloy tray she'd settled back to listen to his idle and amusing chatter while enjoying the unusual scenery as it flashed past her window. The distance from civilisation grew as they headed along a quiet highway towards Mount Ibour. The sun set behind them and the tone of Harold's conversation and jokes changed to include innuendos of sex. She shuddered to think of it, because as he spoke, Harold's chapped and calloused hand had drifted from its resting place on the gear stick to her knee. She'd shoved it away and moved her legs closer to the passenger door to keep them out of his reach. Harold's arm seemed to be made of elastic and had no prob-lem reaching across and finding her knee again. She tried ignoring it, but his hand sliding up the inside of her leg towards her crotch was the last straw.

'Harold, if you don't remove your hand right now, I am going to stab it with my pocket knife.'

Her bluff worked. Harold snatched his hand away.

'Now don't be like that, little lady. I was just being friendly.'

'I don't find being pawed by you friendly.'

He'd muttered something under his breath, but kept both hands on the steering wheel. Just as well – five minutes later, they ran over something on the road. The car fishtailed slightly before Harold regained full control of the vehicle. He eased his speed, pulled over to the side of the road and got out.

He kicked the front tyre on the driver's side and called out to her. 'You might as well get out and stretch your legs. It's gonna to take me a while to change the flat.'

Harold came back to the cab and reached into the pocket of his door and pulled out a torch. He shuffled around to the rear of the vehicle and began fossicking around in a metal toolbox on the tray.

He pulled out a jack and sat it on the bitumen before leaning back in to dig around some more. Annalisa got out and took advantage of the break. She ducked into the bushes to find a spot to relieve herself. She was still squatting with her shorts scrunched around her knees when she heard the vehicle drive away. Annalisa scurried back to the roadside and discovered Harold had driven off without her.

'*Hurensohn*,' she yelled after the departed car. 'I bet that tyre was not even flat.' If her *mutter* had heard her swearing she would've given her a tongue lashing, but her parent wasn't here, so Annalisa let out the curse word at the bastard who had left her stranded in the middle of the Australian Outback.

She groaned, wondering how many kilometres she'd have to walk to the nearest town? Snatching up a small stone, she hurled it after the long-departed Harold and yelled more rude words into the night. To alleviate her anger Annalisa stomped along the edge of the road, slamming her feet down in temper and stumbled over the strap of her backpack. Harold had tossed it into the middle of a spiny-leafed bush. Cursing him further, Annalisa carefully fished her backpack out of the spiky spinifex plant. Well at least he hadn't driven off with her gear.

The night was aglow with a ghostly silver light shed by a bright full moon. Visibility was good and it meant she needn't waste the batteries in her torch. Annalisa trudged along the asphalt praying for another car to come along. The bitumen road ticked and crackled as it radiated the heat it had absorbed from the day's fierce sun, the warmth it emitted warding off any chill. Scurrying noises coming from the bushes beside the road worried her. Annalisa quickened her step. Everyone knew Australia has some of the deadliest reptiles in the world and she didn't want one to leap out of the dark at her. She kept up the fast pace until the first light of dawn peeped over the horizon. In the daylight things looked better. By the time the sun had cleared the distant hills she'd spotted Kelly Creek Roadhouse. Throughout her long night-time trek there had been no passing vehicles and as Annalisa staggered into the café she vowed she was going to stick to hitching rides with truck drivers from now on. They'd always been willing to offer a comfortable seat in exchange for her company and the drivers had always acted honourably.

Annalisa was fit but the long walk had taken its toll and she was weary. So for now she was happy to sit in the shade and wait. According to Stacy, the woman who worked at the roadhouse, the regular Broome to Mount Ibour freight truck came through every second day. Annalisa had missed the last one by twelve hours. Another was due again late tomorrow afternoon. In the meantime there'd be other opportunities for a ride. The usually quiet road was busy at the moment because cattle trucks were taking stock to the abattoirs. There had been an upsurge in the beef market and Mount Ibour Abattoirs, known locally as MIA, had geared up for the influx as the surrounding cattle stations took advantage of the best market prices in two years.

'The drivers call in regularly to fill up on the Roadhouse special – The Humungous,' Stacy announced with a half-smile on her chubby face. 'A steak burger with two thick fillets of steak, a ton of fried onions, eggs and bacon dripping with melted cheese and sauce. You need to dislocate your jaw to take a bite. Which isn't a problem for the guys around here, being they have such big gobs anyway?' She chuckled so hard at her own joke the loose skin under her chin wobbled. 'Do you want one?' she asked.

Annalisa smiled and shook her head. She studied the chalkboard above the counter and settled on a ham sandwich and coffee.

While Stacy wrapped her purchase in a piece of white paper she announced, 'I'll check with the blokes when they come in, see if one can give you a lift. That's if something else doesn't come along first, of course. Take a pew out on the veranda, where it's cool. You'll be able to see the road from there.'

'Thank you, Stacey.' Annalisa was grateful for her friendly help and went outside to sit and wait.

A bush fly tried to settle on her face. Irritated, she impatiently brushed it away. The movement dislodged a swarm of flies that had taken root on her arm. Startled, they took flight and started a game of find the moisture on her brow. One fly even buzzed the inside of her ear lobe. She scrunched her shoulder and used it to rub the annoying bastard away.

Bloody hell! She gave a chuckle. She'd only been in Australia four months and she was already swearing like one, she'll have to watch herself when she returned home to Munich. Annalisa smiled and settled back into her chair to sit as still as a statue and allowed the flies to resettle on her bare arms and her light blue tee-shirt. It was too hot, even for them, to play the game for any length of time.

With a slow careful movement Annalisa eased a map from the back pocket of her shorts, unfolded it and spread it across her lap. She began to study the region and found Kelly Creek. It was a tiny dot in a vast expanse of what looked like nothing. Using her fingertip, she traced a pale red line and calculated the distance north to Mount Ibour. It was approximately two hundred kilometres. Much too far for her to walk in this heat. According to the chalkboard outside the dining room, today's day-time temperature was predicted to reach at least 38 degrees Celsius. No, she'd just sit and wait to see what came along.

Annalisa returned the map to her pocket and pulled out her mobile phone. There was no signal. She sighed. She would have to text her mother later when she got to Mount Ibour. Annalisa slid her seat further back as the shade moved with the advancing morning sun and closed her eyes to doze. A warm puff of air, carrying the unique scent of the bush, played across her sweaty brow, but sleep eluded her. It had been like that for two weeks now, ever since she'd had the big bust-up with Stefan. Her gut was still churning with anger as she remembered the years she had wasted on loving someone who always put his own addiction first. His latest stint in rehab seemed to have worked and he had been more like the Stefan she'd fallen in love with. When they'd first arrived in Perth they'd had a wonderful time travelling around the city, taking in the sights and checking out the night life. Then Stefan began to fob off any discussions of travel plans to see the rest of Western Australia by saying he had a job. Her money rapidly dwindled and Annalisa saw no evidence of Stefan's income. In fact he kept helping himself to her cash, promising to give it back when he got paid. He also promised that they would move on, go north, where there was work for both of them, at the end of the month. But it turned out he'd been lying. She caught him using drugs at a Perth nightclub. Annalisa had blown her stack. But how can you reason with someone who was so stoned out of their brain they would just stare at you and say stupid things like, *whatever*! So she'd told him to shove it and left him standing like the idiot he was at the club entrance and hurried back to their hostel. She had texted her mother and explained Stefan had broken the promise he'd made to her and his own family to stay clean. She had no problem asking her mother to inform Stefan's family he was using again and they needed to come get him. His family lived on the same street in Munich as her mother and were lifetime friends. Annalisa had put up with a lot from Stefan over the years and had tried her best to help him but she'd finally had enough. Leaving him was the best thing she could do for herself. I bet Mrs Shultz will send Stefan's brother, Gunter, to Perth to hold his hand and help him through another stint of rehab. Gunter as usual would blame Annalisa – Stefan could do no wrong in Gunter's eyes. All the while he would insist she do the bulk of the work in caring for both brothers. Well, she wasn't going to stick around to nursemaid either of them. Stefan was a grown man who'd made his choice not to stop the drug spiral he was on, all the while sucking the life from everyone around him as he destroyed his life. Without looking back, Annalisa had packed up her possessions, taken the last of their money and hightailed it out of Perth heading north.

She'd received a text from her *mutter* early yesterday morning.

I am so proud of you my Annalisa. Leaving was the right thing to do. Go out into the world and enjoy yourself. In your travels you may even find a good man, one worthy of your love. Ich liebe dich das Muttertier.

Annalisa felt the weight of guilt lift from her chest and immediately texted her mother back.

I love you too mutter.

Her mother's words of love and support had helped ease some of her pain.

The hum of tyres on asphalt grew louder. Annalisa opened her eyes and watched as a silver four-wheel-drive slowed down before pulling off the main road and rolling to a stop in the shade of a tree growing next to the rest rooms. The car was so clean it sparkled in the bright sunshine. She rose to her feet and walked to the end of the porch to watch the driver dash into the toilet block.

She waited, the driver came out. Annalisa continued to stare. Acknowledgement came with the nod of a head and a smile. She quickly hitched her pack onto her shoulders and noticed the German flag badge sewn on one of its straps had taken on the colour of the Outback.

The driver climbed back into the silver car. Annalisa quickened her step. The driver's electric window hummed as it rolled down.

The occupant said in a soft voice, 'Hi there. Where are you off to?'

Having difficulty hearing Annalisa leant forward with her forearms on the roof of the car and her head just inside the driver's window.

'Hello, my name is Annalisa. I am hoping for a lift to Mount Ibour before I melt in this heat.' It's always good to let a driver know that you are hot. They may take pity and put on the air-conditioning. 'Are you going...'

A semi-trailer snatched at her words as it rolled past. The trailers on the vehicle rattled and banged as the wheels bounced and shuddered along the corrugated dirt strip leading up to the fuel bowsers. Hot dirt, given flight by the tyres and exhaust, swirled around her ankles and bare shins bathing her in a cloud of red dust. The truck's air brakes hissed like a snorting dragon and the truck squealed to a halt. The silence made her ears ring. Annalisa glanced over her shoulder. The semi-trailer looked familiar, just like the one she'd hitched a ride in from Perth. The driver had been really nice – what was his name? Oh that's right, Darryl Harper. His rotund belly had shaken like a bowl of jelly when he laughed. Most of the time he'd worn a baseball cap to cover the bald patch at the front of his hairline that glowed when he sweated. Darryl had entertained her with some fascinating stories about the history of the Broome pearling industry. She had returned the favour by telling him some wickedly funny things that had happened at last year's Munich Oktoberfest. She turned towards the truck, Darryl would see her safely where she wanted to go but paused when the car's driver spoke the magic words and grabbed her attention.

'Jump in. I'm on my way to Mount Ibour. I can give you a ride.'

'*Wunderbar*. Thank you very much,' said Annalisa, giving the driver a happy smile.

Her fingers brushed over the shining Toyota emblem at the back of the vehicle as she lifted the tailgate to sling her backpack inside. It landed next to a large black and yellow plastic toolbox with wheels. Annalisa quick-stepped her way around to the passenger door knowing that drivers could be fickle and quick to change their minds.

As she settled back in the comfortable seat, the driver switched on the air-conditioning, smiled and handed her a bottle of water.

Chapter One

November 2019

The bodies of two young women lay entwined – one was dead, the other hovered on the cusp of consciousness. The ebony skin of the aboriginal girl no longer glowed with health and vitality. Its smooth texture resembled dried matted paint, cracked and peeling from neglect. A layer of fine dust had settled like a lacy web across her distinctive square cheekbones. Fast-moving black and green bush flies ran gleefully along her lifeless limbs, breaking the stillness.

The strawberry-blonde haired woman cradled the girl's lifeless body against her chest, unaware of her fate. A sliver of light cut the gloom in which they lay entombed and revealed pale, bluish-tinged lips, a small straight nose smeared in blood and honey coloured eyelashes. The closed eyelids fluttered for a moment but remained shut. A quiet breath stirred the dust which had settled on the delicate fine hairs just below her nose. The mid-morning light progressed along its path unaffected by the reaction its presence had caused.

Time passed and the next day the sliver of light returned. As the beam pierced the black pool of darkness it touched the woman's pale face. Her eyes opened to reveal startling dark green irises framed by almond-shaped lids. The eyes were the only colour in an otherwise gloomy world. She blinked and her pupils, black and intense, widened to focus on the retreating beam. As the light touched the chocolate brown of the dead girl's eye, it revealed a dull-white film that diminished the colour. The woman held her breath and waited for the girl to react to the light, but her pupils remained fixed, staring at a distant point. The green eyes swam in a pool of tears. She let out a small sob and closed her eyes. A lone tear escaped the corner of her eye and cut a wet trail through the dust and dried blood on her narrow cheek. The tear dripped from her jaw and fell to the ground beside her. Irritated she twitched and rubbed her cheek against the body she was cradling, wiping away its salty wetness.

Opening gritty, sore eyes she studied the world around her. Rising on each side of her were four sandstone walls, rugged and unevenly bricked. They'd been stacked to form a vertical shaft that ended in a square of apricot-tinged blue light, high above. As she stared a small white cloud drifted past her field of vision.

Where the hell am I?

She moved her head to study the floor. The movement stirred up the layer of dust on her cheek. Her nose began to tickle and itch, she sneezed. The sound didn't echo as expected, it just deadened and died. She waited, but there was no response to the noise. She focused her hearing and listened intently but not even a breeze disturbed the quiet. The silence was oppressive and pressed down like a smothering wet blanket. She sucked in a deep breath through her nose and gagged. The smell and taste of death burnt a foul trail down her throat.

The woman eased the girl's body away from her embrace. The movements disturbed a swarm of flies and they took flight. A loud humming filled the air as they formed into a swirling dark cloud, circling in a spiral to ascend halfway up the shaft before descending and resuming their greedy investigations of the body.

The quiet returned.

She sat up and her world began to spin. Bubbles of colour flashed and exploded behind her eyes and a stabbing pain made its presence known at the back of her skull by drumming a ferocious tattoo against its confines. She stuck her smallest finger in her left ear and gave it a wiggle, trying to reduce the loud thump as the blood pulsed past her eardrums making her head pound. The world around her spun, nausea swirled in her stomach and she gave an acidic heave. Reaching out a hand she steadied herself against the stone wall and waited for everything to right itself. When the world came back into focus, she lifted a cautious hand and touched the painful spot at the back of her head. Her fingers jerked when the pain intensified and her eyes blurred once again.

Crap! That hurts.

Her probing fingers touched her hair. It was stiff and matted and hung down in a dried clump like a bamboo curtain. With the back of her hand she lifted the mess and ran a gentle finger along what felt like a jagged gash. She looked at her fingers, no fresh blood tinged them. With infinite care she lifted her hair again and gently pushed at the bone beneath the cut. It didn't crunch or move.

It doesn't feel like my skull's fractured.

She glanced down to where her head had been and saw a piece of brick coated in a dark stain. It was sticky.

I guess that's what's given me the headache.

Pulling her knees towards her chest, she rested her forehead on them and waited for the thumping pain in her head to abate. She dozed off and was rudely awakened when her body toppled sideways. Jerking up straight caused a sharp pain in her neck.

'Crap,' she croaked. A sore, dry throat made swallowing difficult. *Great! Is there any part of me that doesn't hurt?*

Being careful not to injure her battered body further, the woman lowered her head and began to take stock of her woes. Her long, thin legs protruded like matchsticks from plain, black cotton shorts and were covered in small cuts and scratches. Her very pale skin was smeared in red dust. On her feet were yellow ankle socks, the soles of which were also stained a rusty red.

No shoes? How'd that happen?

An inquisitive fly began buzzing around her eyes and nose. Annoyed, she waved her long slender fingers and chased the slow-moving fat insect away. A flash of colour on her arm caught her gaze. She examined her left arm. A trail of livid jagged scars ran along it. They glowed like silver in the gloom. She studied the marks, tracing her finger along the old injuries, trying to recall their history.

Nothing – her mind was engulfed in a silent grey static.

She glanced at her companion and her heart twisted in pain. The girl looked to be around twenty years of age and had the most beautiful face. Leaning forward she brushed the writhing gluttonous yellow maggots away from the staring eyes and placed two fingers to the side of the girl's throat to check for a pulse. The action only confirmed what she already knew from the smell. Death has a distinctive sickening odour. Her movements stirred up a wave of rancid air. The smell grabbed her in the back of the throat and she gagged. To reduce her reaction to the smell she took small shallow breaths through her mouth, pinched her nose and ran gentle fingers over the girl's eyelids to close them. She sighed as a wave of sadness washed through her like a river of water sliding down a pane of glass.

I can't leave her exposed like this. I need to cover her.

She cast her glance around but it was too dark to see anything clearly, so she ran her fingers over the surrounding hard-packed dirt floor, searching for some sort of clothing to cover the girl's naked-ness. Her hand found a bulging smooth surface. She paused and with investigative palms traced a globe-shape with something like wool attached to its surface. It was loose so she picked it up to take a closer look.

'Shit...,' the word exploded from her mouth. She fumbled the globe. It fell from her fingertips and hit the floor with a clink and rolled away to settle next to her right knee. Sucking in her breath, she closed her eyes and waited for her pounding heart to steady before looking again at the grinning skull with its small tuft of knotted black hair coiled on the back of the scalp.

Oh, God.

Scrabbling backward she stopped when her back slammed hard against the stone wall. Her breath rushed in and out of her lungs in a panicked pant. The nausea returned and swirled in her gut as she fought hard to control the scream that threatened to erupt from her open mouth. She closed her eyes and began a slow steady count, matching her breathing to the numbers.

In – one, two, three.

Hold.

Out – one, two and three.

It became a mantra. Breathe in, hold, and breathe out.

It worked, her heart rate slowed and her fear slowly ebbed away. She reopened her eyes, rubbed at them with the heel of her hand before lowering her face close to the floor. She studied the ground and slowly began to make out images. The area was littered with skeletal remains. All of which had been picked clean of flesh. Some of the bones were animal. She could tell that by their shape and the fact they had four legs, but some looked human. She looked but found nothing that would identify the poor unfortunates – no clothing, shoes or indeed possessions of any kind. She was the only one who wasn't naked.

Why am I different?

The grey static in her mind remained thick and dense and offered no answer to how or why she was here. In fact, there were no memories at all – not even a name. She leaned back on the wall and stared up the stone shaft towards the sky. What to do? Do I wait for help? Her gaze returned to the bones and realisation dawned – there would be no help.

A heavy burden settled on her shoulders like a heavy mantle and a small fire flickered to life in her belly, she stoked the flames until her determination to escape roared.

It's up to me. I must tell someone of this well of bones - give these people and their families' peace.

Chapter Two

'Dad, I'm going riding on Rainbow today. I've missed him. Do you have anything in particular you want done on the eastern track?'

'You could check Dry Gulch water trough and give the pump a service. It'll save me a trip,' answered Charlie watching in amusement as his fourteen-year-old son devoured his breakfast.

Eli wrapped his mouth around an entire Weet-Bix bar while eyeing off the stack of hot toast that Charlie set on the table.

A dimple appeared in his cheek as Charlie Morgan's lips twitched in a crooked smile. His heart glowed with warmth and love. It was so good to have his son home again. Eli had been away at boarding school in Perth. It had been six months since Charlie had last seen him. The day before the start of the September school holidays the airport workers had gone on a two-week strike and all air travel had been at a standstill. Eli couldn't come home to their Kimberley property and Charlie couldn't leave the station for the week-long drive to Perth. Lucky for both of them his sister and nephew lived in Perth and Eli had spent his holiday at their home. In his time away, Eli had grown from a short, wiry, pre-pubescent child to a rangy, loose-limbed teenager. Dark hair, the beginnings of a fluffy beard, dusted his cheeks and gave testament to the rapid approach of manhood. Eli so closely resembled Charlie in looks and mannerisms that if it hadn't been for the age gap they would have been considered twins.

Charlie recalled his own time living away at boarding school and the thrill of his homecomings. His mum would cook up a storm before his return, stocking up the freezer with delicious homemade cakes and biscuits in a valiant attempt to keep up with her son's capacity to inhale food. Eli was following in his father's footsteps in more ways than one.

'Will you be okay riding that far on your first day home? Remember you haven't thrown a leg over a horse for a couple of months now, you'll be out of shape.'

'Nah dad, all's good. I did heaps of sport this year and ran track with Bren every day after school helping him train, and weekends I competed with the rowing team. I'm fit enough.'

'What sort of track is Bren doing?'

'Long-distance. Mr Muscles, he's our phys ed teacher, reckons I should join the athletics team as I'm the only one who can keep up with Bren but I'm not interested. I only did it to keep cuz company.'

Eli spread a generous smear of vegemite over his buttery toast with one hand, while grabbing the jar of homemade plum jam with the other.

'How is Bren?'

'Moody. Aunt GG is always in his face, fussing. He can't go outside without her permission, and then she hovers at the door until he's back inside. She's smothering him and he hates it.'

'Hmm.'

'It's no fun spending weekends there anymore. The September hols were the pits. Bren sulked in his room most of the time and Aunt GG sat staring at the front door. When they did see each other they argued about stupid things. I had to tiptoe around them both hoping not to set them off. It was such a relief to get back to school. I'm so glad I only stay over one weekend a month during term.'

'Bren didn't tell me things were that bad.'

'That's 'cause Aunt GG stands over cuz, even while he's on the phone. She didn't used to be like that. Dad, what's wrong with her?'

'Uncle Josh.'

'Ahh – I don't suppose you can convince her to let Bren come here for the Christmas hols? He's busting a gut to get back to Rivers Run and a normal life.'

Charlie tousled the long black corkscrews that had sprouted wildly on his son's head.

'Time for a haircut, mister.' Eli grinned and pointed to Charlie's similar locks.

'You first,' he said, before reverting to his former question. 'Chrissy hols, dad, what do you reckon?'

'I'll work on it, Eli, but don't be unkind about your Aunt GG. She's having a tough time. Uncle Josh died walking to the local shop for a loaf of bread. The car that ploughed him down did it on the footpath right outside the house. It takes a lot for someone to get over something like that. At the moment your aunt's worried the same thing could happen to Bren. Losing him as well would totally destroy her.'

'Yeah I know, but Bren's suffocating. At least you don't fuss and smother me.'

Eli let out a deep sigh, picked up his milk glass and stared at the dregs in the bottom. He refilled the glass and took a large swig. While he did his eyebrows scrunched in thought. Charlie wondered what was running through his mind.

'I'll give Aunt GG a call this morning and see if I can convince her to come home as well. She needs to get out of that damn city,' said Charlie. To lighten the mood he began his finest John Wayne imitation. 'In the meantime, young man...,' spittle caught him in the back of the throat and he choked.

Eli cracked up laughing and almost upended his glass.

'That's shocking, Dad!'

Pretending to be offended, Charlie stuck his nose in the air and gave Eli a stinky eye. His son chortled as he shoved more toast in his mouth. Charlie's gut churned at the thought that life could be fleeting and to lose something as precious as his son would tear him to pieces.

'Eli my man, as you're the only child I'm ever likely to have and I need you to be fit and healthy so you can take care of me in my dotage, I'm gonna fuss,' he held out a finger and thumb in a gesture to show a small amount. 'I want you to take extra care today. We've had a few problems.'

The smile left Eli's face, his eyes widened in curiosity.

'What's up? Is everything okay on the station?'

Charlie was careful with his tone, he didn't want to scare his son but he did want him to take what he was saying seriously. 'Things are pretty good at the moment. The beef market's finally on the rise. Our orchard is producing well and we've just had a good lambing season. Added to all that there's rain on the horizon. There's nothing major wrong, mate. It's just that we've had a couple of yahoos taking pot shots at cattle in the district.'

'Mongrels,' the word exploded from Eli's mouth.

'Yeah I agree. We've been lucky so far and have only lost one steer. That was about a month ago. Zentra Flats Station lost four last week. But some of the cattle stations closer to Mount Ibour have really copped a hammering. The cops are really taking the shootings seriously. There's now a detective stationed at the police station to look into it all.' Charlie dropped two more slices of bread into the toaster and decided a quick reminder of the ground rules wouldn't go astray. He settled into his seat across from his son and said, 'Don't forget to take a fully charged radio from my study with you today and remember to check into base every two hours. Be cautious, Eli. If you see anything unusual or run into trouble of any kind, don't be a hero, call me. Okay?'

Eli nodded. Charlie took a long and satisfying pull of strong black coffee and smacked his lips together as it hit the right spot. Eli sculled a full glass of milk, imitated his father before running his tongue over his milk moustache and giving a contented burp. The toaster popped.

'Do you reckon it's safe for me to grab lunch from the camp kitchen? You know how cranky Cookie gets. I don't want to get on the wrong side of him.'

Charlie rose from his seat, plucked the two pieces of hot toast from the toaster, tossed one across the room at his son, who caught it deftly in mid-flight. His knife loaded with butter, Eli scraped it across the crunchy surface in a rapid flicking motion, as he waited for his father's permission to approach the volatile cook.

'Cookie's not in charge of the kitchen anymore. He threw one too many knives and I had to sack him. Naomi's taken over the kitchen as well as the camp and I have to say she's the best manager we've ever had. She certainly knows how to keep the hands in line, that's for sure. If you ask Naomi nicely and give her one of your winning smiles I'm sure she'll do a packed lunch big enough to get even you through the day.'

Eli's face broke into an enormous grin, a triangle of Vegemite toast clenched in his teeth. He bit, working his jaw around the food, and said, 'Cool. Naomi's the best. Remember when she used to come in and keep house for us – *awesome* food.' Eli rubbed his belly, swallowed and jumped subject. Charlie laughed – the boy wasn't your typical introverted and sullen teenager. 'Righto, Bull, breakfast is done and the sun's up, so I'm off. I promise to stick to the eastern inland track and will radio in. I shouldn't run into any yahoos out along there, it's too far from the main road for them and who knows what the day will bring. Maybe I'll come home with a desert nymph for you,' he said with a cheeky grin on his youthful face.

The use of his station hands' nickname for him took Charlie by surprise. He lifted his eyebrows and looked down his nose at his son. The boy, ignoring his father's twitching brow, leapt to his feet, pushed his chair neatly into place and saluted Charlie.

'I'll see you at dinner you cheeky bugger,' laughed Charlie as Eli raced towards the door, grabbing his hat from the rack as he dashed past. He slapped the Akubra onto his head and paused with his hand on the screen door.

'Ah...Dad?'

'Yeah mate?' asked Charlie, cup paused halfway to his mouth, waiting for the next curler Eli was about to throw his way.

'Can we have a coupla T-bones, loaded with chips and eggs for dinner? I really miss a good steak.'

Laughter exploded from Charlie in a loud bark. Whoever claimed an army moved on its stomach must have been talking about teenage boys.

Eli flashed him a winning smile and dashed out. The screen door slammed closed behind him.

Charlie rose from his seat and peered out of the kitchen window. His son's long, lanky stride rapidly ate up the distance between the main house and the camp kitchen.

It's great having him home. Such a good kid, who enjoys life. You sure missed out there, Amelia.

Six years of marriage and parenthood and then she was gone. He'd known immediately the marriage was a mistake but by then

Eli was on his way. For the boy's sake, he'd done all he could to make her happy, but for the glamour girl nothing he did would ever be enough.

She'd been gone in total eight years now, and after the first day was missed for none of that time. A scribbled note from her had arrived in the post three days after she'd left. It had been short, blunt and to the point.

I'm off to live a better life without you. I've taken my share. You can have the kid. Amelia.

She'd emptied their personal bank account. Taken over two hundred thousand dollars. Thank God she'd not had access to the business account or she would have taken all that as well and destroyed him. He'd searched but found no trace of the money.

Her rejection of their amazing son killed any affection that remained inside Charlie.

There'd been no divorce.

I wonder if she'll ever surface? Charlie mused as he drained his coffee.

Chapter Three

Charlie slid his sunglasses into place to cut the early morning glare, before slapping on his Akubra in an identical gesture to his son's. The worn and battered hat moulded perfectly into place on the back of his head. He gently closed the kitchen door behind him and strode down the rocky path through the garden of native plants and roses with long deliberate steps. He breathed in a tangy perfume as his shoulders brushed past the hanging branch of a Leichardt pine. Charlie smiled in satisfaction. The garden had been his mum's pride and joy. She'd nurtured and raised the seedlings that formed the foundation of the house's lush grounds. She'd done the same with the trees they'd planted in the south paddock orchard which were producing an abundance of fruit at present. Her vision for the future had changed the station's harsh landscape to an attractive, sweet-smelling and bountiful one. It pleased Charlie that the garden and the station were once again moving towards better times. The previous two seasons had been tough. A drought, poor markets and finances not quite as they should be had put a great strain on him, but with hard work and diversification into new markets things were improving. Charlie didn't intend hanging a millstone around Eli's neck when his son was ready to take over managing the million-plus acre property.

His nose twitched. He paused and studied the horizon. A movement to his right distracted Charlie from his musings about the weather. He glanced over and lifted a hand to wave to his son. Eli, sitting astride a handsome, coal-black gelding, doffed his hat. Charlie watched in admiration as the sixteen-hand, four-year-old Rainbow moved with an elegance that was more commonly found in a thoroughbred than a stock horse. Charlie never worried about Eli when he was out on the horse. His son was a skilled horseman, having been raised in the saddle and had formed a unique connection with Rainbow. Eli kicked the gelding into a trot and the pair headed east toward the bridge crossing at Annie River.

Charlie returned his gaze to the distant hills and studied the mountains again. He quickened his pace. His long legs ate up the distance past the married quarters where his station foreman Jimmy Donald lived with his wife Naomi. Charlie gave a smug smile when he caught the scent of the sickle leaf wattle trees and recalled the day they'd been planted. At ten years old his sister, GG, had always tried to outdo her older brother in everything. That year mum had drawn up the landscaping plans for the accommodation area and set her children the task of planting the one hundred wattle trees before the seasonal rains set in. Charlie, being the superior twelve-year-old brother, decided to take advantage of his sister's competitive nature and had challenged her to a tree planting race. He'd taken his time digging each of his holes and planting trees, letting GG race ahead doing the bulk of the work. Poor GG, she'd had a sore back for a week after that, never cottoning on to his tactics. To this day she still boasted about winning. Mum knew though, nothing ever got past her eagle eye. She had given him such a lecture about the importance of family and the need to care for each other. His father dying later that season showed him the importance of her words. Since then Charlie had very discreetly watched over all the members of his family. In later years his brother-in-law Josh had taken over some of that responsibility but Charlie had never fully relinquished his role and always kept an unobtrusive watch. Since Josh's death in June Charlie made a point of being much more active in his sister and nephew's lives.

His morning phone call with GG had gone better than expected, although his sister had been a little odd.

'Good morning sweetheart, how are you doing today?'

'I'm fine,' said GG, but she hadn't sounded fine. Her voice was soft and breathy, like she was distracted and her attention wasn't in the present. He decided to plunge straight in with his request and in the process hopefully pull her away from her dark thoughts.

'Sweetie, how soon can you get time off work? I want you and Bren to come home.'

'When?'

That had come as a surprise and was not like GG at all – she always argued and questioned everything. Today she just acquiesced.

'Next week? Is that enough notice for you to get leave from your employer?'

'They don't need notice. I quit yesterday.'

Charlie was astounded. 'You quit? But you love your travel agency job. What happened?'

'Nothing.'

'Well why quit then? And when do you leave?'

'My boss wouldn't let me go. She told me to take three months off, longer if I need it,' muttered GG. Her voice suddenly became stronger, more the forceful woman of the old days. 'Look, there's some stuff I need to discuss with you but I'm not going to talk about it over the phone. I'll come home and stay until the New Year. Is that okay with you?'

'Of course sweetie, stay as long as you like. Stay for good if you like. You know I love having you home and it will do you both the world of good.'

'Oh Charlie,' she sobbed, 'I've ruined everything – Bren doesn't love me anymore.'

'Of course he does.'

'We don't speak anymore. Bren hides in his room when I'm home. I'm sure he's sneaking out but he only grunts at me when I question him.'

'You have to realise GG that smothering Bren isn't the answer. He's an energetic teenager and needs to live his life without oppressive restrictions. You need to get things back to normal. Can you do that, Sweetie?'

'You're right – again! I am trying. I think with the stuff I've just discovered that will happen very soon. I'll go book the flights now and email you the details. Love you.'

'What stuff, what are you talking about?'

There was no reply, GG had already hung up.

A soft breeze brushed his cheek carrying with it the distinctive smell of penned cattle and something wilder. His nose twitched again. Charlie lengthened his stride and headed towards the transportable building they used as an office and control hub for the day-to-day running of the property. At the main stockyards one of his jillaroos, Darcy, was just closing the pen. He paused to study the fats gathered there. The cattle stood clustered around the cement feeding bin, jaws masticating to a slow tempo on the specially prepared feed Darcy had just dumped into the trough. The herd gave the impression they were having a chat at a stop-work meeting. He lifted a hand in greeting to the pretty, blonde haired, grey-eyed jillaroo. 'Morning Darcy, looking good,' he said nodding towards the cattle. Her wide, bright-white smile could have lit up a dark night.

'G'day, Bull,' she answered dropping the bucket and coming to lean on the rail beside him. Her elbow brushed his as she copied his stance, one foot on the bottom rail, hands clasped and resting along the top of the galvanised fencing. Bull, aware of her closeness, casually stepped back and hooked his thumbs through the loops of his jeans.

'You settling in okay Darcy, enjoying the work?'

'Yeah Bull, I love it here. Good rooms and the crew's great. I can't believe it's been four months already.'

'Four months hey, I swear it seems longer,' said Charlie with a laugh. Darcy smiled up at him, pleasure for his joke showing in the cute dimples that appeared in her cheeks. 'Well,' he said, 'don't let me hold you up. We've got a full day ahead of us.'

The wattage of her smile dimmed and she stepped back from the rail to head back to the abandoned bucket. Charlie, after taking another long look at the fats, turned and strode away, his heart racing. The mob had been sold to a five-star restaurant chain and Mac had instigated a special feed program to fatten them for slaughter. By Mac's estimation each steer would average two hundred and eighty kilograms dressed. The truck from MIA was due in late this afternoon to collect the herd. Charlie would be on tenterhooks until that happened. This was an important contract and a game-changer for Rivers Run's future. It would open up a prestigious market for their beef and lamb. The excellent sale price would go a long way to putting the finances back into a better position – which hadn't been the case for quite a while. Charlie blew out a small sigh and the knot that sat low in his gut tightened as he remembered there was a cattle killer on the loose.

He leapt over the three metal steps leading up to the office and glanced in through the glass sliding door. His foreman, Jimmy Donald, sat inside. Big Mac, as he was known to all the station hands, had lived at Rivers Run all his life. As teenage boys, Charlie and Mac had often sneaked away from their assigned tasks to go fishing and swimming together in the river, but they'd never gotten out of doing the chores – they were always waiting for them when they got back. Mum and Jimmy's father Colin had seen to that. Colin Donald had been foreman in those days, until the lung cancer got him. The job now sat on Big Mac's competent shoulders.

Charlie watched in amusement as his friend, elbow propped on the desk, cupped his head in one hand and pulled hard at his rusty blond hair with the other before snatching the pen from between his clenched teeth and starting on the mountain of paperwork on the desk. Charlie felt no pang of sympathy as his own book work was a similar torture. At least the accounting side was taken care of. After Amelia had taken all his money Charlie had employed a local book-keeper to sort the mess out. MI Accounting had looked after him well for five years until selling the business to Gil Connors. So for the past three years Gil had been coming to Rivers Run once a week to deal with the invoicing and employees' pay. Charlie knew of a least four other local graziers who used Gil's services to look after their finances so he had no qualms about letting him install a software program to keep track of everything and organise the major portion of his finances. While Gil's services were appreciated by Charlie the same could not be said about the man himself. Gil had a belittling and superior way of speaking to the station hands that made it hard to like him. He looked at the desk where Gil usually sat. It was empty. The only paperwork was a small stack of timesheets sitting in the in-tray waiting for him to deal with.

The radio squawked and Jimmy nearly ate the radio mouthpiece as he answered the call.

'This is the Big Mac go ahead Tangles.'

Indistinguishable garble squawked over the airwaves.

'Calm down, mate – say again.'

The chatter slowed but was too soft for Charlie to hear. He removed his hat, used it to whisk the flies away from his face and slid the glass door partially open. He stepped in and slammed the door shut before the pesky bastards could follow. Cocking one ankle over the other, he leant on the grey metal filing cabinet with his arm splayed across the top for balance and waited for the radio conversation to end.

Jimmy leapt abruptly to his feet.

'Gotcha mate, do what you can for now. I'll be there shortly – over and out.'

Throwing the mouthpiece down on the desk, Jimmy's eyes were ablaze with fury as he glared at Charlie.

Jimmy worked his mouth a couple of times before growling, 'Shit, Bull.'

'What's up, Mac?' asked Charlie, straightening his stance.

Jimmy scrubbed his finger vigorously through his scruffy hair. His usually dark leathery face was sickly pale.

'That was Tangles...you know Rhysand. The boys have nick-named him Tangles because they're having trouble pronouncing *Ree-sand*. Anyway – not important,' said Jimmy waving his hand in the air. He closed his gooseberry-green eyes for a moment and took a deep breath. 'I sent Tangles out to Rocky Waterhole at first light. I needed him to check the highway fence. I got a report our cattle were out on the main road. He's just radioed in. Bull, it's the yearlings, mate they've been shot.'

'Fuck.' Charlie's amusement changed to anger in a heartbeat. 'How many, Mac?'

'It's bad, mate. There are at least twenty dead. The mongrel's left about a dozen badly wounded. *Fucking cruel bastard!*'

Charlie's rage, a constant enemy that he'd fought hard all his life to control exploded in a red mist behind his eyes. He clenched his fists tight and his knuckles went white. It didn't help and his control snapped. He lashed out with his right foot and kicked hard at the filing cabinet. The metal side buckled and the cabinet took on a drunken lean.

'Lucky you're wearing your steel caps,' was Jimmy's only comment to the display of rage.

The release was like a bucket of cold water had been poured over him. Lashing out always had that effect. Charlie was at constant war with himself not to strike out because sometimes he couldn't repair the damage.

'Sorry,' he muttered staring at the cabinet. 'I'll get a new one next time I'm in Mount Ibour.'

Jimmy shoved his chair into position at his desk and said, 'I'd better get out there. The shooting must have happened a day or so ago because the wounds are infected and fly-blown. Tangles asked for the humane killer, reckons the mob are suffering.'

'I'll put a call into the police and come with you.'

Chapter Four

Rosie Bloom, short, stubborn and tenacious, never let the jokes her name evoked stand in her way, especially when it came to police work. She worked hard, was blessed with good deductive reasoning and had used it to rise rapidly through the ranks of the Western Australian Police Force to the position of senior detective. The job suited her penchant for order and justice. While her blunt no-nonsense approach offended some of the more delicate personalities that surrounded her, she got results and for that the district superintendent forgave her a lot.

Rosie grunted at the duty constable, Trevor Harrow, indicating he should put down the newspaper he was reading and push the electronic door release. He took his time, a small mean smirk on his face. He folded the paper in such a way to make the headlines obvious to her.

SILVER DINGO ON THE HUNT

Rosie snorted in disgust. Her short, silver hair, cut into a bob that framed her sharp features had once captured the media's poetic side, now the stupid nickname dogged her every footstep.

Why'd I expect it to be any different in Mount Ibour?

She tucked a bundle of files under her arm and glared fiercely at the small-minded constable. When the door finally buzzed Rosie pushed her way through slamming it shut behind her. Her booted feet echoed on the cement tiles as she strode with authority along the corridor towards the meeting room she'd seconded as the investigation office.

Rosie's partner, Constable Mark Bayden, earphones clamped around his head, was sitting with his feet up on the table sipping coffee from a mug entitled *Police Officer because badass cop ain't an official title*. He was listening to what looked to be the recording of last night's interview. The fresh-faced twenty-six-year old was a local lad who had been assigned permanently to his home town of Mount Ibour to help keep the peace. Sergeant Noah George, who was in charge of the police station, had ignored her loud and vocal protests at him being assigned as her partner while she was on assignment here. She didn't object to the constable as a person she just didn't want to be lumbered with a partner, especially a rookie to detective work. The sergeant's only comment, once she'd paused for breath, was he wanted the young officer to benefit from her vast experience. It took the wind right out of her sails. How could she argue with that? After due consideration, Rosie decided having a lackey might prove useful and to give him credit, Bayden was a quick study. He was also a great source of local gossip. Rosie conceded they worked well as a team and was beginning to mellow towards him.

After listening to Baden prattle on for numerous hours about the local yahoos, she was able to identify two particular individuals she wanted to have a chat with in regards to the killing of the district's prized cattle. In the early hours of yesterday morning she'd issued an invitation to one Greg Manning and Craig Knox for a friendly natter about their newly acquired gun licences. A rudimentary background check on Greg Manning revealed he was an unemployed labourer who couldn't hold down a job for more than a few weeks and had not worked anywhere in over twelve months. Craig Knox was currently out on bail and due to face court the following week on drug charges. Despite it being obvious that the primary producer advice letter (PPL) had been forged in the application, Constable Harrow had still issued both men with a gun permit. Sloppy police work or doing mates a favour? Rosie wasn't sure which category Harrow's actions fell into but his poor judgement didn't reflect well on him as a police officer. It wouldn't surprise Rosie to learn this was why he was being so petty about opening the door this morning. It was just his style of brainless thinking.

Rosie had no problem in getting a blustering Manning to confess to the forging of the documents. She only had to show him the inconsistencies in his version of the PPL and all the piss and wind went out of his sails, but she couldn't get Manning to admit to killing the cattle. Not so Knox, he cracked as soon as she asked him about his involvement. He blamed Manning for the actual shooting of the animals, saying that his mate wanted to punish the graziers for not giving him a job when he asked for work. Manning denied Knox's claims, stating his mate, high on drugs, had borrowed his rifle and ute and gone out and committed the deed under his own volition. The fact that Knox couldn't drive and his hand shook like an alcoholic having withdrawals made Manning's version of events unlikely. Rosie charged both men under the Animal Welfare Act and had Bayden lock them up for the night pending further discussions in relation to the firearm breaches.

Rosie hooked her hand around Mark's worn but nicely polished black boots and pushed them off the scarred surface of the conference table as she marched past dropping the files into the space vacated by his feet. She picked up a black whiteboard marker and with a few deft strokes wrote 'Missing' on the blank whiteboard attached to the wall.

Her partner's thin, black eyebrows rose in surprise. He tugged at the headphones, left them dangle around his neck and asked, 'Have we got a new case, Boss?'

'It's a cold case constable – a missing tourist. I need to speak to a jackaroo and get some first-hand details of the circumstances of her disappearance. You don't happen to know where I can find him, do you?' she asked running her finger under a name in the file.

Mark nodded his head, putting down his coffee mug and picking up a pen. 'Yeah, sure. He works at Rivers Run out on Settlement Road, about an hour's drive from here.'

The phone on the desk shrilled. Rosie ignored the annoying instrument and left it for Bayden to answer. He pressed the speaker button with the end of the pen he'd been twirling over his knuckle and announced, 'Criminal Investigations.'

'Getting a bit up yourselves aren't you, Bayden – Criminal Investigations indeed.' The tinny sound of Harrow's scoffing voice echoed around the room. Rosie glared at the speaker but held back her initial response to his sarcastic comment waiting to see how her offsider would handle the office bully and his petty jealousy. If Bayden foundered she would step in and give Harrow an earful.

'What do you want, constable?'

'Is the Silver Dingo there?'

Putting emphasis on her title, Bayden said, 'Senior Detective Bloom has just come in. Why?'

'Some irate cattle baron wants her doggy nose.'

Bayden's voice was ice cold when he replied to Harrow's witticism. 'Trevor, you're not doing yourself any favours here. Act like the professional police officer you're supposed to be will you, not a petty, jealous school boy. Now give me the details.'

Rosie's lip twitched. Good, Bayden wasn't about to be intimidated by the mealy-mouthed, overweight wannabe.

'Charlie Morgan at Rivers Run – he's just rung to say he's got a slaughtered herd in his south-west paddock – the one that backs onto Zentra Hill Road. Looks like the animals were targeted early hours of yesterday morning. Anyway, he wants you guys out there pronto.'

Bayden, busy writing down the details, grunted, 'Yesterday, you sure?'

'Oh boo-hoo, have you arrested the wrong guys? It sounds like you two might need to go back to detective school.'

Rosie opened her mouth to let fly, but before she could threaten to rip Harrow's tongue from his throat, Sergeant Noah George stepped into the room holding a pristine manila file. He calmly handed it to her, lent towards the phone's speaker and said in a cold voice, 'Harrow, my office...NOW.'

* * *

Bayden drove. Rosie read. The file the sarge had handed her contained a single sheet of paper.

'Well, here's a turn up for the books. Seems we've had an anonymous letter advising us we should conduct a murder investigation,' said Rosie, studying the words and letters that had been cropped from magazines and newspapers before being glued into a precise, neat row across the page.

'Who's been murdered?' asked Bayden, his eyebrows once again disappearing under his hairline in surprise.

'Amelia Morgan.'

5

Chapter Five

This was to be her third attempt at climbing the rough brick wall to freedom. If she fell again it would break her. The cuts and scrapes she'd suffered in the last fall joined the raft of other injuries that still ached abysmally and she was ready to concede defeat.

The grinning skull was so mocking it fired her up.

'No, I won't join you. I'm getting out of here – just you watch,' she yelled. Jumping to her feet she attacked the climb again, only this time taking extra care to ensure each grip and foothold was safe before she trusted her weight to it. In an opening just above her head she nestled the raw bloody fingers of her right hand into a small crevice and took a firm hold. Wedging her foot firmly into a hole located about knee height, she took a deep breath and straightened her right leg. She rose higher up the wall in a slow painful crawl towards the patch of darkening sky. Her cheek scraped painfully against the rocky surface as she claimed each small victory. Locking her knee into position, she held her breath and made sure of her balance before sliding her opposite hand up to grasp a new handhold. Concentrating on her left side, the woman found a new position for her foot and wriggled her toes into a small gap where the mortar was chipped away. She tested its stability before committing her full weight to her leg. As she pushed up again her thigh muscles shook with fatigue and threatened to give out. A bad sign, after all she'd achieved. She took a moment to rest and breathe deeply, drawing in the fresher air that trickled down from above. To distract herself from her tired body she began to count. Her internal clock ticked over five minutes before she felt it was safe to take her left hand off the wall and slide it into the pocket of her cotton drill shorts to grasp the digging tool that nestled there. With trembling fingers she removed the jagged piece of rib bone that she'd borrowed from the human skeleton. The tip was worn to a rounded point and was ideal for her purposes. Reaching up she positioned the bone in the join between two uneven stones. Closing her eyes to prevent the falling dust getting in them she began to scrape. Sweat ran in a salty river down her brow and dripped from the tip of her nose as she rubbed back and forth with the bone attempting to wear away the mortar and create a new grab point for her fingers and toes.

Even though the mortar had softened over the years the rib-bone was being worn away by the constant scraping. It was now half its original size. The smaller the bone got the harder it was to use. She was worried that it would wear away fully before she reached the top. Then what would she do? She certainly couldn't climb back down and get another one. She didn't have enough strength left to make the climb again.

'Please God,' she murmured to the wall.

A large chunk of dirt gave way, raining down on her in a stream of loose soil and small pebbles that rolled down her hair and wedged in the neck of her tee-shirt. The dust stuck to her sweaty face and began to itch. She waited, ignoring the irritating prickle of her skin and the dryness that coated her throat as she breathed in more dust, all the while praying she didn't sneeze and unbalance herself. The annoying tickle eased as the dust settled. Cocking her little finger, she ran it around the place she'd been digging and found a small loose rock that when removed would leave a big enough gap for her fingers and foot. She carefully returned her tool to the security of her pocket before reaching up to grab the stone. A mathematical formula popped into her brain.

In physics s=1/2gt squared.

Puzzled she tried to analyse the thought but was too tired. She let the rock fall and stared after it as it fell. It was too dark for her to make anything out. The woman refocussed her attention back to the climb. She straightened her left leg while stretching out with her right hand. In her excitement she rushed the move and began to teeter. Fright exploded in fiery sharp needles that stabbed painfully in her gut. Sweat stung her eyes. Adrenaline coursed through her veins in a hot prickly flush. Terrified she used sheer willpower to force herself hard against the wall. In the process she banged her mouth against rock and tasted blood. Clinging on tight with her toes and right hand she held her breath and forced her body to stop its rocking motion and still. In response her heart thundered so hard against her ribs it dislodged fine particles of dust from her shirt and the rush of adrenaline caused her legs to shake.

No.

She locked her knees and elbows and held on tight. With closed eyes she began to recite her mantra.

Breathe in...one...two...three.

Hold.

Breathe out...one...two...three.

The soothing process calmed her. Working her lips over dirt en-crusted teeth she discovered her canine tooth was chipped and lip split. Using her tongue to root around in her mouth she found the piece of broken enamel and spat it out. A sob escaped her lips.

It's alright. It's only a tooth, not the end of the world. Now, get your butt into gear and get out of this place then you can get it fixed.

The fire of determination in her gut burned brighter. Carefully sliding her hand above her head, she searched for a new handhold. The fingers of her right hand scrabbled in a void of nothingness. Confused, the woman tilted her chin upwards and stared. Just below her searching hand was a plank of wood that delineated the edge of the shaft. Beyond it was liberty. Freedom, or so she hoped, was within her grasp, she only had to reach out and take it. Tension churned in a sour swirl around her chest as her heart thudded in excitement.

She took a steadying breath.

I'm nearly there, nearly out. Be bloody careful, if you fall you're dead.

Taking her time she dug her numb toes as deep as she could into each foothold and made sure of her stability before lifting her right hand and making a grab for the shaft's edge. Her palm slapped against the rough and weathered wood. She gripped it hard. With confidence she moved her left hand up to position it at shoulder width beside her right one. Gathering her strength she pushed upwards with her elbows and straightened her legs. She flew up, and as she cleared the edge of the shaft she dropped her left shoulder allowing her body to roll away from the mouth of the well. Landing flat on her back, arms and legs spread wide she faced a night sky ablaze with a billion stars that glittered and shone like polished crystals. She let out a gasp of surprise. Cool fresh breeze played along her body and into her mouth, refreshing and cleansing her lungs as it raced to clear the stuffiness and dust she'd been breathing.

Her strained ligaments and muscles twitched like floppy wet noodles as they tightened and relaxed in relief. Drawing her gaze away from the view she quickly scanned the flat ground around her for any signs of danger. It would be terrible to go to all this effort only to fall straight back into the clutches of whoever had thrown her away like a piece of unwanted garbage. There was stillness around her, only disturbed by a light breeze. In the starlight she could see she was lying in a small copse hedged by stumpy shrubs and large boulders. The well's shaft was positioned in the exact centre of the grove but had no distinguishing features to make it stand out from being a hole in the ground. The shrubs danced with the breeze and the air vibrated with the clicking and humming of insects so loud it was almost deafening. A loud screech made her heart jump as a nocturnal bird flew past. She became aware of another noise, a panting that throbbed in breathless intensity. Fear scorched her. She froze, held her breath and took a rapid look around. The noise ceased. She let out her breath and the panting started again as her chest heaved up and down.

Stupid, that's you making that noise.

She let out a sobbing laugh. Suddenly, all the sounds around her ceased and a whisper rose up from the depths of the well.

Glancing towards the void, she answered the question from the deep.

'I promise to get help and return you to your families.'

The whispers fell silent. The night noises returned.

* * *

She staggered up on tired wobbly legs and they protested by giving a shudder. Sucking in a deep breath she waited for the twitching to stop. With stiff, tired legs she forced one foot in front of the other making her way over to the nearest shrub. With searching fingers she scrabbled underneath until she located the items she sought. Still warm from the day's sun, she selected three small flat rocks and carried them to the entrance of the shaft. There she stacked them into the shape of a pyramid. Not satisfied she checked under another bush and found some more stones to add to her pile. Grabbing the hem of her tee-shirt she lifted it to her face and wiped the sweat away as she studied the grove, memorising the area and the positioning of the pyramid at the shafts entrance. Satisfied, she turned and hobbled across the uneven rocky ground and made her way towards the animal track that ran between two large boulders. Squeezing through she began to follow the trail as it meandered around a spiky bush, past a clump of stunted shrubs and zigzagged down a steep incline. A full moon blazed and bathed the hillside in a ghost white light, bright enough for her to see as she tentatively shuffled along the rocky track in her socked feet.

The silhouette of a large boab tree loomed ahead. She hobbled to its base and found a freshly dug pile of dirt. Flattening the soft earth at the top of the mound she sat and drew in the warm, clean air deep into her lungs. Lifting her face to study the sky she frowned at a weird shape that hung from a branch overhead interrupting her view. Puzzled she took a closer look. A boab fruit – and it was within her reach. She wondered if it might be editable. Tempted, she stood on her tip-toes and plucked the round, hard nut from the tree limb. Running her hand over the pod's rough surface, she searched for a way of cracking the fruit open. Finding no easy access for her fingers she slammed the nut hard against a rock. The casing split apart revealing a powdery white flesh surrounded by large black seeds. Sticking her index finger in her mouth, she wet it and gingerly touched the white powder allowing a small amount to cling to its tip. In a tentative gesture she put this on her tongue. It tingled and a rush of saliva filled the insides of her cheeks as a pleasant taste of dried apple and citrus invaded her mouth. She continued licking the small fruit casing long after the fruit's powder had been consumed. Disappointed there was no more flesh she popped a seed in her mouth to suck and eyed off the tree's branches searching for more fruit. There was an abundance of fruit that the timid scaly tailed possums hadn't yet devoured but they were so high up the giant tree she had no hope of reaching them. Disappointed she spat out the dry and now tasteless seed and replaced it with another.

Leaning back against the wide and bulging trunk, she dozed as she waited for the eastern sky to change colour and announce dawn's arrival. When a ray of light touched her eyelid it drew her from a deep sleep. Opening her eyes, she rubbed at her stiff neck as she studied the horizon. The black of night had faded to an almost colourless white-orange, and even as she watched, expecting the yellow sun to announce dawn's arrival, a burst of glorious red burnt its way heavenward and then out across the world. The morning light raced across a red-dirt landscape chasing the long shadows of the night into oblivion. It revealed distant rugged ironstone hills covered in spindly trees. Panning out before her was a treeless semi-arid savannah. The plain was dotted with tussocks of tufted kangaroo grass and native millet, both common species of the far north-west of Australia.

Where the hell am I?

Her mind remained a grey haze of nothing. Sighing she rose to her feet. It was time to find some help and get some answers. Selecting a long, smooth, fallen boab branch as a walking staff, she turned her back to the rising sun and positioned it behind her right shoulder. In a measured step she hobbled directly west.

One, two, three...

After a thousand steps she paused to build a pyramid of stones. Every thousand steps she built another. The morning passed and the heat began to build as a blazing sun rose to its zenith, scorching everything it touched. It began to take its toll. Putting one foot in front of the other became a major battle of grim determination. Sapping humidity drained her body of its moisture and her skin burned and blistered under the sun's fierce rays. The scorching ground punished her feet but she knew to stop was to die.

Her mind began to play tricks – the horizon seemed to darken and then the words of a song began scrolling around in her head.

And then a hero comes along,

Concentrate and count – One, two, three...

With the strength to carry on,

The unrelenting sun pounded down on her uncovered head and it too began to pound. Running a dry tongue over cracked lips she forced herself to concentrate on the numbers.

Seventeen, eighteen...

And you know you can survive...

What number am I up to? Oh right, thirty-three...no that's wrong.

Strange I can't remember my name or anything about my life but I know the words to a Mariah Carey song.

The tune scrolled through her mind like an iPod stuck on repeat. She shook her head, trying to dislodge the annoying repetition and staggered. Her knees hit the ground.

I should rest...no, no...get up or you die.

She caught a glimpse of movement from the corner of her eye and jerked her head up hoping it was someone who could help. Rubbing away the salt that encrusted her lashes with the back of a sunburnt hand, she focussed on the movement. A mob of emus, their long legs extended, were gracefully dancing like a troop of ballerinas towards a towering cluster of woollybutts. Her gut knotted in despair as she watched them disappear into the clump of trees.

Trees! The fifteen-metre-high woollybutts meant a canopy and a canopy meant shade. Come on, get up. The ground is too hot to stay kneeling here. Get your butt into gear and moving, you can make it.

Digging the end on the walking stick into the ground she leant hard on it and hauled herself to her feet. The allure of the shade gave her the incentive to go on. Pausing for a few precious moments she snatched up a few loose pebbles and stones and built a small pyramid before altering her westerly course. After lining herself up to the tallest reddish-brown trunk, she took a step in its direction, staggered, almost fell but fought hard for control of her legs and won. She forced her feet forward one step at a time and kept going.

Indeterminable time passed. The bite and glare of the sun eased and was replaced with a cooler dappled light. She raised her gaze from the ground and squinted up – a tree, she'd made it. She collapsed against its trunk in relief and slid to the ground where she curled up into a ball and closed her eyes. Shades of light and grey played over the inside of her eyelids, and she drank in the soothing, fragrant scent of eucalyptus like it was a balm. Exhaustion overtook her and the world faded away.

Chapter Six

Charlie dropped the phone back in its cradle.

'Cops are on their way,' he said.

Jimmy nodded and paced behind his office chair like a caged tiger.

He stopped, looked towards Charlie and spat out, 'Thank God it wasn't the fats, Bull.'

Charlie nodded as he unlocked a cupboard and grabbed the keys for the gun safe from their hook. He threw them to Jimmy and said, 'Yeah, we have to be grateful for small mercies Mac. Is Tangles okay?'

Jimmy rocked his hand from side to side. 'Says he's okay...'

'Yeah, but we both know finding the herd like that can do your head in. Even the most experienced stockman, which he's not, would be sickened by what he's found and have nightmares. Shit, Mac, I hope this is it and they didn't go further inland and hit the second contract herd out in north haven paddock,' said Charlie, clenching his fists and seeing the rosy future he'd been imagining this morning being flushed down the gurgler.

'I reckon we should send Steve up in the chopper to check,' Jimmy said.

'Yeah, good idea – but there's to be no hot-dogging this time or it's the sack.'

Jimmy cracked his first smile since Charlie had entered the room. 'I was going to talk to you about that – been pretty rough on the aircraft lately. I've never had so many maintenance issues.'

'Well, last chance, and Mac...the weather forecast, it needs to be checked. There's a storm brewing over the ranges. I can smell it.'

Jimmy rolled his gooseberry-green eyes and his sun-chapped lips quirked as he muttered, 'You and your bloody nose.'

Charlie crossed his arms and gave his mate a crooked half-smile.

'Kept us out of trouble a time or two – but I still can't follow a track like you.'

'Too true, Bull – must be something lacking in your expensive education.'

Jimmy rounded his desk and headed for the door.

'I'll go get the crew started and send Steve south, away from the ranges. Roscoe and Pod can cover north haven paddock and fence line. Mimi and Darcy can finish stripping the last of the fruit trees in the orchard. Rather not lose all that wonderful produce.'

'Mac, get Pod and Roscoe to record everything with one of the drones will ya. I want to see if there are any unexplained vehicle tracks.'

Jimmy gave him a thumbs-up. Slapping a hat on his dusty blond hair he paused at the door and said, 'I hate having to put animals down.'

Charlie placed a consoling hand on Jimmy's shoulder and said, 'I'm with you on that, mate, but it has to be done. I'll grab the camera and join you out front. The cops and insurance will need a record of everything we find.'

* * *

Sun-bleached grass rippling in the soft, warm breeze was flattened by the tyres of the fast-moving Rodeo as Mac guided it across the paddock towards Rocky Watering Hole. He leant forward over the steering wheel and peered intently towards a small hilly outcrop. Spotting his quarry, Jimmy redirected the vehicle towards the man and quad bike parked in the shade of a cabbage gum and didn't ease up on the accelerator until they were level with the tree. He slammed on the brakes, stirring up a cloud of dry red dust, and brought the Rodeo to a halt in a patch of shade.

The man known to his fellow station hands as Tangles presented an iconic picture of a hard-working jackaroo – a long lean frame, dressed in tan moleskins, blue and white checked shirt, and Cuban heeled riding boots which he was studying studiously. Tangles lifted his head at their approach, unfolded his crossed arms and removed the Akubra from his white-blond hair to wave the dust and flies away from his sweaty face. With a long, slow, deliberate stride he walked towards the driver's door and nodded his head in greeting.

'Big Mac.'

Charlie watched Jimmy nod in return before hooking a thumb in his direction. Tangles glanced in the window and said, 'Good *morgen*, Bull,' he said in a mix of Norwegian and English.

'Whatcha got, Tangles,' asked Jimmy, as he leapt from the driver seat.

Charlie rolled from his seat and made his way around the bonnet of the car. He stood behind his foreman's left shoulder remaining silent. This was Jimmy's territory...what he paid him for. Charlie let him get on with it.

'I was checking the fences, as you asked. The gate to Zentra Hill Road was open. That is how the cattle got out onto the road. I rounded them up and pushed them back in through the gate. A few popped back out onto the road again. I walked along the fence line and found a section of the wire was down. It looks like a vehicle has been driven through it.'

Tangles used his hat to point to an area of the fence where shrubs and fallen tree branches had been piled up to deter escaping animals.

'And?' asked Jimmy, rubbing the tip of his nose with the back of his hand.

'I did a temporary fix on the fence. It is the best I can do until I can get more wire from the storeroom. I found these at the fence line and was just about to come back to the homestead and report in when I noticed the birds circling.' Tangles handed over a handful of shell casings. With a loud gulp, Tangles shoved his hat onto his head and stared back down at his booted feet.

'You alright, mate?' asked Jimmy, resting a hand on the young man's shoulder.

'*Ja*,' said Tangles with a slight catch in his voice. 'I found a big portion of the mob wounded and twenty dead steers.'

Charlie placed a consoling hand on the young stockman's other shoulder and stared ahead. He could feel the rage beginning to build again. He gave himself a shake – not good Charlie you can't afford to lose control. Sucking in a deep breath, he said, 'Tangles, you up to showing us, mate?'

Tangles gave another loud gulp, '*Ja*.'

'Mac, we'll have to photograph the carnage before we put 'em down,' said Charlie through gritted teeth.

* * *

Sick and dispirited, Charlie packed his camera into its bag and slid it under the driver's seat of the Rodeo. The photographs had been necessary for the police and insurance company. Nausea swirled in his gut – none of the animals could be saved and they had lost an entire herd to needless cruelty. The stench of burning flesh didn't help. It fouled the air leaving a bitter taste in his mouth. Setting fire to the carcasses had been necessary to prevent the spread of disease, but it was a sickening task. As Jimmy poured fuel over the last beast, Tangles cleared the area of dry brush. All they needed was a bushfire and the day would be complete.

The radio squawked.

'Bull, you on air?'

'Yeah Naomi, what gives?'

'Mayday from the chopper...'

Crackle.

The radio went dead.

'Naomi, come in Naomi.' There was no reply. The radio remained silent. 'Fuck, Jimmy we've got problems back at the homestead. We gotta get back.' He bent to collect his knife from the ground.

A police vehicle, in a squeal of tyres, came to a screeching halt on the main road. Before the vehicle was at a complete standstill, a silver-haired woman dressed in black cargo pants, tight black tee-shirt, and vest with police emblazoned across the front had opened the door and leapt out. She started yelling.

'What the fuck do you think you're doing?'

The vixen features of her sharp angular face were twisted in fury and a dark blue vein throbbed visibly in her neck. . . Not a strictly beautiful face but definitely unique thought Charlie as he watched her charge over the temporary fence towards him. Straightening his back with a clear plastic bag in one hand and a sharp and bloody bowie knife in the other he waited for her to come within speaking distance.

'You idiot, you're burning evidence,' she yelled.

He held out a ziplock bag containing bullets. 'Dug 'em out before firing the beasts.' The stomp of her feet was a telltale sign that her temper was not yet under control and with a wry smile on his face, Charlie pointed to the fence she'd just bolted over. 'You might wanna watch where you're putting your feet, officer. You've just tramped all over the shooters' lair,' he said and held out another bag containing the shell casings that Tangles had collected from the fence line.

The detective halted her mad charge.

Chapter Seven

Something cold and wet splashed on her face and startled her awake. Precious water, the life-giving fluid her body was crying out for, was falling from the sky in a torrential downpour. Large streams ran from the branches above, she opened her cracked sore lips to one and gulped. A slight eucalyptus flavour gave the water a unique taste, but she was so thirsty she could have drunk mud and enjoyed it. Again and again, she swallowed.

If you don't have a bottle, the best place to carry water is in your stomach, she thought, *so drink.*

At last, her thirst was abated, and with a full belly she stood under the stream letting it run over her head and face, washing away some of the grime.

BOOM!

She fell to her knees as thunder reverberated around her. Flicking her gaze up at the fast-moving black clouds she watched them tussle and roll over each other in their rush to move towards the west.

Her skin was stinging from sunburn, so she sat in a pool of water that had collected at the base of the tree and bathed her neck and cheeks in mud hoping it'd stick and act as a shield.

As suddenly as it had started the rain stopped.

It was time to move and find some shelter, maybe there was a hollow tree or a rocky overhang that would offer some protection from the storm that was heading in from the east. Using her walking stick she pulled herself to her feet. Muddy water ran in rivulets from her wet shorts, down her legs, creating dirty trails. Mud-filled her ragged socks. Her feet burned and protested at being stood on again. She studied them for a moment, not much left of the soles of her cotton socks, but going barefoot was a bad idea, her feet needed as much protection as possible. She removed the socks one at a time, stuffed them with as many green leaves as would fit, and pulled them back on. Taking a hesitant step forward, she tested the improvised shoes, the cushioning helped.

CRASH!

Her heart leapt in fright as a shrub nearby toppled to the ground.

Moo...

Her back hit hard against the tree's trunk stopping her backward flight. An enraged steer charged into the open space between her and the fallen shrubs. The animal stopped, swayed its head from side to side and snorted, looking confused. Wide-eyed she watched as the beast's eyes rolled up under its lids to show only the whites of its eyes. It bellowed again, stomped its front leg once and shuddered. The large bovine seemed to be fighting an internal demon.

Terrified she held her ground, not wanting to draw attention to her presence. She quietened her breathing by sucking in long slow breaths through her nose and allowing the air to trickle out of her mouth. The steer shook its head hard, like a dog shaking rain water from its ears, before snorting and glaring at its flank. Her glance followed the beasts and she saw a wound that was crawling with maggots and seeping yellow, bilious pus. It looked painful. No wonder the steer was enraged.

Why hasn't the owner done something to help the poor creature?
SQUAWK.

A long-billed corella, its white and yellow wings moving in maniacal determination, flew low across the plain heading in her direction. The bird halted its mad flapping and glided over the steer's head in a teasing circle before letting out another loud, penetrating screech. The steer's eyes bulged. It spun in a full circle searching for the threat. Not finding the source of the noise it gave up its cavorting and stood on cocked legs, poised for flight. The nerves along its back quivered and twitched. The bird swooped onto a tree branch and screeched again.

The startled steer charged.

Chapter Eight

'It's all right, detective. Tangles has already messed the area up. He fixed the fence before realising there was anything wrong.'

Removing an oversized calfskin glove from his work-hardened hand, Charlie reached forward and offered it in greeting.

'Hi, I'm Charlie Morgan. I guess you're the Silver Dingo!'

The detective's face took on an interesting pink tinge, her lips tightened and thinned as if her temper was only just under control. She glared at him.

'Damn press, giving out friggin' nicknames everybody insists on using.'

Humour bubbled deep in Charlie's gut at her words, but not wanting to give her temper something to focus on he kept the amusement from his face. She reached out and took Charlie's offered hand, her long slender fingers tightened as she gave it a hard pump in a good strong handshake.

'*Detective* Rosie Bloom,' she said by way of introduction. 'Tell me what we've got here.'

Charlie waved to the police vehicle and pointed to the Zentra Hill entrance gate. The four-wheel drive headed off in that direction at a more sedate pace than when it arrived. Once the vehicle hit the dirt track, it altered course and headed straight for them.

Charlie looked down at the trim and fit-looking woman before him and wondered how good a detective she was.

BOOM!

Thunder clapped overhead and was followed by a sizzling streak of lightning that bounced off the paddock next to them. The day darkened and the wind picked up speed, whipping up the dry dust of the fields to form fast-moving, swirling, willy-willies. The police Landcruiser halted next to Charlie and Detective Bloom.

Charlie spun around and yelled, 'Mac...Tangles...*Storm*...get in the police vehicle...*now*.'

* * *

Thunder rattled the cab, the noise almost deafening its five occupants. The wind roared and howled as it rocked the vehicle side to side trying to overturn it. Blobs of rain pelted against the windscreen blurring the occupant's vision of the outside world.

THUD.

A chunk of ice the size of a man's fist landed in the centre of the four-wheel drive's bonnet making a character dent in the pristine white panelling. A thumping drum announced the arrival of more frozen water as hail beat a loud tattoo on the roof. Charlie hoped the vehicle's skin would be tough enough to protect them from Mother Nature's awesome display of fury.

Lightning lit the cab. Charlie flashed Jimmy a toothy grin.

'Told you,' he mouthed.

Jimmy lifted his middle finger. A bark of laughter erupted from Charlie, lifting his mood from black to grey. It had been a pretty shitty day so far.

As suddenly as it arrived the hail rushed past, moving with rapid haste to fall across the parched landscape. The silence it left behind was almost deafening. The sun made a temporary appearance but Charlie knew it wouldn't be for long. He could see the rain heading their way like a misty grey curtain. It was time to go before they got stranded.

'Detective, there is nothing more we can do here. There's more weather coming, probably a flood. The station's radio has gone down and we need to get back to the homestead to find out what's going on. You and the constable should head back to town before you're caught by the rising waters.'

Rosie turned and stuck her head between the two front seats and glared at the three men sitting shoulder to shoulder on the rear bench seat.

'Not yet,' said the detective, 'I need to speak with you, Mr Morgan.'

'We don't stand on ceremony out here, Rosie. Call me Charlie or Bull. This is my foreman Big Mac,' he said, pointing to the man seated in the middle, 'and that's Tangles on his right.'

The detective seemed to ignore the introductions. 'Mr Morgan, I need to take a statement from you about the shooting and...'

'We're kinda in the middle of an emergency, can't this wait?'

'Nope.'

From his position behind the detective's seat Charlie had a good view of Constable Bayden as he sat behind the steering wheel and he saw the man's eyebrows lift and his lip twitch.

'Well, it'll have too.' His temper rising Charlie pulled on the handle to open the door. Nothing happened, the door stayed locked.

The detective shrugged in amusement, keeping the smile off her lips but not out of her eyes.

Charlie clenched his fists and opened his mouth to curse her out. Jimmy elbowed him hard in the ribs and Charlie reigned in the rude comment that sat just behind his teeth.

He took a deep calming breath and said, 'Follow us. We'll sort it out at the other end.'

* * *

The sight that welcomed their convoy of vehicles didn't improve Charlie's mood. The satellite dish and radio tower, which normally graced the roof of the stockman's common room, was lying in a twisted and tangled heap on the ground. A large hole in the roof gaped up to the black storm clouds allowing the heavy rain to pour in. The galvanised stockyard fences were flattened and had been trampled into the mud. The cattle were gone. Footprints in the mud indicated the herd had stampeded. It was going to take a miracle to get them back in time for the transport this afternoon.

A bolt of lightning split the sky, bathing the landscape in stark white light before fading into obscurity. The wind was making itself felt. Naomi, running from the office had a rolled-up blanket under her arm and she was carrying the medical box. She had her head down and was fighting her way against the wind to the jeep. She tossed her burden onto the pile of gear already stowed on the back seat and turned as Jimmy halted their vehicle next to her and buzzed down the window.

'What's happening, *Bunji*?'

Holding her rain hood in place, Naomi raised her voice to be heard over the whistling wind. 'The chopper's gone down, near the stand of swamp blood trees in the south paddock. Steve managed a mayday, just as the storm hit and took the tower out. I don't have any other details'

'Jimmy, go with Naomi and take some cutting tools. God knows what you'll find.' Charlie said, waving his hand towards the jeep. 'I'll round up the rest of the crew, make sure everyone's safe. Naomi, what about Eli?'

Naomi shook her head, 'No word. He called in at ten this morning, Bull. He was taking a breather at the paperbarks just short of Dry Gulch.'

Jimmy put a comforting hand on Charlie's shoulder, 'He'll be fine. Eli's a smart lad. He'd take shelter in the fence riders' hut. The sandstone walls have stood up to many a cyclone and we've just reroofed it.'

Charlie gave a single nod, his priorities conflicted – take off and find Eli or stay and find the crew.

No conflict.

'Tangles,' yelled Charlie, leaping from the vehicle, 'get up to the orchard, check Mimi and Darcy are okay. Then try and get hold of Roscoe and Pod. Tell 'em to get their arses back here on the double. Get everyone boarding up the camp and homestead.' Tangles, holding his hat clamped to his head, nodded and took off at a fast jog towards the orchard. 'Detective Bloom, you and Constable Bayden are welcome to hole up in the house. We'll talk when I get back.'

'Where are you going?' asked Rosie

'To find my son.'

'I'll come with you. Two sets of eyes are better than one. Bayden, you stay and give the crew here a hand.'

Before Charlie could argue, the pint-sized copper was in the passenger seat. He took possession of the driver's seat and planted his foot on the accelerator. The Rodeo sped towards Annie River Bridge. As the front wheels hit the crossing he slammed on the brakes.

'Fuck.'

He stared out the windscreen in despair. Water lashed the railing and splashed across the road, except for the middle section. That was missing...washed away.

9

Chapter Nine

The steer bellowed and rushed past her, racing towards the treeless plain. A deep ragged breath caught in her throat and she coughed in sobbing relief. The walking stick was clamped so tight in her hands her knuckles were white and fingers numb. Working her fingers, she eased the tension in them and they began to tingle with pins and needles. Sighing in relief when the weird sensation had passed she leant her forehead against the top of the staff and closed her eyes.

What a day.

A cool breeze played over her hair bringing with it the smell of rain on hot dry dust. Glancing up into the tree she noticed the cheeky bird dancing about the branches above her, 'Thank you my friend, you almost gave me a heart attack.'

The long-billed corella ignored her, being more interested in its investigation of the tree's upper canopy for seeds or ripening fruit. Finding nothing of interest, the bird screeched its disgust and took flight.

The click of metal striking stone was followed closely by the whinny of a horse. She whipped her head around searching for the source of the noise. Her heart gave a mighty heave when she spotted a black colt, with its saddle askew, limping its way in her direction. She watched the horse's hesitant steps as it avoided stepping on the trailing reins. She was puzzled as to where the rider was. When the horse was close enough she clicked her tongue to alert it to her presence. It snorted, picked its way in her direction and stopped just out of reach.

'Come on boy, there's a good lad,' she murmured. At the sound of her soft words the colt froze in a stiff-legged stance that indicated it was ready to bolt at the slightest sudden move. She watched in fascination as the nerves along its flanks quivered. The flies that had been hitching a ride took flight, circled and resettled. In slow motion she held out her fingertips and clicked her tongue again.

'Who's a beautiful boy? Gently now gorgeous, I won't hurt you.'

The horse stared at her with beautiful chocolate brown eyes surrounded by long dark lashes.

'Come on my handsome...there's a good lad.'

The soothing tone acted like a balm and the horse began to relax. It took a hesitant step forward, followed by another and then as if a decision was made, the horse trotted over to place its muzzle into her waiting palms. Its nostrils flared as it snuffled and sniffed at her hands and the front of her shirt. The colt gave a soft whinny. She grabbed hold of the dangling reins and using a slow soft tone she spoke inane words as she ran a hand along his glossy muzzle before stroking his neck in a long firm motion. The horse nodded and snorted to indicate enjoyment. When he seemed calm she looped the reins over the branch of a nearby shrub and tied it off, allowing the horse enough lead to graze. With concerned eyes she stood back and studied the open wound on its left flank. It looked to be a fresh injury, not more than a few hours old, because while the blood had begun to crust it still looked soft.

'Hmm that doesn't look too bad, boy. What have you been up to hey?'

The horse lifted its head and stared at her with its glorious eyes as she continued her one-sided conversation. 'Where's your rider, hmm?'

The horse snorted, pawed the ground once and resumed grazing.

'Sorry, I don't speak horse. I think I'd better take a look around, while you wait here.'

Leaving the stand of trees, she followed the horse's trail for a short distance and scanned the area. Nothing. No signs of life, not even the crazy steer.

* * *

She tried to straighten the cross-breed saddle hanging askew on the horse's back. It defied her and slipped further towards the horse's belly. This seemed to unsettle him and he began to dance and snort in annoyance. She gave up and released the cinch holding it in place. The saddle and rug slid to the ground with a resounding thud. In her tired state the saddle was too heavy for her to lift above her knees so she didn't bother to attempt to get it back on the animal's back, instead she dragged the saddle away from the horse's restless hooves to a clear patch of ground. Kneeling she unbuckled the flaps on the saddlebags to check out their contents and found a scrubbing brush, bottle of glass cleaner, and a neat bundle of clean rags. Well that's not what I expected, she thought and shoved her hand in deeper to feel around for anything that might have been missed.

'Aha,' she croaked as her fingers closed around a long smooth object. Pulling it out, she discovered a pocket knife. Flipping open the various multiple tools revealed a very sharp looking flat blade plus a small serrated one, along with a corkscrew and various other implements the purpose of which defied her imagination. She slipped the knife into her pocket and opened the second flap.

'Jackpot,' she cried when her gaze landed on a large water bottle and a plastic lunchbox. Lifting the box lid she saw it was stuffed with enough food to feed an army. Three big fat sandwiches cut into triangles had been jammed in next to fat wedges of fruit cake and two apples. Lifting a corner of the bread revealed a generous slather of butter, thick slabs of meatloaf and a fine scraping of mustard.

Wow this smells amazing.

A fist sized knot of hunger clenched in her gut. She grabbed a sandwich. Resisting the urge to cram the food into her mouth, took a small bite. Her stomach let out a loud growl of anticipation. Chewing in a slow methodical rhythm and keeping the food away from her chipped tooth she took her time, savouring the taste of each mouthful and enjoying the sensation of eating. When the first triangle was finished she denied herself another because she didn't know how long the food had to last before she found help. Removing an apple, she ensured the tucker box was properly sealed before crunching into the crisp, juicy fruit. Chewing away all the flesh, she then sucked the apple core dry. Guilt at enjoying the delicious fruit, while the horse only got to graze on spindly dry grass, she offered him the remains. The horse nuzzled the core gently from her palm and in three crunches demolished it.

It was time to move. Piling everything from the saddlebags, including the food and water, onto the centre of the horse blanket she tied it into a bundle before feeding the walking stick through the knot and hoisting it onto her shoulder. She looked like an orphan on the run. Gathering the horse's reins, she clicked her tongue to get him moving and began following the trail of hoof prints left in the mud. As she shuffled along the trail, she studied the black clouds that hung heavily overhead. They looked like they were about to dump a heavy load so she picked up the pace hoping to find the horse's rider before the hoof prints were washed away.

* * *

A strong breeze shoved her along as the rain pelted down in large, cold drops. The storm had long ago washed away the track she'd been following. With no sun as a compass, she had no idea of the direction she was taking. The horse, head hanging in misery was unhappily following where she led, but to where?

With her chin tucked down on her chest in an attempt to ward the rain from her eyes she walked a straight line towards what looked like a group of paperbark trees. Night was falling and the gloom caused by the dark clouds darkened. She urgently needed a place to shelter and rest up. The search for the missing rider would have to wait until dawn.

A distinctive track came into view and ran through the clump of trees. She quickened her pace. Hoping to find a road sign or something to indicate the direction she should take to find help. As she stepped onto the trail a small bush growing at the base of one of the paperbarks rustled. Startled she halted and tentatively took a closer look.

A booted foot protruded from under the shrub and wiggled.

'Hello,' she said. Her voice croaked and failed. She tried again, this time the words had some volume. 'Is anyone there? I need help.'

'Lo, that you, Dad?' said a young, male voice.

The horse whinnied, bumped past her and headed towards the voice. She had no choice but to follow as the reins tugged her into motion. The horse halted at the shrub and snorted.

'Rainbow?'

She pushed some branches aside to reveal a handsome dark-haired lad, who was on the brink of manhood. His eyes resembled polished silver but were etched in pain. His left leg was twisted at an odd angle.

'You're not Dad – who are you?' he asked, opening his eyes wide and giving her a startled look.

She stared at him wondering what to say, opened her mouth, paused and waited for the cloudy grey static in her mind to shift.

A name popped out of her mouth before she had time to stop it. 'Kelsey. I think.'

The teenager stared at her, his silver-grey eyes crinkled with curiosity. She was conscious she wasn't looking her best and tried to smile but felt her lip crack and a coppery taste of blood touched her tongue.

The boy lifted himself to an elbow and said, 'Hi ya, Kelsey. You don't look too good, are you okay? You've broken a tooth, did you know? I'm Eli by the way. Where'd you come from?'

Kelsey, dazed by the raft of questions, didn't know which one to answer first so she pointed in the direction she'd just walked and said, 'I found your horse.'

'Bloody, micky bull,' growled Eli.

Confused by his comment Kelsey knelt down next to the shrub and inspected the young face before her. 'Is your leg broken?'

'Don't think so. I think I've just twisted my knee. Hey...thanks for finding Rainbow. Are you a desert nymph?'

Kelsey felt her lips split as a smile came unbidden to them. What a delightful boy.

Boom.

She lifted her head and stared at the watery sky. Thunder cracked again in the distance.

'Eli, we've got to find some better cover. That storm sounds bad.'

'Yeah, that's why I was under the shrub, best I could do.'

'Can't you walk?'

'Not without help. I had to crawl here.'

Shit, how was she going to carry the boy – she could barely carry herself.

'Kelsey, there's a line riders' hut about five hundred metres that away,' said Eli indicating to the right of where she knelt. 'We can shelter there. I was going to wait there for Bull. He'll come searching for me soon and that's where he'll go first.'

Bull?

A flash of stark white lit the gloom as lightning zigzagged across the sky.

She held out a hand to Eli and helped him slide out from under the shrub. There was more of him than she'd expected, his long frame kept coming. Eventually all of him was out and she noticed he matched her for length.

He must be from tall stock.

'Hang on, this might hurt,' she warned as she ran her hand over the leg and cupped his calf.

'Ahh...shit,' yelled Eli, as she straightened his leg. He grabbed her hand, 'Sorry, I shouldn't swear in front of a lady.'

'I won't tell,' she said, touched by his manners.

Eli's smile bloomed and Kelsey's heart began to glow.

Here was someone easy to love.

'I think you're right Eli, your leg doesn't feel broken but your knee cap is swollen, so I should splint it. Here cut me some ties.' She untied the bundle and handed him the rags, before reaching into her pocket and pulled out the knife.

'Hey my pocket knife, fantastic. Are you a doctor, Kelsey?'

The thick cloud in her head remained unyielding and unhelpful. No new information emerged. 'I don't know,' she said, shaking her head.

'What do you mean...?'

'It's all grey static up here at the moment,' she said, tapping a gentle fingertip to her forehead. 'Now, I need to find some straight pieces of wood ...' She glanced around, searching the ground. Eli, leaning back on his hands with his legs straight in front of him, nodded towards the paperbarks.

'There's some over there.'

Kelsey rose and hobbled along the wet muddy track to the cluster of trees. She spotted some straight sticks that would be perfect. As she stepped off the track she stood on something hard. Lifting her foot to investigate she almost stopped breathing.

A radio!

In excitement she bent down and snatched it up. It rattled in her hand. She twiddled the on-off button – nothing. She shoved the sticks under her arm and hurried back to Eli. Falling to her knees at his side she held out her find.

'Look, I found a radio. Do you think you can fix it and call for help?'

Eli took the black leather covered transmitter from her hand. 'I wondered where that got to,' he said and started to fiddle with the dials. While he was distracted, Kelsey went to work on his leg, tying the sticks into place with the strips he'd cut from the rags.

Her doctoring complete, Kelsey wedged her shoulder under Eli's arm to support his weight and helped him up. It was an exhausting struggle but he finally found his feet. Panting, with his arm draped heavily over her shoulder and beads of sweat standing out on his forehead they took an exploratory step forward. Eli nearly toppled to fall flat on his face. Kelsey shot in front of him and managed to catch him, but the effort made her dizzy.

'This isn't going to work, Eli, you're going to have to get on Rainbow,' said Kelsey, 'I don't have the strength to carry you.'

She watched as Eli eyed the horse's injured flank, opened his mouth to protest, eyed her and closed his mouth again.

Good lad.

She gave the horse's reins a small tug and Rainbow moved closer to them. She knelt down on her hands and knees next to the horse and said, 'Come on, Champ, use me as a step and get on.'

A lot of grunting took place, the weight on her back wobbled then eased and when she looked up, Eli was laying along Rainbow's back, holding his injured leg away from the horse's wounded flank. He clutched a handful of mane and had his face snuggled into Rainbow's neck.

'Alright Google Maps point me in the right direction.'

Eli chuckled and stuck a finger out. Once more she lined herself up to an landmark and prepared to hobble on, only this time she was accompanied by a walking stick, a bundle, a horse, a teenage boy and a name.

Chapter Ten

Charlie shrugged on a backpack and tugged the straps tight. He locked the guns and humane killer away in the gun safe before heading out to where they garaged all the vehicles. The damage to the Annie River Bridge was a major pain in the butt for him. Now he'd have to travel downstream to the Zentra Hill Bridge, cross the river there before swinging southward towards Dry Gulch. The quickest route was the dirt trail by the river and the fastest mode of transport was by motorbike. Detective Bloom had argued with him about going alone, she demanded to go with him, but Charlie didn't have time to play nursemaid to her or anyone else.

'Look Rosie, I know the country around here like the back of my hand – you don't. The last thing I need right now is to be slowed down because you don't know where you're going. It's not an indictment on your abilities – but I need to find my son, fast.'

'I understand, Mr Morgan...'

'Bull, please.'

'Alright, Bull. But are you sure about this plan?'

'Yeah, I'm sure. Look, all the station hands are back in camp now. I've set them to work battening down the buildings and homestead.

Once that's done, Mimi will have a shot at getting the radio working. She's brilliant with electronics. I need someone strong and sensible to keep an eye on everyone until Mac gets back from the helicopter crash site.' Placing a hand on the detective's shoulder, he looked her straight in the eye and said, 'You've got this...'

Charlie kicked the motorbike to life and gave it full throttle. Rubber chirped on the garage's cement apron. As the tyres grabbed hold of the wet ground, the back wheel slid sideways into a skid. He fought the slide, righted it and the bike surged forward, rapidly leaving the homestead behind. The strong wind had eased but rain was falling in a heavy deluge and his sodden jeans flapped and snapped around his legs as the air whistled past. His leather riding jacket repelled most of the wet, keeping his arms and upper body warm and dry. Mud sprayed up in a fountain behind the bike as he sped towards the river crossing.

Charlie's imagination had kicked into overdrive and nothing short of holding Eli in his arms was going to ease the worry that burned hotly inside him.

The rushing air chilled his legs and they went numb with the cold. So tight was his grip on the throttle that after two hours, cramps started to knot his fingers and palms but it was worth it because the crossing was finally in sight. Charlie prayed the tree that had taken out Annie Bridge hadn't come from this far upstream and wiped out the Zentra Hill Bridge as well. Standing up on the footpegs he allowed the bike to roll forward, while he eased his aches and pains and through narrowed eyes studied the wooden bridge. With relief he saw there was no sign of damage.

He grabbed the handlebars and gunned the engine. As the bike started to cross Charlie heard a mighty roar. He glanced to his right.

Oh Shit.

A fast-moving wall of foaming water, littered with branches and other debris, sped down the river threatening to engulf him. He twisted the throttle to full power and lay low over the handle-bars. The bike shot forward.

Crash.

The water hit the bridge in a pounding, devastating wave.

* * *

Kelsey kept her head down and watched her feet move forward, one step at a time. She moved at a steady pace, pushing hard into the headwind. It was hard work and just when she thought her strength was going to give out, Eli spoke.

'We're here.'

She raised her head and took in a squat, old sandstone building with a new tin roof. She staggered to the open archway in the centre of the building. It was large enough for a horse and rider to pass through. The whistling of the wind that had been blowing past her ears ceased and they rang in the silence left behind. Giving her head a quick shake to ease the sensation, she glanced around the rectangular-shaped room. It was weatherproof and sparse. Against the nearest wall, bales of hay leant in a drunken heap along with a small stack of dry firewood. Recessed in the far wall was a stone fireplace, it gaped with a toothless smile at an expanse of stone floor littered with dried leaves and wisps of hay that had been blown in by a swirling breeze.

She smiled. *Well, that's the kindling for the fire taken care of.*

Kelsey led Rainbow to the far corner and built a step beside the horse out of the hay bales. Eli spun around sideways on his stomach and with her assistance slid from the horse's back to stand on his good leg. Kelsey hooked his arm over her shoulder and they staggered over to the fireplace. Exhaustion was nudging her hard but Kelsey knew they needed to start a fire and eat before she could rest.

'Hey Champ, do you know how to light a fire without matches,' she asked her young companion.

'I do...but it's easier with this,' said Eli. He reached into his pocket and pulled out a disposable lighter. His grin was infectious and she felt her cheeks dimple in response.

Feeling self conscious about her damaged tooth, which was silly considering all the other injuries she was sporting, Kelsey held her fingertips in front of her lips to hide it as she spoke. 'Awesome...you unpack the bundle and spread the blanket for us. I'll get the fire started.'

They set about their tasks and in no time at all a cheery fire was blazing in the hearth. They settled close together on the rug and held their hands up to the flickering flames warming themselves.

'I'm so glad you found the tucker box, I'm starving,' said Eli, rubbing a hand over his trim belly. He opened his mouth wide and took a massive bite of his sandwich.

'Your lunch certainly saved me, I don't think I'd eaten for quite a while,' said Kelsey, taking a small delicate bite and savouring the taste of the peppery meatloaf in her mouth. 'You up to telling me how Rainbow found me?'

'Yeah sure, *and* I really want to hear what happened to you.'

'Love to tell you all about it, Champ, but I've got no idea. I don't know who I am, where I am, or even how I got here.'

Eli's jaw paused and his eyes widened. Around a mouthful of food he said, 'That sucks. You're not an international spy or anything like that are you?'

'Maybe,' Kelsey chuckled, 'but I don't think so.'

'Well, I can answer one of your questions and tell you where you are. You're on my family's cattle station, Rivers Run. Our property line runs from just south of Mount Ibour across to the Northern Territory border and out into the Tanami Desert. My great grandparents settled here in the Kimberley over a hundred years ago.'

'Wow. That's a huge area. It must take some work to manage all that land.'

'Yeah, we own over a million acres. To make it viable we've had to diversify over the years by running sheep and cattle as well as growing fruit. We now have our own brand of jams and preserves. I want to introduce a holiday stay program that included things like horse riding, jackaroo lessons, fishing and all that jazz. I reckon that has a real future.'

'Sounds interesting, Eli. What do your parents think about that?'

'I haven't had a chance to really discuss it with dad yet. I only got home from boarding school Friday.' Eli crammed a wedge of cake into his mouth. His jaw worked up and down hard and fast and he thankfully swallowed before continuing on with his story. 'Today was my first ride in months. I was heading for Dry Gulch water trough, to give the pump a service and clean and check the solar panel and camera. Dad says it's been offline this week.'

His food finished, Eli wriggled to get comfortable. He leant forward then back on his hands all the while avoiding moving his injured leg. He propped himself up on one elbow but looked uncomfortable. Kelsey patted her thigh in invitation. He lay down with his feet towards the fire and nestled his head in her lap before going on with his story.

'At ten o'clock this morning it was time to report in. I found a nice shady spot under one of the paperbarks and looped my reins and leg around the saddle horn so I could relax while I spoke with Naomi on the radio.'

'Who's Naomi?'

'Only the best cook ever. She runs the camp, and Big Mac. Been here all her life, he has too.'

'Big Mac?'

'Uncle Jimmy, dad's best friend, and Rivers Run's foreman. They're married...' Kelsey narrowed her eyes, trying to take in all the fresh information and names.

Her confusion must have been evident because Eli said, 'It'll make more sense when you meet everyone.'

Kelsey nodded, settled her back against the wall to relax. In an unconscious motion she began to stroke Eli's unruly mop of hair away from his face.

'Go on with your story, Eli.'

'I turned to slip the radio back in my saddlebag when a bloody...sorry, a mickey bull came charging from the scrub. It frightened the hell out of Rainbow and he reared. I was nearly thrown. That's when I grabbed for the reins and dropped the radio. I was still trying to get my leg back over and into the stirrup when the steer's horn got tangled up with the girth strap and grazed Rainbow. He bucked to shake the bull. I remember flying through the air and woke up with a sore knee and no horse. When I heard the storm coming I crawled to the bush and then you found me.'

'Lucky.'

'Yeah, sure was...you're nice.'

Kelsey felt a blush heat her cheeks. This boy was going to be a heartbreaker.

'What about the radio, Eli. Do you reckon you can you fix it?'

'Nah, the insides are smashed. Looks like it went under Rainbow's hoof.'

'Bugger.'

Eli's lips lifted in a small smile at her curse.

'Don't worry, Bull will find us.'

He closed his eyes. Kelsey continued to stroke his hair and closed hers.

Sleep grabbed her.

* * *

The tyres bit hard into the wooden planks and the bike shot forward. Charlie glanced over his shoulder without easing back on the throttle and watched as the crossing disappeared. Water splashed high and wide, as the flash flood pounded the bridge, drenching him in a cold wave. The bike skidded and fishtailed before shooting free. Charlie's heart banged hard in his chest.

Shit that was close!

Taking a deep breath he slowed the bike and glanced back. The water was over the crossing. Night had fallen and in the gloom he couldn't tell if the bridge had been destroyed or not. It was irrelevant because with the river raging over the crossing they couldn't return home this way. Charlie stood erect on the foot-pegs letting the bike idle its way forward as he dug around in his pocket for the compass. His numb fingers had trouble getting a grip, so he stopped the bike and dismounted. Charlie took a moment to stretch the stiffness from his body then moved to the front of the bike and held the compass and map in the headlight beam to read. He calculated that he was only a kilometre from the trail south. Then it was a straight run to the hut.

* * *

Kelsey awoke with a start. A loud buzzing had disturbed her dreams. She opened her eyes and looked around the room. It was softly lit by dwindling firelight. Not noticing anything out of place she looked down at Eli still cradled in her lap, he seemed to be asleep. She studied his handsome face and ran a gentle hand over his brow.

Crunch.

Her head shot up and she stared towards the door. A scream formed on her lips which took some effort to hold back as she stared at the tall, handsome, older but intimidating version of Eli who stood in the archway glaring at her. Her heart sped up as he took a step forward. She sucked in a startled gasp. He halted.

The head in her lap moved.

'Hey Bull, you took your time.'

'Eli, mate you okay...?'

'Yeah, I twisted me knee. You got any food on ya, I'm starving.'

The man at the door let out a warm and comforting laugh that cracked slightly at the end. Kelsey heard him draw in a deep breath as he moved towards them. She stiffened, uncertain of his intent. He knelt his giant frame in front of her and placed a huge mitt onto Eli's chest. The boy clasped it and squeezed.

'I was worried, son.'

His voice, deep and calm, warmed her frayed nerves and she began to relax.

Eli smiled at Bull and said, 'I'm fine, my desert nymph has been looking after me.'

Kelsey saw the lines around Bull's eyes, the same colour and brightness as his sons, crinkle in a smile. He raised his gaze from his son's face and studied her. The smile dropped away and was replaced with a frown.

'Hi, Charlie Morgan,' he said, holding out a mud-splattered hand.

Kelsey's fingers tingled as she placed her hand in his.

'Kelsey.'

Something flashed in Charlie's eyes...was that surprise?

He looked down, sucked in a small breath, and began to examine the cuts and grazes on her fingers. He lifted his gaze and studied her face.

'You look like you've been in the wars.'

'I have rather.'

'Kelsey walked out of the Tanami, Dad,' said Eli. His glance danced between the two adult faces above him. 'She doesn't know what happened to her or who she is.'

Charlie's brows lifted, his lips tightened.

'I don't suppose you know who I am, do you?' asked Kelsey, wondering if his cold suspicious look was because they'd come across each other at some time and it hadn't been a pleasant experience.

'No.'

He let go of her hand and with a gentle finger lifted the hair hanging over her cut scalp. She flinched, expecting him to push at the damage and hurt her. He didn't touch the wound but leaned nearer for a better look. He smelt of wood smoke and spice. It was enticing.

'You've had a bad bang to the head, it's all bruised. There's an open cut, might need stitching but it's not bleeding. I won't touch it.'

'That would be from the broken brick.'

Charlie gave her a quizzical look but said nothing, just waited.

Kelsey glanced down at Eli in her lap and decided not to be too graphic in front of him. 'Mr Morgan...'

'Call me Charlie or Bull if you prefer.'

'Charlie,' said Kelsey. She liked the way his name rolled off her tongue, it sounded as if it belonged there. 'Would you be able to help me? I need to get to a police station.'

He studied her face for a moment before speaking. 'Sure, but we have a few obstacles to overcome first. Annie River's in flood and the bridges are gone. The radio and satellite phone dish was damaged in the wind, so we have no communication. It's all repairable but will take time. For now, our first priority is to get you both across the river and back to the homestead.'

'How do we do that with no bridge?' asked Kelsey.

'Flying fox, Dad?' asked Eli, his grey eyes sparkling in the firelight.

'Yeah, mate,' replied Charlie, the same gleam in his own eyes. 'Flying fox.'

* * *

Charlie eased back on the throttle as Annie River came into view. He flexed his shoulders and enjoyed the warmth of the woman seated before him, her thin frame fitted perfectly below his chin and against his chest. She felt like she belonged there. Eli straddled the seat behind him and had his injured leg wedged across Charlie's hip and tucked under Kelsey's arm. She'd held it in place for the entire journey and never once complained about the uncomfortable trip.

Casting his mind back to his arrival at the riders' shack he could still feel the unexpected frisson of enchantment that had greeted him. The tension he'd held in check during the ride had eased somewhat when he spotted the firelight glowing from the shack's archway. The only person known to be in the area was Eli. Charlie presumed he was the one holed up there.

He'd rushed in the door to be confronted by an unexpected sight – a blonde beauty, looking battered and fragile cradling his son's head in her lap. His heart took a mighty leap, how bad was Eli hurt? And a pang of jealousy slammed him in the chest as he watched Kelsey stroke his brow.

He moved his feet and her head jerked up, the terror in her glorious emerald green eyes obvious. The eyes rocked him as they drew him in with their beauty and made him want to swim in their depths. His knees went to rubber and he took an involuntary step forward. Her startled gasp halted him in his tracks. Eli spoke and the world righted. His laugh, even though it cracked slightly, covered the sob of relief he could feel welling in his chest at finding his son safe.

After examining the woman's injuries he dug out a thermos of soup from his pack. While Kelsey and Eli took turns to sip the hot liquid, he grabbed an armful of wood and stoked up the fire. It guzzled the fresh fuel with hunger and then burst into a merry blaze. Charlie stood with his back to the fire, waiting for his pants to dry, and watched the interchange between the boy and woman. They seemed to have bonded. Amelia would never have shared her cup like that – he'd have been lucky if he was allowed to kiss her.

He squatted down and checked Eli's knee. Kelsey had taken good care of it and until he could get it checked by the doctor and X-rayed he would leave it in the splint.

Eli took a big gulp from the cup. 'Dad, that micky bull that surprised Rainbow...' Charlie gave a nod to show he was listening and waited for Eli to continue. 'It had been shot.'

Charlie sighed. 'I'm not surprised. We've had quite a few dramas today. Lost a herd of steers, and the helicopter.'

'Shit Dad...'

'Eli, mouth,' growled Charlie.

'Sorry...' Eli looked up at Kelsey as he apologised, 'You don't mind do you, Kelsey?'

Charlie watched in fascination as she gave his son a sweet smile that revealed a badly chipped canine tooth. 'Not my call, Champ.'

His lip gave an involuntary quirk. Wow, she had Eli's measure already and handled him beautifully.

'Eli, we'll go hunt the steer when the storm's over. There nothing we can do for it right now, besides you're in no fit state to be hunting, so rest. I'll just stable Rainbow properly and he can shelter here until we can get back and collect him.'

Eli nodded and said, 'He needs some first aid, Dad.'

Charlie dug the medical kit from his bulging backpack and wandered over to examine the horse's flank. The wound was clean, no sign of infection, and didn't need stitching. Relieved, Charlie set a filled bucket of rainwater and a biscuit of hay within reach of the horse before rubbing him down with a handful of hay.

Tired, Charlie settled down on the rug in front of the fire, lifted his son's legs into his lap, and closed his eyes.

'We'll head out at first light. Get you both back to the homestead and check out your injuries properly,' he murmured.

His comment was met with silence. Opening one eye he looked over at his two charges. Eli gave a soft snore. Kelsey stared at the fire, a tear leaked from the corner of her eye which she quickly brushed away. Charlie wondered what it was that Kelsey wouldn't talk about in front of Eli, and how she came about her injuries. He opened his mouth to speak but her eyes closed and he thought it best let her rest. There'd be plenty of time to talk once they were home.

Dawn's light arrived late because the sky was enveloped in heavy black cloud that pressed down on the earth like a thick blanket blocking the sun's access. Yesterday's tempest had passed, leaving the landscape littered with fallen trees and branches, mud, large bodies of water and the promise of more to come. Charlie stood watching the horizon and breathed in deeply through his nose, smelling the weather. A faint tickle pushed him into action.

He wheeled the bike into the shack and parked it in front of the waiting pair. Kelsey poured the last of the soup into a cup and held it up to him.

He smiled his thanks, chugged it down, and said, 'We need to get going. There's heavy rain on the way.'

'Your nose, Dad?'

'My nose, mate.'

Kelsey's eyes widened, startled. Eli laughed and turned to her. 'Bull's nose is famous for never being wrong about the weather.'

* * *

Charlie, sandwiched between his two passengers, drove with as much speed as he dared until they reached the loud and fast-moving Annie River. He halted the bike and flipped out the kickstand. He murmuring to the woman nestled under his chin, 'Kelsey, can you hold the bike steady. I need to get off.'

'Sure,' she said taking hold of the handlebars and bracing her feet on either side of the bike.

'Got it?' he asked. At her slight nod he slid out from between his two passengers and dug around in the pack that was perched on Eli's back. He pulled out a black, hard-plastic carry case he'd secreted there before leaving the homestead.

Eli glanced over his shoulder to see what he was doing and said, 'Cool, Dad. You've got a new generation drone with 1080HP imager.'

'Thought you'd be impressed, mate,' smiled Charlie.

'Does it have a good range?'

'Sure does. It's also got hand trajectory flight with a gesture sensing camera that not only takes photos and videos but will also sync with my phone and tablet.'

'Awesome,' breathed Eli.

Charlie set the drone up and sent it skyward. It zoomed across the river heading towards the homestead. He'd asked the detective to keep a watch out for it this morning. When the screen displayed the kitchen door Charlie settled the drone on the door mat.

'And now we wait.'

Chapter Eleven

Ten minutes later Kelsey stared fascinated as two four-wheel drives fishtailed and skidded their way through mud and slush on the opposite side of the river. The vehicles came to a halt and people spilled from the doors.

Eli leant forward, pointed to a fit-looking, sun-tanned man dressed in dusty jeans and a checked button-down shirt.

'That's Uncle Jimmy, Big Mac to the crew, and that's his, wife, Naomi, next to him.' Mac settled an Akubra on his scruffy blond hair and lifted a hand in acknowledgement to Charlie.

Kelsey looked with interest as a tall and shapely aboriginal woman emerged from the vehicle. So this was the woman Eli had described as the best cook ever. She had a bright toothy smile on her face and was flapping her hand in a mad wave at them. The corner of Kelsey's mouth lifted in a smile at Naomi's display of happiness at seeing them. Eli, not so restrained, waved with boyish enthusiasm.

'Who are the other two?' Kelsey asked, studying the short, silver-haired woman who was all sharp angles and a tall and thin, dark-haired, square-shouldered man dressed in khaki trousers and shirt.

'No idea,' said Eli, cocking his head left and eyeing the pair.

'That is Constable Mark Bayden and Detective Rosie Bloom,' said Charlie, hooking his thumbs into the belt loops of his jeans. 'They arrived with the storm.'

Kelsey's heart gave a hard thump and a knot formed in her stomach.

The police were here. What do I tell them. Oh God, I'm not prepared for this yet.

Big Mac pointed down-river. Charlie nodded and slid back onto the bike. He pulled her closer, made sure they were balanced, and lifted her thigh with a gentle hand. She enjoyed the sensation until she realised he needed the room to reach the motorbike's kick start. The bike lurched forward and they rode the short distance towards a massive ironwood tree. She stared up in amazement at the spikes that encircled the tree's trunk forming a spiralling ladder. Her heart sank. She realised she would have to climb up the structure because strung across the river and secured to another large and solid looking ironbark was a zip line for a flying fox.

Kelsey leapt in fright when Charlie spoke with a soft murmur in her ear.

'It's quite safe, we've done this before,' he said, giving her waist a gentle squeeze.

She sucked in a deep breath vowing not to shame herself in front of him. Eli's enthusiasm and excitement brought a timid smile to her lips.

'Can I go first, Dad?'

Repeating their earlier manoeuvre Charlie slid off the bike and lifted his son from the bike. He cradled Eli in his arms and carried him over to the tree and propped the boy against the trunk. Eli smiled at her while Charlie gave Big Mac some sort of complicated hand signal before commencing to climb the spiral ladder. Kelsey flashed a quick glance across the river at Big Mac. He was standing on a platform at the top of the tree opposite parroting Charlie's hand movements.

She returned her focus to Eli's father. He had scaled the ladder with ease and was now returning Big Mac's thumbs up. He pulled on a guide rope and two harnesses attached to the zip line zinged across the wide expanse and into his waiting hand. He detached them and climbed back down to his waiting son.

'Hold this mate,' he said handing Eli a bundle of black webbing and alloyed steel buckles that clinked whenever they touched each other. Charlie ran his fingers along all the straps checking their condition before doing the same with each of the buckles and carabiner. Satisfied, he helped Eli carefully feed his injured leg through the leg loops and once fitted adjusted the harness so it was a firm fit. He did the same for himself.

'All set?' Charlie asked Eli.

The boy nodded enthusiastically. 'Yeah.'

Charlie slung Eli onto his back, piggy-back fashion, and started to re-climb the tree. Kelsey's legs shook in fear and fatigue as she watched the pair trust their weight to the strategically placed metal bars.

They were halfway up when Charlie stopped and cursed. Kelsey's hand flew to her mouth, *Oh no, what's wrong?*

'Bloody hell, Eli, what paddock have you been grazing on?' he growled.

The boy's laughter reached her ears and she let out the breath she didn't know she'd been holding.

They finished the climb without incident and Eli made the crossing look easy and enjoyable by giving a loud yahoo as he zinged across the expanse above the river and into the waiting arms of Mac.

Now it was her turn. Charlie nodded at the harness he held out in a cradle shape for her and said, 'Just like Eli did, put your legs through here.'

She obeyed his command and stood rigid as he secured the buckles around her and double-checked each one was secure and tight. With a gentle hand he spun her around to face him. He massaged her shoulders with soothing fingers and looked deep into her eyes.

'You okay?' he asked.

'Yeah, I'm okay,' she nodded. A crack in her voice betrayed her.

Charlie smiled and a small dimple appeared in his cheek. Her heart flipped and butterflies swirled low in her stomach. She took a deep calming breath.

'I won't let anything happen to you.' His quiet and strong tone instilled her with a strong sense of security. He spun her around again, this time to face the ladder. With a final squeeze on her shoulders he said, 'Now up you go. I'll be right behind you.'

Kelsey nodded and carefully took a step up onto the first rung and then climbed to the next. She didn't look down or any further up than her fingers clutching tightly on the next rung. Her weary body did as it was told as she slowly took each step but she could feel her strength and resolve running out. She sighed in relief when she finally reached the platform. On hands and knees she crawled forward and sat with her knees tucked under her chin looking down at the man who was following close behind. When Charlie got to the top rung he pointed to the zip line, so Kelsey stood and hooked her carabiner onto the trolley. She screwed up the latch and gave it a tug to ensure it was hooked on properly and was secure. She felt a pull behind her and heard another click. She looked over her shoulder at Charlie.

'A safety line,' he murmured in her ear. The small hairs on her neck stood up and a sensation ran up her spine, she wasn't sure if it was fear or something else. 'Ready?'

Kelsey nodded.

A hand pushed her and she fell forward.

Zip.

The noise was long and drawn out. She sucked in her breath, blinked fast and watched the clouds above her head. They had hardly moved before a calloused hand was placed over hers and she was drawn into a strong embrace. Startled Kelsey looked into a pair of dusty green eyes.

'Hi,' she said.

'Hi yourself,' said Mac, and he reached behind her to unhook the harness.

The zipping noise started again.

'Bloody hell, Bull, give us a chance,' Mac swore as he unfastened her harness and helped her onto the first rung of the ladder.

The zipping noise stopped. Kelsey peered up at Mac who was frantically tugging on the guide rope. The flying fox had ceased moving halfway over the raging river leaving Charlie stranded in mid-air. She held her breath and her nerves began to twitch.

'Hang on Bull, the rope's tangled.'

'Take your time, Mac, the view from here's great,' was the calm reply.

Kelsey heard some colourful language being muttered in a soft voice. Mac gave the rope another shake and the flying fox recommenced its trajectory across the river.

As her feet touched the ground Kelsey's world swayed. She fell to one knee.

'Kelsey...?' Eli called out.

Two strong, warm brown arms embraced her and helped her to her feet.

'I'm okay...tired...' she swayed again, the grey static dimmed and went black.

* * *

Charlie's heart sank when he saw the woman collapse. What the hell?

Ignoring Jimmy cussing him out, he scrambled down from the tree two rungs at a time and rushed towards Naomi and the bundle she struggled to hold up.

He could hear Eli explaining to the detective who was supporting him, '...she's walked a long way and has no memory.' His son's voice was very shaky.

He scooped Kelsey up in his arms. She was as cold as ice.

He yelled, 'Hurry up, Mac. We need to get these two home and warmed up.'

Mac was down the tree in an instant. He scooped Eli up in his strong arms and lifted him onto the back seat of the Rodeo. Charlie climbed in beside his son, clutching his precious cargo against his chest. Eli's teeth began to chatter with cold and shock. Charlie freed up an arm from under Kelsey's legs and drew his son close.

The boy snuggled into his father's embrace and asked in a wobbly voice, 'Is Kelsey alright?'

'I think so mate but she's had quite an ordeal. We need to get you both warm.'

'You know, Dad, I've never met a girl like her...not one complaint.'

'Hmm, strong huh.' Charlie felt Eli's head nodding up and down madly.

The vehicle slid to a halt and the door next to him flew open. Jimmy carefully lifted Kelsey from his arms and made his way rapidly up the path towards the kitchen door. Charlie slid out and turned towards Eli.

'Come on, mate, let's get you warmed and doctored.'

'And fed?'

'Yeah, I'm sure there's a steak somewhere with your name on it...' he laughed, in relief. Charlie knew Eli would be okay. It was only when the boy was off his food he'd have to worry.

* * *

Charlie turned from tucking the blanket securely around the inert body of Kelsey on the couch and nearly stood on Rosie. She held her ground and stared up at him, her eyes hard.

'Who's your friend, Mr Morgan?' she asked.

So she's back to calling me mister.

'Don't know detective. I think this might be your department.'

A fleeting look of curiosity crossed her face before it went blank.

'How so?'

'Look, once I've seen to Eli...we'll talk.'

Naomi bustled into the room, putting a halt to Rosie's intense questioning. Naomi held a bowl of warm water with a cream flannel floating in it. In the other hand she carried the RFDS medical kit. With gentle fingers, Naomi squeezed the wet cloth and laid it across Kelsey's forehead, then began a long slow inspection of each of her injuries. When she removed the dirty, threadbare socks from Kelsey's feet, a bunch of squashed eucalyptus leaves and red dirt fell onto the carpet.

'Smart girl,' said Naomi, brushing away the last of the insulation Kelsey had used to protect her soles. Washing first one foot then the other, Naomi began applying antiseptic cream. 'She's got some bad damage to the soles of her feet. They're raw. It could have been much worse if it hadn't been for the makeshift shoes.'

Charlie and Rosie stared over her shoulder. 'How the hell did she walk on those?' Rosie asked, staring at the bloody soles.

'Guts,' said Charlie.

Kelsey's eyes fluttered and she murmured, 'Need help.'

'Shhh. You're safe now,' said Naomi in a soft voice.

Kelsey sighed and stilled.

* * *

All the chairs around the kitchen table were occupied and the plates in front of everyone were empty.

'What happened at the crash site?' asked Charlie. He was angry with himself for waiting this long to ask about the welfare of his pilot.

Jimmy snorted in disgust. 'Steve clipped a tree with the tail rotor and dropped the chopper on the deck. Choppers a mess but Steve is fine. Sporting a couple of bruises but that's it.'

'Hot-dogging?'

'Denies it...but yeah I'd say so.'

Charlie shook his head – now he had to find enough funds for helicopter repairs. Bloody Steve – an irresponsible ego on two legs who thought the station chopper pilot was indispensable. Wrong, of course.

Rosie started fidgeting with her cutlery, tapping the knife against the plate. Her impatience to question Eli was obvious. Charlie had told her in no uncertain terms that she was to leave the boy alone until after the meal.

Eli gave a belch of satisfaction, pulled the dark blue mink blanket tighter around his shoulders, and smiled.

'Better?' asked Charlie.

Eli nodded.

'Okay, I want you to tell Detective Bloom everything.'

And that's exactly what Eli did. He gave a detailed description of his adventure, the trek to the shack, and all his conversations with the woman sleeping in the next room, word for word. He provided so much detail that instead of asking questions, Rosie had to hold her hand up to stem the flow. Charlie hid his amusement. Serves her right he thought.

When Eli's chatter finally ran down, Jimmy, who wasn't hiding his amusement, said, 'Sounds like she walked across the northern plain, coming from Zentra Hill direction. If she'd gone south-east she could have followed the inland track to the main road and found us.'

Charlie nodded.

Jimmy continued to reflect.

'Zentra Hill inland track – the gate was open.'

Charlie nodded again

'The two-year-old steers were shot near the gate.'

Jimmy stared at Charlie. Charlie stared back at Jimmy.

'Awe come on, Dad...' Charlie held his forefinger up to Eli to halt the flow of words and rolled his hand for Mac to continue.

'The cattle were shot after she was dumped...someone thinks she's dead,' said Jimmy as he looked around the table at all the watching faces. 'She's in danger until she remembers what happened to her and can tell us.'

Charlie nodded again.

The detective leant forward and spoke, 'I'm here in the region to investigate the disappearance of some young women...'

Charlie stared at her. 'Not the cattle.'

Rosie shook her head. 'The cattle are only one of my briefs. Sixteen hundred people are currently missing in Western Australia. I was sent to Mount Ibour to look into two open cases. You don't think they'd send a detective to sort out a few dead steers do you?'

'So why do you need to speak with Tangles?' asked Charlie.

Rosie gave him a puzzled look.

Constable Bayden spoke for the first time, 'Tangles is Rhysand Archerson, boss.'

Rosie's confused look cleared, 'Oh, I see. Well I don't know if you're aware or not but your boy, Tangles, arrived at Mount Ibour Airport in June 2018 in the company of a woman named Britt Larsen. A week later she was reported missing.'

Chapter Twelve

Dishes washed and put away, the kitchen was reasonably tidy – or as neat as Charlie could get it considering all the people in the room. At the request of the detective he wheeled the whiteboard from his office into the room and positioned it against the crockery sideboard. Constable Bayden braved the torrent of rain that had been hurling from the sky for the last half an hour to collect a stack of files from the police vehicle parked in the garage.

He dashed into the room shaking water from a reflective police raincoat and handed the case notes to Rosie. 'Britt's is the top file, boss.'

Rosie extracted the colour photo clipped inside the cover and studied it. She flicked it across the table to Mark and said, 'Draw up an incident board, Bayden.'

The constable leapt to his feet and started to section off the whiteboard with the black marker pen.

Eli, his injured knee packed in ice and his leg propped up on a stool, was sitting back watching the preparations with boyish delight written all over his face. Charlie didn't have the heart to send him to bed.

'Mac, do us a favour and go fetch Tangles for the detective?' said Charlie.

Jimmy gave a thumbs-up, rose to his feet and said, 'Will do, and then I'll get on with the tech repairs. See if between us Mimi and I can get some communications back online. Something tells me were gonna need them real soon.'

Rosie slipped gold-framed, half-moon reading glasses onto the end of her nose, opened a red folder and flipped through the pages. She glanced up over the top of the lenses at her young and eager subordinate.

'Bayden, I want you to take notes of everything that's said.' The constable stopped drawing lines on the board and unzipped his computer bag. He dug around inside and with a grunt of success pulled out a large notebook and pen. Rosie glanced over at Eli and said, 'A good investigator keeps a record of everything they see and hear. Also a task list, that way nothing falls through the cracks.'

Eli nodded, drinking in the information like a sponge. Charlie, also curious to see the workings of the investigation, settled into a chair next to his son.

Rosie leant forward and read out loud from the file. 'Britt Larsen. Nineteen years old. Norwegian. 165cm tall, long wavy russet-brown hair and dark-chocolate eyes. She went missing June 2018.'

Reaching out to pick up the photograph that lay face upwards on the table, constable Bayden sighed. 'She's extremely beautiful.' He stared at the picture before laying it face down on the table top.

The screen door gave a quiet click. Charlie watched Rosie's glance dart across the room to the entry and focus on the man hovering just inside the door. Tangles, looking scared, stared down at his boots waiting to be invited in. Charlie noticed raindrops stood out in beads on his short, white-blond hair as if repelled by Scotchgard. With a slight tremor in his hand, Tangles brushed the drops away.

He'd changed his dirty work clothes for a clean blue-checked, long-sleeved button-down shirt and close-fitting black jeans that hugged his athletic frame.

Rosie slid her mobile phone on the table and set it to record while waving to a vacant chair. 'Come in, Rhysand and sit down. I want to talk with you about Britt.'

Tangles' chin came up in a rush, his blue eyes zeroed in on the detective and his golden, tanned cheeks paled. The Adam's apple in his throat leapt up and down like a ball bouncing madly on a trampoline.

'Have you found her?' he asked in a choked voice, his Norwegian accent more pronounced than usual.

Rosie didn't answer the question. Instead, she asked one of her own.

'Did you kill her?'

Wow, no touchy-feely with this woman, thought Charlie. Bang, straight to the heart of the matter. He decided that maybe Eli shouldn't be here, but before he could make a move to remove his son from the room, Tangles answered the question.

'*Nei*...no, detective, I didn't kill her. I loved her.' He let out a soft sigh and went on, 'Finding Britt is the main reason I'm still here in Australia. Is she dead?' His voice cracked when he asked the question.

'I don't know Rhysand. Sit down and tell me about her.'

Tangles lowered himself into a chair, his movements slow and laboured. 'Britt and I live in a town called Lillehammer. Have you heard of it?'

'1994 Winter Olympics, right?' said Bayden.

Tangles nodded his head, '*Ja*...sorry, yes and also the 2016, Youth Winter Olympics. We work together at Lysgardsbakkene the ski jump arena. We *vedlikeholde*...sorry I must speak English, yes.' He took a deep breath and continued, 'Together we maintain the skiing equipment.'

'How long had you been together?'

'All our life,' said Tangles. A puzzled frown creased the detectives face, it cleared when he continued. 'Britt, she is my cousin, you understand, my family. Last year a small *gruppe*...sorry...our small group of cousins, Britt, Astrid, Frida and myself came to Australia on holidays. They also are family. You understand?'

The detective nodded. 'Yes. So tell me in which city did you start your holiday?' asked Rosie.

'We had one week in Perth.'

'And after you left Perth, where did you go?'

'We came to Mount Ibour.'

'So, you were only in this country for seven days before Britt disappeared?'

'*Ja.*'

Rosie sat forward and clasped her hands together in front of her on the table. 'You can see my problem here, Rhysand. You and your cousins are the only people who knew Britt's itinerary, and only hours after arriving in our remote community she goes missing. She didn't have any family or friends here or in Perth?'

'No, but she did meet someone.'

'Tell me about that.'

'Britt was happy and excited. On our second night in Perth, the girls wanted to go to a nightclub. I went along to fetch the drinks from the bar for them and make sure they got home safe. When we arrived Astrid and Frida went off to find a table. Britt went with me to the bar to carry some drinks. The dance floor was crowded, the young they move wildly...all arms and legs. A strobe light, it flashed on, off and on and the music was all thump, thump, thump...it was like being hit in the head with small fists. You understand.'

'Yes, the music pounded loudly,' said Rosie.

A clear image of a crowded, stuffy and noisy nightclub rose in Charlie's mind. Beautiful Amelia, arms locked around his neck, her lips parted in a sultry smile, gazing up at him adoringly. He remembered he had to pinch himself as they swayed to the music locked in each other's arms, not believing that this glorious creature was his for the taking. He placed his lips over hers...

Tangles spoke and jerked Charlie back from his memory.

'The people seemed to enjoy it but I thought it was horrible, it gave me the headache.'

'Tell me what happened at the nightclub to make this outing important.'

'Britt took two of the drinks I bought and pushed hard to get through the crowd. I turned my back to her, to pay the bartender and wait for my change. Britt tripped. She was saved by a strong pair of arms and fell in *dybde*...sorry...urm, depth with an amazing pair of eyes. No...that is not right either.'

'I understand,' said Rosie, 'she was caught by someone with lovely eyes.'

Tangles nodded and continued with his story. 'I didn't see the person, you understand. This is just what she told me, afterward. For the rest of the week, she would disappear for long periods, instead of coming and sightseeing with us. When she did return from these absences, she always had a smug smile on her lips. When I asked her about where she was going and who she was seeing, she told me and my cousins to mind our own business, she was just having a *flort*...a fling. That's all she would say. My cousins and I, we didn't get to learn anything about the person.'

The kitchen light reflected off the beginnings of a bald patch on the crown of Constable Bayden's head as he hunched over his notebook writing in a quick and untidy scrawl. Charlie felt sorry for him, trying to keep up with the detective's rapid inquisition.

'What was his name?'

'No name, and I cannot say it was a man.'

Charlie lifted an eyebrow at this comment and flicked a quick glance at the detective to gauge her response. Her face remained blank as she asked, 'Why do you say that?'

'She has always rebuffed the men who made advances towards her...before. Britt always seemed to prefer women's company. But I am not sure. Britt never spoke of this side of her life, to me or anyone else in the family. It was not important to our feelings for her. You understand?'

Rosie's head moved up and down in a nod and her short silver hair brushed her jaw-line. 'Tell me what happened next?' she asked, tucking the hair back behind her ears.

'Britt and Frida asked that we come to the Kimberley to sightsee. There is so much to see and do they said, and if we needed jobs there were good prospects for work. So we booked accommodation at the Nambung Gorge campground and took an airplane to Mount Ibour. When I unbuckled my seat belt to get off the airplane, Britt was just hanging up on her mobile phone. She announced she was not going to come with us to Nambung Gorge, she was going to stay with a friend for the week. When I asked who this friend was, she just gave me that same smug smile and said she would meet us at the airport on our day of departure. We did not argue but I was not happy. She was the one who pushed us to come to Mount Ibour, to go camping at Nambung Gorge. I asked her to wait while I went to pick up the keys for the hire car because I wanted to know where she was going so we could stay in touch. She agreed but while I was busy she left.' Tangles shook his head and covered his face with a hand. Charlie could hear him taking long slow breaths that hitched at the end. Finally, he peered up, ran the hand down his chin and sighed. 'I should have been more insistent. Asked, *nei*, demanded to meet her friend. I promised my family, her father and mother, my uncles and aunts that I'd look after all my cousins. The girls were very angry about that. Norwegian women they are strong – they have no weaknesses and are fierce about their independence. They don't enjoy being watched over. I was upset with Britt for leaving us that way, we all were, you understand, but I did not think she would come to harm. I am angry with myself for having failed in my duty.'

Rosie acknowledged the sentiment with a nod of her head but did not comment on the futility of hindsight. Eli squirmed in his seat. She glared at him and said, 'Do you have a question, Eli?'

'Yeah, I was wondering how Britt got from the airport to wherever she was going without being seen? The airports five kilometres from the town, taxis have to be pre-booked and there's no airport shuttle like in the city. The terminal and car-park usually have lots of locals hanging around waiting to pick up family and friends – someone must have seen her leave.'

Rosie smiled, a glow of satisfaction on her face at the insightful question. She turned to her partner and said, 'That, Constable Bayden, is what we call an excellent question. Well done young man.'

Charlie watched in amusement as a faint rosy blush tinged his son's cheeks. Bayden's head dropped closer to the page he was writing on but he didn't comment. The smile left the detective's face, as she studied the distressed features of the jackaroo across the table.

'Would you be able to answer that, Rhysand?' she asked.

'*Ja*...I mean yes. When we were loading the bags into the car, I saw someone who looked like Britt climb into a four-wheel drive.'

'What type of vehicle?'

'A RAV4. I can't be positive it was her, you understand, it was too far away for a good look.'

'Did you see the driver?'

'No, the windows were dark, tinted I think you call it.'

'Shit,' said Rosie. Charlie glared at her for using the profanity in front of Eli. 'Sorry for the swear word. Rhysand, what can you remember about the car. For starters, are you sure it was a RAV4?'

'*Ja*. It was silver. Very clean, it sparkled in the sunshine. No dents or scratches. I did not see the number plate. I know it was a RAV4 because Bull has one just like the one I saw.'

Constable Bayden's head shot up and he gave Charlie a startled look. He opened his mouth to comment then let out a gasp. He leant forward to rub his leg. Charlie suspected that the detective had just kicked his shin to keep him quiet.

'Is that the last time you or any of your family saw or heard from Britt?'

'*Ja*,' said Tangles. 'I have asked many times at the pub and around Mount Ibour when I have been there. No one remembers seeing Britt after she left in that motor vehicle. She has never answered my phone calls or text messages.'

'All right Rhysand, that will be all for now. Let me know if you remember anything else.'

'You didn't answer my question, detective. Have you found her, is she dead?'

'We don't know, Rhysand. That is why I'm here, in Mount Ibour, to take a fresh look at her disappearance – but I think you and your family should prepare yourselves for the worst. It has been over eighteen months. I don't hold out much hope of us finding her alive.'

Tangles nodded, a tear slid down his cheek. He gave it an impatient swipe and stood up. 'Bull, I will go back to work now, if that is okay with you?'

'Sure, mate. There's more bad weather coming in, would you get Roscoe to secure the shutters on the shearers' shed and if you could, check on Bindi. I'm worried she's going to drop her litter of pups tonight'

Tangles nodded, 'Do not be concerned, Bull. The dog she can bed down in my quarters,' he replied.

'You spoil those damn dogs,' said Charlie with a smile, pleased his stockman had something to distract him from the sadness in his life. Tangles flapped his hand, gave a small smile before heading out into the rain.

Charlie noted Eli trying to suppress a yawn. It didn't work and his face nearly split in half as he displayed a gaping chasm of teeth and tongue. Charlie turned to him and said, 'It was a long day and an even longer and more uncomfortable night, mate. It's time for you to get some rest.' Before Eli could protest or the detective could ask any questions that might upset his son, Charlie lifted him from the chair and carried him away from the inquisition.

Chapter Thirteen

The laughter scared Kelsey and she sat bolt upright in fright. Sweat was pouring down her face. Terror had a firm grip on her throat and was squeezing the breath from her chest making it hard to breath. She held back the scream that formed on her lips, worried that any noise might draw the wrong attention.

She darted her gaze around the room in an effort to take in the new situation she found herself in. She was on a couch in a room with soft translucent light coming from slim-line strips that ran around the skirting boards giving it a warm and friendly ambiance. Landscape paintings and photographs depicting cattle station life from all eras decorated the walls and blended well with the electronics of the modern world. Deep in the house a clock ticked. Sinking back into the comfort of buttery-soft brown leather she tugged up the white and lavender hand-stitched quilt and tucked it under her chin. The quilt smelt of fresh-cut flowers. Kelsey took a long calming breath and waited for understanding to surface.

Where am I?

The grey static in her brain cleared and a memory returned. A handsome black horse called Rainbow. A boy's infectious laughter

– Eli, and a handsome and desirable man, hanging over the raging river with his zip line tangled. Her heart began to race. Was he all right? She was sure she heard the line zing before a smooth hand had stroked her brow and a woman's gentle voice had whispered words of comfort.

Is this Rivers Run Homestead?

Kelsey threw the quilt aside. Her legs and hands were still dirty. Being careful not to stain the beautiful patchwork anymore than she had, Kelsey swung her feet to the floor. She yelped and hissed as fire shot up her legs like a thousand burning needles. She snatched her feet up from the floor and let them cool, before tentatively putting them down again. In a slow deliberate movement she applied pressure until the pain became bearable and she could stand.

The nightmare disturbed her – a shadow had held her at the bottom of a shaft with its inky black arms, while high above a faceless image had laughed. Was it a dream or a memory? The terror it evoked in her was slow to fade and her nerves still jangled from its effects. She needed answers. Deciding to start with the most immediate questions she took half a dozen shuffling steps towards the two archways at the far end of the room. The door to the left was closed but a thin line of light shone along its bottom edge. The door to the right stood open. Curious, she glanced in. A night light at the far end of the corridor shone on a Kaswar Persian carpet that ran its entire length. The hall was watched over by a grandfather clock and acted as an artery to five closed doors and a carpeted wooden staircase.

Bong, bong.

The noise made her jump, but the slumbering house remained undisturbed.

It must be 2am. Kelsey turned and shuffled towards the door showing a strip of light. She twisted the knob and pulled. The door swung quietly open to reveal a large square foyer. The exquisite

Persian carpet matched the one in the hall. To her left a door stood ajar. The room was lit by a standard lamp, its cream woollen shade tamped down the harshness of the bright globe. The light illuminated a floor-to-ceiling bookcase. The untidy shelves were stacked with a huge assortment of ledgers, books and periodicals, some of which had leached onto the floor in piles as though waiting to be re-shelved. A large oak desk stood in the centre of the room and was littered with piles of papers and envelopes. Tucked into the desk was an oversize black leather office chair.

The tantalising aroma of coffee wafted into the hall. She closed her eyes and sucked the smell in. Her stomach growled in anticipation. With slow careful footsteps she followed her nose and crossed to another open doorway and found herself in a large country-style kitchen. The benches were covered in gleaming appliances and in the centre of the room stood a well-used, ten-seater jarrah dining table with five chairs a side.

Sitting in a central chair at the table, surrounded by paperwork was Charlie Morgan. He thumped the laptop computer in front of him and cursed its existence.

'Damn stupid bloody thing. Why won't you do what I want?'

The harshness of his voice scared her. She sucked in a startled gasp and his head shot up.

'Sorry, Kelsey...did I wake you?' he asked, rubbing the nape of his neck. She watched fascinated as a rosy pink colour tinged his cheeks.

'No,' she said, shyness making the words more a mumble. 'I had a nightmare.'

'I'm not surprised. You've had an eventful few days,' he said, rising to stand tall in stockinged feet. His hair was tussled and untidy and he had a sheepish look on his face. Kelsey thought how handsome and at home he looked.

'Do you want to talk about it?' he asked, hooking his thumbs into his belt loops and rocking back on his heels.

'Thanks, Mr Morgan, but there's nothing to talk about. It was just a vague image. Do you mind if I have a cup of coffee?'

'Call me Charlie, please,' he said, a small smile touching his lips. 'Go ahead and help yourself to anything you want. Treat this like your home, Kelsey.'

'Can I get you one? You look like you need it?'

Charlie nodded but when she started to shuffle forward he growled, 'Shit, I'm sorry...' He swooped around the table and lifted her from her feet. He carried her to his chair, and in a gentle gesture deposited her on the warm seat. 'My bad, I was so wrapped up in my own disaster,' he said pointing to the laptop, 'I forgot about your injuries. You sit and relax, I'll get the coffee. How do you like it?'

Kelsey's body tingled where he'd touched her. She took a moment to enjoy the wonderful spicy scent he'd left behind before replying.

'I don't know...black?' While he busied himself at the coffee machine, she looked at the mess on the table in front of her. 'Why were you beating up the poor computer?'

'I'm trying to catch up on my bookwork, find some cash to repair my helicopter but the stupid spreadsheet won't co-operate. I'll have to wait and ask my book-keeper next time he's here as this software stuff of his defies me.'

'What's your main problem?'

'I was trying to clean up some of my accounts and get a handle on my finances but I can't get the columns to tally. There a glitch in the formulas and the more I try to fix it the worse it gets. Gil Connors, he's my book-keeper, usually takes care of this stuff but I find of late I'm relying on him too much and I've lost track of my expenditure. Anyway, my attempts have messed up the worksheets and they've stopped talking to each other. Gil's going to go ballistic because I've stuffed it up good and proper.'

Kelsey pointed to the half-closed laptop and said, 'Can I take a look?'

'Do you know spreadsheets?'

Kelsey paused, cocked her head, and stared at the man before her in puzzlement.

'You know, I'm not sure but this seems familiar.'

'Well give it a go...you can't do any damage. I've already done that.'

Kelsey opened the laptop. With a blank mind, she laid her fingers on the keyboard and waited. They started to dance across the keys.

Taking a small bite from the delicious cheese and tomato sandwich that Charlie slid next to her elbow, she pointed to the screen and said, 'I've corrected and protected the formulas, so you can't damage them again. There was some weird logic in some of them and it was sending your numbers to the wrong places. I can password protect the whole lot if you like then they can only be changed by a deliberate act.' When Charlie nodded his agreement she completed the task and said, 'Just enter your figures, here or here and save. The program will do the rest.'

Charlie leant forward and kissed her on the cheek. 'You're a lifesaver...can I keep you?'

Her heart flipped in excitement, then a small pain pierced it and her lips stopped smiling. *Oh, I'd love to have a man such as you in my life, but you're already married.*

'I'm sorry. I didn't mean to embarrass you. You probably have a husband or a string of boyfriends waiting for you...'

'No...I don't think so. It doesn't feel like there's anyone...' Kelsey stopped, stunned by the gleam of light coming in through a small window in her mind. A memory of always being alone and the pain of loneliness, she lifted her arm and studied the white scars. 'My family died in a car accident when I was a child.'

Her soft words were raw and broke as they left her lips. Charlie used his forefinger to tuck a wisp of hair behind her ear and said, 'I'm sorry. Is that how you got the scars?'

The window slammed shut.

'I don't know.'

Along with the first blush of dawn Detective Rosie Bloom stepped into the room.

Chapter Fourteen

Charlie glanced up from the distressed face of his guest at the detective who was standing in the doorway. He silently pointed to a cup and a chair. She nodded and took a seat.

'Kelsey,' Charlie said, keeping his voice soft and calm, 'this is Detective Rosie Bloom. She'd like to ask you some questions, would that be alright with you?'

Kelsey lifted a tear-streaked face. 'Yes, I need to speak with the police...it's important.' Charlie watched as she slid her hand into the pocket of her shorts and drew something out. In a slow deliberate movement she set it in the exact centre of the table.

The detective's eyebrows rose. She picked it up and held it up to the morning light streaming in through the kitchen window.

'Human?'

Kelsey nodded once.

'Are there more?'

Kelsey nodded again and said, 'And a body.'

Charlie's hand shook at her words, spilling the coffee he was drinking over the side of the cup. He sucked in his breath.

The detective's fingers danced over the screen of her mobile phone. She slid it onto the table and in a cool, calm voice, commanded, 'Tell me.'

Kelsey closed her eyes and brought up her first memories. Her voice refused to work at first. She gave a cough to clear her throat, before she could try again the detective said, 'Take your time.' Kelsey nodded and took a deep breath. She felt Charlie move away from beside her. She flicked a glance his way and watched as he left the room. Her heart fell, she felt bereft without his support. He was gone only a moment before returning carrying the lavender quilt. He wrapped it around her, sat down and draped his arm across her shoulders. She felt safe and cared for in the warm cocoon he'd created.

Closing her eyes for a moment she took a deep breath and said, 'When I opened my eyes I was lying at the bottom of a shaft. I think it was once a well because it was vertical only, no tunnels. The body of a young aboriginal woman, she looked to be about nineteen, was clutched in my arms.' Kelsey watched the detective's bright-blue eyes blink but her gaze didn't move from her own. So, she held the look and with meticulous care described the scene of her first memories in graphic detail. She then went on to describe the effort taken to escape the well and her adventures up until being found by Charlie. When she'd finished, the detective asked her repeat it. As the last words left her lips, the woman before her leant forward and said, 'Did you kill the girl?'

'No.'

'How do you know?'

Kelsey opened her mouth to explain that just the thought of taking such an action made her feel ill, but the words would not come. Instead she just shook her head.

The detective changed tact, 'What's your name?'

'Kelsey...'

'Who?'

'Kelsey...' The window in her mind remained shut.

A small sob left her lips and the man sitting beside her growled, 'What are you doing?'

The silver-haired woman glared across the table at him and lifted her slender shoulders, 'Sometimes being put under pressure like that activates or triggers an automatic response, Mr Morgan.'

'How many times do I have to say it, Rosie? My name is Bull. I'm beginning to feel like a suspect.'

Eli hopped into the room, his injured knee held out in front of him for balance. Wearing short PJ boxers and an oversize tee-shirt, his hair was endearingly rumpled just like his fathers, except Eli presented the perfect image of someone who had enjoyed a deep and satisfying night's sleep.

The detective ignored his entrance and said in the same abrupt tone, 'Well, there is your wife.'

'Amelia...what's she got to do with anything?'

'Is she one of the bodies? Did you kill her?'

Eli's hand stopped just short of a breakfast bowl he was reaching for and he swung around to stare at his father. Pain etched lines on his face. Kelsey's heart hurt at the sight.

The telephone in the office rang, breaking the silence in the room. Charlie rose to his feet, his face a dark storm of anger. He walked across the room and gathered the boy into his arms.

'No, Detective Bloom,' he growled, across the top of Eli's head. 'And it's wrong of you to say such things in front of Eli.'

'See – automatic response, protect your son, not defend yourself – tells me a lot.'

'Well, it was cruel and insensitive.'

The phone continued its incessant demand to be answered. Charlie chucked Eli under the chin with the knuckle of his forefinger and left the room. He was back in a moment.

'It's for you, detective. Sergeant George, Mount Ibour police station.'

Rosie picked up her mobile phone and checked the screen.

'Jimmy and Mimi have managed to fix the satellite dish, but you won't get mobile coverage out here until the telco's been to fix the tower,' Charlie said.

Rosie nodded, shoved her chair backward and hurried from the room. Charlie walked over to his son and cupped his chin. 'Eli, look at me son.' Eli's pewter grey eyes bore into Charlie's. 'This has nothing to do with your mother, or me for that matter. Okay.'

Eli continued to stare at his father, eyes flitting left and right as he studied Charlie's face. Even as she watched, Kelsey saw his body relax and the smile and trust returned to his face.

'Sure, Dad.'

'Come and sit down, you look like a scraggy stork hovering there by the cupboard.' The warmth and affection in Charlie's voice was evident as he spoke.

Eli hopped over to the chair across from Kelsey and said, 'Morning, Kelsey. How ya feeling today?'

'I'm good, Champ. What about yourself?'

'Starvin,' he growled, rubbing a hand over his flat belly.

Kelsey watched in fascination as a smile formed on Charlie's face and the resemblance of father and son became more pronounced. He pulled a box of cereal from the cupboard and slid it and a bowl in front of his son. Eli tucked in. Charlie flung open the fridge and started loading his arms with bacon, eggs and tomatoes.

'Dad, maybe after breakfast we should get some of Mum's old clothes out for Kelsey, so she can have a bath. It must be awful to be still wearing the same grungy stuff.'

'From the mouth of babes...' said Charlie, shaking his head and giving her a contrite look. 'I'm sorry, Kelsey, I should have taken care of you sooner, instead I've had you sitting here all night solving my computer glitches. Let's get you both fed then you can have a nice long soak in the tub.'

'Sounds like heaven,' Kelsey declared.

* * *

Rosie lifted the telephone receiver. 'Sarge?'

'How's it going out there? I was worried when I didn't hear from you.'

'Yeah, we got hit bad by the storm. It knocked out the entire comms system here. The foreman...'

'Jimmy Donald...'

'That's him. He worked all night to get the satellite phone working but the rest is still down. So don't bother with the mobile for now. Bayden and I will be sticking around – the case has just gotten bigger.'

'What do you mean bigger? Isn't a missing tourist, some dead cattle and an anonymous letter big enough?'

'I can't help it Noah, shit happens. Do you have a missing persons report on a woman, emerald-green eyes, shoulder length blonde hair, around 174cm tall. First name of Kelsey...last name, unknown.'

'Not locally.'

'What about an Aboriginal girl? Approximate age nineteen. Very pretty. I've got no other details.'

'Why? What's going on?'

'I've got an injured woman, carrying what looks to be part of a human rib bone and one hell of a story...take a listen,' said Rosie. Setting her mobile to play she held it to the telephone and allowed Kelsey's interview to play over the airwave. When it finished she held the receiver back to her ear and asked, 'Still there, Noah?'

'Yeah...shit Rosie, sounds like we've got a serial killer on our hands. I'll get the reports filed straight away and contact the Coronial Investigation Unit. They are going to need to send the specialist team your way.'

'Yeah, well don't mobilise them yet...we still have to find the grave and confirm her story. She seems genuine and doesn't seem delusional but I'd hate for us to end up with egg on our face by jumping the gun and not doing our due diligence first.'

'I can't hold them off for long, how much time do you need?'

'Well, we are flooded in here. Charlie Morgan reckons there's more rain on the way today, then it should ease.'

'Well believe him, his nose is never wrong. We didn't cop the wind you did but we are getting the rain. The highway to Broome's flooded as is the road to Rivers Run. That will help buy us some time. You probably have a week before the roads open and traffic can get through. See what you can accomplish in that time. Get Bull to fly you to the crime scene in that chopper of his...'

'Can't – pilot crashed it in the storm yesterday.'

'Bloody hell, Rosie, it just gets better and better. Well do what you can and do it fast. You do realise we won't be able to keep this out of the press, so be careful, especially when the road opens. The killer is not going to be happy knowing one of his victims is still alive.'

* * *

Kelsey was floating along in Charlie's strong, safe arms, drinking in his wonderful warm spicy scent. With a long steady stride, he carried her through the lounge room and straight across the grandfather clock hallway into a large and feminine room. He set her down carefully on the edge of a king-size bed that had been dressed in a handmade patchwork quilt. To hide the flush that had risen in her face at Charlie's closeness, Kelsey ran her finger over the beautiful stitching that formed one of the quilt's panels. It had been crafted with a Japanese sense of detail, colour and design.

I wonder how I know about quilting she asked herself as she scratched around in her brain for an answer. Nothing surfaced, so she flicked her gaze around the rest of the room with interest. There were delicate lace doilies protecting the Queen Anne single-draw bedside table. An exquisite beaded crystal bottle set lived on the matching dressing table across the room and the spicy, sweet scent of Lily of the Valley seeped from the perfume decanters. A wall caught her attention. It was covered with a variety of photographs. Each picture represented a milestone moment in the history of family life. Kelsey pointed to a black and white wedding photo of a handsome couple, who strongly resembled the man standing before her and asked, 'Are they your parents, Charlie?'

Charlie smiled, 'Yeah, and grandparents,' he said, indicating another older grouping of people in sepia tones. 'My mum's folks. That's her as a baby. She was born here at Rivers Run and died here. Dad too, he was the only son of the station's foreman. Dad died in a cattle stampede when I was twelve and my sister ten.' Charlie adjusted a colour photo of two cute toddlers, both with corkscrew black hair.

'Is that you and your sister?'

'Sure is.'

Kelsey studied the pictures with interest. Over a hundred years of history was on display on that one wall, capturing weddings, births, graduations and the intermittent changes of what looked to be a happy family. The gallery's story line ended with the wedding photo of Charlie's sister.

'This was my mum's room and that wall was her portrait gallery. She told me she loved talking with dad and her folks every night at lights out. She'd keep them up to date on all the family events.'

'Your own wedding and Eli's birth aren't here.'

'No, mum died before any of that happened.'

'Oh, I'm sorry. Why do you keep all this wonderful history hidden away? They'd look great out on the wall in the kitchen, in the heart of family life?'

Charlie didn't answer the question instead he asked one of his own as he tossed aside an assortment of throw pillows to give her more room.

'Do you want me to ask Naomi to give you a hand to take a bath?'

'No, I'll be fine,' she answered, looking up into his face as it hovered above hers. He stared back at her, the tension between them crackled. She wondered if he was going to kiss her.

Charlie's face suddenly went blank. He stepped back and nodded. A small wave of disappointment passed through her.

Silly girl...he's not interested in you. With everything that's going on you're just another complication.

He crossed the room and slid aside a full-length mirror. Behind it was a walk-in wardrobe. Charlie strode in, rummaged around, and returned carrying two large fluffy towels, the colour of burnt brass. He hesitated for a moment, came closer, and set them on the bed next to her hand. Their fingers brushed.

In slow-motion he withdrew his hand, held it up and pointed towards a door. 'The bathroom is through there. I'll be back in a minute,' he said and with a brisk step stalked out of the room.

Kelsey carefully got to her feet and taking the towels with her, took the half dozen steps across the cream carpet to the bathroom door. She opened it and peeked in. Her mouth dropped open in surprise – beige marble tiled the walls and floor, contrasting beautifully with a dark brown marble that surrounded an oversized double sink. Glancing behind the door, her lips lifted into a smile of delight. A spacious, glass-enclosed shower cubicle butted a generous, white claw-foot bathtub.

So much nicer than the stingy shower nozzle over the chipped tub at home.

Her fingers tightened on the door frame.

Oh, a memory.

The bedroom door swung open. She jumped in fright. Charlie paused and studied her face. In one hand he held a suitcase and in the other he clutched two pairs of thick woollen work socks. She allowed her features to relax and loosened her grip on the door frame.

'Sorry. Is it okay to come in?'

'Of course, it's your house.'

'Kelsey, this is your room, your own private space. You say who can and can't enter.'

He strode into the room, dropped the case onto the bed and flipped open the locks.

'Use anything you like. Most of it is new and never been worn.'

'She won't mind?'

'Who?'

'Your wife.'

A range of emotions crossed his face – pain, anger, and something indefinable but all that came out of his mouth was an abrupt, 'No.'

* * *

After lathering a generous amount of the rose-scented soap over her body for the third time, Kelsey lay back in the tub and floated in the hot water. It was a relief to be clean. The smell of flowers filled the steamy air. She smiled and closed her eyes, the warmth of the water soaked deep into her bones. It was glorious. Her thoughts wandered. She was safe for now, but how long could she stay hidden from whoever was out to get her? Once she'd shown the police the 'well of bones', it would be time to leave. She couldn't remain here and be a burden to these good people – but there was still a killer out there.

I must remember.

Tiredness seeped in and she began to drift into sleep. The water cooled and chilled her. A laughing dark shadow formed and tried to force her under the water. She sank into its depth. Her heart began to pound loudly in her ears. She couldn't breathe. The smell of death touched her nose. Her hands flailed and found the edge of the tub. She grasped hold and pulled herself up. A scream came unbidden from her throat.

Her bedroom door crashed open.

'Kelsey,' Charlie roared.

She coughed and spluttered and managed to choke out, 'I'm okay.'

A loud knocking sounded on the bathroom door.

'Kelsey, it's Detective Bloom. Are you decent, can I come in?'

'Just a minute.'

With a sigh Kelsey pulled the plug and tentatively climbed out of the tub. She slipped her arms into the silk floral kimono that hung on the back of the door, wrapped a towel around her wet hair. It was time to go out and explain.

Chapter Fifteen

'I wish I could draw,' growled Rosie, pacing the room like a caged dingo. 'We could then do an identikit. It's no good asking Bayden, he's about as useful as tits on a bull in that department. I don't suppose you can draw?' She swung around and stared at Charlie, who was still standing in the open doorway.

His dark brows rose and a look of bewilderment passed over his face. He shook his head.

'Bugger,' snarled Rosie and resumed her pacing.

Eli bounced up beside his father, placed a hand on Charlie's shoulder for balance, and said, 'I can draw graphic stuff. I don't know about an identikit. Cartoons are more my style. Do you want me to give it a try?'

'Anything's better than Bayden's useless stick figures,' grumbled Rosie pausing her restless circling and staring at him in consideration. Being confined to the house by the bad weather was hampering her from working the case and it was driving her crazy. Maybe the boy could get a clear picture from Kelsey's memories. That would be a step in the right direction. She spun around and peered at Kelsey clutching the towel wrapped around her wet hair. 'Do you want to give it a try?' The woman nodded.

'Good girl...' said Rosie, patting her warm and damp shoulder. She looked towards Eli. 'Go get your drawing gear young man and we'll get started straight away.'

'How about we give Kelsey some time to get dressed first,' said Charlie in a husky voice.

Kelsey peeped down at her outfit. The kimono she wore clung to the warmth and dampness of her body, revealing every contour and curve. She might well have been standing naked. Her cheeks began to burn in embarrassment.

'Come on Eli, while Kelsey gets dressed we'll go collect your sketch pad,' said Rosie amused by the undertone going on in the room. 'See you in the kitchen in ten minutes, okay Kelsey?'

Rosie gently pulled the door closed after them as they left the room to give Kelsey some privacy. She smirked when she heard Eli whisper to Charlie, 'Kelsey looks beautiful in that robe.' Charlie's voice rumbled softly. The words were unclear but to her they sounded like, 'Yes son, she is.'

* * *

Eli threw his pencil down in disgust. 'I'm sorry, Kelsey. I'm better at designing in my head than drawing someone else's description.'

'That's fine, Champ, no biggie,' said Kelsey. Tucking her dry, flyaway hair behind her ears she picked up the pencil and began to doodle on a clean sheet of paper. 'I see it more like this...'

The pencil took on a life of its own and her dream began to take shape on the page. In a few bold strokes, the walls of the well rose. A forbidding figure emerged at the head of the shaft. The faceless figure radiated menace and bore down on the observer invoking a sense of dread.

Eli breathed out a long, soft, 'Cool,' as he studied the picture that had emerged on the paper. 'How'd you do that, Kelsey?'

'No idea, Champ,' she said, staring at the pencil clutched in her battered fingers. 'It just seemed to come to life on the page.'

Rosie snatched the drawing away from under Eli's hand and eagerly devoured the sketch. 'There's no face on the figure,' she said, glaring across the table at Kelsey in disgust.

Kelsey shrank back in her seat. 'I'm sorry, I haven't remembered a face...yet,' she whispered, hoping the detective wasn't going to yell at her.

Rosie lay the drawing face down on the table, reached across and patted her hand gently.

'Don't mind me. I'm just wound up tight. Can you draw the girl for me?' she asked in a softer tone pushing a fresh page toward her.

Kelsey's hand shook as she reached out for the paper. She took a deep breath and closed her eyes. Her hand steadied and the girl's face rose before her. 'I'll try.'

The screen door behind her gave a soft click. Eli looked up and the animation left his face, replaced by a blank mask of politeness. Kelsey flicked a glance over her shoulder to see who had caused the change in his demeanour. A tall, svelte woman with bronze hair that hung over her shoulders in a wave of lustrous curls was removing a wet yellow raincoat. She had a tiny waist and prominent breasts.

'Hello sweetie. Welcome home,' the woman purred.

'Oh...hello,' said Eli, his voice flat and holding no inflection. It was as if all the joy had been sucked out of him.

The woman strode across the room with feline grace and paused level with the boy. She reached down and cupped his chin in her long slender fingers. In a gentle movement, she eased his face up and kissed his cheek. 'I missed you, precious.'

Eli pulled his chin away and rubbed his cheek against his shoulder. 'Dad's in the office.'

Kelsey watched the beautiful woman's face change. It turned sour then went blank. She turned her magnificent hazel eyes to Rosie, narrowed them and asked, 'Who are you?'

'Detective Bloom – and you are?'

The woman's left cheek twitched. She ignored the question and glared at Kelsey.

'No need to ask who you are – you're the one with no memory. Huh, he won't fall for that bullshit, you know,' she sneered.

Kelsey dropped her own gaze under the intense scrutiny she was being subjected to and flicked a glance at Eli. She didn't like the change this woman had caused in him. She also didn't like the domineering stance she was trying to impose on the room's occupants.

Something rose in Kelsey's breast, a strong urge to protect Eli from this oppressive woman. In a gesture that felt foreign to her normal reaction to confrontation, Kelsey lifted her gaze and spoke out. 'Well, it's lucky I don't bullshit isn't it.' She reached across the table, patted the back of Eli's hand and said, 'Hey Champ, can you show me some of your Dragoart?'

Eli gave her a dazzling smile. It warmed her heart. As he took up his pencil Kelsey noticed the woman's top lip curl up into a snarl, before she turned on her heel and stalked from the room heading towards Charlie's office.

Well, I didn't make a friend there, thought Kelsey.

Rosie met her glance over Eli's bent head. 'Well, she seems nice...' said Rosie in a dry level tone. Kelsey felt her lip twitch in amusement at the understatement.

* * *

'Hello, darling. You wanted to see me?'

Charlie moved his attention from the papers in front of him to study the woman framed by his office doorway. The light was on in the hall behind her. It glinted off the highlights in her hair and silhouetted her toned body.

Funny, I don't remember flicking that light switch on.

Charlie rose to his feet and pulled a chair forward. He indicated the woman should sit.

'Yes, I did want to see you. How are you?'

He kept his tone level and polite, not giving her an opening to take the conversation to a more intimate level. Her lip quirked in a sultry smile, it reminded Charlie of an alley cat after devouring a bowl of stolen cream. She trailed her fingers along his arm and casually brushed her body close to his as she passed by to take the seat.

'I'm a little stiff darling and I have a slight headache, but nothing that some careful TLC couldn't fix.'

There it was again – innuendo. To think it had once attracted him. Lucky for him his good sense kicked in before his hormones had allowed her to ingratiate herself too far into his life. *I'm not making that mistake again. She's too much like Amelia was.*

'Good, you make sure you give yourself that,' said Charlie, resuming his seat behind the desk. A slight frown touched the corner of her mouth. 'The telephone's working again so we need to call and file a report with the Civil Aviation Safety Authority.'

A deep frown marred her features. 'But darling, why bother CASA? There's only a little dent in the damn chopper and a slight bend in the rotor. We can fix it and forget about it can't we?'

'I'm not your darling, Steve. I'm your boss. Call me Bull.' Charlie was careful to keep a lid on his temper, which was simmering like hot lava just under the surface. 'I will not lie to CASA for you, just so you can maintain an unblemished record. Now tell me what happened.'

She pouted her lips like a spoilt child and said, 'I was flying over the southern pasture, doing a grid search, just like Mac asked. I caught a glimpse of something near the stand of swamp bloodwoods down by Rusty Creek. I took the chopper in for a closer look and a strong blast of wind rocked the old girl. The chopper tilted, spun on its tail and clipped a tree branch. I went down, a little hard I'll admit, but it wasn't a crash, more a forced landing.'

'Okay, write it up for me,' said Charlie. He pushed an incident report form – kept on hand for such occasions – in front of her and offered her a pen. She stroked his hand as she took the pen from his fingers in a deliberate act of seduction.

'Look I'm sorry about the chopper, darling. You're not really going to report this are you?'

He gave her a small smile, 'Indulge me, fly girl. We need to have everything documented correctly, just in case there's a query.' The endearment always seemed to work with her. He sat back and watched as she wrote in a bold flamboyant hand the tale she wished to weave. A small smirk of complacency creased the corners of her mouth. She signed the report with a flourish and pushed it across the desk with her forefinger.

'There you go, darling. Why don't you just file that away as storm damage and forget it ever happened.'

Charlie's cheek creased on one side as he tilted his lip in a half smile. She pouted with a smug come-to-bed look in her eyes until he picked up the phone. While he spoke to the investigator at CASA he watched in fascination as the seductive look left Steve's lips then her eyes. She now resembled a furious alley cat.

'The investigator will drive out from Broome and check out the crash site when the floodwaters drop. Until then you're grounded,' said Charlie standing up and indicating the door.

Steve rose to her feet and snarled, 'All this is so unnecessary. It's not my bloody fault the storm knocked me...'

'No, it wouldn't be if the chopper crash had been caused solely by a gust of wind, but we both know that isn't exactly what happened. So consider this your final warning, Steve. Mess up again and you're outta here – for good. Understand?'

Her eyes narrowed to resemble silky tiger-eye gemstones. The clenching around her jaw chased all the beauty from her face and the flush of her cheeks hinted at the anger being held in check. He wondered if she was going to hand him the solution he sought by losing her temper and then her job. Instead, she stalked from the room without a word. Moments later the kitchen door slammed.

Chapter Sixteen

Charlie watched Rosie flip over the whiteboard so the photographs and profiles of the victims faced the wall before lodging the board behind the dining room door. She closed the files she'd been reading and stalked across to the sink where he worked.

Ignoring her restless fidgeting he spread a garlic and mustard glaze over the sirloin roast and slid it into the oven. 'Do you think the second girl...what was her name – Annalisa is it?' he asked. Rosie nodded to confirm he had the name correct so he went on with the thought that had been worrying him. 'Is Annalisa's disappearance connected to what's happening here at Rivers Run?'

Rosie stared at him, her face blank. Charlie wondered if she was checking her internal clock before she spoke. While he waited for her to make a decision on what she was actually going to tell him, Charlie opened the pantry and gathered together the root vegetables he wanted for the roasting pan. When he returned to the sink he noticed she had a file open in her hand.

'Kelly Creek Roadhouse,' she announced.

He waited and when no more information was forthcoming he commented, 'That's four hours south of here,' and pointed in the direction with the vegetable peeler that was clutched in his hand.

The detective nodded her head as though agreeing with his assessment before holding up a photo for him to look at.

'Annalisa Wagner,' she said, 'was last seen at Kelly Creek Roadhouse, January 2019.'

He studied the picture she waved in front of his face. The smiling young woman about eighteen years of age held a beer stein aloft looking happy and fancy free.

'Her family sent us that photo. It was taken in Sydney, a month before she and her boyfriend arrived in Western Australia on their backpacking holiday.'

'She's a lovely looking girl. What happened to her?'

'Annalisa caught the boyfriend, Stefan, dealing drugs at one of Perth's nightclubs. Witnesses to the event say she had a hell of an argument with him over it. They don't exactly know what was said as most of it was carried out in German. Though everyone agreed Stefan answered *'was auch immer'* to everything Annalisa yelled at him.'

'Translation?' asked Charlie. His knowledge of German was non-existent.

'*Was auch immer* means *whatever.*'

'God, how infuriating. Did he have anything to do with her disappearance?'

'Wouldn't that be convenient? Stefan was not only selling drugs, he was also using heavily. He dipped into the supply he was supposed to be selling. Not a smart move. Two nights after Annalisa left Perth, he wound up in Royal Perth Hospital. Someone gave him a touch up to remind him that the drugs were not for his use – not without paying for them anyway. Stefan spent a few days recovering in RPH before being discharged. The next day he overdosed and was found dead in the backpackers where he and Annalisa had been living. He died the same day she went missing.'

'Did he overdose or was it a hot-shot by his supplier?'

'I don't know, Bull.'

'Did Annalisa know he died?'

'I don't think so. The family sent her lots of phone texts but she never replied.'

'So how do you know where she was or the direction she was heading?'

'Annalisa hitched a lift with a semi driver by the name of...' Rosie glanced down at the file in her hand, 'Darryl Harper. He was hauling frozen goods to the North-West and picked her up on the Great Northern Highway just outside of Perth. They travelled together all the way to Broome. According to Mr Harper they had a great old chinwag along the way, all about what to see and do in the Kimberley and the best places to pick up work. Seems she was a bit short on cash. To return the favour for his stories Annalisa told him all about the beer festival they hold in Munich every year – Oktoberfest. Says he dropped her off at Roebuck Plains Roadhouse.'

'Not Broome?'

'No, she didn't want to go into Broome, which can be an expensive place to visit. Harper told me she intended heading inland to Mount Ibour looking for work and would live it up in Broome on her way back. Anyway, Harper had just finished his deliveries when he got a call from his boss. It seems Mount Ibour Abattoir's freezer truck had broken down and they had a load of beef they urgently needed to get to market. He promised Harper double pay if instead of taking a three-day break in Broome until his return load was ready he head inland and do the rush job. Harper agreed – I mean who wouldn't for double pay? When I spoke to him on the phone last week, Darryl Harper told me he'd stopped at the Kelly Creek Road-house on his way to Mount Ibour for a feed. Waffled on about how they do the best burgers this side of the black stump...'

'...and steak sandwiches, they're Eli's favourite. We always take a break at Kelly Creek ourselves whenever we do the run to Broome,' said Charlie, scooping the carrot peelings from the chopping board and dropping them into the chook's feed bucket.

'That boy of yours is a bottomless pit. I've never seen anyone inhale food like him. Are you sure he doesn't have worms?'

Charlie let out a deep belly laugh at the description of his son's eating habits. 'That's how I know he'll be okay – the day he's off his food is the day I'll worry.'

'Yes, well, anyway...the roadhouse staff told the investigators that Annalisa arrived with the dawn, dusty and tired. It seems some mongrel had dumped her by the roadside in the middle of the night when she wouldn't put out for him.'

'How'd she get to Kelly Creek?' asked Charlie drawing a large knife from a wooden block on the bench. It was sharp and slid through the onions with ease.

'According to the woman behind the counter, it was a full moon and she walked. Annalisa was still at the roadhouse around noon because Darryl Harper saw her talking to the driver of a silver four-wheel drive, when he pulled into the roadhouse's truck bay. He ordered his burger and then went looking for her to offer her a lift but she was gone. The attendant confirmed his story. That's the last time she was seen.' Rosie's lips turned down at the corners and she said, 'We tried tracing her mobile...nothing.'

Rosie stared at the photo in her hand then walked over to the board behind the door, flipped it over and stuck the photo under a magnet next to the one of Britt Larsen. She stood studying the images. Not wanting to disturb her train of thought Charlie stopped asking questions and got on with peeling the potatoes.

'Bull, when will it be possible to cross Annie River and follow Kelsey's trail?'

He peered out the kitchen window and studied the sky. The blanket of cloud was now a light grey and in places it had started to break apart, revealing tantalising glimpses of blue. 'The rain's stopped for now, so if it stays dry, and I think it will, we should see a drop in the floodwaters tomorrow. I'll get Jimmy to send someone out to check the Zentra Hill crossing. You can tag along with whoever goes out if you like.'

'Sounds good to me, I'm going stir crazy stuck in here. Being idle doesn't suit me,' said Rosie. 'It's all right for Bayden – he was born a social butterfly. He's having a grand time hanging out with your crew shooting the breeze. Useful to me too...who knows what snippets of gossip will bear fruit.' She came to stand next to him at the kitchen bench and started tossing a potato from hand to hand.

Charlie sighed. She reminded him so much of Eli whenever he wanted to ask something awkward.

'What?' he asked, in the same tone he'd use on his son.

'I need to conduct a search of your RAV4. I can get a warrant.'

Charlie lifted his eyebrows in surprise. Up until now, the detective had ploughed on ignoring the impact her actions had on the people around her. What had changed?

'It's parked up in the vehicle shed. Keys are in it.'

'Are the keys always in your vehicles?'

'Well yeah, otherwise you can't use them.'

Rosie eyes looked heavenwards at his logic. A small chuckle caught in his throat which he turned into an amused cough.

'So anyone can help themselves to any of your vehicles anytime they like?'

'Yeah, sure. Everything has a logbook but the crew rarely bother to fill in the exact details of where they go with the day-to-day running around they do. They just write up the total mileage at the end of the day. Oh, and the monthly trip to Mount Ibour is just written up as The Pub Run...not who goes in the vehicle or for how long.'

'And this once-a-month pub visit, when did that last happen?'

'Weekend just past...' said Charlie. He studied her blank face and picked his words carefully. 'We took three vehicles to town that time. I took the Rodeo because I had to collect Eli from the airport Friday night. His flight got in at midnight. We stayed at the Boomerang Motel and drove home Saturday afternoon. Steve drove one and I think Darcy the other. The crew didn't return until early Sunday morning, and yes the keys were left in all three vehicles while we were in town.'

'Don't you ever lock up?'

'Why?'

Rosie did another eye roll.

'What happens if someone takes your car.'

'Then they get to use it until they don't need it anymore and return it. Look detective, we are a community and up until recently the worst problem we had in town was a few yobbos with a belly full of beer, dropping wheelies in the main street.'

'Did Rhysand go to Mount Ibour?'

'As far as I know everyone went, except Mac and Naomi, they stayed home. Shit, you don't think...'

Rosie ignored his unfinished question and said, 'Will you come and witness the search of the vehicle and record everything with that fancy camera of yours? I don't want accusations of evidence planting if I find anything.'

Charlie gave a silent nod of his head. Rosie placed the potato back on the chopping board and said, 'I'll go get Bayden and meet you at the garage in fifteen minutes.'

Charlie finished preparing the vegetables and went up to his room to collect the camera bag. Not sure how long the detective's search was going to take, he decided to seek out Eli and ask him to chuck the tray of veggies in the oven in an hour's time. The upstairs lair was the main lounge area they used to relax in. It had a big-screen television on one wall and a floor-to-ceiling bookcase, jam-packed with DVDs and Play Station games, most of which were of the high-octane adventure variety – Eli's favourite. A second bookshelf held a huge selection of musical recordings ranging from classical to the latest head banger. Soft leather couches and reclining armchairs that cradled you in their warm embrace had been positioned to take full advantage of the audiophile's dream room. Charlie found evidence of his son's recent occupancy but no Eli. The Play Station was on pause, *Foo Fighters* screeched from the surround sound speakers that had been wired into not only the television but also a state-of-the-art stereo system, and his son's size thirteen sneakers lay abandoned next to the couch. They fouled the air with eau de teenager. A small thud sounded out on the balcony. Charlie went to the glass sliding door and took a peek outside. A feeling of rightness warmed his belly. Occupying a wicker two-seater daybed each, Eli and Kelsey slept peacefully in the fresh air. A novel had slipped from Kelsey's hand and had made the noise that attracted his attention. He glanced at its title and was surprised to see she had chosen one of his favourites, *From Strength to Strength* by Sara Henderson.

A study of her face showed that the scratches and bruises as well as the sunburn were beginning to fade. The lines of stress and fear around her eyes had diminished somewhat and she was looking slightly better – physically at least. It seemed a shame that Rosie was about to make Kelsey relive her trauma but once the floodwater receded enough for the river to be crossed safely there would be no stopping the tenacious detective from dragging the poor woman across country in an attempt to find the well in which she'd been dumped. Well, Kelsey's not going alone, Charlie decided. He would tag along because he needed to keep an eye on the investigation and get a grasp on how this situation was going to affect him and his family. He took another look at the sleeping pair and tiptoed away. The vegetables could wait. On his way past the oven, he flicked the temperature dial down to the lowest setting.

With a grunt he slid his feet into the raggedy, old grey gumboots that hadn't been out of the mud room since the last wet season. They didn't smell the best but would do the job he thought as he squelched his way across the yard with the boots slapping against his claves. Over at the stockyard, bright bubbly Darcy, Steve and one of his jackaroos, Roscoe, were re-erecting the galvanised fence panels. The skinny, bandy-legged Roscoe wasn't much chop to look at but he was an experienced jackaroo – strong, hardworking and reliable. His long, scraggy, grey hair had been neatly braided with a leather thong and it hung down the middle of his back and finished level with the waistband of his jeans. His wispy beard was a similar length and Charlie often thought he looked like a ZZ Top reject.

Pausing, he called out a greeting, 'Afternoon everyone.'

Roscoe, looking eighty instead of his actual forty years, straightened his back and gave Charlie a gappy-toothed smile. Steve glared at him. I guess I'm not forgiven for the CASA report, he thought in amusement. Darcy dropped her tools and rushed to his side.

'Hi ya, Bull. Yesterday's storm was a doozy wasn't it,' she giggled. 'Are you joining us for dinner tonight? Naomi's cooking lasagne.'

'Sounds good but I've got a houseful of people and a roast in the oven.'

At that moment he caught sight of Rosie and Bayden footslogging their way through the tacky mud. The detective's combat boots were covered in sticky clumps of it. Charlie shook his head. *I suppose I'll have to find her some gumboots.* He doffed his hat to Darcy and gave Roscoe and Steve a casual wave before quickening his step towards the detective and her partner. As he reached Rosie's side her foot slid sideways and she lost balance. She fell into his arms nearly landing on her arse in the mud. Bayden grasped her elbow and helped her to rebalance. She shook their hands off with an impatient gesture and stomped off towards the garage.

Bayden gave a small smile and said, 'That was close.'

Charlie smiled and noticed Darcy and Steve watching with thunderous looks on their faces. He wondered what had upset them. Had they been having words? He gave a mental shrug and peered down with interest at the box-like briefcase clutched in Mark's hand.

'What's in the case?'

'Crime scene stuff. I always keep it in the vehicle, along with a spare set of clothes. You never know what you're going to be faced with in this line of work.'

'Not only in your job, mate,' said Charlie chuckling as he recalled some of the grungy jobs that needed to be dealt with on the station.

In companionable banter they made their way along wombat track towards the garage to find Rosie. She was standing with her hands on her hips staring at the parked-up mobile equipment. Charlie took a fresh-eyed look around and realised that for someone with no experience in primary industry all the tractors, trailers, cars and motorbikes along with the heavy machinery might seem excessive but he knew they were all essential for the successful running of his property.

'Bloody hell, Bull. I'd hate to have your fuel bill,' said Bayden.

'Tell me about it,' replied Charlie, removing his hat and running his long fingers through his thick hair.

'There's more than one silver RAV4 here,' said Rosie circling a pristine vehicle parked in the employees' car area. She tested the door. 'And it's locked.'

'That's not one of my fleet – I think it belongs to Steve or maybe Gil, if he's around.'

Rosie grunted and murmured to Bayden, 'We'll need to find out and get permission...'

'How do you want to handle this, Rosie?' asked Charlie, not wanting to get tangled up in a discussion about his least popular employees. He moved towards a dusty Toyota RAV4 and mentally added a chore to the upcoming jobs list. The rains had come so there would be enough water to clean up all the equipment. 'This vehicle's mine.'

Rosie gestured to the camera bag hanging from his shoulder and said, 'Follow us and record everything we do. We'll start by identifying ourselves, you included, as being present. I want you to film a panorama of the garage, make sure you capture a good image of that other vehicle. After that, focus on the Rivers Run Toyota and all our movements.'

A search of the vehicle's cab yielded some lose change, an assortment of work-gloves, fencing tools and a dirt encrusted butter menthol lolly. Everything was covered in a thick layer of red dust. Zooming the lens in on the rear door of the vehicle Charlie waited for Mark to open it. They'd been here over an hour and he was bored by the tedious and meticulous examination the detective was conducting.

The door was flung open and Rosie shone a small torch light inch by inch over the cargo area. She started on the ceiling and working her way down to the floor. As she examined the rubber matting she gave a small grunt. 'The back of this vehicle had been meticulously cleaned.' The detective ran her gloved forefinger along the edge of the mat and held it up. 'See, no dust.' She swept her light around again, the black rubber matting shining with cleanliness in its beam. 'Bayden, bag,' she commanded, sticking out a hand and wiggling her fingers.

Mark carefully placed one in her palm. Charlie took a step forward zooming the camera lens closer. Rosie put her torch down and fished around in the join between the back seat and the floor.

'Gotcha,' she exclaimed holding up a gold cross hanging from a broken filigree chain. She opened the neck of the clear plastic bag and dropped it in before handing it to Mark to seal. He wrote some details on the outside of the bag and locked it in his briefcase.

* * *

Charlie hosed the mud from their boots, kicked his off and put them to dry in the mud room at the rear of the laundry. He left Rosie and Bayden fighting with their wet boot laces and headed into the kitchen to put the vegetable tray into the oven. He sniffed the air expected a tantalising aroma of roasting beef, that's not what he got. He quickened his step. Opened the kitchen door and was confronted by a room filled with dense, grey smoke. He rushed to open the window and veranda door. The draft created by the openings sucked the acrid cloud outside. He turned his attention to the oven. The oven dial had been switched to 250 degrees Celsius. He flipped the switch off and opened the oven. A new cloud of smoke billowed out into the room. He grabbed an oven mitt, pulled out the shrivelled black mess that was once a beautiful sirloin and threw it out into the garden for the dogs to devour later.

'Bloody hell, Bull...don't you have a fire alarm?' asked Bayden as he rushed into the room.

'Yeah, I do,' he said, pointing to the white dome in the ceiling.

Rosie stood at Bayden's elbow and cocked her eyebrow at Charlie. He looked up as a puff of breeze moved the swirling grey smoke that hung at ceiling level. The smoke detector was hanging open.

'Won't work without the battery,' she said. Sarcasm dripped from her words.

Charlie's rage started to simmer just below the surface and a red haze made a fleeting pass across his eyes.

A thump from overhead was followed by a pounding on the stairs. Charlie raced for the door into the main part of house. He reached the hall just as Eli, clutching the railing for support, came bouncing one-legged down the stairs. Kelsey was close on his heels.

'Dad,' yelled Eli, 'I smell smoke.'

Charlie made a decision he hoped wouldn't cause problems later. 'Everything's fine mate, I burnt the roast.'

Eli roared with laughter. 'You dope – and I was hungry too.'

It was so worth the lie when he saw a smile light up Kelsey's face. He felt a stirring near his heart, one that had been missing from his life for a long, long time. His rage started to retreat.

'Not to worry, stockman's stew do ya?'

'Awesome.' Eli breathed as he glanced over his shoulder at Kelsey. 'You're gonna love it...' His brows drew together suddenly and his lips tilted down to form a frown. 'You're not vegan or anything stupid like that are you, Kelsey?'

Charlie watched as Kelsey studied Eli's face with her beautiful emerald eyes. Her head was cocked to the right and her nose wrinkled in amusement. He felt another stirring, this time it also included his groin.

Charlie you stupid bugger, she's not interested in you. With everything going on you'd just be another complication.

'No, I don't think so, Champ. I certainly enjoyed your meatloaf sandwiches the other day,' Kelsey said in a warm voice that filled the rest of the emptiness inside him. It was like a soothing balm. His rage disappeared.

* * *

The stockman's stew, a braise full of hearty vegetables and tender chunks of steak, had been a great success with everyone, even the accompanying odour of burnt meat that still hung around the kitchen hadn't killed the taste or anyone's appetite. Charlie left the windows and doors open while they ate and a soft cool breeze played around the roomful of people.

He was reaching forward to start clearing the plates when a warm gentle hand covered his. The hairs on his arm stood up.

'You cooked, Charlie,' murmured Kelsey, 'We'll take care of the dishes. Besides I think Eli is anxious to talk to you about something.'

Rising from her chair before he could protest, she started collecting the plates and shuffled between the table and the sink. Mark leapt to his feet and took over, while handing her a tea towel and sitting her up on a clear spot on the kitchen bench. Over the noise of running water and the clank of cutlery, Bayden began recounting to her a humorous tale about his two children.

For some reason the scene gave Charlie a feeling of contentment. He turned his attention to his son and began to tease him. 'Did you enjoy your sleep today, mate?'

'Sleep, I didn't sleep. I may have been contemplating the back of my eyelids as I thought deep thoughts but I don't reckon I slept.'

'So, the snoring was just a sound effect, huh?'

Eli's cheeks went a bright pink. His gazed flitted to where Kelsey sat wiping a plate and whispered, 'I didn't snore in front of Kelsey did I, Dad?'

Amused Charlie felt for the lad and decided not to make a sport of the crush he could see Eli was developing over their unexpected guest. 'I don't think she heard you, she was snoring too.'

A look of relief crossed Eli's face. 'She's nice, Dad. You should marry her.'

Charlie felt his jaw sag. He was shocked that Eli could trot out a comment like that without even blinking. A hundred thoughts roiled through his mind, none of them suitable for discussion with his son or the detective who sat across from them watching with interest. 'Don't be cheeky, Eli. Kelsey is a nice lady with some serious challenges in front of her. You are not to add to those by voicing your silly ideas. Besides, I'm still married to your mother.'

Eli's cheeks burned bright red and he lowered his gaze to study the hands that were clenched in his lap. 'Sorry, Dad,' he whispered.

Charlie squeezed his son's shoulder with a gentle grip and in a low voice murmured, 'This is not a game, Eli. There's a killer out there and for whatever unfortunate reason, Kelsey is involved. We'll offer her our friendship, do our best to help and protect her but anything else is inappropriate.'

Eli glanced up through his long dark eyelashes. His grey eyes were shining with unshed tears. He nodded and Charlie wanted to gather him into his arms. A burst of laughter from across the room broke the tension and drew the attention of everyone in the room.

Mark was leaning with his back to the sink, dish mop in hand, chuckling as he finished his tale, '...and then the kids presented me with this coffee cup which reads *Police Officer because badass cop ain't an official title*. Best Christmas present ever.'

Kelsey's face glowed with amusement. It dazzled and shone in the kitchen light. She looked relaxed and at home.

'What about you, what's your best Christmas ever?' Mark asked her.

'The last Christmas I ever had with my family I was five years old. Mum sketched a picture of my dad giving my sister and me a piggy-back ride at the picnic grounds on the shores of the Swan River. I got to feed bread to the black swans. It's the only picture I have of them. They died the next week in a car accident. After that I went into foster care and never had another nice Christmas...oh.' Her eyes widened and she clamped a hand over her mouth. 'A memory and it's a good one. Thank you, Mark.'

Rosie leant forward, tapped Charlie on the back of the hand and said, 'See I told you Bayden and his chatter has its uses.'

Chapter Seventeen

Kelsey watched Charlie and Mark load the police vehicle and the Holden Rodeo with camping equipment and enough food for a week. She was nervous and the butterflies in her stomach screamed to be let loose. Eli stood beside her at the front gate clutching his Akubra to the front of his blue and white checked shirt. He'd rolled his sleeves up to his elbows and had a pair of sunglasses perched on the top of his head. On his lips was an uncustomary pout.

'But why can't I come too, Dad? My knee is almost as good as new.'

Charlie stepped close, put out a hand and brushed a lock of unruly hair away from his son's eyes.

'Remember our discussion about this not being a game?' Eli nodded. Charlie continued, 'You're in charge while I'm away. I've left you a list of jobs but the two most important ones are that as soon as the road opens you need to get the cattle truck out here – the fats have got to get to the abattoirs before the contract date expires. Mac and the crew are out rounding the mob up now. Make sure each animal meets the buyer's stringent requirements. You'll find a copy of the contract on my desk. Also get the fruit that's boxed up in the cool room to the factory. We've a conserves run booked and I don't want to miss it. Otherwise it will be three months before we can get another scheduled. I'm relying on you, son. I know you're on hols, but this is all part and parcel of running the station. We graziers don't always get to do what we want, though sometimes we can slope off for a short while...' He gave Eli a cheeky smirk. 'So, when I get back you and I are going fishing, okay?'

'Right,' grinned Eli, the sulk leaving his face.

'Mac and Naomi are going to sleep in the house with you at night.' Eli's brows rose, surprise registering across his features. He opened his mouth but Charlie held up a finger and said, 'Not negotiable. You're far too important to me. Now one more thing – an outline of your business vision, can you have something ready for me by the time I get back? Then we can sit down and discuss what is achievable in the short term.'

Eli's shoulders straightened and his smile bloomed. 'Sure, Dad, you can count on me.'

Charlie nodded, 'I know I can, and I promise to bring Rainbow home with me. Roscoe's been across on the flying fox and checked him out. He reckons the injury's healed well and your horse is quite contently chomping his way through all the feed we've left him.'

'Thanks, Dad. That'd be awesome.'

A silver four-wheel drive zoomed into the yard. Charlie eyes narrowed a fraction as he muttered out the side of his mouth to his son, 'I thought he'd left.'

'He did, Dad. He headed over to Zentra Flats Station the morning the storm hit.'

The vehicle slid to a halt and a good looking, medium sized but slightly pudgy man, dressed in a white polo shirt and tan moleskins slid from behind the steering wheel.

'Morning, Bull. I was heading back to town from Slab Johnson's place and discovered the main road's been closed to all traffic. You'll give me a bed for the night won't you? The usual one in the house?' he asked, and gave a toothy, disenchanting grin.

'Sure, but you'll have to put up in camp, the house is full.' The man raised his blond eyebrows in an unasked question which Charlie ignored.

His eyes slid past Charlie and fastened on Kelsey. He stepped forward, a smarmy smile plastered on his face and said, 'Hi, I'm Gil Connors, book-keeper extraordinaire.' Taking her hand in his soft, stodgy fingers he gazed intently up at her while stroking the back of her hand with his thumb. He was standing a little too close for her liking, right in her personal space. She stepped back slightly. He winked and his mouth tilted in a playful boyish grin as he confessed, 'I'm really here to keep these boys honest and make sure they pay their dues...'

'Well, we certainly pay...' said Charlie cutting him off. 'Gil, go on over and check in with, Naomi. She'll see you right for a bed for the night.' He kissed his son on the forehead and climbed into the waiting vehicle.

'Was it something I said,' whispered Gil leaning in too close to Kelsey. Uncomfortable with his obvious flirting and not wanting to prolong the encounter she tugged her hand from his grip, gave him a timid smile and turned towards Eli.

'I'll see you in a couple of days, Champ,' she said and patted his left cheek with the tips of her fingers in a gentle gesture of farewell. She smiled at the result her display of affection caused. Eli had taken his father's kiss in his stride but blushed pink at her slight caress.

'Bye, Kelsey,' he said, and coughed to clear the crack in his voice. 'Take care of dad for me.'

'Sure,' she said and climbed into the Rodeo's passenger seat. She ignored Gil and gave Eli a small finger wave. In return he lifted his hand in a two-fingered salute and pulled his sunglasses down to cover his eyes. After slapping on his Akubra, Eli brushed past the watching Gil and limped away, heading towards the stockyard.

'That's a lot of responsibility you've placed on his shoulders, Charlie,' said Kelsey following Eli's progress with her eyes.

'No more than he's capable of. Mac will keep an unobtrusive eye on him and keep him grounded.'

'Oh, I'm not criticising, I think it's marvellous you have so much faith in his capabilities, besides I would never forgive myself for subjecting him to what we are about to see. No one should have those images in their mind – especially not a fourteen-year-old boy. I'm so sorry I've brought this trouble to your home.'

Charlie turned the key in the ignition and waited for the engine to fire before he replied. 'You didn't – the killer did.'

He backed the vehicle up, slid out of his seat and went around to hook up the horse float. She sat mulling over his words. The killer. Painful jitters started bouncing around in her stomach and chest. Why had someone tried to kill her?

* * *

The Rodeo fishtailed in the slick, slushy mud as they crossed a water-filled dip in the road. Kelsey saw the muscle in Charlie's jaw tighten as he changed the vehicle down a gear. The engine roared. Water churned creating white frothy foam around them. The four-wheel drive gave a sudden jolt as the tyres found purchase and pulled forward to dry land. When they reached the top of the ridge, Charlie braked and checked his mirror. Kelsey turned in her seat to watch the police vehicle that followed in their wake. It struggled in the same spot. Water sprayed in a high, arcing spout behind the Landcruiser as the tyres spun at top speed trying to grab a solid grip. The spin of the tyres slowed, the vehicle shuddered and shot out of the floodwater.

'Is it going to be this bad all the way?' Kelsey asked, turning to the square jawed man beside her.

'No. The roads around here are hard packed from constant use, but this section here is new, only put it in about two months ago. It hasn't had time to fully compact. Now I know that spot will flood, I'll get a team in to install a culvert and lift the road over the top of it,' said Charlie. 'We'll be alright, Kelsey. Don't forget Tangles and Rosie made it to Zentra crossing and back again yesterday without a problem and the floodwaters have had time to drop even further since then.'

'Oh right.'

'Trust me, I won't let anything happen to you.'

'I do trust you, Charlie. I'm not worried about myself, I was more concerned about the strain all this must be having on you.'

Charlie looked over at her and his bright white teeth flashed in the sweetest smile. Butterflies flip-flopped low in her belly. He reached over and patted her hand. Her heart give a tremendous thump – not good, Kelsey. He's a married man.

'Sweet girl. It's been a long time since I was fussed over.'

It had to be said.

'What about your wife, she must fuss over you and Eli. How can she not?' The animation left his face and the grip on her hand disappeared. Kelsey's breath caught in a slight hitch as she asked, 'I'm sorry, did I say something wrong?'

'No...' he answered, but his voice sounded cold.

The police vehicle pulled to a halt on the driver's side of the Rodeo. Charlie wound down his window.

Rosie cocked an arm on her door frame and propped her chin on her fist.

'That's the last bad patch between here and the crossing, Bull,' she said.

Charlie nodded. 'Alright, you guys push on. We'll meet at the stockman's hut. I'm just going to make a pit stop.'

From the driver's seat, Mark gave them a cheeky smile and a wave. Kelsey watched the vehicle shoot forward and disappear over the edge of the rise. She continued to stare out the windscreen long after it was gone. If she looked at the man beside her she'd start crying. For some reason her words had hurt him and she's only meant them as a gentle reminder of his status. She didn't know how to rectify the blunder. Charlie made no attempt to get out of the vehicle or drive on. Instead he glared out his open window.

It came as a shock to her when he began to speak. His voice was icy and remote. 'Amelia was a fashion model – perfect face, perfect hair, perfect figure. She loved to surround herself with beauty, materialistically as well as in her friends and lovers. So you can understand how a young and gullible Charlie Morgan, taking a six-month sabbatical in the city, was flattered when he found his attentions were well received. He courted her, gave her everything she asked for and more. Then his mother died unexpectedly and he needed to return home to take up the mantle of Rivers Run grazier and run the station full-time. The night before he was due to leave the city, Amelia fell into his arms in tears. Her career was in ruin, she was carrying his child and no one was going to employ a pregnant model. He was thrilled by the news and delayed his return to marry her. Amelia became mistress of Rivers Run. Ten months later Eli was born.' The third-person synopsis was delivered in a flat almost bored tone.

Kelsey lifted her gaze from her lap where she'd been staring unblinking at her clasped slender fingers. She studied the face of the man whose blank gaze now stared out of the front windscreen. The emotion in his eyes was masked by his sunglasses. Two words in his story stood out as inconsistent.

'Ten months?'

'Yeah, ten months. I quickly worked out that Amelia was ambitious and greedy. She thought being a grazier's wife would make her one of the country elite, an aristocrat of Australian society with unlimited wealth. The reality of life on a cattle station was not something she was prepared for. She grew to hate it and me. When Eli was six years old she emptied our bank account and left.'

'Does she ever see him?'

'No...we've not seen nor heard from her since the day she walked out. I can forgive her leaving me but not her rejection of Eli,' said Charlie.

* * *

The fence riders hut came into view. It had sustained no damage from the storm. Washed clean from the dust of summer it looked warm and welcoming.

'We'll stop here for the night. I need to exercise Rainbow before we head out. Then it's up to you, Kelsey. Do you think you'll be able to guide us from here?'

'Yes, I marked a trail.'

'You did? How?'

'Using rock pyramids.'

'Clever girl, how'd you know to do that?'

Letters and words formed in her mind. HSAM – high functioning autism with a photographic memory. The diagnosis was delivered in a cold clinical tone and the words were tainted with envy, resentment and revulsion that made her feel uncomfortable. More words appeared only it was her voice this time, warning her to hide this ability, dumb it down and not to tell anyone. An image formed. She was cowering against a wall while some kids threw the contents of a rubbish bin on her. She clutched two books to her chest with the spines face up. She read their titles. *Surviving the Australian Outback* and *How to Draw Australian Mammals.*

'I must have read about it.' It wasn't a lie but also not the entire truth. No don't do this Kelsey, Charlie deserves the truth. 'I think I...'

'Bull,' Mark exclaimed loudly as he stuck his head in through the car's side window causing her to jump and the rest of the words died in her throat. 'The boss's got a bee in her bonnet. She wants to know if you remembered to bring any spare batteries for the radios.'

'Yeah, course' replied Charlie. He calmly removed his glasses and tossed them onto the dashboard. 'Tell her not to get her knickers in a twist. We've got a satellite phone, a couple of two-way radios *with* extra batteries and a charging station. I've also bought the drone and a generator to power everything. It's not my first rodeo in the bush you know.'

'I'll tell her – but I'm not mentioning her knickers. I prefer my head where it is.' Mark chortled as he strode away.

'Drone?' asked Kelsey.

Charlie, his laughing eyes sparkling like polished pewter, winked at her. 'Yeah, it will save us a lot of legwork. I'll give you a lesson and you can retrace your steps from the comfort of the car?'

Kelsey heaved a sigh of relief. The well-polished and sturdy riding boots Eli had presented to her this morning might fit comfortably, but even with the two pairs of socks she wore, her feet were still too tender to cope with another long hard trek. She reached across to the man whose place had become cemented in her heart and gave his hand a squeeze. 'Thanks, Charlie. I wasn't looking forward to another long walk.'

Her heart lurched when he lifted her fingers to his lips and gave the tips a gentle kiss.

* * *

'That way, about a thousand paces.' Kelsey stood in the shade of her salvation, the large and towering woollybutt and pointed in the direction they needed to send the drone. Rainbow's saddle no longer leaned like a drunken traveller against the tree trunk. 'Eli'll be glad to have this back,' said Charlie as he slung it into the back of the float with the quiet and patient horse. 'It was a gift from my B-I-L. His last gift in fact.' There was an odd note in his voice.

'B-I-L?'

'My brother-in-law, Josh.'

'Josh...that name seems familiar to me,' said Kelsey closing her eyes. She tried to push aside the barriers in her mind. They resisted. She opened her eyes to see Charlie looking at her with curiosity written all over his face. 'No, sorry, nothing. The static is being resistant. It would be really bizarre, wouldn't it, if we knew the same Josh.'

'Josh is dead. He died six months ago.'

Shit, Kelsey just open your mouth and change feet why don't you. 'I'm sorry, Charlie.'

Charlie tilted his hat to settle it at the back of his head and wiped the sweat from his forehead with the sleeve of his green and white checked shirt. Tight denim jeans and button down cotton shirts seemed to be the fashion around here, along with fit healthy bodies. The toned and athletic frames of everyone she'd seen at Rivers Run was like eye candy and the one standing next to her was the sweetest of them all. There was a lot to be learnt from eating fresh, getting out in the open air and exercising. Her nerve endings started to flutter with desire and carnal thoughts creating some interesting images in her mind. Charlie's reply brought her down to earth and back to the moment.

'Don't worry about it. Here, take the drone control and guide it on the path you think we should follow. We can watch on this screen and see everything the drone sees. Now tell me, what exactly are we looking for?'

'A small pile of rocks, stacked in the shape of a pyramid,' Kelsey replied, indicating with her hands the approximate size of her trail markers.

Charlie moved to stand in close behind her and leaning over her shoulder he handed her the controls. She could feel his body warmth along the length of her spine. A rush of goose bumps lifted the hairs on her arms and the back of her neck. It made concentration difficult as all she wanted to do was lean back into his embrace. She took a deep breath and refocused her attention on following his instructions in getting the drone airborne.

In a buzzing whirl the machine lifted and hovered. She applied some light pressure to toggle the joystick forward and the drone sped away. Kelsey quietly counted, establishing a time reference to use as a baseline for the distance between each marker. She had reached one hundred and twenty seconds when Charlie asked, 'Is that it?'

Kelsey released the pressure on the toggle and allowed the drone to hover. She examined the pile of rubble he was pointing to on the screen and nodded, 'Yes.'

Charlie gave her shoulder a gentle squeeze. 'Fantastic, keep the drone hovering over the top.' He lifted his head and called out to Rosie, who was sitting with her chin cupped in her hand watching the drone in flight. 'First marker detective.'

Rosie removed her elbow from the window frame, pointed and said, 'Let's get this show on the road, Bayden.'

The Landcruiser rolled away, its tyres leaving deep wheel ruts in the soft mud. When the vehicle arrived under the hovering drone, Kelsey allowed it to settle on the ground to conserve its power.

'Good job, Kelsey,' said Charlie placing a warm hand on the small of her back and guiding her to their vehicle. After helping her in and closing her door he moved to slide into the driver's seat. The keys were hanging in the ignition and he fired up the engine. Matching their tyres to the tracks left by the police vehicle, the four-wheel drive easily coped with the soft ground. They came to a gentle halt and Kelsey alighted to take her bearings. When she was sure of the direction she repeated the drone procedure.

At twilight Charlie called a halt. Kelsey was relieved. The drone's last battery was almost flat and her neck ached from being hunched over the controls. She climbed from her seat with a sigh, stretched and stared back at the tyre tracks that stood out like a highway across the plain. It was pretty obvious she hadn't walked in a straight line.

Rosie clomped her way over to stand beside her and said, 'That must have been a hell of a walk.' The hard to please detective's voice was full of admiration.

'Oh well, if I have to do it again I'll at least have a road to follow,' said Kelsey. 'Not that I'm planning any long strolls for a while.'

Rosie flashed her a smile that highlighted the sharp bone structure of her face and Kelsey's fingers itched to capture the image. She really must get a camera so these moments didn't get lost before she could transfer them onto canvas. Oh, wait you idiot, aren't you supposed to have a photographic memory? Use it. Kelsey closed her eyes, created a picture wall in her mind and bonded the image to it. She would test it out later as they sat by the campfire to see how effective it would be. Mark and Charlie opened the back of the Rodeo and started discussing what to unload and how to set up camp.

'How much further to the well?' asked Rosie, her bright-blue eyes an intense colour in the twilight.

Kelsey turned a slow, full-circle, taking in all the landmarks around her. She closed her eyes and turned the same circle again, this time pulling up the earlier pictures from her memory. She scrolled back towards the image of the knoll and boab tree. With her mind's eye she moved forward and counted until she reached the spot on which they now stood. Her eyes popped open, and she pointed in the direction they should travel, 'That way, it's not far.'

Rosie raised her voice and cut into the men's discussion. 'Bayden, Bull, stop unloading, we're moving on.'

The men glanced around looking startled and Charlie's back stiffened. Kelsey could see he was about to protest so she smiled across at him and his shoulders seemed to relax. She raised her hand and pointed. 'If we drive in a straight line that way, approximately two kilometres we'll find the boab tree that grows at the base of the knoll.'

Portraying a strong resemblance to a silver dingo with her hair shining in the twilight, Rosie patted her shoulder. 'Good girl. Okay boys, let's go.'

* * *

The fat bulbous boab was right where Kelsey said it would be. Pleased her memory was working as it should be – for recent events anyway – she ran a gentle hand over the soft spongy texture of its trunk. In that moment she decided that one day she would paint it with its silver-grey branches glowing in the moonlight guarding the spirits of the dead. She stepped back and peered intently up at the animal trail that ascended the side of the knoll. A gentle breeze touched her brow and with it came the whisper of voices.

'I've bought help,' she whispered back to them. The breeze died away and the voices fell silent.

She turned and walked straight into a solid wall of muscle. Arms encircled her to preventing her from falling.

'Are you okay?'

She looked up into the pewter-grey eyes of a tall, broad-chested, handsome Charlie. A feeling of security filled her.

'Yes thanks. I was just speaking with the dead.'

Stupid, Kelsey. Now he's going to think your crackers. Charlie nodded and gazed up at the brilliant night sky.

'Spirits watch over the living but who among the living act for the souls of those who are lost?'

The corners of Kelsey lips lifted in a smile. He understood.

He slid a strong muscular arm around her shoulder. She leant into its warmth and drew in the tantalising scent of spice that was his unique smell, along with the tang of smoke and the meat cooking on the fire.

'Dinners almost ready,' he said, misinterpreting her action. 'Hope you like barbequed sausages and chops.'

* * *

A large campfire bathed them in a warm yellow glow. Kelsey sipped her coffee and made some final touches to the sketch of the girl's face she had been working on for Rosie. Mark settled beside her and studied the drawing over her shoulder.

'You're very good. Are you an artist?'

'No, I work with numbers but art is my passion.' Her hand stopped its activity and she looked at him startled. 'Oh...you're very good at getting me to remember things, Mark. Ask me something else.'

Dimples appeared in his cheeks as the corners of his mouth tilted up. 'Probably won't work if you push it...but okay.' He scrunched his nose up as he thought about what to ask.

'I know, let's go for something simple. Do you like your beer in a can or a stubby?'

The pencil dropped from her fingers and a wave of black despair washed over her. Large tears began to flow down her face and a loud sob escaped her lips.

Rosie, turning the meat on the barbeque hotplate swung around and growled, 'Bayden, what have you done?'

'I don't know. Kelsey remembered something and then started crying.'

Through the tears Kelsey saw deep concern etched on his face. She took a hiccupping breath and tried to stop sobbing. Mark took both her hands in his own and said, 'Kelsey, please tell me what's wrong.'

Her throat was tight but she managed to push the words out. 'He wore a scruffy, dirty white singlet and reeked of perspiration and stale beer. A fat gut hung over the top of tight shorts, and his cheeks and chin were covered in grey and mousey brown bristles.' Kelsey took another uneven breath, shuddered and said, 'He was my foster father.'

Mark nodded, his hazel eyes tinged with flecks of brown and green gazed deep into her own. Kindness seemed to radiate from him in a comforting wave.

Rosie came over and sat on the other side of her. Kelsey's body warmed when the detective placed her arm around her waist, gave a gentle squeeze and said, 'Don't stop, Kelsey. Let it out.'

Kelsey broke eye contact with Mark and looked beyond the firelight. Charlie, who had been grooming Rainbow before bedding him down for the night was showing signs of agitation. With swift steps he was thundering over to where they sat. His gaze locked onto hers, she tried to smile but failed. Rosie forestalled whatever he was going to say with a raised hand in his direction and a loud, 'Be quiet, Bull.'

Shame filled Kelsey. She dropped her chin to her chest and closed her eyes. How could anyone love her now.

Rosie gave her waist another squeeze and whispered in her ear, 'Your safe, Kelsey. Just let it out.'

The words dragged themselves from her lips. 'I'd hide from him every night. I didn't always succeed. But if I was quick I could lock myself away in the back of my bedroom cupboard so he couldn't get to me. One day I arrived home early from school, it was one of those teacher development half-days...anyway, my foster mother was out. My foster father took advantage of the fact we were alone and cornered me in the hall. He tried to put his horrible bulbous lips on mine and shove his fat stubby fingers up my skirt. I yelled at him and pushed him away. Furious at the noise I was making, he broke the stubby he was holding against the wall just above my head. Glass and beer showered down on me. With his free hand he grabbed me by the throat. I can see his face...so close to mine. He had a mole growing next to his left eye and his cheeks were a patchwork of broken red blood vessels. When his breath hit my nose it was rancid and the heat of it seemed to burn my face.

He began yelling, 'Shut ya cakehole, you worthless, stuck-up bitch.'

I couldn't breathe. The world started to go black. The grip on my throat was so tight it made the blood pound in my ears like a drum. I remember it felt like my eyeballs were trying to pop from their sockets. I couldn't let him win so I kicked out as hard as I could and caught him plumb on the shin with the sharp heel of my shoe.

In retaliation he shoved the broken bottle into my stomach but my school bag got in the way and saved me from being gutted. With the last of my strength I made a grab for his wrist and tried to push the bottle away. He let go of my throat, pulled back and raked the broken glass down my arm. I remember screaming as blood spurted everywhere. He threw me to the floor and began to kick me.

As I was blacking out I heard my foster mother yelling, 'What have you done you, stupid man. How the hell am I going to get all that blood out of the carpet?'

Kelsey paused, took a deep breath and finished recounting the memory. 'I was twelve years old.'

'And is that how you got the scars on your arm?' asked Rosie.

'Yes,' whispered Kelsey.

'You know, there should be some sort of a police report. The hospital would have made one. I'll be able to trace it and get you some of the answers you need. Like for instance your last name.'

A drawer gently eased open and name popped into her head. 'Delaney. Try Kelsey Delaney.'

Rosie tucked a gentle finger under Kelsey's chin and lifted her face so she was staring straight into the detective's sharp blue gaze. Kelsey, feeling soiled and unworthy of the concern she saw in them, tried to pull away.

'You have nothing to be ashamed of, Kelsey. You did nothing wrong.'

A tear rolled down her cheek.

'Men like that should be castrated and eradicated from the face of the earth,' growled Charlie, sitting down on the other side of Rosie and looking directly into Kelsey eyes. He took her breath away when he added, 'and in spite of his brutal abuse, look how you turned out – a beautiful, strong, resourceful woman with a warm and caring heart.' A warm glow replaced the sour, unclean sensation that had invaded her heart. With those few words the knots of shame inside her began to unravel leaving a feeling of self-worth and confidence in its place.

Chapter Eighteen

At dawn the following morning, the sun cleared the distant hills in a glorious burst of colour. It was still early when they set off to climb to the top of the knoll but the day promised to be a scorcher. Following the twists and turns of the track Charlie, carrying a loaded pack strapped to his back, strode effortlessly along in front of Kelsey. His long legs ate up the distance to the first bend in the path. Even though it was already hot and he was wearing jeans – he didn't seem to break out in a sweat and Kelsey wondered if after a lifetime in this environment he even felt the heat. Rosie giving a sure-footed imitation of a mountain goat raced ahead of the group eager to be first to the top. Kelsey took her time, following the trail with small cautious steps, aware that her healing soles needed to be treated with care. Charlie turned and held his hand out to her.

She took it and said, 'Sorry, my feet are still a bit tender.'

'No rush,' he said, smiling down at her.

When Kelsey drew level with him, Charlie tucked her hand into the crook of his arm and matched his step to her pace.

She looked up and saw Rosie had made the top and was looking down at them, impatience written all over her face.

'Hurry up, Bayden,' she yelled down at them.

Kelsey laughed when Mark, who was following along behind, brushed past them, picked up his pace and said in a soft voice not meant to be heard by the woman above, 'We are not all super fit ninja dingos you know.'

Kelsey and Charlie followed along at a comfortable pace. With reluctance Kelsey let go of Charlie's muscular arm when they reached the summit and limped between the two large boulders that marked the access to the glade where the well was located. She took a moment to glance around at the shrub-lined clearing not having seen it in daylight before. It was very pretty, the native cotton shrubs had burst into flower and the insects zipped gleefully from plant to plant feasting on the nectar. Her feet gave a small twinge so she made her way over to the rock pyramid and sat down.

Mark, still puffing and panting from the effects of the climb, slumped to the ground beside her and groaned, 'My wife's too good a cook and it's beginning to tell.'

Kelsey smiled and patted his shoulder. 'Here, have a drink.' She handed him an unopened bottle of water.

'For God's sake, don't anybody mess up the scene.' Rosie holding a camera was darting around the edge of the clearing like a madwoman, photographing everything in situ. No blade of grass, overturned leaf or scuff mark was safe.

Kelsey snorted when she saw Mark do an eye roll.

'It's only been raining for what...a week? That shouldn't have washed any evidence away,' he whispered.

'Shush, you'll make me laugh.'

Charlie dropped his backpack beside them and pointed at the ground on the other side of Kelsey. 'Can I watch the show from here?'

Kelsey giggled. 'Stop it you two. You'll get us in trouble.'

Rosie turned to the trio of spectators and asked, 'How were the bodies transported here?'

The smile left everyone's face. The reminder of their mission caused the nerves in Kelsey's stomach to re-knot.

'As far as I'm aware no one has been here for three or four years. Obviously, I'm wrong of course,' said Charlie, pointing to the well and then Kelsey. 'This was the original homestead site. My great grandparents set up camp here when they settled the property but the well is in the wrong position to draw in underground water, so they sealed it up and moved. They named this knoll Heartbreak Hill. About four years ago I gave prospectors permission to use the knoll as a base camp for some work they were conducting further inland.' Charlie pointed in the opposite direction to where they had come from. 'Through that clump of trees is the overgrown dirt track that was the original access road. If Kelsey had hiked that way instead of going the way she did, she would have come across the main road to Mount Ibour.'

Rosie strode over to where he pointed. She examined the ground, took some photos and said, 'There are some faint tyre tracks and what looks like they may be drag marks. Bayden, do we have any casting powder so we can make an impression of these?'

Mark shook his head.

'Right, well make a note will you – we'll get the CIU to bring some with them, and anything else we need. Tape that area off for now. Everybody is to stay away, okay?' They all nodded their heads at the directive and Mark rolled to his feet. He dug around in his police bag and pulled out a roll of blue and white barrier tape.

'What is CIU, Rosie?' asked Kelsey

'Coronial Investigation Unit. They'll provide the specialist support we need and work with the coroner, pathologist and chemistry centres in Perth to process any evidence we find,' Rosie replied. She walked over and stood with her hands on hips. 'Right, Bull we need to confirm the existence of the body or any skeletal remains before I can call them in.'

Charlie nodded, opened his backpack and pulled out the drone. He inserted fresh batteries and did a test flight.

'We're going to need to get one of these Bayden for future investigations. Put it on the list will you. I'll fill out a purchase request and justification form when we return to the office,' said Rosie watching the drone do its thing. 'Bull, I want you to record a panorama of the area, showing its remoteness, before we tackle the well. I'm positive we're looking for someone with local knowledge.'

'Yeah sure,' said Charlie.

He settled his back against the pyramid and fiddled with the control stick. Kelsey had a clear view over his shoulder and watched the monitor with interest as the drone completed a full circle of the area. The images were crystal clear and the bush looked magnificent. Fresh green shoots sprouted on the surrounding shrubbery. A kaleidoscope of butterflies fluttered and swirled above the new growth feasting on the succulent nectar being produced in abundance as new flower buds burst into a glorious display of colour. Sheets of water that had been left by the deluge of rain were being utilised by flocks of water birds that were enjoying a delightful game of splash.

Kelsey leant forward putting her mouth close to Charlie's ear and asked in a soft voice, 'Can you pause and print a photo from your recordings, Charlie?'

His lip twitched with a smile and said, 'Yeah, why?'

'I'd love to capture some of those wonderful images so I can paint them.'

'Consider it done, my lovely.'

Kelsey's heart did a small flip at his new name for her. She gave his shoulder a gentle squeeze. He patted her hand then went back to his task. She took a deep breath and decided not to read too much into it, Charlie was just being kind.

To distract herself from his closeness, Kelsey glanced over at the detective. She watched with curiosity as Rosie pulled a tube of plastic from her backpack and unfurled it along the ground so it ran from the well to where they sat. It looked like a VIP carpet only black instead of red. 'Everyone is to walk on that,' Rosie said, pointing to the makeshift path. 'That way we don't mess up the area, destroying potential evidence, okay.'

Once again everybody's head nodded in agreement. Rosie came and squatted next to Kelsey. She took her by the hands, her eyes an intense sparkling blue.

'Are you ready for this?'

Kelsey's heart began to race, nausea churned in her belly and her breakfast formed into a hard rock. Kelsey squeezed the hand holding hers. She considered shaking her head but a soulful sad voice called to her from the shaft. She gulped in a lungful of air and nodded.

'Good girl,' said the detective, patting her knee. 'Okay Bull, time to take the drone down.'

Everyone rose to their feet. Utilising Rosie's makeshift path, they moved to the head of the abandoned shaft and looked down. The bottom section was dark where the sunlight didn't cut through the gloom. The gruesome jumble of bones Kelsey knew to be there wasn't apparent to the naked eye. Charlie draped his arm around Kelsey's shoulder and gave her a soft squeeze. She patted the comforting hand before it was returned to the controls.

Rosie peered around Charlie's other arm peering intently at the screen. An eerie red light thrown out by the drone reflected off rough, uneven stone walls.

'Stop,' said the detective.

Charlie lifted his finger from the joystick and the image on the screen became stationary. Rosie pointed to a shallow hole. It was half-filled with fresh, sandy-red soil and showed signs of recent digging. 'Did you do that, Kelsey?'

At her nod, Mark exclaimed 'Bloody hell, not much to hang onto.'

'It's all I could manage,' whispered Kelsey reliving the fear of the moment when she had wavered and almost fallen.

The drone recommenced its descent and rotated in a slow circle. The record button glowed so Kelsey knew everything they saw was being captured for viewing later.

'Right Bull, point the camera angle down, I want to see that floor.'

Kelsey took one look at the screen, turned and ran. She made it to the edge of the clearing before her stomach contents heaved themselves from her mouth.

* * *

A bloated body, rotting and maggot ridden, lying in a pool of water.

Kelsey racing away didn't distract Rosie from the image on the screen. She became aware of the restless movement of the man beside her so she reached out a hand and held him in place.

'Bayden,' she said, 'go and check on Kelsey. Bull, stay where you are. Keep recording and zoom in.' She looked up to emphasise her words and noticed he looked pale under his tan. He nodded at her command. She slipped her half-moon reading glasses onto the tip of her nose and pushed her face closer to the image, studying it in minute detail.

'It helps not to think about what you see in terms of being human,' she murmured. 'Try to concentrate on the small details and finding anything that could be evidence. Oh, and don't forget to breathe.'

Charlie grunted in reply to her pearls of wisdom.

'Alright Bull, spin the drone around and let's see what else we have.'

She could hear Charlie deep breathing through his mouth as he guided the aircraft in a slow circle that showed the bottom of the well was covered in a sheet of water. She was disappointed there was nothing else to see but also realistic. Stepping back she indicated to Charlie to raise the drone back to the surface.

'It looks like we'll have to stick a pump down there to get rid of all that water and see what else we've got. Thank God bloated bodies float, because it means I have enough evidence to justify a call to the retrieval specialists.'

Charlie didn't reply. She looked up at his face. His lips were pinched and his nostrils flared. 'You did well mate. Not an easy thing to see.'

'No, it's not,' he replied, fiddling with the drone controls.

A twig snapped and dry leaves crunched and rustled as though being walked upon.

Rosie's scrutinised the taped off area. 'Did you hear that?' she asked.

Bull nodded. 'Could be a roo or maybe Mark is taking a leak.'

Rosie was sucking in a deep breath to yell at her partner when she realised he was on the other side of the clearing attending a sick looking Kelsey.

The sound of an engine firing had her leaping towards the noise. 'Bayden,' she yelled, 'get your arse into gear, we've got company.'

Rosie pumped her arms and dashed towards the noise. She leapt over a small boulder to avoid going through the taped off area.

Spinifex and cotton shrubs scraped against her bare arms leaving long scratches on her skin as she forged her way out onto the overgrown track. From the corner of her eye she caught a flash of silver and peered over in time to see the roof of a vehicle disappearing over a rise. She was too late.

'Shit...shit, shit, shit,' she snarled.

'What's up, boss?' asked Mark as he slid to a stop beside her and rested his hands on his knees panting.

Rosie pointed down at the fresh tyre marks on the track. 'Someone was watching us. Silver vehicle. Could be our perp.'

'Even if it's not,' said Mark, 'word must be out. How soon will it be before the killer hears that Kelsey is alive and we're investigating the well on Heartbreak Hill'

'Hmm, good point. Get on the sat-phone Bayden. We need CIU here ASAP. We can't afford to leave this site unguarded until they arrive... and get me some photos of these new tyre marks so I can compare them with the ones behind the tape.'

Chapter Nineteen

Charlie watched in amazement as the detective yelled 'Bayden', and leapt into action. She was as agile as any of his working dogs and cleared the boulder with no difficulty. He flipped the toggle on the drone and it flew up out of the shaft to land on the black plastic. Placing the hand-held controller next to it he marched over to the emerald-eyed beauty standing with her back against the large rock with her face to the sun. Her eyes were closed and her face was as white as a ghost. Without a word he gathered her into his arms and breathed in her unique floral scent. She responded by snuggling in against his chest. His heart swelled and long suppressed urges filled the empty void within him. He forced himself to take a small step back before he overstepped the mark and gave rein to his desires. Not happy to lose total contact he reached down and with a gentle finger stroked her cheek. Her magnificent eyes sparkled and shone in the sunshine.

In a desperate attempt not to lean forward and kiss her with all the passion he possessed, he said, 'Did you see the Silver Dingo giving a brilliant display of agility?'

Kelsey snorted. Her cheeks returned to their normal pale rose colour.

'What's going on?' she asked.

Charlie didn't want to dispel the animation that had returned to her face but he also didn't believe in not being straightforward with people. 'Rosie thought she heard a vehicle.'

He waited for the tint of colour to leave her face again but instead all he got was a nod and a statement that took his breath away.

'So, the killer has found me.'

The shrubbery rustled, he swung around and put himself between Kelsey and the noise. Charlie relaxed when an unfeminine curse heralded the return of their companions. Mark made a beeline for his backpack, lifted the flap and pointed to the bag's contents.

'Okay to use the phone, mate?'

Charlie nodded and took Kelsey by the hand. She clung on tight as he led her over to the rock pyramid which had become their perching spot.

Mark was talking into the phone receiver. Charlie paused to listen but he was only reciting a list of equipment Rosie wanted. The constable nodded his head in confirmation to the tinny voice on the other end of the phone.

'Hang on a sec, I'll put her on,' he said, and held out the phone to Rosie. 'Sergeant George wants a word.'

Rosie grabbed the instrument from his hand and wandered away with it clamped to her ear. Charlie caught only snatches of her conversation as he watched her march to and fro updating her colleague on the events that had unfolded during the morning. Charlie had attended primary school with Sergeant Noel George, but had lost touch during the years he'd boarded away. They had renewed their acquaintance when Charlie had taken up the reins as grazier of River Run. Since that time he had been a keen supporter of the local policing programs introduced by Noel. Always one for community policing, Noel had a tendency to sort out the wilder element of his town in a practical way, only using jail time and the courts as a last resort. Over the years Noel George had earned the deep and abiding respect of Charlie as a good police officer and community man. So it was quite a shock to hear Rosie tearing strips off him for incompetence.

'How the fuck could you let that happen...' As she listened she took half a dozen stomping paces away from them, swivelled and paused. 'I specifically asked you to keep it quiet.' Red fury tinged her cheeks and the tips of her ears. As Noel continued to talk the colour made a slow retreat from her face. 'I see...and it's been dealt with?' Rosie nodded her head in agreement at whatever was being said. 'Good,' she barked and resumed her pacing giving an occasional grunt. 'Well do the best you can to mobilise the troops, and get me that equipment pronto. Yeah, I'll see if Bull has a pump we can use, much faster than trucking one in from Broome. No, everything's under control here.' Rosie hung up without any adieu and tossed the phone over to Mark's waiting hand.

He stowed it neatly away in the backpack and raised his brows to his cranky boss. 'What's going on?' he asked.

'Your mate, Constable Trevor Harrow has earned himself a nice little retainer from the media.'

Mark's eyebrows shot up and his eyes widened. 'Shit...sorry Kelsey...what's Harrow done now?'

'The bastard's only gone and leaked the story of Kelsey's survival. I hope he enjoys the money he's been paid because he's qualified for a place in the unemployment queue.' The fury in her voice deepened her normal tone to an almost baritone level and her words came out choppy and hard. 'Bull, we need to set up a camp here, next to the well, to keep an eye on the crime scene. There's not going to be much sleep for any of us because we'll be taking turns to guard the site. Three hourly intervals for the three of us...'

'Four,' said Kelsey.

A loud 'No...,' spewed from Charlie's mouth at the same time as Rosie said, 'Not happening.'

'But I want to help,' said Kelsey.

Rosie took a hold of Kelsey's hands and gave them a small shake. 'Listen, you're not to go anywhere or be anywhere by yourself – not even to take a leak. Someone is going to stay with you at all times. You are too important, not only to this investigation but also to us.' Rosie pointed to the three of them in turn. Her comment surprised the hell out of Charlie and Mark, judging by the owlish, round-eyed look on his face. It wasn't like the terse and no-nonsense detective to display her feelings of affection in so obvious a manner.

Kelsey's face hardened with determination. 'I can't sit around doing nothing and expect you all to take care of me,' she argued.

'You won't be idle. For starters I need you to finish that sketch of the girl, so I can get a missing persons enquiry started.' Rosie let out a loud sigh and added, 'We might as well put the press to use and get her image out into the public arena. Someone must know who she is. Secondly, you're about to draw out the killer...' And there it was, thought Charlie, the detective's hardness and focus for the task at hand was back.

He shook his head in disgust and snarled, 'You can't use Kelsey as bait.'

Charlie felt a soft touch on his forearm. He glanced down at Kelsey. She gave his arm a gentle squeeze.

'She's not, Charlie. I'm already a target and I always will be, until I remember something that will catch this mongrel.'

Rosie's lips thinned into a hard grimace. 'And it's not just the killer we have to worry about...'

'What do you mean? What's going on?' asked Charlie.

'Our peace is about to be shattered. The media not only has been fed Kelsey's survival story but also that your wife is missing...it's being splashed all over the networks. Accusations are rife. The newspaper and television reporters are clamouring for access and interviews, and knowing their resources they'll probably arrive before CIU can. My biggest concern is that they'll get in the way, and muddy the waters giving the killer an opportunity to get to our girl here...'

'My wife is not missing, she left,' growled Charlie. His anger began to rise and his vision blurred.

'Be that as it may, but until we find her or she makes contact the media are going to speculate all sorts of theories and bust a gut to get out here to Rivers Run to talk with you both. And who knows who'll show up with them...that's why, Kelsey, you must always have one of us three with you. I don't trust anyone else.'

'I understand,' said Kelsey. She looked like a deer in the headlights with her eyes wide and her face devoid of emotion. 'While I'm alive I'm a danger to whoever threw us away like unwanted refuse.'

Rosie's nodded. Charlie's heart sped up and the nerves in his gut knotted at the thought of an invasion of strangers on his land, especially if one of them came with murderous intent.

He bent and began to rummage in his backpack, searching for the phone Mark had just returned.

'I'm phoning Mac...he can get all the property gates chained and padlocked. That might hamper anyone trying to sneak in through one of the back roads. The gates already have cameras. Eli can set up the home computer to monitor and record any movements. If some smartarse decides to cut the lock and get in we'll know. I'll get Naomi to give the crew a lecture about the gravity of their actions should they give any stickybeak directions to our location. She can be terrifying if crossed. If they do, word travels fast on the bush tele-graph and they'd never work on a station again. It's not worth the risk to their livelihood.' Pointing to the well he added, 'As for the bas-tard, who did this, all I can do is make access as difficult as possible but you know as well as I do, where there's a will there's a way. We just have to be hyper-vigilant, especially with your safety, Kelsey.'

Rosie nodded. 'Excellent,' she said. 'The sarge is mobilising CIU as we speak. He's organising a helicopter to get them here. So what I need from you, Bull, are GPS co-ordinates that I can pass on to the pilot and a landing site for the chopper. Kelsey, can you help him with that?'

From the corner of his eye Charlie saw Kelsey's head nod up and down in rapid agreement. The assignment pleased him. He intended to keep a good watch over her starting with getting the pistol from the lock box under his driver's seat. No way was a killer going to strike on his watch.

'You guys stay here for now, watch the well,' said Rosie rubbing her hands together. 'Bayden and I'll lug up some equipment for a watch camp.'

Charlie began to feel sorry for Mark and the steep learning curve Rosie had him on. He cleared his throat to get her attention and said, 'Umm...why don't you load what you need into the police cruiser and drive around the base of the knoll. There's a track around the other side that joins up with the Heartbreak Hill one. I followed it when I went for a ride on Rainbow this morning. You'll save your-self a lot of grunt work.'

Rosie gave a snort, winked at him and with a sly grin tapped Mark on the forehead with her index finger. 'Now why didn't you know about that, Bayden?'

Chapter Twenty

The rattling of the marble in the spray paint can didn't distract Kelsey from the interesting and insightful conversation she and Charlie were having about the future of Rivers Run.

'The old ways are under serious threat. That's what so impressed me about Eli's vision of the future. He has embraced modern life and come up with a variety of sound business ideas to preserve our lifestyle while moving with the times.'

'He's a smart boy, Charlie. Do you think you'll be able to make the transition to the changes he's suggesting?'

'It will take time, but yeah, I think we can make it work. Take, for example, the Jackaroo Home Stay...no, we need a more inclusive name...ahh, Stockhand...no boring,' said Charlie, rubbing the back of his neck and gazing off into the distance for a moment. He gave a grunt, leant forward with the paint can in his hand and pressed the spray nozzle. Pink exploded onto the ground adding colour to the line he was working on.

'Hmm how about something like JacknJillaroo Station Stay or just stick with something basic that won't, in people's minds, box you in to being one sort of holiday experience,' said Kelsey gazing at all the beauty around her and imagining tourists enjoying a camp-out. 'Rivers Run Camping Resort.'

Charlie peered over his shoulder at her and said, 'Good thought. No rush to come up with a name just yet. Anyway, where was I?' Kelsey opened her mouth to provide a prompt but it wasn't necessary. When he was on a flow Charlie could chatter as much as Eli. 'We have the beginnings of the accommodation. I've already got some new transportable buildings under construction that I'd intended adding to the crew quarters, but we could establish a camping and caravan ground at Rocky Watering Hole instead and install them as cabins. Eli is going to crunch some numbers, develop a draft budget. I suppose I had better run it by Gil as he's the book-keeper.'

'You don't sound keen on discussing it with him.'

'No, I'm not. I can't put my finger on it but I get a weird vibe talking about my finances with him. Stupid I know seeing as he's looked after my accounts for a couple of years now.' He hesitated then continued, 'God I miss, Josh. He was good at interrogating concepts, seeing problems and looking outside the box.' Charlie sighed and continued squirting paint on the ground. 'Anyway, we need to think about how to keep the visitors entertained, maybe with workshops and day trips, perhaps. You know the stuff I'm talking about, horse riding lessons and treks, mustering experiences, whip cracking – which by the way we don't use on our beasts but a display of the old skill would be fun for the tourists to see. I suppose I'll also have to consider how we'd entertain tourists after hours, and what staffing we'll need. Oh hell! It's a lot to get my head around.'

'Well Charlie, from what I'm hearing, you've made a good start. Thinking about what people would like to experience and how you could provide that, is important. Don't limit your thinking to just the stock work, though. Artists and photographers for instance, would give their eyeteeth to come here. The unique beauty of your landscape, the day-to-day workings of the station and the glorious flora and fauna of the Kimberley will sing to them in ways you cannot imagine. You also have access to a magnificent river – I presume it has fish?'

'Oh yeah,' grunted Charlie.

'Then what about a fishing and campfire cooking experience.'

'Wow...yeah...all good ideas,' said Charlie reaching over to grab a new can of paint. 'I think we need some help to plan this out.'

'Well, you have your sister...she's a travel agent isn't she?'

'Yeah. How did you know that?'

Now there was a puzzle thought Kelsey. How did I know that?

'Eli must have mentioned it when he gave me a rundown of everyone involved in his life. He told me so much when we first met that I don't think I absorbed it all.'

'Yeah,' laughed Charlie, 'that sounds like him.'

Kelsey shook the can in her hand and squirted. The bitter tang of paint overpowered the soft mellow scent of eucalyptus that drifted on the breeze. It stung her nostrils. She rubbed her nose at the stench and sneezed. One more spray from the can and the task was finished. She stood, stretched her back and gazed around, satisfied that the police helicopter now had an obvious landing zone not far from the main camp. She flicked her gaze around searching, for any movement around them or anything out of place on the horizon. She'd been keeping a constant vigil ever since this morning's unannounced visitor because she had no intention of letting anyone sneak up on her.

Charlie's lips were pulled back in a smirk as he strolled over from his completed work. He handed her a rag. She looked down and she saw that not only were her hands covered in paint, but she had somehow managed to accumulate pink kneecaps and shins. Trust her to make a goose of herself she thought and rolled her eyes.

Charlie chuckled at her gesture, which gave his face a real Eli cheeki-
ness. He turned and bent to pick up her empty cans. Jealous that
Charlie didn't have a hair out of place she gave in to temptation and
squirted a large cross on the seat of his pristine jeans. He looked over
his shoulder and stared in surprise at his rather nice looking butt.

He lifted his glance, eyes narrowed and a slight smile played
on his lips.

'So you want to play huh...'

Kelsey dropped everything and ran. Giving a carefree laugh she
raced towards the Rodeo, planning to lock herself in the cab. The
sound of Charlie's feet pounding on the earth behind her drew
closer and she realised with his long legs he would catch her before
she made it. She wove to the right and headed towards the boab tree
hoping to get the advantage on the slope up to the well. She looked
ahead and stopped dead. Her gut knotted in fear and she spun to
face the man racing up behind her. He swooped on her and crowed,
'Gotcha.' Her feet left the ground as he spun her around.

'Stop, Charlie,' she yelled, fear made her voice crack.

He put her down like she had slapped him across the face. The
laughter drained from his eyes to be replaced by a blank look. He let
go and took a rapid step back. Kelsey, scared he'd misinterpreted her
fear, reached forward and grabbed his wrist.

'Someone's coming,' she said, pointing to the curve of the knoll.
A slow moving four-wheel drive was heading towards them. Charlie
grabbed Kelsey's shoulder and gave her a gentle push.

'Come on, move – get to the Rodeo,' he said.

She followed his long-legged stride at a fast trot that ate up the
distance to the parked vehicle. Charlie flung open the driver's door
and rummaged under the seat. When he turned around he held a
handgun.

Charlie's voice was cold and hard when he said, 'Stay behind me until I see who it is.' With a deliberate step he positioned himself between her and the new arrival. The action blocked her from view. His back muscles were stiff and his spine was ramrod straight. The sound of the vehicle became louder as the vehicle drew close. Kelsey tried to peek around Charlie's large frame but he put out his left arm to stop her.

'But...'

'Please, Kelsey. Stay behind me and out of sight. I don't want you getting in the way of the gun. If I tell you to run...run as fast as you can. Don't look back, just go. Rosie and Mark are up at the well, make a beeline for them if you can. Okay?'

'Yes, but what about you.'

'I'll be right behind you.'

Her heart gave a painful squeeze as it tightened in her chest. She felt her bottom lip begin to quiver so she clamped it between her teeth and leant her forehead against the middle of his back. She told herself to get a grip. The internal lecture worked and she felt her courage return. If Charlie thought she would just run away and leave him behind to face danger alone, he had a lot to learn. Silence descended, broken only by the sound of the approaching vehicle. It dragged on for what seemed like an eternity. Kelsey was about to ask what was happening when the tenseness left Charlie's muscles and his shoulders relaxed.

'What the fuck...' he murmured.

Kelsey straightened her spine and stood ready to run. Staying hidden, she patiently waited for instructions. The rev of the engine slowed and the crunch of tyres ceased. A soft voice that almost purred with pure sex floated in the air, 'Hello, Bull. I've bought you a present.'

'Steve,' said Charlie, taking a step forward. He slipped the gun into the waistband of his jeans, where it nestled against the small of his back. He flipped his shirt tail over the top to cover it before he turned to face her. 'Kelsey, it's okay, it's just one of the crew.'

His face was devoid of expression, cold almost. Kelsey glanced towards the smirking woman standing next to the silver RAV4, its engine ticking as it cooled. Once again Steve had dressed to enhance her body shape, tight blue jeans tucked into fancy dark-brown leather boots. Her long-sleeved green-checked shirt was knotted under her voluptuous breasts which threatened to spill out in all their glory with every move she made. Her copper-bronze hair gave off a dazzling shine in the sunshine and had been artfully arranged into a long ringlet that cascaded over one shoulder and hung down to her waist.

Steve gave Kelsey a small finger wave and a smile that didn't reach her eyes. Kelsey gave a polite nod and returned her focus to Charlie.

'I'll go lock myself in the Rodeo while you deal with this. One less worry for you,' she said, not at all upset at not having to spend time in the company of this woman. There was something about her, other than the obvious that made Kelsey's skin crawl. A look of relief crossed Charlie's face as he nodded in agreement to her plan.

Kelsey settled back in the seat and watched the couple in the side mirror. Steve, in a casual gesture dusted a speck from the shoulder of Charlie's shirt. She said something that brought a small smile to his face. He reached around her and opened the rear of her vehicle. Her breasts brushed against his arm causing Steve to laugh. She placed a hand on his upper arm before taking a tiny step back. Charlie pushed the door fully open and began examining whatever was in the back of the vehicle. He and Steve stood close together and began to talk. Kelsey watched the two heads held so close to each other they were almost bumping. She could feel tendrils of jealousy snaking their way around her heart and doing a tap dance in her chest. Charlie stepped back and held out a hand. Steve placed hers in his and lifted a foot to climb into the cargo hold. Somehow, she stumbled and fell to the ground. Charlie leant down to the fallen woman and she wrapped her arms around his neck, placed her face in tight against his chest. He removed her arms from his neck and cupped her face with his palms. Kelsey could see tears sparkling on her cheeks. As Charlie placed a hand on her ankle she yelped as though in pain, so he scooped her up in his strong arms. Cradling her like a baby he carried Steve towards where Kelsey sat waiting.

Sighing she unlocked her door and slid from her seat. As they drew near Kelsey could hear Steve's pitiful, 'I am so sorry darling. It's not like me to be so clumsy.'

It wasn't the satisfied look on Steve's face that hurt Kelsey but Charlie's reply.

'You'll be right, fly girl. A bit of TLC and you'll be as good as new.'

* * *

Kelsey sat inside the tent unobtrusively peeping out the flap. From her position she had a perfect view of the scene taking place at the campfire. Steve was settled in one of the camp chairs, her leg propped on top of the car fridge with a bag of ice packed around her ankle. A pathetic look of pain was painted on her face. Charlie patted her hand, strolled to the Rodeo and leant against the driver's door with the car two-way in his hand.

'Yeah, Mac she's turned an ankle,' he said.

Jimmy's voice crackled over the airwaves but the words came through clear enough. 'Do you want me to send someone to collect her?'

'No...it's not too bad, we'll keep it iced and she should be right to drive herself back in the morning.'

'Roger that. Radio me if the plan changes.'

'Yeah, will do mate. Out.'

Charlie turned and returned the two-way's mouthpiece to its cradle in the cab. A small smirk momentarily touched Steve's lips. It was so quick Kelsey wasn't sure if she'd seen it or not. She sighed and opened the medical box sitting on her lap. After extracting two paracetamol tablets, Kelsey locked the box again and crawled out of the tent. She strode over to the injured woman.

'Some painkillers for you, Steve,' she said holding out the medicine and a bottle of water.

'Thank you, sweetie,' said Steve, the saccharine so thick in her voice you could have made jam.

Charlie smiled over at Kelsey. 'Thanks, that's very thoughtful of you.' He turned his attention to Steve and said, 'The detective's screaming for the pump that's in the back of your vehicle. I need to go and set it up. I'll just pop you on the back seat and repack the ice around your foot.'

Steve's face went totally blank. 'No don't bother, Bull. The jostling of the vehicle wouldn't be good for it. I'll just sit here and let the ice do its work. Don't fuss darling, I'll be fine.' Her words totally surprised Kelsey. Her body language since arriving had all been about seducing Charlie – now she was letting him out of her sight. Strange.

'Are you sure?' Steve nodded and he shrugged. 'Okay, but keep this next to you in case you need us.' He held out a two-way radio. Steve quirked her lip in a lopsided, almost intimate smile and ran her fingertips down his arm before taking the radio from his hand. 'We won't be long, fly girl. Kelsey, you're with me.'

Kelsey's mood lifted at his words. Good, a least she wasn't being left with the care of this woman.

* * *

Kelsey finished duct taping the sieve handle to the hose just as the pump fired to life. The discharge hose stiffened in her hand and a slow trickle of water began to flow from the nozzle through the makeshift screen and down the side of the knoll. Rosie watched with a smile of satisfaction on her face.

'Fantastic, that should catch any small pieces picked up by the suction. Good job, Kelsey.'

'It's nice to be useful.'

Rosie patted her on the shoulder. 'Crank her up a notch, Bull,' she yelled.

Charlie nodded, fiddled with the throttle and the discharging water increased to a steady flow. Charlie, wiping his greasy fingers onto a rag clutched in his hand, wandered over to check out Kelsey's makeshift sieve. He smiled at her and said, 'Simple but effective, very smart, Kelsey.'

'I hear we have a visitor in camp, Bull,' said Rosie. 'Make sure she stays away from here. I don't want her wandering through the scene messing it up.'

'Not a problem, Rosie. Steve's sprained her ankle so she won't be wandering anywhere.' He turned away to high-five Mark who wandered over to join them.

'Yeah right,' said Kelsey under her breath. Rosie must have heard because she glanced down, her crystal blue eyes sharp and eyebrow cocked.

'Problem?' she asked.

Kelsey studied the detective's face, shrugged her shoulders and said in a low voice so the men wouldn't hear. 'You've met her, what do you reckon?'

Rosie gave a snort. She straightened her features, looked at her watch and interrupted the men's discussion about the local cricket team selections.

'Okay, boys, its three o'clock, I'll take first watch. Bayden, you and Bull head back to camp. Rest up, eat, or whatever. One of you, come back at six o'clock and relieve me. The other can have the nine to midnight shift. I'll guard Kelsey tonight. We can share the back of the police vehicle.' Both men nodded. Rosie put her hand out and helped Kelsey to her feet. She didn't let go. 'Stay, I want to talk. See if between us we can't get that old brain box of yours working.'

Kelsey felt her top lip twitch. She was happy to avoid being in the company of the Rivers Run sex kitten but unsure how gruelling Rosie's inquisition was going to be.

'How long do you want to keep up this security vigil, Rosie?' asked Charlie, 'I've still got a son at home who needs me, a property to run and my sister and nephew are due any day now.'

'CIU will be here tomorrow. Once they take over the scene, you and Kelsey can go.'

Kelsey's heart sank. So, it was finally happening. She'd have to leave.

'But where is home for me?' asked Kelsey.

Rosie patted her on the shoulder. 'You're not going home where there's nobody to protect you. Bull, is it still okay if our girl stays at the homestead for a while longer? If not I'll make some alternative arrangements.'

'Kelsey you're welcome at River Run for as long as you want or need,' said Charlie giving her a reassuring smile.

'Good, excellent.' Rosie flapped her hand at the two men, 'Go on then you two, bugger off. Kelsey and I are going to settle back and have a chat.'

'Righto boss,' said Mark with a flash of teeth. His happy smile gave the impression he'd had an early release from school.

Rosie, always one to keep him on his toes waited until he'd turned away before in a deceptively mild voice said, 'Oh Bayden.'

Mark stopped mid-stride, his shoulders slumped and he turned. 'Yes boss.'

'Keep your radio handy – in case you're needed.'

Charlie smiled, thumped Mark on the shoulder and said, 'Come on slugger, let's go fire up the barbeque.'

The happy smile returned to Mark's face.

* * *

'I don't suppose your sergeant has learnt anything about me has he?' Kelsey asked when the men had driven away in the police vehicle. She was eager for some details, anything that might help kick-start her sluggish memory.

'Not much, that's why we need to talk.'

Kelsey leant forward but Rosie's raised hand forestalled her. 'Let's see what you can remember.'

Kelsey shoulders sagged and she gave the detective a reluctant nod. Rosie slung a friendly arm around her and led her to a camp chair set out in front of a dark-blue one-man tent.

'Come on my girl, grab a pew in my fancy new office, where we can enjoy a nice cuppa and a chat.'

Rosie dug around in an esky and pulled out some mugs, a thermos and a packet of Tim Tam biscuits. Using the lid as a table she poured hot liquid into both cups before handing one to Kelsey.

Taking a giant gulp of the black, tart coffee Rosie sighed, 'Ah, all the essentials of life.' She crossed her legs at the ankles, took a large bite of a biscuit and held her face up to the sun.

With her eyes closed, Rosie's jaw worked slowly as she hummed a small tune. Kelsey crossed her own legs and watched in fascination. She was seeing another facet of the strong, driven woman.

As if feeling the penetration of Kelsey's gaze, Rosie began to speak. 'You know, I don't get many chances to sit and relax. People think I'm a workaholic and don't know how to unwind, but nothing is further from the truth. Solving puzzling cases, for me, is a form of relaxation and my work fulfils that need in me. Don't get me wrong, I am driven and I admit to being very competitive. That comes from being surrounded by the high achieving men in my family. My mother died when I was very young so I was raised by my father, Chief Superintendent Robert Kettle and my two older brothers – Alex and Tom. Both my brothers, along with five of my cousins who lived around the corner from us growing up, took a great interest in my upbringing. I was used by them to make up the football team after school and I can tell you they didn't hold back just because I was a girl. I was Tom's practice partner for Tae Kwan Do and Alex's lackey at the gun club, as well as his athletics training partner. I got interested in detective work because dad used to sit with me of an evening, reviewing old case files while I did my homework. As I grew older we'd discuss his cases and what each piece of evidence could mean. He told me once that my perspective, young though it was, helped him solve some very puzzling problems.'

'Sounds like a great way to grow up.'

'Yeah, it was. The Kettle family...'

'Kettle, Rosie?'

Rosie sighed, 'Bloom's my married name. I never it changed back.'

'Divorced?'

'No, widowed. I married at seventeen and was alone again at nineteen. Ian and I had twenty glorious months together before he died. My husband was the one who convinced me to join the police force, but he never lived to see me graduate.'

'I'm sorry, Rosie.'

The detective flapped her hand as if waving Kelsey's words away. 'Don't be, it was twenty-two years ago and while I still miss him, the pain of his passing is more a familiar friend than overwhelming grief.'

'That's an excellent description. I feel like that about my family, like some tasty ingredients been left out of the recipe but the meal is still okay.'

Rosie smiled. The contours of her face softened. She took a small sip from her mug and said, 'Why weren't you in the car with your family when they had their accident?'

'I was staying at a specialist centre, taking tests to do with my Highly Superior Autobiographical Memory.' Kelsey drew in a deep breath and a lead weight formed in her stomach. Oh crap, now the disgust will come, just as I was beginning to make a friend.

'Having a brain like that must have been challenging for you growing up. The jealousy and pettiness of others would have been awful,' said Rosie, her tone remaining even with no trace of anything except friendliness. 'Am I right?'

Kelsey looked at her in surprise. 'You're not disgusted?'

'Why would I be disgusted?' asked Rosie reaching over, taking Kelsey's hand with one of her own and giving it a gentle squeeze. 'You have a marvellous gift. Own it and be proud.'

A memory of puzzled and unkind stares, curled lips and rolled eyes, and the words know-it-all, formed in her mind. Kelsey told Rosie about it and said, 'Disgust has been the major reaction to my photographic memory all my life. So I tone down my intelligence and hide it. I don't remember ever having friends.' An image flashed in her mind, so quick she wasn't sure what it meant, of a tall, blond-haired boy with a bright, even-toothed smile. He held out a hand to help her up from the ground. The picture of the boy merged into a man, with a worried frown creasing his handsome face. He handed her something.

Before she could say anything, Rosie spoke, 'Well you don't need to tone down the smarts for me. I like and respect you for who you are.'

A warm glow ignited in Kelsey's belly. 'Do you think the others will feel the same?'

'If by others you mean Bull...,' Rosie smirked, 'I don't think he will have a problem with you being brilliant. He's not a man to be threatened by intelligence no matter what form it takes. Kelsey, your brain is an awesome machine. Embrace what it can do. If others don't like it then let them lump it.'

'Oh...,'said Kelsey. She had never thought of it like that. So practical, but what was Rosie thinking, saying that she had a special interest in Charlie. That would never do. She could feel the colour rushing to her cheeks, 'I don't especially mean Charlie...'she stammered, 'he's not interested...'

'Please,' Rosie snorted, 'that man has fallen for you hook, line and sinker.'

'But he's married.'

'Kelsey, Kelsey, Kelsey. That boat has well and truly sailed. She left him and the boy high and dry eight years ago. I don't reckon either of them is pining for her.'

At her words Kelsey felt a surge of relief. It didn't last. She stared at the hose running down the shaft and a feeling of dread made her blood run cold. She had to ask.

'Rosie, the other day you asked Charlie if he had killed Amelia.' Kelsey pointed to the well and asked, 'Do you think...?'

'I'd be very surprised.'

'But you had an anonymous letter...'

'Yeah, interesting that...' Rosie's eyebrows drew together in a puzzled frown. 'I think someone is out to make trouble for our prize bull and it's made me very curious as to what they're after.'

'What do you mean? And how can you be sure she's not down there?' asked Kelsey, nodding towards the well.

'Three maybe four years ago the well was unsealed by the prospectors and they found nothing. Amelia's been gone for eight. I'll double check, of course, but it would be a stupid thing to lie about.'

Rosie picked up the packet of Tim Tam's and waved them under Kelsey's nose. Tempted she took one and dipped it into her coffee. The chocolate coating softened and she sucked the goo from the biscuit.

'Hmmm...yum.' She almost purred in enjoyment.

Rosie smiled, took another biscuit for herself and copied Kelsey's actions.

'Hmmm...yum.'

They looked at each other and burst into a fit of laughter.

'This is a great way to conduct a stakeout. Should be more of it,' said Rosie settling back in her seat and stretching her legs out in front of her. Kelsey followed suit and found herself gazing up at the late afternoon sky. Fluffy white clouds edged in soft grey, lazily traversed the blue expanse. A lone bird of prey on the hunt, glided on silent wings in ever decreasing circles. A sweet scent coming from the pinky-lavender mulla mulla flowers that bloomed around them in abundance helped relax her even further. The peace and quiet was only broken by the distant hum of the pump. Her eyelids became leaden and began to droop.

She came awake with a start when Rosie spoke. 'I have five questions I want you to think about,' she said. 'Don't try to answer them now. Just let them rattle around in your head for a while. We'll talk about other things. I'll ask you for your impressions later and I want you to tell me whatever comes to mind.'

Kelsey nodded and waited.

'Question one...Why Mount Ibour? What was it that attracted you to that fair town?' Rosie sat up and leant forward to place her empty mug down on the top of the esky. 'Question two. How did you get to Mount Ibour? Car, bus, plane or did you walk? Questions three, when did you arrive? And question four, where were you staying? Now question five I'm very interested in. Was anyone with you or were you meeting someone?'

'Wow, you're not asking much, Rosie,' said Kelsey cocking her head and staring off into the distance. 'I'll start by thinking about the easy one first – mode of travel.'

Rosie nodded her head and patted Kelsey on the knee. 'Good. Now have you finished that sketch yet?'

'Yes,' said Kelsey and drew the sketchpad out from her backpack. She handed it over and Rosie took her time to study every page.

When she came to the sketch of herself Kelsey asked timidly, 'You don't mind?'

'Oh no, not at all. You've captured so much more than my hard exterior – there's so much life below the surface. Can I have it, my dad would love it.'

'I'd like to put it into oil first. Would that be alright for your father?'

Rosie let out a breath of delight, 'Yes.'

Chapter Twenty-One

At the sound of footsteps climbing the track Rosie hurriedly rose to her feet. She positioned herself so she was hidden from view and stared down the side of the knoll. She was surprised to see Bayden staggering slowly up the hill weighed down by an overfull backpack.

'God Bayden, how much food do you need for a three-hour shift?' she asked in amusement when he finally slumped on his haunches beside their small fire.

Mark flashed a friendly smile, his teeth dazzled in the firelight.

'It's the drone, our laptop and all the evidence we've collected so far. I thought I would spend the evening downloading the video. At the same time I want to make sure the logs are all up to date. Besides, if the stuff is here with me it's safe. I'd hate for someone to sneak into camp and knock anything off.'

A glow of satisfaction burned in Rosie's breast. Her young partner was beginning to shape up in a very satisfactory manner.

'Good man,' she said and checked the time on her watch. 'You're a half hour early.'

'Yeah, I was beginning to feel like a third wheel.' Rosie lifted her brows in surprise at the comment. 'You can cut the sexual tension in camp with a knife. I think Steve has major designs on Bull – she's all over him like a rash. Give me a nice, wholesome, friendly girl any day. I don't know how Bull stands it to be quite honest.' He peered at the napping Kelsey for a long moment before continuing in a soft voice. 'Maybe he can't – that's why he's spent so much time grooming that damn horse. While he was doing that she began bombarding me with questions, wanting to know every detail about what's going on up here on top of the knoll. I thought it best to come away before I let anything slip.'

'Good plan. Well, as you're here, Kelsey and I will go and sort out some dinner for ourselves. I trust you guys didn't eat all the food.'

'Heaven forbid,' Mark snorted, 'Bull's got enough meat in that car fridge to feed an army.'

Rosie grinned at him. 'Kelsey...,' she called softly to rouse the woman asleep in her chair, 'It's time to for us to head back to camp.'

'Is it that time already?' asked Kelsey, springing to her feet and collecting her gear. 'Hi, Mark did you have a nice dinner?'

'Best T-bone steak ever.'

Kelsey grinned. 'Everyone around here loves their beef. Do you know Eli asked me if I was a vegan? The look of disgust on his face at the thought was hilarious. Can imagine what a challenge that would be when you live on a cattle station.'

'Doesn't bear thinking about,' said Mark with a shudder.

'True, but it is something Charlie and Eli will have to think about if they're going to run a homestay.'

Rosie smiled to herself and gave Kelsey a gentle push in more ways than one. 'Well, that's something you can help him with, isn't it,' she said, and pointing towards the track added, 'Come on, let's hit the trail. All this talk of food has got the old gastric juices churning.'

Kelsey gave Mark a finger wave and disappeared between the boulders.

Rosie put on her boss's hat for a moment. 'Bayden, keep your radio close. Call if anything disturbs you and I mean anything. I don't care if it turns out to be a false alarm. I have no intentions of explaining to your wife and kids why you're a dead hero.'

'Righto, boss,' said Mark giving her a salute and a cheeky grin.

She shook her head, glanced up at the darkening sky and flicked on the torch to follow Kelsey.

'Come on,' she said to the woman waiting at the top of the trail, 'let's leave this fool to his own devices.'

She took the lead, and remembering the soles of her companion's feet, set a slow pace. Rosie gave the woman marks for her fortitude, she'd never once complained about the injuries she carried, or about anything that had been asked of her. Rosie admired that.

'It must have been hard climbing down here in your socks,' she said. 'What happened to your shoes?'

She glanced over her shoulder and in the gloom could just make out the expression on Kelsey's face. Her lips were twisted sideways in a gesture that Rosie was learning meant she was digging around in her brain for a memory. Rosie didn't rush her.

'They were white, bright white, so probably new.' She paused, cocked her head and nodded to herself. 'Yeah, they were a pair of Sketchers. I'd never owned Sketchers before. The first time I wore them they glowed in the evening gloom. I remember taking small, fast steps. Not running but definitely hurrying along a footpath. It was gloomy, the street lights, few and far between, were a dull yellow. I remember the strong scent of eucalyptus as I brushed past a shrub overhanging the footpath on a quiet street. I started to breathe fast, panting almost and my heart was pounding. I had just met someone or I was going to meet someone and I was worried.' She scrunched up her nose. 'I had something small in my hand...'

Rosie turned and flashed the torchlight onto Kelsey's left hand. She held it clutched to her breast. The fist was closed and the thumb and forefinger rubbed together like she was feeling something in her grip.

'What were you holding?' she asked.

Kelsey shook her head. 'I don't know, but it scared me. Sorry. The rest is blank.'

Frustrated Rosie ground her back teeth. This was taking too long. She was impatient to move the investigation forward and needed something more to go on. Rosie didn't hold out much hope of finding any evidence in the well. From what Kelsey had said, the bones and body had been stripped bare and anything else was going to be tainted by the storm's runoff. Kelsey's clothing had been through too much after her escape from the well to be of any use. She'd still send them to the lab for testing but didn't expect to get anything useful back. Rosie turned to continue her descent. As she flicked the torch its light reflected like silver from the branches of the boab tree.

'I sat on a soft mound of freshly dug dirt under that tree,' said Kelsey, her voice held a soft almost dreamlike tone as she painted the picture in words. 'The moon was full and bathed the landscape in a silvery mystic light. The sky was ablaze with stars that looked like pinpricks of dazzling crystals and a swirling nebula cloud was producing some amazing colours. It was a humbling and awesome sight. For a short period I felt safe and at peace.'

Rosie halted and Kelsey bumped into her. 'Show me,' she demanded.

Kelsey studied her face for a moment and without a word strolled with confidence to the far side of the tree.

'Here,' she said, patting the ground. A puzzled expression crossed her face. 'Why?'

Rosie ignored the question and flashed her light over the area. Earth, devoid of plant life and darker than the surrounding soil had been mounded into a compacted heap. It was perfect for sitting on. She handed the torch to Kelsey and sank to her knees next to it.

'Shine the light here,' Rosie ordered, pointing to the side of the mound. Using her fingers she scratched and dug at the pile to loosen the topsoil. The crust gave way and she worked her hands until they sank deep into soft earth. Rosie felt around with her fingers and delved deeper.

'What are you doing?' asked Kelsey.

Rosie grunted, not bothering to waste her breath. Something brushed her fingertips. She twisted her hand, grabbed hold and pulled hard. The dirt gave way and she fell backwards, landing in an inelegant heap on her butt.

'Are you okay, Rosie?'

Rosie took a hold of the hand that Kelsey was holding out to her and used it for balance as she stood.

'Yeah, not my finest hour,' she muttered.

She snatched the torch from Kelsey's hand and shone it on the disturbed ground. A dirty olive-green strap, threaded through a stainless steel buckle protruded from of the side of the mound. Rosie sank to her haunches and brushed away the dirt with the side of her palm. She sat back on her heels to study her find.

Kelsey leant over her shoulder for a closer look. 'That's a German flag,' she said, pointing to a hand sewn badge on the strap.

Excitement fizzed around in Rosie's gut.

She looked up at her companion and said, 'Not a word of this to anyone. Not even, Bull. I'm going to cover this back over and after dinner you and I are going to move the police vehicle here and stand guard.'

'But...'

'No buts. I need to keep this find secret.'

'Why?' asked Kelsey.

'Because there's a woman in the camp, who will blab to all and sundry about everything that's going on out here when she gets back. I don't want the killer to know what we've found.'

'What have we found?'

'The mother lode of evidence,' said Rosie, rubbing her hands together in delight.

'Okay, but won't everyone be suspicious about us camping out here?'

'I'll tell everyone we're sleeping here to guard the track.'

* * *

With a massive set of barbeque tongs in her hand Kelsey turned two huge steaks on the grill. Charlie was supervising. Men never believe women can cook a good barbeque, Rosie thought in amusement as she collected together the bedding, a battery-powered hurricane lamp and a flask of strong hot coffee to take on their sleep-out. Task complete, she strolled back to the camp fire. The grounded pilot still had a bag of ice on her foot and was glaring at the laughing couple. Rosie found it interesting that whenever Charlie glanced her way she had the most angelic look on her face. Rosie decided to prod the viper just for the enjoyment.

Dragging her chair closer to Steve's she said, 'They make a nice couple don't you think?'

Steve flinched at her words but said sweetly, 'Oh they're not a couple. Bull is always nice, to everyone.'

'Are you sure? It looks like it's heading in that direction.'

'I'm sure. I've known him for a long time. We actually have an understanding but we haven't made it public yet.'

'And here I thought he was already married?'

Steve look flummoxed for a moment then said, 'He's working on getting a divorce. Besides, there's Eli to consider.'

'You don't think he'd like to see his father happy?' asked Rosie curious to see how far this woman's delusion went.

'Oh it's not that. Eli is a teenager and it's such a challenging stage in life. I told Bull he needed to ease Eli into the idea of us. Christmas is a good time to announce an engagement don't you think?' She had a hard glint in her eye and a fake smile on her lips. 'Anyway, I've said too much,' and changing the direction of the conversation said, 'Your constable was telling me you've spent the day gathering evidence. Did you find anything interesting?'

'Not a great deal and nothing I can talk about,' said Rosie, keeping her face blank. Didn't hurt to spread misinformation that might bear fruit – make the killer careless. 'I was wondering – do you or any of the other stock hands get away from the station much? Go to Broome or Perth?'

'The last time I was in Broome was for a three-day break back in January.'

'Oh, did you fly?'

'No, we drove...'

'We?'

Steve gave a smirk and a meaningful nod in Bull's direction.

'Surely you didn't take the old Rodeo ute? That would have been so uncomfortable,' said Rosie fishing for information without being obvious.

Steve gave a small snort of amusement, 'Course not. No, the three of us went in the RAV4.'

'Three?'

'Yeah, us two love birds and Eli.'

'So, Eli travelled with you.' Rosie held up her forefingers, formed them into quote marks and gave them a wiggle. '*Awkward*. Having a teenage boy around wouldn't be conducive to a nice romantic getaway.'

'No, it wasn't, not really, but that was a busy time for us. I remember Bull and Eli spent most of the day in a meeting. I took care of some personal business then drove the car home.'

'What sort of meeting?'

'Some mining company. I'm not really sure.'

'And did you get to enjoy a night out on the town?'

Steve shook her head.

'That was a bit lousy of Bull.' Rosie put an inflection of horror in her voice, trying to make it seem like Steve had been hard done by on the romantic stakes.

Steve gazed across at the subject of their conversation. A look of disappointment crossed her face. 'Bull wasn't around. He and Eli caught the 6pm flight to Perth. Eli had to get back for the start of a new school year.'

'Leaving you to drive back all by yourself in the dark. That must have been fun.'

'I stayed the weekend and went back on the Sunday morning.'

'Did you put up in a nice hotel?' asked Rosie, leaning forward and peering intently at the woman next to her.

'I stayed with a friend. He...' Steve halted with whatever she was about to let slip. 'Hey, what's with all the questions?' she snarled.

Her gaze must have been too intense, thought Rosie. She improvised an answer to allay Steve's suspicions. 'I'm only asking because when I leave here I was planning to stop in Broome. I wanted to stay somewhere discreet.'

'You got a fella on the back burner?' Steve asked, arching an eyebrow and leering.

Rosie went with it, 'My husband...' she said, and feigned embarrassment by looking down and flicking some imaginary dust off the leg of her cargo pants.

Rosie watched Steve from the corner of her eye. The woman's lip twitched in contempt before reeling off the name of the some of the most expensive hotels in Broome. 'My favourite is the Blue Seas Resort with its luxurious self-contained apartments, hot tub and jacuzzi and it's only 600 metres from the beach. But remember you're anonymous when you're just a face in the crowd.'

All that local knowledge just screamed of more than one visit to Broome in the last 18 months. 'Thanks Steve, that's a great tip. What about in Perth or do you never go there?'

'Sometimes but not very often, I was there in June. Before that it was at least two years ago. I prefer flying out of Darwin to Bali and Singapore for my breaks.'

'June, isn't that when Bull's brother-in-law died?'

'Yeah, I flew back straight after the funeral.'

'Wow that's a long way to go for one day. I bet Bull and his sister, Georgina were glad of your help. Did you stay with them?'

Steve shook her head, her face devoid of expression. 'It wasn't just one day. I'd been in the city for the fortnight before as I needed to renew some of my pilot accreditations.'

Interesting thought Rosie, not a subject she was comfortable discussing. I might just give her a little push and see what falls out of her mouth.

'Which hotel did you stay in?'

'I didn't stay at a hotel. My friend has an apartment in the middle of the city...' Steve paused, the look of suspicion returned to her face.

Rosie kept her face blank. 'My husband doesn't take me out much and the city's not his cup of tea. Were you close to the night life? What did you do for fun?'

Steve gave a snigger. 'Went to a couple of nightclubs, a tad provincial for my taste but better than anything Mount Ibour has to offer. Now, Singapore is the place to go for an interesting clubbing experience.'

Oh great, she's just given me the opening I need thought Rosie.

'I hear the Rivers Run crew have a break in Mount Ibour once a month. What sort of things do they get up too?'

'I don't really know. I don't associate with them much as they're a boring lot. They play a lot of darts and talk shit with the local losers at the pub. Mimi's the one to ask, she's always the centre of attention, so I don't bother sticking around. I've other fish...' A chortle of laughter came from the couple huddled at the barbeque. Steve glared in their direction, leant forward and removed the ice pack from her ankle. She gave her foot a wiggle. 'That feels a lot better.' She pulled on her sock and boot and made a big show of hobbling over to the laughing couple.

Chapter Twenty-Two

It was midnight. A soft snore came from Rosie. She was curled up in her swag in the cargo hold in the back of the police Landcruiser. Kelsey sat on the tail gate, with her bare legs swinging in the warm evening air and watched Charlie as he climbed the track towards the well. She glanced over to the quiet camp. In the firelight she saw Steve adjusting her shirt as she left Charlie's tent and stride past the campfire, showing no signs of a limp.

Kelsey's heart ached. It seems she wasn't as important to the burly grazier as he was to her. She stared off into the darkness and decided there was no place for her here anymore. Being the other woman didn't sit well with her and no matter what Rosie said, there must be something going on between Steve and Charlie for her to be welcome in his tent this late at night. When she was allowed to leave Kelsey would ask Rosie and Mark to take her to Mount Ibour and from there she would return to the city. It would be sad to say good-bye, she'd grown to love the station and its people, in spite of the terror stalking her. She'd especially miss the rambunctious Eli and his desirable father but staying would only cause her more pain.

She needed her memory and decided to start pushing at her brain and force it back into working order. She'd start with Rosie's first question. How did she travel to Mount Ibour? Kelsey folded her legs and sat Indian style, with the soles of her feet tucked under her cotton shorts. She relaxed her limbs, took a deep breath and held it for a long moment before letting the air gently trickle out her nose in a long slow exhale. Closing her eyes she emptied her mind of all thought and waited. In the dark recesses of her mind a drawer slid open and a white fluffy cloud seeped out. It settled to resemble a carpet of snow in a clear blue sky. The image was framed by an oval porthole. A background hum deadened the voices around her to indistinct murmurs. She was sitting in the window seat of an airplane. The seat next to her was occupied by a stranger. Underweight, all bones and angles, he looked to be in his early twenties and had a hoddie pulled low over his forehead and ear buds cutting him off from all social interaction. To further emphasise the point that he wanted no contact, his eyes were closed.

Kelsey looked down at her feet. They were encased in a pair of white athletic shoes – the Sketchers she'd told Rosie about – clasped around a plum-coloured leather satchel. This must be her bag. The white cover on the mobile phone, encouraging her to be *Fearless,* was being rotated over and over by her nervous fingers.

She jumped, startled when a male voice announced, 'This is your captain speaking. We have commenced our descent into Mount Ibour, where the local time is eight am and the weather is a balmy thirty-two degrees.'

Kelsey obsessively triple checked that her seat belt was fastened low and tight, just as the flight steward had instructed. She was jumpy. Not because she was about to start a new job but because it was an undercover job for someone very important to her.

Kelsey's eyes popped open and she sucked in excited breath. 'Rosie...'

'Hmm,' murmured the woman snuggled deep in her swag.

'I flew into Mount Ibour. It was eight o'clock in the morning when we landed and it was a very hot day.'

The swag sat up. 'What else?' came Rosie's muffled voice.

'Someone was supposed to meet me at the airport. A man. I can't see him clearly –yet. But he is very important to me. All I'm getting at the moment is an image of a sandy coloured fringe that flops forward no matter how many times he pushes it back into place.'

'Name? Age? How important? Why Mount Ibour?' The questions poured out of Rosie without pause.

Kelsey held up her hand to stop her, 'I don't know...yet. The name's hovering just out of my reach. I must know him because the gesture with the fringe is familiar and brings a warm feeling to my heart. He asked me to come here to do a job.'

A light from a torch caught her in the eye and broke her train of thought.

She sucked in her breath, tension knotted her gut.

'Rosie, someone's coming.'

'Kelsey, is the boss awake?' asked Mark, relaxing the tension that built up in her by his movement down the path.

Mark sounded upset. Rosie still encased in the swag wriggled forward, stuck her head over Kelsey's shoulder and asked, 'What's up, Bayden?'

'Boss, do you have the bullets and shell casings? The ones Bull gave us from his slaughtered cattle.'

'No, I put them in the evidence box,' she said, freeing her arms from her covers and sliding to a seated position on the tailgate with the swag still hugging her lower half. 'Why?'

'They're recorded in the database but the bags are missing.'

In the gloom Kelsey could just make out the lines of worry on Mark's face. Beside her she felt Rosie stiffen.

'Shit, Bayden! Who had access to the box?'

'The four of us, and Steve. She's been alone in the camp all afternoon and the box was unlocked and unguarded in my tent. Also,' Mark continued as he took a seat beside them on the tailgate, 'anyone who's been at the homestead in the last couple of days. The vehicle was parked unattended in the vehicle shed with the box on the back seat. It wasn't always locked. I didn't check to see if everything was still in there before we left the homestead.'

'And there's our mystery prowler from this morning,' growled Rosie, adding to the list of suspects. 'Who knows how long they were hanging around before we heard the vehicle? They could have searched the camp before coming up the hill to see what we were doing. Is that all that's missing?'

'As far as I can tell.'

'Well, what was so important about the shell casings and bullets that someone would risk getting caught to remove them?'

She stared at Mark and rolled her hand, encouraging him to theorise.

'Well, they were a different calibre to the ones used by those idiots, Manning and Knox who we currently have locked up in the poky for the other cattle shootings. Without them we can't prove or disprove they weren't responsible for Red River's losses. It also puts a dark cloud over their arrest.'

Rosie rolled her hand again, 'And...'

Mark tugged at his ear lobe and stared at his boots, deep in thought. A thought struck Kelsey and she said, 'Can you trace bullets back to a particular gun by the rifling?'

Rosie snapped her fingers and jabbing her forefinger forward in approval at the question. 'Yes, you can. The spiral lands and grooves of a rifle barrel leave unique marks on the bullet as it passes down the barrel's length, and the firing pin and ejector have their own distinctive marks that imprint on the shells. If we have the gun we can match it to the shells and the spent bullets. As far as our killer is aware, they've just gotten rid of the only piece of traceable evidence we have against him or her.'

'Well that true. We haven't found anything else, have we?' said Mark.

Rosie's teeth glinted in the moonlight as she grinned.

Chapter Twenty-Three

It was a relief to watch Steve drive away. Kelsey turned away from the sight and gathered the dirty breakfast dishes the woman had left behind. Rosie, carrying a shovel hitched high on her shoulder, marched towards the boab tree. Her rapid stride halted at the sound of a helicopter. She cupped a hand over her eyes and stared up. Kelsey followed her gaze and watched a white chopper, with a logo on the tail, circle the area.

'Shit, it's the bloody media. Kelsey, get out of sight.'

Kelsey ran and ducked through the nearest tent flap. She stopped, startled. Bull was sprawled on top of a swag wearing only briefs and was oblivious to the action unfolding outside. His soft snore spoke of a deep sleep. Kelsey's stomach flipped at the sight of his naked torso. Charlie's toned stomach muscles rippled as he breathed in and out. He twitched under her hot gaze. She quickly turned away and squatted down just inside the flap to watch the scene outside. It would never do to be caught ogling him as he slept.

Outside Rosie was yelling at someone on the satellite phone as she pointed heavenward.

'What's going on.'

Kelsey nearly jumped out of her skin at the sound of Charlie's sleepy voice. Remembering to keep her eyes off the glorious sight of him she continued to stare outside and murmured, 'There's a media helicopter hovering overhead. Rosie told me to get out of sight. Yours was the nearest tent. Sorry.'

The sound of an amused chuckle reached her. 'You're welcome, anytime, sweetheart.'

Trapped, Kelsey watched the chopper as it slowly circled the camp. She kept her back towards him and her mouth shut. Suddenly the helicopter diverted, taking a direct line over the well and heading west.

'They're leaving.'

'That's a shame. I enjoy waking up with you here. We should do it more often.'

'Well, I don't think your wife and fiancée would agree,' she said and before Charlie could reply Kelsey bolted from the tent. She raced over to join Rosie, who was cursing like a sailor at the retreating aircraft.

'Bloody nosy bastards.'

Charlie emerged from his tent. He had on a pair of jeans that hitched low on his hips, nothing on his feet and fury on his face. He hadn't bothered with a shirt.

'Oh my...,' said Rosie, appreciation written all over her face as she ran her eyes over him. Charlie ignored the sensation he was causing and stormed over to join them.

'What the hell...' he yelled, glowering at Kelsey.

Kelsey's legs began to shake. Images of raised fists flooded her mind. She flinched and lifted her hand to protect her face. Her action was followed by silence. Gentle fingers touched her shoulder, she jerked and she looked up to see Charlie with an appalled look on his face, 'Sweetheart, don't be frightened. I'd never hurt you. It's just that you can't say stuff like that to me and leave.'

Her other hand was taken and squeezed. Rosie. She'd be safe with Rosie here. Kelsey returned the squeeze and told herself to be courageous. Even though her insides shook like a bowl of jelly, she let the hurt out. 'Stuff like what? That your fiancée – even though you are a *married* man – wouldn't appreciate another woman sharing your tent?'

'Yeah, stuff like that.' Charlie's hand shot out and before she could react he'd grabbed her wrist and jerked her hard against his chest. His arms engulfed her in a tight embrace. 'I don't have a fiancée and I've not had another woman since my wife left. I don't play games.'

'You don't? You haven't?' stuttered Kelsey, lifting her gaze from the deliciously smooth, honey-coloured skin at eye level to stare up at his handsome face in confusion. 'But what about, Steve? She says you two are secretly engaged, and I saw her leaving your tent last night, right after you went up to the well.'

'Did you just? I wonder what she was up to? She wasn't in my tent while I was there, I'd have turfed her out on her ear. As for being engaged, it's all in her mind.'

'Told you,' Rosie whispered close to Kelsey's ear, causing the hair on the back of her neck to stand up – or was that because of the words Charlie muttered at the same time.

'No, my desires run more towards a certain blonde with magnificent green eyes and a courageous heart.'

'Oh my, I think I'm having a hot flush,' breathed Rosie, fanning her face with her hand.

'Shut up Rosie,' said Charlie, an amused grin tugging at his lips.

He leant forward and captured Kelsey's mouth with his own. Her toes curled, and heat sizzled throughout her entire body. She lifted her arms and locked them tightly around his neck. The kiss deepened and she experienced the hot flush that Rosie spoke of.

'About bloody time,' said Rosie, breaking the spell. 'Now break it up you two. CSI is here.'

The distinctive whomp, whomp, whomp of rotor blades announced the arrival of the forensic team's helicopter.

* * *

Kelsey perched on the edge of a camp chair and let the tears roll down her cheeks unchecked. Her heart ached as she watched a tall, white clad, forensic investigator heave on the rope that was looped through a pulley and dangled into the well. The investigator's paper overalls rustled with his every movement. A stretcher with a black body bag strapped to it came into view. Kelsey closed her eyes against the sight of him manoeuvring the bag over the shaft edge and dragging it over to join the other two small bags already laid out on the ground. The sound of the zip being drawn back made the hair on the back of her neck stand up. She rose to her feet and turned her back. Nausea burned the back of her throat.

Kelsey looked over to where Mark was making careful notes and said, 'I'm going down to join Rosie.' Mark gave her a distracted nod.

Kelsey headed down the trail, thankful that her feet were now healed enough to cope with all she was asking of them. A flock of birds trilled past, the blue and white cloud swirled and circled like a school of fish, before settling high in the branches of the boab tree. The activity going on at its base startled them back into flight. They rose and swarmed away, taking their high-pitched chatter with them. Rosie stood, hands on hips, talking with a short middle-aged man. He pushed wire framed glasses up his nose with his index finger and nodded at what she was saying. They were both clad in the same rustling white overalls and blue booties as the other investigators. The detective handed the man a shovel and glared up at Kelsey.

'Why aren't you up top with, Bayden?'

'The bodies are being recovered. It made me nauseous.'

Rosie nodded and the hard look on her face softened. 'Understandable, but I don't want you wandering around by yourself.' She pointed over to the camp. 'Why don't you go help our ruggedly handsome grazier pack up the camp? Once we finish here you guys can head home. Bayden and I'll follow the forensic team with the evidence we've collected to headquarters in Mount Ibour. We'll see you at Rivers Run homestead in a day or so, when I have some more information. Besides, I'm sure Bayden wouldn't mind spending a night or two at home with his family.'

Head home, Kelsey liked the sound of that...home.

* * *

'That's everything,' said Charlie, removing his Akubra and wiping away the sweat on his brow with the hem of his shirt. 'It's as steamy as hell, there's more rain coming in the next day or so. How about we go for a swim before we head off?'

'A swim? Where?' asked Kelsey, glancing around. She knew the river was a long way from here and she hadn't come across any creeks or waterholes on her long trek.

'About twenty minutes that way is a billabong,' said Charlie, indicating with his hat towards the east of where they'd been camping. 'Bunyip Gorge we call it. We probably won't see the bunyip – she's been a bit shy in recent years.'

'A bunyip, Charlie?'

'Yep. According to local Aboriginal legend the creature would prowl across the land, hunting for women and children to eat. Its mournful howl has been known to carry through the night air at the billabong, terrifying people and making them afraid to enter the water. The locals steer clear of the gorge when the wind is howling, not wanting to take their chances.'

'Really? You're not just making that up?'

'Nah, not at all. If you don't believe me ask Naomi. She'll tell you the full story and if you're lucky she may even take you to see some of the rock art. She and her family are custodians of some wonderful areas on the property that we don't tell many people about because we want to keep the art safe.'

'That would be a marvellous treat,' sighed Kelsey. It would be awesome to have a chance to admire some of the local artwork and hear about the Dreamtime from someone with cultural knowledge. 'Are we walking or taking the Rodeo?'

'Neither, we'll ride. Rainbow needs a good stretch before we load him into the float.'

'Ride Charlie – I'm not sure if I know how.'

'You don't have to do anything,' he said, handing her the horse's reins. Rainbow snorted a greeting and began to nuzzle the front of the blue tee-shirt Eli had lent her to wear. 'I'll just let Rosie know where we're going.'

Kelsey stroked the horse's silky neck and tried to calm the butterflies that fluttered wildly in her belly.

* * *

She sat with her back pressed against Charlie as they rode towards the swimming hole. The reins dangled from his left hand, the palm of his right hand lay flat on her stomach, anchoring her against him. Her skin was covered in a layer of goosebumps caused, not by the shade thrown out by the rock walls of the canyon they rode through, but by his touch. She was hyper aware of his closeness and the sweet desire that was flooding her system. A strong urge to turn in his embrace and give in to her needs was at war with the taint left by the memories she had of her stepfather. She sighed. Charlie must have misinterpreted her action because he leant forward, kissed her in the sweet spot just below her ear and whispered, 'Relax, sweet girl. We're almost there.'

The hairs on the back of her neck tingled as they stood up. Her nipples hardened and became obvious through her lacy bra and even thinner tee-shirt. The nervousness in her belly swirled and cranked up a notch along with the aching need deep inside.

With a slight flick of his wrist Charlie guided Rainbow to the left and they rode out into bright sunshine and the thrumming of water falling from a great height. The sun glinted across the crystal blue surface of a large gorge surrounded by steep sided rifts of banded orange and black sandstone. At the far end of the fully enclosed gully an opening high above the gorge allowed a waterfall to cascade onto a circular rocky shelf and feed the large pool of water that formed there. The overflow ran along the face of a huge limestone boulder and down to the gorge below.

'Oh Charlie, this is magical,' exclaimed Kelsey craning her neck to take in all the views at once. Rainbow picked his way carefully along white sand and flat limestone to halt at the water's edge.

'One of the many special places I'd like you to see,' said Charlie. His hand left her stomach and he pointed to the right. 'In those low caves and the ones above there is a vast array of pools that never dry up. Some are deep and cool, while others are shallow and tepid. It's a perfect place to sit and while away a hot summer's day. We won't go in and explore today as our time here is limited. We'll save that adventure for another day, when we don't have to rush.'

Kelsey shivered in anticipation that there would be another time. Charlie slid away from her and off the back of the horse. She missed his closeness. He was back almost immediately, and reaching up to place his hands gently around her waist, helped her to dismount. As her feet touched the ground their lips met. Her fears melted away. Hot burning desire filled her and scorched its fiery trail though her veins. She ran her palms along his muscular chest before burying her fingers deep in his thick black hair. Their tongues met and performed a sizzling hot dance. Kelsey's limbs turned to jelly but before she could meld her body into his the war that was raging inside her made its presence known. She began to shake. Their lips parted and Charlie stared down at her in concern.

'I'm sorry, Charlie. I don't know if I'm ready...'

'Understandable and don't apologise, Kelsey. With everything you've been through in the last ten days I'm not surprised. Let's just get to know each other better, enjoy each other's company and see where it leads.' He cupped her cheeks in his large hands, smiled down at her as if she were the most precious thing in the world and dropped a kiss on the tip of her nose. 'Come on, sweet girl let's go and wash the grime of the day away,' he murmured with a rasp in his voice.

Charlie stepped away, grabbed the neck of his shirt and in a swift movement tugged it over his head. His smooth, honey coloured chest and stomach muscles rippled as he leant forward and kicked off his boots. In a flash, his socks and jeans joined the growing pile on the ground. Kelsey's heart pounded hard against her rib cage. Shyness at exposing herself for a skinny dip had her turning her back and silently tugging off her own footwear.

At the sound of a mighty splash she spun around and saw Charlie was already in the water, striking out in a strong over-arm, propelling himself across the water's surface towards the waterfall. Glancing down she saw the Beretta he'd been carrying lying on top of his jeans. There didn't seem to be any underwear in the pile of clothing and that made her feel slightly better.

Removing her shorts she folded them neatly and set them on the ground next to Charlie's untidy pile before doing the same with her tee-shirt. As she set her boots in a neat row with the socks folded inside, a tingle started on the back of her neck. She swung around and scanned the area. It felt like she was being watched. Kelsey studied the mouths of the low-level caves, but saw nothing. She chided herself, how could anyone be watching? Rosie was the only one who knew where they were. Rainbow snorted and whiffed at a nearby shrub, his lips plucking at delicate morsels of green shoots. He seemed unconcerned. Kelsey took another swift glance around and seeing nothing, she carefully picked her way barefooted across the hot sand in her lacy bra and knickers to the water's edge. She slid into its cool and refreshing embrace and gave a sigh of delight before gliding towards the middle of the pond. Kelsey let her gaze roam over the rocky cliffs trying to absorb the magnificent beauty of the billabong. But she couldn't settle. Something didn't feel right. The heebie-jeebies still plagued her as if she was being stared at by unfriendly eyes. Knots of stress and anxiety began to coil tight in her chest.

A low grunt sounded.

What the hell was that?

It came again.

She glanced towards the waterfall thinking it must be Charlie fooling around, pretending to be a bunyip but he was scaling the rock face making his way towards the upper pond and the loud pounding by the falling water muffled any noise he made.

Rainbow snorted and then gave a distressed whinny. She spun around. The horse was nervously tugging on his tethering lead. The whites of his eyes were showing as he pulled backwards trying to free himself.

Kelsey struck out, swimming as fast as she could towards the shore. She needed to stop Rainbow before he bolted.

As she stepped onto the hot sand a mournful howl echoed around the canyon.

* * *

Charlie stripped and dove into the cool water. He slammed his arms over and over in an attempt to cool his ardour. He cursed himself for acting like a clumsy schoolboy and rushing things. Kelsey had been through so much recently and was struggling to remember anything good from her life. She didn't need to have a randy grazier adding to her woes, even though she meant more to him than just a quick romp. She needed time to get to know him and realise that he wasn't anything like her bastard foster father or whoever had attacked her. It's a fine line, and only time and friendship would show her the genuine feelings of affection he'd developed for her. For now he would carefully support and protect her and when she was ready then they'd look at taking this, whatever this was, to the next level. He decided to climb the cliff face and take a gander at the pool known far and wide as the home of the bunyip.

'CHARLIE!'

Hearing Kelsey scream he immediately leapt from the wall into the water below and began to swim rapidly to shore.

As he dragged himself ashore he realised he was too late. Rainbow was rearing, his front legs pawing the air, squealing a trumpet of rage.

* * *

Kelsey's heart leapt into her throat. She dashed forward and snatched up Charlie's pistol remembering to flip the safety off.

She pointed the gun around as she turned a half-circle seeking the perpetrator of the howl. There was movement at the mouth of the cavern on her left. Rainbow reared and pawed the air, trumpeting in rage or fear she couldn't tell.

At a deep fierce bellow Kelsey swung the gun and took aim, pointing the weapon into the air. She pulled the trigger. The resounding boom echoed around the canyon and startled the charging animal. It veered and missed both her and the horse. Rainbow broke free and backed away from the animal. It swung it head and glared through pain filled red eyes. It was foaming at the mouth and its flank was a mess of festering sores. She knew this beast. It was the mickey bull she'd encountered at the base of the woollybutt tree the previous week. Amazing that it was still alive even though its flesh had wasted away, leaving the poor animal's skin to sag on it like an overstretched pullover.

Rainbow neighed and the steer began tossing its head from side to side.

'Shush, Rainbow,' said Kelsey, not letting her gaze leave the bovine.

'Kelsey, slowly back away,' came Charlie's soft voice. 'Don't run. I'll circle around and come up behind you. Please don't shoot me.'

Her top lip hitched in a slight grin at his last words. She took a slow careful step backwards, followed by another. When she reached Rainbow she grabbed his halter making him back up with her. She could hear Charlie leaving the water somewhere behind her, so she kept going. The steer stood and swayed from side to side. The sunshine in its eyes seemed to have blinded it. Her foot caught a stone and it clattered as it rolled across the surface of a limestone rock. She halted and held her breath. The steer took a step towards her and both its front legs gave way. It sagged to its knees and gave a mournful bellow.

A hand slid along her forearm, and fingers circled the wrist holding the pistol. Charlie breathed in her ear as he removed the pistol from her tight grip. 'Good girl, well done... you're safe.' She sagged back against him for a moment. He kissed her temple and said, 'Do me a favour, lead Rainbow over to the cave while I take care of the steer.'

She nodded without taking her eyes off the animal. He squeezed her shoulder and stepped around her.

'So, mate, this is where you've been hiding,' murmured Charlie as he slowly moved towards the downed steer. 'Rainbow and I have been looking everywhere for you. Relax buddy let me take all that pain away.'

Kelsey turned and led Rainbow towards the cave. At the crack of the gun being discharged she didn't look back.

Chapter Twenty-Four

Kelsey was amazed at all the activity going on at the homestead. A large refrigerated truck was backing up to the cool room. Two jillaroos dressed in jeans, red shirts and work gloves, stood in the open doorway, hands on hips, surrounded by boxes marked Rivers Run Produce. So, this was Mimi and Darcy thought Kelsey – nice looking girls, and judging by the laughter and banter going on between them, friends.

To the right of the cool room at the stockyard, a road train was parked at the cattle ramp. Jimmy and a blond Nordic looking jackaroo in a red shirt, were herding beasts up the race while the station's working dogs ran around the rear of the mob encouraging forward motion in their own unique and vocal manner. Standing on the steps outside the office, Eli, clad in dusty blue jeans and a green and white checked shirt with a very pregnant dog sitting at his heels, was pointing to a map and talking with a dark-haired man who looked to be a mixture of trades in his white business shirt, dark trousers and rubber boots. Steve, her red-checked shirt knotted under her large breasts, hovered below them with a thunderous scowl on her face. When the visitor lifted his well-groomed head she gave him a sweet smile and said something. He nodded and held out his hand to shake hers. Eli looked calm and in total control as he spoke with the pair. He handed Steve a radio and glanced at his watch before making a note on the clipboard he carried. In a dismissive gesture he shook hands with the visitor and strode away. An obvious statement of who was in charge. Steve narrowed her magnificent eyes at Eli's back but without a word she headed towards a white four-wheel-drive that had the letters CASA emblazoned on the door. The stranger climbed into the driver's seat. Eli turned towards their approaching vehicle, gave a happy grin and a small wave, before marching towards a blue and white van parked outside the stables. He spoke to the occupants through the driver's window before handing over a piece of paper. He pointed beyond the fruit shed to the recreation room. As the van drove away Kelsey saw the words Mount Ibour Electrical in neat, reflective lettering splashed across the door.

As Charlie and Kelsey drove up to Eli, Charlie leant out the open window and said, 'Hey ya, Sport. Looks like you've got everything under control.'

'Hi, Dad, g'day, Kelsey, welcome back. Everything's cool. The road reopened yesterday, so I told this lot to hustle before we copped another storm. The weather jonnies reckon not, but I erred on the side of caution. My knee has begun to ache.'

Charlie smiled and slid out of the vehicle. Kelsey followed suit and watched as he turned towards the hills and took a long slow sniff. 'Looks like your knee's become a weather vane son – my nose is twitching.'

'Awesome.'

Kelsey chuckled to herself, maybe these two should rent themselves out to the weather bureau.

The air was alive with the sounds and smells of a busy working property. She allowed her gaze to sweep the yard, taking it all in. A relay team was now underway outside the cool room, the boxes were being passed in rapid succession along the line and the girls were singing while they worked. Over at the stockyard, the road-train driver was securing gates on a full trailer. A mob of fats bellowed and kicked up the distinct odour of fresh manure as they milled around the pen. Jimmy yelled at the working dogs to ease up, before cantering his horse towards the next herd the stockmen were circling on the far side of the paddock. The dogs raced after him competing to be first. The electrician whistled a catchy tune and untied a ladder from the roof of his van. Kelsey drank it all in, capturing the picture in her mind. She would paint this. It was the perfect antithesis to all the horrors she'd witnessed at the well of bones.

Something solid bumped hard against her knee. She looked down in surprise. Bindi, the pregnant cattle dog, peered up at her with her tongue hanging from the side of her mouth. It was a happy sight. Kelsey bent down and gave her a gentle rub on the head. If a dog could smile Bindi did.

'I brought you home some lost property, son,' said Charlie, nodding towards the horse float. Eli was talking non-stop as he raced around the float. He slung open the back door and clambered in.

'Awesome to have you home, Rainbow. How are you boy? Thanks, Dad. How's his injury?' Before Charlie could reply, Eli exclaimed, 'Hey, cool, you found my saddle! I thought I'd lost that for sure.'

A four-wheel drive whizzed into the yard and came to an abrupt halt beside Kelsey. With the sun behind him, the man who leapt from the driver's seat dressed in tan moleskins and red cowboy shirt, looked as if he wore a halo around his blond head. Charlie's book-keeper Gil gave her his version of a sexy smile and ran his gaze up and down her body. He sauntered over to stand too close to her.

'Hello gorgeous, it's lovely to have you back. The place hasn't been the same without you.'

'Oh, hello Gil, you're still here,' she said, taking a small step away from him. 'I though you would've gone back to Mount Ibour now the road's open.' She was not terribly enamoured of his flirty ways.

'Yeah, I did but I had to come back. There's been a snafu with the book-keeping program. The formulas in the spreadsheet have gone all skew-whiff and for some stupid reason I'm locked out from changing them. So I've returned to rebuild the entire thing.'

'Oh, I thought I'd fixed that.'

'You?' he asked, startled.

'Yeah...' her brain gave a buzz and before she could filter her words, 'I'm a forensic accountant,' slipped out. Wow, another memory. I must tell Rosie. 'I'm very good with spreadsheets, Gil. I'll tell you what, let me get settled tonight then I'll go through the accounts with you and Charlie tomorrow. Between us we should be able to get the glitch fixed. It's probably something really simple.'

* * *

'There was someone in the house while you were gone, Dad.'

Charlie sat on his bed and peeled the socks from his sweaty feet. He was looking forward to a nice hot, cleansing shower. The swim at the billabong had been refreshing but he'd had to put on the same clothes and the smell of death clung to them.

Eli's words gave him pause. 'When?'

'Two nights ago.'

'Naomi or Jimmy?'

'Nope, it wasn't either of them. Naomi had just left to do the weekly bread bake and Jimmy was supervising the poker match. No, whoever it was tried to be very quiet.'

'Explain.'

'I was upstairs, playing *Assassin's Creed Valhalla*. I had the headset plugged in even though I was alone. I know the noise annoys you, so it's become a habit to wear them. Anyway, in *A Fury from the Sea*, I'd just cleared out the shipyard and broken through the gates with some awesome moves...' Charlie rolled his hand to encourage Eli to get on with it as he had no idea what the boy was babbling about. Eli laughed, 'You're such a techno challenge, Dad. So, anyway, I paused the game to call Bren to brag to him that I was the GOAT,'

'Goat, why is being a goat important?'

'Daaad, it means *greatest of all time*. Don't you know anything?'

'Obviously not.'

Eli snorted in amusement. 'I also wanted to know what time cuz and Aunt GG would be here tomorrow. Oh, I didn't tell you they are on their way. Aunt GG's driving and they are in Broome at the moment.' Charlie nodded, pleased that his sister and nephew were on their way. 'When I lifted the upstairs extension I heard someone whispering on the line. It was a male voice and he said, 'Don't do anything stupid,' then the line went dead. I thought you'd come home, but it was a weird thing for someone to be saying to you. Anyway, I headed down to the study to check things out. Just as I got to the bottom of the stairs I heard the back door click shut. By the time I made it to the kitchen there was nobody around.'

'What time was this?'

'Old grandad had just chimed 10pm.'

'I'll check with Naomi. Nobody should be coming into the house, especially that time of night. The stock office phone is always available if anyone needs to call home.'

'Yeah, but that's monitored by a security camera. What I want to know is what they were doing in your office?'

'That is a good question, Eli. I'll just go take a look and check to see if anything is out of place,' said Charlie, rising to his feet. He slipped on his favourite sheep skin slippers and strode from the room. His feet made no noise as he jogged down the stairs. The grandfather clock chimed the quarter-hour. He glanced down the hall. Kelsey was standing outside her room staring in, her face ashen white.

'Are you okay, sweetheart?' he asked, rushing forward.

She gave a small start and lifted her finger. 'I have a visitor.'

Curled in the centre of the bed was a king brown snake. Charlie took her gently by the shoulders and pulled her into his arms.

He kissed the top of her head and said, 'Go upstairs. I'll deal with this.' She sagged and leant into his chest with a sigh. Before his arms could tighten around her she drew back.

'Thank you, Charlie. I think I've had just about enough for one day.'

He watched her climb the staircase, her back straight and un-yielding. After everything she'd been through it was going to take more than a snake on her bed to break her. The admiration he had for the spirit she'd shown since they'd met rose another notch.

Charlie stepped into the room, closed the door and moved to-wards the reptile. He grabbed a corner of the bedspread and flipped it over the snake, then raced to the other side of the bed gathering quilt corners as he went. When it was bagged he dragged his bundle out the door. In his office he held his cargo in one hand and lifted the phone with the other.

'What's up, Bull?' asked the surprised voice on the other end of the receiver.

'Got a visiting king brown, Mac. I need a hand.'

'Shit, I'll be right over.'

Charlie hung up and dragged his bundle out onto the slate lined veranda. Jimmy came tearing down the path, shotgun cracked open over his forearm and a box of cartridges clutched in his hand. His dusty blond eyebrows shot up when he saw the bedding clutched in Charlie's hand. A range of emotions flitted across his face but he didn't give voice to any of them, saying instead, 'I'll go get the ute. We can release the bugger down the road from here.'

The vehicle skidded to a halt just outside the gate. Between them, Charlie and Jimmy lifted the snake bundle into the tray-back. Bull returned to the house and pulled on some work boots.

As Jimmy drove he chatted. 'A kilometre should be far enough away from the house don't ya reckon. We'll chuck the bugger from the tray, that way he can't swing back and latch on.'

Bull nodded, but didn't speak.

'You okay, mate. You've got that look again.'

'What look?'

'The one you had when that useless wife of yours left.'

Charlie glared at his best friend. Jimmy quirked his top lip at him, as if expecting an explosion of the famous temper and was entertained by the thought. Jimmy had always taken Charlie's tantrums in his stride never doubting he had the ability to rein it in before he did any harm. Charlie wasn't so sure he could have that level of control, not if something really important to him was under threat. Only once in his life had Charlie ever lost total control and for that he would always carry a burden. Charlie remembered Kelsey's reaction to his mild display of anger. The fear she'd shown. It was like a dose of cold water to the simmering heat in his veins. Charlie sighed, his anger subdued once again.

The vehicle halted and he rolled out of his door and clambered into the bed of the ute.

'On the count of three we launch,' said Charlie unknotting the bundle and handing Jimmy two corners of the quilt. 'One...two...three.'

The snake sailed through the air and landed with a dull thump next to a small clump of spindly spinifex. The snake didn't move, probably because it had a gaping hole in its belly.

'It's dead! Where'd you find him, mate?' asked Jimmy, his tone low and eyebrows knotted in a puzzled expression.

'It was on Kelsey's bed.'

'Holy shit! How the bloody hell did it get into the house?'

'Now you know why I have that look, it was put there deliberately,' said Charlie, scrubbing his hands through his unruly mop of hair.

'Fuck, Bull,' said Jimmy. He turned, squinted into the setting sun and glared towards the road leading in from the highway.

'Yep,' nodded Charlie, 'someone is as mean as hell and moves fast.'

* * *

Showered and over her shock of finding a snake in her room, Kelsey decided to go for a walk. It was a lovely evening to take a stroll and investigate the layout of the homestead and its surrounds.

'Eli, I'd like to go out and do some sketching.'

'Righto Kelsey. Steve and the CASA guy have just gotten back from the chopper crash site. I just need to catch up with them and get a copy of the report then I'll take you down to our fishing spot on the river if you like.'

'That'd be lovely, Champ.' The grandfather clock whirled and struck five o'clock as they passed it at the foot of the stairs. Kelsey paused to admire the maple wood casing. 'That's a beautiful timepiece, Eli.'

'Sure is. We call him old grandad. I miss his chiming voice when I'm away at school. He's got a secret compartment you know.' Eli grinned up at her, looked around as if the walls had spies. He must have decided it was safe. 'Wanna see?' he asked.

She nodded.

Eli cast a furtive glance around before opening the glass panel in front of the brass pendulum. Kelsey expected him to reach around the swinging weight but he didn't. Instead he slipped his fingers inside the lower lip of the doorframe and pressed the bottom panel of the timepiece. A section of wood clicked and slid back revealing a shelf about the size of an A4 page. It was an ideal place for storing small packages, documents or envelopes. It was empty.

'Wow that's awesome, Eli. Do you use it much?'

'Not now. As kids we did. Bren and I used it to play a secret spy game. Uncle Josh would hide coded notes in here for us to follow and solve. If we worked the puzzle out we'd find a reward in here.'

'Sounds like fun.'

'Yeah, he would create the most awesome adventures for us. I really miss him.' Kelsey heard the sadness, but what can you say. He would always miss the terrific uncle who added such fun to a boy's life. She patted Eli's shoulder in comfort.

'Come on, let's go have an adventure of our own down at the river.'

Eli smiled and nodded. When they got to the kitchen door he flung it open and bowed her through. It made Kelsey laugh. She did a dainty curtsey and strolled down the path that took her through a beautiful and sweet smelling garden.

The white CASA vehicle was parked outside the stock office. Kelsey could hear Steve flirting outrageously with the chubby, middle-aged investigator. She decided to avoid the woman. 'Eli, you go ahead and take care of your business. I'm going over to the stables to check on Rainbow.'

Eli flashed a smile of understanding and headed towards the duo. Steve saw him coming, said something to her companion and stalked away. The set of her shoulders and head screamed contempt to the authority the young man had over her. Eli laughed as she stomped along wombat track towards the accommodation blocks. Kelsey grinned, positive Steve had heard Eli's amused chuckle and didn't like it.

Kelsey enjoyed the warm evening sunshine on her shoulders and took her time to stroll over to the stables. As she put out a hand to open the door a low moan caught her attention. It sounded like someone in distress. She quickened her pace and hurried along the cobblestone floor, peeking into each stall as she passed. Horses stuck their heads over some of the doors but none were showing any signs of distress.

The noise sounded again. 'Hello. Is anyone there? Are you alright?' she called out.

There was no answer but there was rustling in the second last stall. Kelsey swung open the door. Bindi lay on a bed of hay, her chest heaving as she struggled to whelp a pup.

'Oh, you poor thing,' cried Kelsey and raced over to check on the dog. The emerging pup was coming out tail first and seemed to be stuck. She knelt beside Bindi and spoke soothing words to her as she ran a hand down the dogs heaving flank. Bindi gave a soft whimper. Kelsey gently massaged around the dog's vulva to help ease the birthing pup out. The sac spat out like a cork from a bottle and landed with a plop into her waiting hand. Kelsey held the newborn up close to Bindi's inquisitive nose and waiting tongue. The mother gave the pup a thorough inspection as she cleansed away the birth sac. A small wrinkled pup, banded along the spine with tan and brown stripes emerged. It gave a yelp of protest at the rough treatment it was receiving from its mother. A warm glow filled Kelsey's heart, the pup was alive and judging by the noise it was making, raring to face life. She settled its wriggling form next to three others already feasting at their mother's teats.

'There you go, Banjo, meet your brothers and sisters,' she said, before leaning over and stroking the watching mother's head. 'Beautiful babies, Bindi, you're a clever girl.' The dog panted a happy smile and licked Kelsey's hand.

A slight noise outside the stall broke the spell. Bindi growled. Kelsey glanced around in time to catch a flash of red, before something hit her.

* * *

Her cheek was cold and something sharp was digging into it. She moved to ease the annoyance and her head began to pound. Nearby a dog's incessant barking added to the pain. She heard her name called from a distance. Kelsey tried to call out but could only manage a moan. Her mind began to drift towards a dark hole but was jerked back when the dog let out a long, loud howl.

'What the hell's going on?' It sounded like Charlie's deep voice.

'One of the dogs is howling in the stables, Dad. We might have another snake.'

'Go check the horses, Eli.'

'Dad, Kelsey went in there to visit Rainbow...'

Hurried footsteps echoed as booted feet scuffed along the stone floor.

'Darcy, what's going on?' yelled Eli.

'I don't know. I saw the stable door swinging open and came to shut it.'

There was a thudding as stall doors were flung open. Someone must have hit a light switch because a bright light burned a trail into her brain. Kelsey groaned against blinding pain. Bindi barked. The footsteps sped up. Air swirled around her as the stable door was flung open.

'Kelsey...' came Eli's frantic cry.

Kelsey moaned. The noise was making her head worse.

'Shit Dad!' yelled Eli. Kelsey could hear running. 'A plank of wood's fallen and hit Kelsey on the head.'

A warm hand touched her cheek. The familiar spice that was Charlie's unique smell soothed her.

'Eli, run and get Naomi.' Lips close to her ear whispered, 'Hang on sweet girl, I've got you.'

Feeling safe Kelsey drifted into the darkness.

Chapter Twenty-Five

Kelsey was floating in a foggy cloud as Charlie carried her to the house.

Déjà vu struck when Naomi's soft hand stroked her brow and in a soothing voice crooned, 'Relax, your safe.'

Something cool pressed against the painful spot on her forehead, the scent of lavender eased the ache in her head and she realised she was lying on the couch wrapped in the quilt. This time she wasn't alone though, the room was full of people who were all talking at once.

'Do I need to call the flying doctor?' asked Charlie.

'I'll go get the RAV4, we can set a bed up in the back and take her to the hospital...' said Jimmy.

'I'm so sorry, Dad. Kelsey was alone while I dealt with the CASA investigator...' whispered Eli. Kelsey could hear the threat of tears in his voice and her heart ached. It wasn't his fault she forgot to be careful.

'Shush the lot of you. Bloody men...you're like a stampeding mob in a glass shop,' growled Naomi. 'The poor girl's probably got a hell of a headache and you lot are only making it worse.'

Kelsey raised a hand and pushed the icy wet cloth away from her forehead. 'I'm fine, stop fussing. Yes, I have a headache, but that's all. You don't need to call a doctor,' she said furrowing her brow. 'Are Bindi and her pups okay?'

'They're fine, *Tidda*,' murmured Naomi brushing soft fingers down Kelsey's cheek in a gentle soothing stroke. 'She has four strong sturdy pups, thanks to you.'

'*Tidda*?' asked Kelsey, here was a new word to her.

'Sister. He loves you, so you're family,' said Naomi jerking her thumb in Charlie's direction. A cheeky grin lifted Naomi's chubby cheeks and gave her face a warm glow.

Kelsey's felt her own face flame in embarrassment. She decided to change the subject. 'I'm glad the dogs are safe. Bindi saved me you know.'

'What do you mean?' asked Naomi.

The conversation around her stopped and everyone was staring at her. 'Whoever hit me didn't get another shot because of her.'

'What do you mean hit you?' squeaked Eli, the octave of his voice going almost soprano in his surprise. 'A railing fell, didn't it? It was right there next to you...'

'No, Eli. Someone crept up behind me. Bindi growled a warning just in time. As I turned, I caught a flash of red, a shirt sleeve I think. I was only hit with a glancing blow because I was moving. I did more damage to myself by banging my forehead on the floor. Anyway, Bindi stood over me, snarling at my attacker and stopped them having another go. I don't think anyone would be brave enough to take on those teeth of hers.'

'Shit,' snarled Charlie, grabbing her hand. 'This is getting out of control. First the snake, now this. I'm going to move you up to the family floor where we can keep a better eye on you. Naomi, would you and Eli please go pack up Kelsey's clothes. Take everything up-stairs to my room. I'll move to the spare.'

'You don't have to move out of your room, Charlie. I'll take the spare,' said Kelsey.

'No you won't. Mine has an ensuite. You do not want to be sharing a bathroom with Eli and Bren. I wouldn't wish that on my worst enemy.'

'Awe, Dad...'

'Also, my room has a *lock*.' Charlie glared around the room at everyone, daring them to argue. 'From now on, all the house doors and windows are to be kept locked, and Kelsey, I'm sorry but you are not going to be left alone.' Everyone nodded agreement with Charlie's plan. Kelsey shook her head in despair. How had her life come to this where she needed protection every moment? Charlie took her breath away. 'Mac, you and I are going to hunt this bastard down.'

'You're not wrong, Bull. Enough is enough. I'll go check out where everyone was while we were wrangling that snake.' Jimmy slapped his Akubra onto his thinning blond mop and strode from the room.

Charlie gently nudged Naomi aside and picked Kelsey up in his arms. 'This seems to be becoming a habit Mr Morgan,' she said nestling her aching head in the crook of his neck.

'Well, the next time I carry you up those stairs it will be to our bed permanently.' His comment left her speechless and Naomi chuckling. She thought she heard a soft 'Yes' from Eli but wasn't sure if her ears were playing tricks or not. It all flustered her, so she looked for a safer topic. 'Charlie, can I have Bindi, Banjo and the other pups upstairs with me?'

He gave her a gentle squeeze as he strolled towards the staircase. 'You'll spoil that dog, having her in the house.'

She lifted her face and peered into his pewter grey eyes. 'Please...'
A smile twitched the corner of his mouth. 'How can I deny
you anything? Okay, but not tonight. Tangles will check the pups
over and make sure they're feeding properly. Which of the pups
is Banjo?'

'The one with the stripes along its spine. He yips like an out-of-
tune Banjo.' A thought struck her. 'You won't blame Eli will you,
for what happened? I shouldn't have wandered off to the stables like
that but I thought I was safe as I was in the homestead yard.'

'No, I don't blame Eli. I blame myself. I was slow on the uptake
with the snake.'

'What do you mean?'

'That snake was already dead. Someone put it on your bed to
scare you.'

'It didn't work.'

'No, you're one tough cookie.'

Charlie placed his lips gently over hers. She closed her eyes and
enjoyed the warmth and tingling that spread along her limbs. He
broke off the kiss before it deepened and gave a small cough, 'Tomorrow after work, I'll bring over your new dog.'

'My dog?'

'Yeah, Banjo, he's my gift to you.'

Kelsey smiled in delight and feeling bold placed a butterfly kiss
on his cheek.

* * *

Since she'd received the bang on the head Kelsey hadn't been left
alone – except to sleep of course. At Charlie's insistence she kept
her bedroom door locked, especially while she slept. When Charlie
was working, Eli stayed with her. If they both had something to
do, Naomi would settle in one of the Lair's comfy armchairs and

chatter. The women shared numerous cups of strong coffee while Kelsey learned a great deal of the history of Naomi's people and life as an extended member of the Morgan family.

A soft breeze skimmed the blush of flowering roses that were putting on a magnificent display in the garden. It swept up their glorious scent before drifting up to touch Kelsey's face as she rested on the daybed on the upstairs balcony. She breathed in deeply, enjoying the warm scented air. The wonderful bouquet soothed the dull ache in her head.

The racket of cattle being penned, gate chains rattling and the work dogs being whistled and yelled at filled the air. Her eyes flew open.

Charlie was back.

She leant forward in her chair and drank in the sight of his muscular body as he dismounted the horse and hitched the reins to a nearby fence. He looked up at her and smiled. She waved. Jimmy rode past him and spoke. Charlie roared with laughter. A tingle ran up her spine and her heart sped up. She snatched up her sketching pad. Her pencil flew across the page in quick confident strokes capturing the image. Strength, dependability and belonging radiated from the faces that appeared under her deft strokes. Kelsey poured her love into those images and the men came alive on the page.

Into this scene drove a dark-blue four-wheel drive. Kelsey had a clear view in through the windscreen. A thirty-something year old woman sat behind the wheel. Her long, corkscrewed black locks had been tamed with a clip at her neck. She had a grim expression on her face but it didn't detract from the beauty of strong cheek bones and plump lips. There was a distinct resemblance to the Morgan men. Slumped in the front passenger's seat with earphones slung around his neck and an expectant look on his face was a blond, muscular teenage boy. He was similar in age to Eli but they were as different in looks as chalk and cheese. The sight of Bren tugged at a distant memory, a boy with a blond fringe that kept flopping forward. He was holding out his hand to help her up from the ground. Before she could capture the image it faded. Kelsey put down the drawing she was working on and rose to her feet.

'Eli,' she said to the boy who was nestled deep in a leather recliner in the Lair, 'I think your Aunt GG and Bren are here.'

He peered up from the laptop he was working on and stared at her. 'Will you be alright here by yourself for a couple of minutes?' he asked, eagerness to be off written all over his face.

'Yes, Eli I'll be fine.' He didn't move but stared at her wide eyed as if unsure if he should leave.

'I'll tell you what, Champ. I'll go to my room and lock the door. I need to rest anyway. I think it's the only thing that's going to shake this blasted headache. You go be with your cousin and I'll catch up with you guys later when I feel a bit better.'

The pounding of footsteps on the stairs announced the abandonment of the spreadsheet Eli had spent the afternoon creating for his business plan. He was proving to have a great head for business matters, it showed with his insightful questions and reasoning as he worked, and she was pleased she'd been able to give him some aid and guidance. Kelsey was sure the future of Rivers Run would be in safe hands.

Talking Eli through how to set up a template gave Kelsey an insight into one of the drivers that was pushing him to make this project a reality – the revenue his mother had stolen all those years ago. He told her they had never really gotten their head very far above water since she'd emptied the bank account – no matter how good a year they'd had. His comment rang an alarm bell within her and Kelsey decided to ask Charlie if she could make an in-depth study of his books. Something didn't feel right. Besides it was the least she could do in return for everything the Morgan family had done for her.

The vehicle below drew to a complete halt. Eli erupted into the yard and flung open the passenger door. Bren launched himself from the vehicle, the boys faced off and fist bumped with a nonchalant, 'Hey Cuz,' in a hilarious attempt at being cool. Bren and Eli were similarly dressed for the hot muggy weather. Their generous sized board shorts and loose tee-shirts, emblazoned with the latest rock band, looked cool and comfortable although the new trainers on Bren's feet looked enormous compared with the rest of him.

Charlie didn't bother to hide his happiness at the arrival of his much-loved sister. He had an enormous smile on his face as he galloped towards the house on an impressively muscled grey work horse. Drawing to a halt he slid from the saddle at a run, pulled the jean clad woman, who'd been slow to emerge from the driving seat, hard against his chest and wrapped his arms around her in a tight embrace. Kelsey was becoming quite familiar with that embrace. It was warm and loving and carried the sweet smell of Rivers Run and Charlie's own unique, spicy scent. GG had on a sleeveless top and her honed, honey tanned arms grasped him around the waist and she began to sob as if her heart was broken. The smile left Charlie's face as he cradled his sister.

Eli asked Bren a question that Kelsey couldn't quite catch.

'I dunno, Cuz. She's been like this for over a week. It's something to do with dad but she won't tell me what. I'm so sick of being mollycoddled...' Bren's voice cracked and squeaked with the approach of manhood. He pushed angrily at his fringe which had flopped forward and turned away from his mother.

'Come on, GG, let's get you inside. A cup of coffee and a chat, we'll soon fix whatever the issue is,' said Charlie. As he started to lead his sister down the path towards the kitchen he called back to the two lads still standing next to the car. 'Bren, it's good to see you, buddy. Now do me a favour boys, stable Ramrod and bring in the all luggage before you start terrorising the station.'

'On it, Dad,' said Eli with a laugh and slung an arm over his shorter cousin's shoulder.

Not realising how far their voices carried the teens started talking ten to the dozen.

'Uncle Charlie's awesome, Cuz. No fuss. He just gets on with the problem at hand and sorts it. Dad was like that too,' said Bren as he swung open the back door of the Prado and grabbed the handles of two large pink suitcases. 'I hope you haven't been slacking off because these cases are heavy. Mum's bought nearly everything we own.'

'Harsh dude, I've been flat out like a lizard drinking. We've been having all sorts of fun and games...,' said Eli and he launched into a long-winded account of everything that had happened in the last ten days.

Kelsey stepped away from the balcony rail, not needing to relive what for her had been a massive ordeal so far. Deciding against going downstairs and intrude on what was going to be a very personal conversation between brother and sister, she collected her sketching gear, made sure the outdoor sitting area and Lair was neat and tidy, and retired to her room. She bolted the door behind her before stripping off the bone-coloured linen shorts she wore and climbing into bed.

* * *

Charlie's hand shook with rage and shock as he filled the kettle. To his blunt, 'Tell me what's wrong, GG?' came an answer that had rocked him to the core.

'Josh was having an affair.'

He hated deceit. The betrayal Charlie felt at Josh's actions was nothing compared to the pain his sister was now living with. He slammed the kettle down and saw red.

Not good, Bull. Get control of yourself.

Charlie closed his eyes and took the half-dozen long, slow breaths he needed to calm down. The red haze receded to a dull pink. He took the last of his temper out on the pile of used tissues that overflowed from the rubbish bin by shoving his foot in to squash them down forcefully. He was positive that before this conversation was over the extra room was going to be needed. Stalking to the pantry he yanked out the cake tin. The process of making coffee and cutting big fat slabs of fruit cake soothed him. He kept quiet and gave GG time to compose herself.

Charlie thought deeply about the man who had been his brother-in-law. Josh had been a good friend and a man whom Charlie had considered honourable and trustworthy – one he was proud to call his brother. Charlie shook his head. Had he, deep down, been just another Amelia? Charlie didn't think so because Josh had always shown by his actions and words that he considered GG and Bren were the most precious things in his life. What had changed? Remembering the man, Charlie began to have doubts.

He set the coffee mugs and cake onto the table, settled into a chair and clasped GG's long slender fingers with his own.

'Tell me...,' he said, making his voice soft and tender in an attempt to coax the story from her. GG studied their coupled fingers for so long Charlie thought she'd zoned out. He let go, took a sip of coffee and repeated the question. This time he was harsher. 'Spit it out, GG. Trust me when I say bottling this shit up does you no good. It'll eat you up.'

GG leant back in her chair, raised her red-rimmed grey eyes and focused on his face. In a voice that was scratchy and wobbled she said, 'Don't swear. You know Mum didn't like it when you did.'

'I'll swear if I want to. My house, my rules. Now tell me.'

The corner of GG's mouth gave a twitch and a small amusement line creased the corner of her lips. It faded quickly when she spoke.

'The week before you asked me to come home, I started going through Josh's stuff.' She gazed blankly ahead. 'It was time. I need to move on with my life.'

Charlie nodded, understanding that part of the grief process. He too had needed time to grieve before clearing away, not only his mother's possessions but also Amelia's. He might not love his wife but he still had to mourn for what might have been.

'While sorting through Josh's clothes I came across a scrap of paper in the pocket of one of his work jackets. It had a landline telephone number jotted on it. I didn't recognise it and thought it must be something to do with his job, so I stuck it in with all the other paperwork piled up on his desk – to sort later. I was going to return any work related documents to his office and leave the new investigator to decide if it was important or not. Then the phone bill arrived, with an overdue charge for Josh's mobile. That's when I realised I hadn't cancelled his phone – another thing to add to the list that I needed to do. I hadn't actually seen his phone since he died and thought maybe the police had forgotten to give it back when they returned his other stuff. I called them and asked, but they assured me they'd returned everything of his. The phone wasn't important, although I would've liked to have passed it on to Bren. It had that great cover on it, the one we gave Josh last Christmas. Do you remember?'

Charlie nodded but didn't speak. He didn't want to interrupt the flow of words.

'Anyway, I called the service provider to cancel the account and was told there were phone calls, from June to November, outstanding. I said that wasn't possible because Josh had died in early June. The girl on the help desk was very helpful. She emailed me copies of all his phone activity for this year, and yes, someone had been making calls and using data in the last six months. As I scrolled through, I noticed Josh had been calling the number I'd found in his jacket pocket on a regular basis. Then the strangest thing, in the two weeks before he died, he stopped calling that number and started calling his office desk phone instead. Why would he ring himself?'

Charlie shrugged his shoulders and wondered where this was going.

'I dug out our landline phone bill for the same period and checked the log. In those two weeks Josh was calling his mobile, late at night.' GG paused and took a gulping breath, and flapped her hand in a hopeless gesture. 'I know it doesn't seem much to go on but there is more. The day after Josh died his mobile was used to call his desk number. I spoke with his secretary, Rosemary, and asked if the person had left a message on his answering machine. She said there'd been a lot of calls, all work related and nothing specific stood out. I don't know if she knew something and was protecting me or if she was telling the truth.' GG stopped talking and stared at Charlie with glazed eyes. He opened his mouth but she refocused and held up her index finger, took a deep breath and continued. 'I called the mobile, thinking maybe a work colleague had borrowed his phone. A woman answered and before I could say anything she said, "Hello Lancelot, I'm here. My plane has just landed and I'm waiting for you. Where are you?" I was so shocked I just hung up.'

Charlie stared at his sister, trying to make sense of what she was saying, but all that came out of his mouth was, 'Lancelot?'

'Josh Lance Elliot. His middle name was, Lance. If you string that with our last name you get Lancelot.'

'I didn't know he had a middle name,' said Charlie knitting his brows together as he tried to make sense of where the conversation was going.

'That's 'cause he hated it. He never told anyone what it was. I was one of the few people who knew about it – but so did the woman on the other end of the phone. She must have had real intimate knowledge of him to come up with a nickname like that.'

Charlie ran his palm along his jaw line unconsciously feeling the growth of the day's bristles and let out a deep sigh. In his mind he was trying to find a better explanation than the one GG had come up with but it was a struggle.

'There's more, Charlie. When I searched Josh's desk, I found all his diaries locked away in the bottom draw. He loved the leather ones where the date on the spine was inscribed in roman numerals. Twenty years of his life, from the age of sixteen was meticulously documented in those books. He'd stacked them in date order tied together with a green ribbon.' Charlie nodded confused why that would be important. 'Well for a man who was a stickler for order and precision it was strange that his 2019 diary was out of place. It was between the 2008 and 2009 books. Then I remembered Josh's old theory, hide something in plain sight. Anyway, I combed the entries and appointments. A lot of stuff was in code. I think Bren will be the only one who could decipher it, but I'm not going to ask that of him. Let him have untarnished memories of his father. I did manage to match up some meetings he had at the Hyatt, Sheraton and The Aviary Perth, with charges on his personal credit card. Josh and I never went to those places together. We preferred to dine at the Italian restaurant around the corner from home. Oh Charlie,' she sobbed, letting the tears flow freely down her cheeks, 'Josh had been quiet and withdrawn for months and I felt so shut out. When I asked him if something was wrong, he told me it was a tough case he was working on. According to his secretary Rosemary that wasn't so, Josh had nothing serious on his desk and all his old cases were winding down.'

The chiming of the grandfather clock deep in the house echoed into the silence as Charlie stared at his sister.

'Did you call the number you found in his pocket or ring his mobile and ask for an explanation?' This to him would have been the next logical step. GG shook her head and opened her mouth to speak, but before she could voice what was on her mind the kitchen door flew open. Eli and Bren staggered in, overloaded with sports bags and suitcases. As the boys passed the table they spotted the cake.

'Food...awesome,' exclaimed Bren and let his load drop with a resounding thump on the floor. He swooped on a thick wedge of cake like he hadn't eaten in years and crammed it into his mouth.

Eli, never one to pass up a feed, copied his cousin. With his mouth chock-full he still managed to garble out, 'Aunt GG we've parked your car up in the vehicle shed. Bren's got the keys in his pocket. Dad, Ramrod's groomed and in his stall, the cops have just arrived, they're heading this way. Oh, and by the way, my knee was right, it's started to rain.'

GG's eyes widened. Charlie leant forward and patted her hand. 'We've been having a few dramas here, ourselves. I'm surprised you haven't heard about it on the news.'

'I've avoided the news ever since that reporter tried to corner me with questions about Josh's accident.'

Charlie nodded, remembering the intrusive reporter who had bailed them up at the funeral home demanding answers. If it hadn't been for the fact that he had one arm around GG and the other around Bren at the time, Charlie would have punched his lights out. Luckily the funeral director had intervened and ejected the man before Charlie could free himself and blows were exchanged.

'I'll explain it all to you later GG but for now all you need to know is that a couple of local yokels have been shooting at cattle, the police are conducting a missing persons investigation and a dead body along with some old bones have been found in the well on Heartbreak Hill. The detective and her partner are staying with us while they make their inquiries.'

'And I found a desert nymph...well actually she found me,' said Eli with a smirk at his father, 'and Dad is...'

'That's enough, Eli,' said Charlie in a tone that halted the flow of Eli's words and made him swallow his food in haste.

'Charlie, the boys...' gasped GG, wide-eyed with concern.

'Are perfectly safe as long as they stick to the rules,' said Charlie. He glanced up at his son and nephew and gave them both a stern look. It wasn't often he laid down the law and the boys stared at him in awe. 'Fishing, swimming and riding are all allowable activities for you lads, as long as you stick together and keep a radio handy. Bren, I know you'd like to spend some time with Naomi in the camp kitchen – that's not a problem. Eli, you can either join them and learn how to cook, which wouldn't be a bad thing, or you work with Mac and me. Neither of you boys are to go anywhere by yourself, and especially not to investigate things that are none of your business. Remember what I told you the other day, Eli...*this - is -not - a - game*. Got that, boys?' The wide-eyed lads nodded. Charlie wasn't satisfied and decided to make any punishment a major deterrent to them getting embroiled in this mess.

'I mean it, if *either* of you break the rules I'll put you *both* on the very next plane to Perth. Right?'

'Yes, Dad,' said Eli.

'Yes, Uncle Charlie,' said Bren his voice cracking and coming out all squeaky.

'Good, now get that luggage upstairs. Bren, you're going to have to share with Eli buddy as we've got a full house at the moment.'

'Yeah, Dad's sleeping in your room because the desert nymph has his, because we found a snake in nan's old room, and the police are using the other downstairs rooms.' Eli didn't pause to breathe and his words came out in a rush. 'Aunt GG your room's ready as always. Naomi put fresh sheets on the bed yesterday.'

She nodded and gave him a grateful smile. The boys gathered together the vast array of bags and staggered out. Eli's voice competed with Bren's in non-stop chatter as the boys banged and clattered their way down the hall and up the stairs.

'A snake, a desert nymph, dead bodies and the police, good God Charlie, what the hell is going on?' gasped GG. Charlie noticed that her tears had fully receded, and except for a few red blotches dotted along her cheeks she looked composed and her old self. A smile even twitched at the corner of her mouth. 'I think you've been holding out on me.'

Charlie was grateful for the intrusion of the boys. It meant he'd have time to assimilate and sort through all that GG had told him. The slamming of the kitchen door announced the next lot of arrivals and interrupted their conversation further.

Rosie and Mark, both freshly showered and wearing clean clothes stood just inside the doorway. Mark's khaki police shirt and trousers had been pressed to perfection. Rosie once again wore her body fitting black tee-shirt neatly tucked into tight black cargo pants. Her polished combat boots gleamed, all traces of the dust and mud she'd picked up on her previous visit was gone.

Charlie smiled a greeting.

'Hey, Rosie. Have you given up the exciting nightlife of Mount Ibour and decided to move in with me?' he asked, pointing to the bulging leather satchel clutched in her hand.

'Why, Bull Morgan if I didn't know better I'd say you're flirting with me,' she replied, a wide smile lighting her sharp features. 'No, I have something for our girl. I think it may be her luggage.'

'Where'd you find that?'

'Under the tree at my new camping spot.'

'I'm just guarding the track, huh! You really had my bullshit meter running on overdrive with that one.' Rosie's smile widened at his comment. Charlie pointed, 'This is my sister, Georgina.'

Rosie held out a hand. 'Detective Rosie Bloom,' she jerked a thumb over her shoulder, 'Constable Mark Bayden.'

'Call me GG, everyone does.' Rosie nodded as she shook GG's hand. 'I know Mark. How's Trish and the kids?'

Mark gave a cheeky grin, 'Excellent. Kids are growing fast and keeping Trish on her toes.'

'Give them my best won't you.'

Mark nodded.

Rosie raised her eyebrows at the interchange and steered the conversation back on track. 'The base of the boab tree was a gold mine, Bull.'

'How so?' asked Charlie.

She waggled a finger at him, looked around to check if anyone was listening before pointing to the whiteboard that still faced the wall behind the door.

'I found a backpack with a German flag sewn onto the strap.'

Charlie's mouth dropped open. 'No...'

Rosie nodded and the smile left her lips. 'I want to have another chat with Tangles.'

'You asking?'

'Sort of.'

Charlie nodded, Rosie's personal skills had progressed but the hard-nosed copper was always just below the surface.

'I'd like to see our girl first, though...about this.' She held up a caramel coloured leather satchel. 'There's a good chance it's hers.'

'I hope you're right,' he said as excitement and apprehension churned around his gut. 'There might be something tangible in it to jolt her memory.'

'My thoughts exactly. Sure, you don't want a job?'

'No thanks. Being a grazier is enough excitement for an old man like me.' Rosie's eyebrows rose. He could see amusement forming in her eyes.

'You're what...thirty-six?' Charlie nodded. 'Nothing old about that my lad, I'm in the decade that's considered the old age of youth but I know that when I reach fifty I'll be in the youth of old age. So I'm actually getting younger and I tell ya there's a whole lotta life in this young girl yet!'

Charlie roared with laughter. He heard GG giggling along with him. He was really taking a shine to this strong, smart and witty detective.

'Now where can I find our girl?'

'She's locked in my room, asleep. She's got a bad headache still. Someone hit her over the head the day we got back from Heart-break Hill.'

The amusement left Rosie's face. Anger had her spitting out the words, 'Fuck, Bull, why didn't you call me?'

'Watch your language, detective,' he growled, flicking a gaze in his sister's direction. Swearing was not to be tolerated, especially in the home. Something his mother had drummed into him. Charlie chose to ignore his own recent slip. 'I did call, but you were unreachable...'

'Fuck, the bloody battery on my phone went flat. It's still in the car charging,' she said ignoring his chastisement of her language. 'Tell me what happened.'

GG's glance zipped from one face to another as she heard for the first time a full account of the previous day's events.

'I'm going to commandeer your dining table for a while, Bull. I need to talk with everyone on your crew.'

'I thought you might.'

Rosie tossed the bag she carried under a chair and took a seat. Mark joined them at the table. The boys came tearing into the room and grabbed another handful of cake.

Charlie rose and refilled the plate, handed it to Eli and said, 'Dinner won't be ready for a couple of hours yet, so you pair might as well go upstairs and give the Play Station a hammering. You can show Bren your fury at the shipyard move.'

'Oh, Dad you're hopeless,' said Eli, rolling his eyes and snorting with laughter.

Bren dropped a pile of magazines in front of GG. 'For Mimi,' she murmured at Charlie's surprised look.

'Travel brochures?'

'Yeah, she wants to go on a cruise.'

'Anywhere in particular?' asked Charlie.

'No, don't think so. I bought a selection of different types and destinations for her.'

Chapter Twenty-Six

The kitchen door rattled.

'Come in,' called Charlie.

Tangles in his usual unobtrusive manner stepped into the room. In his arms he cradled a sheepskin lined wooden box. At his heels Bindi was supervising the movement of her pups. Her tail gave a tentative wag as if unsure she should be in the house. Charlie clicked his fingers and she trotted over to him. He ran a gentle hand over her head and murmured, 'Good girl.' The dog relaxed.

GG rushed over and peered into the box. 'Oh, what a beautiful litter, I especially love the striped guy.'

'That's Banjo, and he's already spoken for.'

Rosie gave a small chuckle. 'Of course he is. How romantic of you, Bull.'

He could feel the heat rise in his face, so he ignored her crack and said, 'GG would you mind taking Bindi and the pups upstairs to the boys. While you're there maybe take the time to unpack and settle in.' GG gave him a curious look. He flicked a gaze at Tangles then back to GG. 'Please sis,' he pleaded.

'Sure.'

She gave Tangles a sympathetic smile and relieved him of the box. 'Come on, Bindi old girl,' she said softly to the dog and together they left the room, quietly closing the door after them.

Charlie rose from his seat and refilled the kettle.

'Take a seat, Rhysand,' said Rosie. 'I need to have another chat with you.'

Charlie could hear Tangles loud gulp from across the room. The young stockman didn't speak, he just slid neatly into a seat and clasped his hands tightly together on the table in front of him.

Rosie placed her mobile phone on the surface between them, pushed record and said, 'Rhysand, late afternoon the day before yesterday, a member of this household was knocked unconscious in the stable. What can you tell me about that?'

The Adam's apple in Tangles' throat was working overtime as he took a series of gulps before speaking. 'Mac told us about the attack on Miss Delaney. I know nothing of it,' he said giving Charlie a frightened look.

'Where were you at four o'clock yesterday afternoon?' asked Rosie.

'I was at the far end of the home paddock servicing the windmill. I told all of this to Mac last night.'

'That's fine but now you're telling me. Were you alone?'

'*Ja*...yes.'

'So you have no one who can confirm your whereabouts?'

'*Nei.*'

'Did you see anyone or did anyone see you?'

'I saw a ute, moving very fast, drive away from the homestead. Maybe ten or fifteen minutes later a white SUV rolled in and parked near the office. Steve and a man I did not know got out. I climbed down from the mill and sorted out some bolts, before climbing back up. I fixed a blade and looked around. Steve was standing at the stock office door, talking to someone. She did not go in and only stayed for a brief moment before rushing away.'

'Which way did she go?' asked Rosie

'She hurried along wombat track to the back of the stables.'

'Did she go into the stables?'

'I did not see, but that path leads past the barn's back door. It also leads to the dongas.'

Rosie turned her head and glanced at Charlie over the top of her shoulder, eyebrow raised in query. 'What's the donga's used for, Bull?'

'The sleeping quarters, detective,' murmured Charlie.

She nodded in thanks and continued with the questions. 'Anyone else?'

'Gil. I saw Gil Connors, the man who does the timesheets and wages. He rushed out of the office about one minute after Steve stalked away and he too hurried in the same direction. He kept looking around like he was looking for someone. It can't have been young Eli because he was talking to the strange man and Gil would have had a good view of him from the office steps. I climbed down from the windmill and packed up my toolbox. Mimi and Pod zoomed past on a quad bike.'

'Where were they coming from and in what direction were they heading?'

'They drove down the wombat track, away from the dongas and the stables. They drove up to the equipment shed. They were still there when I put my tools away.'

'That's a lot of activity on the path.'

'But not surprising, detective,' said Charlie. 'We use wombat track as our main pedestrian, horse and bike thoroughfare. The larger equipment and four-wheel-drives are required to stick to the main roads. It's safer for everyone that way.'

Rosie grunted and stared hard at Tangles. 'Did you see anyone else?'

He nodded. 'As I walked up to the shed, I saw Bull, Mac and Eli walking towards the barn.'

'And when we got to the stables Darcy was already there, closing the back door,' said Charlie.

'Was anyone wearing a red shirt?'

'Everyone, detective.'

'Why was that?'

'The girls, Mimi and Darcy, won the poker tournament this week. They requested a red-shirt day.'

Rosie stared wide-eyed and removed her spectacles from the tip of her nose. Tangles' explanation seemed to flummox her. Charlie took pity and explained.

'We have a tradition here detective. So that there are no ill feelings about losing their hard-earned money, the cash in the pot is donated to the Police Youth Program. In lieu the winners are granted one request that everyone who plays must abide by.'

Rosie nodded and murmured quietly to Mark who was sitting next to her. Charlie pushed the plunger down on the coffee pot and poured out four mugs of the brew. He quietly placed one in front of each of the three people seated at the table and offered milk around. Everyone shook their head, so he returned to the sink. He leant his hip against the bench and took a sip of his coffee. He watched and waited.

Rosie slurped at her mug before accepting the file Mark was holding out to her. She centred it in front of her on the table but didn't open it.

'Rhysand, when we previously spoke you told us the last time you saw Britt was at Mount Ibour Airport. Is that correct?'

He nodded. She pointed to the phone.

'Please speak your answers for the recording.'

He nodded again and said, '*Ja*, detective that is correct.'

'What did Britt's luggage look like?'

'She only had a small backpack, about so big.' Tangles held his hands apart to indicate the size equal to a teenager's school bag, forgetting about the recording. 'It was wine-red in colour, leather I think. It had a large main pocket, two zipper pockets in the front, a cell phone pocket on the side and all sorts of compartments.'

'That's a small bag for a backpacking journey. What was in it, can you recall?'

'I was always amazed at how much Britt could carry in it. Also, she and the cousins all shared clothes. They told me she carried shorts and tee-shirts, one pair of fancy shoes, a skirt for going to the nightclubs, a camera, her mobile telephone and an electronic tablet plus chargers and some beauty products. She took the bag with her when she left but not her sleeping bag. I still have that.'

'Apart from the electronics did she have anything else of value with her? Jewellery, money, credit cards anything like that?'

'Frieda was in charge of the credit cards and passports. Britt had about two hundred Australian dollars in cash in her pocket. She always wore earrings, mostly big silver hoops, and sometimes a *kryss* necklace. On her right hand she wore a ring.'

'Kryss?'

'A religious cross,' said Tangles. He squeezed his fingers tight and began rolling his thumbs around each other in a nervous motion.

Rosie opened the file in front of her and selected an A4 photo. She slid it across the table and positioned it squarely in front of Tangles.

'Do you recognise this necklace?'

The photograph was of the cross with the broken gold filigree chain they'd found in the back of the RAV4. Tangles studied the necklace carefully. 'No, her *kryss* was silver to match her earrings.'

Rosie moved the photo aside and slid another one in its place. Charlie leant forward for a peek and saw this one was of a ring. It looked to be a white and rose gold Celtic knot. Tangles' face paled and tears began running unchecked down his cheeks. He placed a finger gently on the photo and said, 'Britt's father, my Uncle Eric, presented this ring to her upon her sixteenth birthday. *Hun elsket det*...sorry.' He took a deep shuddering breath and translated, 'She loved it. The ring never left her hand.'

Charlie walked over and squeezed the young man's shoulder before seating himself in the chair next to him. Mark handed Tangles a neatly folded, clean, white handkerchief.

'Thank you,' he murmured and used it to scrub at his face, wiping the tears away. He sucked in a long, deep breath, held it for what seemed an age before exhaling. 'Have you found her detective? Is she dead?' he managed to choke out.

Rosie, her face blank of all emotion, reached over and placed her hand over one of his.

'Rhysand, it's my sad duty to inform you that this ring was recovered near the site of a number of human remains.' The breath exploded from Tangles' lungs and he slumped in his seat. 'To identify the remains I would like you to submit to a DNA test so we can ascertain if any of the remains belong to Britt. Would you agree to do that?'

Tangles nodded then he allowed his head to sink onto his folded arms. Charlie put a comforting arm over the sobbing man's shoulder.

'Constable Bayden, will you take care of the DNA collection please,' said Rosie softly and reached over and switched off the recording. She rose to her feet and with her head indicated that Charlie should follow her out into the hall.

'I need to have a chat with Kelsey, see what she remembers before I speak to the other hands.'

Charlie opened the door into the main house. 'I'll come with you?'

'No, stay and take care of that courageous young man.' Charlie's brows rose at her words. 'Tangles has lived with this dread for a long time. He promised his family he would find her and bring her home. That's quite a burden to carry.'

Charlie nodded. 'Yes it is,' he said. 'You'll find Kelsey upstairs, second door on the left. Eli is up there with his cousin. The boys will point you in the right direction.'

Chapter Twenty-Seven

Colours, voices and images floated through Kelsey's mind. A door opened and she stepped into a room full of drawers. Each drawer was labelled but the print was blurred. She chose one at random and peered inside. Bren appeared and held out his hand. He asked if she was okay. He helped her stand up and brushed the rubbish the kids had been throwing at her away from her skirt.

She quietly slid the drawer shut before selecting another. Spread-sheet formulas scrolled past and then column after column of numbers. She flicked her gaze up and down the rows, adding them up. They didn't all balance and it was frustrating because numbers always came easily to her. She slammed the drawer shut. A drawer to her left glowed around the edges so she cracked it open and found herself gazing out of a window that overlooked a congested city street. She reached forward and double checked the window latch before turning and scanning the one room flat to ensure everything was in order and that nothing was out of place. She took a memory photo of the room. If anything was different when she returned she'd know. A bit compulsive obsessive she knew but a hard habit to break. The flat was starkly furnished, bereft of bright colours or decoration. It didn't feel like a real home, but then she'd never had one of those. The round, laminated table was battered and scarred but the worst of it was hidden under a plain brown tablecloth, a bargain from the local op shop. Tucked neatly under the table was a rickety, paint scratched wooden chair. The table was set for one.

A small bar fridge, pristine and white, hummed a soothing background noise. She opened it and stared at the small carton of milk, tray of fresh fruit and a small bowl of green salad, the rest of the fridge was empty. Selecting an apple, Kelsey switched off the silver and black plastic radio that sat on top of the fridge like a gentleman's top hat and slung a plain black handbag over her shoulder.

She flicked her gaze around the room again, obsessively checking that the soft, thick blanket was neatly tucked in around the single mattress that had been pushed hard against the far wall. That blanket represented comfort and safety when she was in need of solace, and travelled everywhere with her, no matter where her job sent her. Satisfied the flat was secure and everything was in its allotted place Kelsey slipped her feet into a pair of plain black flats that sat waiting on a folded towel at the door. It had been raining when she returned home the night before and her feet had been soaked.

Home! So that was where she was. It was so strange that her home was so bland when she loved bright colours and beautiful flowers.

Never one to draw attention to herself she'd dressed plainly for work. A dark knee-length pencil skirt and plain, white cotton button-down shirt was paired with a black suit jacket. Kelsey stepped out the door and the cold air made her gasp. None of her clothing items were thick enough to cope with the cold winter breeze that seeped up the barren concrete stairwell. She gave her door handle a twist, checking it had locked and then did it again just to make sure. For some reason Kelsey's gut felt like it was loaded down with lead. She took a deep breath to prepare herself for the day and in an attempt to warm up she jogged down the stairs.

Kelsey didn't own a car. A thirty-minute brisk trot along St Georges Terrace had her arriving at a city office building. This was where she currently worked. Kelsey didn't question the knowledge, she just allowed the memory to reveal itself. She was slightly out of breath and her jacket had ridden up so she gave it a slight tug and smoothed her hand over the front to ensure it lay flat. The automatic glass door opened to a soulless expanse of grey and white tiles, broken only by two black, vinyl steel-framed benches and a sad looking palm. The ducted heating already on overdrive against the morning chill sent a blast of hot air across her face. It carried a cloying odour of wet wool and mothballs. The air tasted stale and dry in her mouth. It was all very uninviting and she hesitated to cross the threshold. Office workers jostled past her like a herd of sheep heading towards a bank of shiny steel elevators.

Come on Kelsey she said to herself, how bad can it be. After another moment of hesitation she followed the herd. Squeezing into a corner of the elevator she looked at the faces surrounding her. Two women bundled up in thick scarves and coats glared at her before turning away and whispering to each other. Kelsey closed her eyes trying to pretend she was alone but the smell of unwashed bodies, saccharine perfume and stale air made that impossible.

'Level three. Doors opening,' announced the annoying melancholic elevator.

Kelsey surged forward, caught in the flow of people. The doors snapped closed at her heels. Employees disappeared into partitioned hidey holes, the noise level in the open plan room rose to an annoying buzz, as phones purred, fingernails tapped on keyboards and the coffee crowd huddled in a cubicle, laughing and discussing the latest scandal. Kelsey quietly made her way to her assigned torture chamber and sat staring at the blank computer screen. Dread settled in her stomach like a heavy weight.

She hated her current job.

Forensic accountants and auditors were expected to ferret out wrongdoing and right it. She'd done that and her fellow workers hated her. She couldn't quit, the thought of not having an income terrified her. She'd been poor all her life and had struggled to find her place in the world. People were nasty and jealous of her brain capacity and a lifetime of hiding her capabilities had worn her down. Kelsey knew she was depressed and unhappy and needed to find a way to make her life more fulfilling.

Sighing deeply, she leant forward and gingerly pressed the power button to start her computer.

Her phone rang.

'I need you...' said the most important person in her life.

A sharp rap startled her awake and the memory faded. Kelsey opened her eyes and groaned. Her head was still pounding like a bass drum and the light skewered her eyeballs to the pillow. The door rattled again as someone knocked. Not Charlie, he always announced himself when he knocked so she wouldn't be frightened. She struggled upright and shoved her blonde mop away from her face.

'Just a minute,' she croaked.

Her glance fell on the packet of paracetamol and glass of water on the jarrah bedside table. Kelsey reached across and popped a couple of pills from the blister packet and washed them down her throat with the water. She reached out to the end of the bed for neatly folded clothing and climbed into the tailored linen shorts. Even though the price tag had still been on the garment when she selected it that morning it still felt weird stepping into another woman's clothes. Running her fingers through her sleep mozzed hair to give it a brush, she pulled on the crisp white sheets that emitted a pleasant scent of fresh air and sunshine and remade the bed.

Remembering the caution that had been drummed into her by both Charlie and Eli, she approached the door with caution and tentatively asked, 'Who is it?'

'Detective Bloom.'

A small smile tugged her lip and she flipped the lock on the door. 'Hello, Rosie it's nice to see you. When did you arrive?'

'Oh, about an hour ago. Alright if I come in?'

'Sure,' Kelsey said, gesturing past the king-size bed to the two navy-coloured, winged-back armchairs arranged in the nook formed by the bay windows. The chairs had been positioned to take full advantage of the breathtaking views of the river and landscape that the second storey of the house afforded along the back of the house. A small hand-crafted wooden table, its polish glowing warmly in the evening sunshine, separated the chairs.

Rosie glowered as she ran her hot gaze over Kelsey.

'What?' asked Kelsey. She was startled by the intensity of the look on the detective's face.

'You weren't careful,' growled Rosie. 'Tell me what happened when you went into the stable.'

Kelsey sighed and took a seat.

When she finished reciting her recollection of the attack, Rosie asked, 'Did you see anyone wearing red that day? Can you remember?'

'Of course, this is me you're talking about...old computer brain,' said Kelsey, tapping her forehead gently with her forefinger. Rosie smiled and rolled her hand to encourage her to continue. 'We'll start with the jillaroos. I spotted them when we returned from the well. They were loading boxes of fruit from the cool room into a chiller truck. Mimi wore a button up red and black plaid. It had roll tab three-quarter sleeves and turndown collar. It looked cool and comfortable and was suitable as a work shirt. Darcy on the other hand had gone for something a bit more feminine and revealing. A long sleeve, scoop-neck tee that stopped at her midriff, it was really form fitting and rode up to reveal the stud in her naval as she worked. Gil Connors drove in while Eli and Charlie were unloading Rainbow from the horse float. He was wearing what I can only describe as a cowboy shirt that would've been more suitable for a line dance than a work day. Red again. Eli had on green and white, cotton check that buttoned up at the front. The CASA inspector wore a white business shirt. Steve a skimpy white singlet, with a red and white checked cotton shirt knotted under her breast. A couple of stock hands were in the home paddock rounding up cattle, both of them had something red on as well, but I never got close enough to see them clearly. What's with all the red anyway?'

Rosie explained the fortnightly fundraising poker event.

'That's clever. No angst about losses being used to fuel someone's fun night out in town,' said Kelsey. 'You know what Charlie was wearing – you saw his shirt that morning. He hadn't time to shower and change when we got back because he'd been dealing with the snake and had only just returned from disposing of it. Jimmy wasn't wearing red, neither was Naomi. That's it, I didn't see anyone else.'

Rosie sank back in her chair and tapped her lips with a finger. Kelsey wondered what was going through her brain.

'Rosie...I think my memories are coming back.'

The detective looked up and her eyes brightened. She sat forward in her seat and said, 'What makes you say that?'

'Just now when I was asleep, I had a dream. In it I was at work and I was very unhappy. In my role as forensic accountant and auditor I'd uncovered some wrongdoing by the office staff and they hated me for it.'

Rosie nodded her head. 'Well, that matches what your employer at Hardgrave & Associates told me. I had a long telephone conversation with Samantha Hardgrave yesterday and she reckons you're a brilliant auditor. The scourge of white-collar criminals the world over. H&A send you all over the globe to ferret out any wrongdoing in the accounts of a vast array of international companies that are on their books. You had recently returned to Perth from Europe where you'd worked a long and intensive case that involved a criminal consortium. Charges were laid against some very shonky people as a result of your work. Samantha Hardgrave, your boss, told me that ever since you'd returned to Perth, you seemed depressed and she was concerned that you were suffering from burn out – you'd been living in basic hotel rooms and constantly on the move for years. So she assigned you a space in the H&A city office and an easy role to allow you time to get your mojo back. But you, being you, actually discovered that most of the office staff were rorting the expenses repayment system. When you raised the issue with the office manager you became the department's persona non grata. The staff hated being caught out and having their nice little earner taken away. Then one morning, out of the blue, you marched into Hardgrave's office and announced you were quitting.'

'That doesn't sound like me,' said Kelsey wondering what had catapulted her into that type of action. 'How long ago was that?'

'Five months – around the end of May. It was a bad time for her to lose you, as it was coming up to the end of the financial year and the beginning of the audit season. Hardgrave was shocked. In all the years you'd worked for her, you'd never taken a day off, not even for an illness. She asked you to take some time to reconsider. You told her you would do H&A's audit then take six months off. You started your sabbatical three weeks ago.'

A fragment of her dream floated forward. 'I wonder who was on the phone that morning?'

Rosie frowned and looked puzzled by the comment.

'What phone?'

'When you knocked on the door just now, the phone on my desk was ringing...' Kelsey went on to describe what she'd dreamt. 'Unfortunately, I awoke before I had a name.'

'Hmm, every time you remember something we end up with more questions than answers,' said Rosie shaking her head. She reached across and squeezed Kelsey's hand. 'Are you feeling well enough to come downstairs? I want to show you some things.'

'Sure. Give me a minute to grab a quick shower first.'

She left Rosie sitting in the evening sunshine drinking in the view.

The air in the ensuite was filled with masculine notes of lavender and spice, the scent of Charlie's shower gel. It filled her senses and warmed her soul and eased the last of her headache away. Kelsey showered and dressed herself in a white and green floral sleeveless silk shift.

Chapter Twenty-Eight

Kelsey and Rosie trotted down the stairs to the sounds of pots clang-
ing and cupboard doors slamming. As they entered the kitchen they
stepped into a burst of laughter. Charlie with a vegetable masher in
his hand was pounding away at a large pot of potatoes. His sister
GG was spreading a bright cheerful cloth over the dining table and
Mark stood holding a handful of cutlery. He was reciting one of his
numerous and amusing tales as he waited to start setting the table.

'I see Constable Bayden is keeping you entertained,' said Rosie
with a crooked smile on her face. Marks cheeks flushed but his smile
didn't slip. Into this happy scene stepped Gil. He gave a smarmy
smile to the people in the room and made a beeline for GG.

He cupped one of her hands in both his and said, 'Georgina,
welcome home. It's so good to see you again. It's been too long.'

GG gave a gentle smile. 'Hello, Gil. How are you?'

'Much better now I've seen you. I swear you get more beautiful
every time I see you,' he said with a flirty smirk. GG gently extracted
her hand and went back to adjusting the tablecloth.

'How's the book-keeping business going, getting plenty of work?'
she asked.

'Sure am. Did you hear, Peter Forest had a heart attack six months back and had to close up shop?'

GG shook her head, 'No I didn't hear, that so sad.'

'Good for me though, I've picked up most of his clients...so busy, busy, busy. Unfortunately, this flood has hampered me a bit this last week. I haven't been able to get around to see everyone. I'd hoped to have my own book-keeping system set up with them all before Christmas.'

'I hope what you set up works better than it does here,' said Charlie walking over to the fridge and grabbing the jug of milk. 'I've had nothing but problems.'

'Why's that?' asked GG turning to stare at her brother.

Gil chuckled. 'Bull's been flogging around and messing up the accounts again. In the process he's somehow corrupted the program. I wish you'd leave all the financial stuff alone. I can take care of it. As it is I've been here off and on all week trying to sort out your mess.' Gil's words startled Kelsey and she shot Charlie a look. Before she could offer to check Gil's formulas and see if she could fix them, Gil said, 'I've fixed the problem, some of the formulas were pointing to the wrong worksheets and had the wrong links, I just need to access the Rivers Run server and you're good to go. Bull, I want your laptop tonight to put the new program in place. I would have done it earlier today but the doors to the house were locked and I'm leaving first thing in the morning to get to my next job.'

Charlie stared at Gil, then flicked a look towards Kelsey. She gave a slight shake of her head.

'How long will you need the computer for?' he asked.

'An hour, maybe two,' said Gil. He started to walk towards the office but was pulled up short by Charlie's words.

'Sorry to throw a spanner in the works, Gil, but I'm in the middle of something important on my computer and I need to go back to it straight after dinner. You'll have to do it in the morning.'

Gil swung towards Charlie looking startled. 'I won't get in your way. I can work in the study...'

'Bull, I need to use the study...' said Rosie crossing her arms and glaring at Charlie.

'And I need the computer,' said Charlie. 'Sorry mate it'll just have to wait till morning.'

Gil's lips pouted and he began to sulk at not getting his own way. 'Well, I really wanted to get on the road early tomorrow and head back to Slab Johnson's.'

'You can't leave Rivers Run. Not yet anyway,' said Rosie 'I need to talk with you.'

Gil swung in her direction his eyes narrowed, 'What about?'

'You're a regular traveller around the district. You might have seen something that can help me in my case.'

Gil's gaze shifted to his shoes and he blinked rapidly. 'No, nothing that springs to mind. I would have said.'

'And there have been a couple of incidents here at the homestead that need clearing up...'

Gil's spine stiffened. He folded his arms across his chest and in a defensive tone said, 'Nothing to do with me...'

'...so you and I are going to have a little natter before you leave. Take a seat for now. I'll be ready for our first chat in about ten minutes.' Gil looked like a deer in the headlights, his wide-eyed gaze not leaving Rosie's face. She had just bulldozed over all his objections and excuses as if he hadn't said a word.

Rosie turned away and smirked. 'Kelsey, I'd like you to come with me,' she said, grabbing the file Mark held aloft for her and headed towards the study.

* * *

Rosie slid a photo in front of Kelsey. 'Do you know this woman?'

'No who is it?'

'Have you met Tangles yet?'

Kelsey shook her head. 'No, I've only seen him at a distance. Why?'

'This is his cousin Britt. She's been missing since June 2018.'

Kelsey stared at Rosie. Her eyes filled with tears and her stomach began churning.

'No, her face isn't familiar to me,' she managed to choke out.

Rosie raised her gaze above the half-moon glasses perched on her nose. Her blue eyes stared unblinkingly at Kelsey. Rosie's demeanour had changed. Gone was the friendly woman who had treated her with patience and kindness. Here was the Silver Dingo in full inquisition mode, focussed on solving the murder of three people. She slid another photo across the desk.

'What about this one?'

The photo was a happy snap of a young woman smiling up into the camera.

'No. Who is she?'

'This is Annalisa Wagner. She went missing in January 2019, from Kelly Creek Roadhouse. Ring a bell?'

'No. Where is Kelly Creek?'

Rosie ignored the question and said, 'I'm going to show you a photo of a piece of jewellery. Tell me if you recognise it or if it evokes an emotion in you.'

Kelsey brushed her eyes with the heel of her hand and focused on the photo. She took her time to study it and search the recesses of her mind but the necklace was not one she'd seen before.

'No.'

'I'm getting a lot of nos from you,' said Rosie, her frustration obvious. 'Do you remember this one?' she asked, placing a copy of Kelsey's sketch on the table and lined all three faces in a neat row in front of her.

Kelsey relaxed her computer brain, letting it do its thing. A name popped into her mind and with it a flood of information.

'Nari, her name was Nari. She collected me from Mount Ibour Airport because the man I was meeting couldn't.'

'Who were you meeting?'

'He's still being elusive but I was there to do a job for him.' A name popped into her head. 'Zentra Flats Station! My mystery man had made arrangements with a Hector Johnson for me to audit the books.'

'But you're supposed to be on leave from work. Is this Johnson bloke a friend?'

'No, I don't know him.'

'Then why are you auditing his books?'

Numbers began scrolling around her brain. 'There's something wrong with Zentra Flats Station's accounts.'

Rosie stared at her. 'How do you know?'

'The phone call.'

'Phone call...the one you got at work just before you took leave?' Kelsey nodded.

'Who was it from and why is it so important for you to leave your job and come to Mount Ibour to investigate the books of someone you don't know?' demanded Rosie.

Lights began to flash inside Kelsey's head. She groaned as pain seared behind her eyes. She pinched the bridge of her nose and breathed through the pain. 'It's not ready to come out yet, Rosie. Can we talk about something else?'

'Okay. Follow me I have something to show you.'

They returned to the kitchen. Charlie was ladling mash potato over a huge tray of mince stew while GG grated a mound of cheese on top. Mark was just heading to the door that led into the main part of the house. 'I'm going to round up the troops,' he said pointing upwards to where Eli and Bren were smashing bad guys and saving the world. 'According to our chef extraordinaire and his able assistant, our dinner will be ready in ten minutes.'

'Before you go Bayden, where's that bag we bought with us?' asked Rosie.

Mark pointed to the chair where Gil was sitting on his hands, looking like a naughty school boy waiting outside the principal's office. Rosie strolled over and reached underneath his seat. He squirmed in his seat as she held up a leather satchel. Kelsey's breath caught in her throat and a drawer opened in her mind.

'I've seen that before or one just like it.'

A self-satisfied smile appeared on Rosie's face. 'I'd hoped you had,' she said handing it and a plastic bag containing a pair of white shoes to her. 'Open the satchel and tell me about the contents.'

Everyone stopped what they were doing to watch Kelsey. She stuck the bag of shoes under her arm and opened the flap of the satchel. Her fingers wrapped around a book. She pulled out the tatty paperback entitled *Follow the Rabbit Proof Fence* and ran her hand lovingly over the book's cover. 'This is the true story of three young Aboriginal girls who in 1931 were forcibly removed from their families. They were taken from Jigalong to Moore River to a government settlement. They escaped and trekked the 1,600 kilometres home. Those kids were so full of guts and determination. I really admire their fortitude. Have you read it?'

Rosie shook her head, 'Saw the movie,' she murmured.

'Not the same as reading about it...I love this book.' She opened the cover and a memory stick slid out of a slot cut in the pages and into her palm. Startled she clasped it in her fist.

What the hell!

A feeling of dread settled in her gut. She folded her lips and stared blindly at the page in front of her. What to do. She stood in a room full of people holding information she'd promised to keep secret and safe.

I need to hide this until I can see what it contains.

Kelsey looked around, everyone was staring.

'Sorry...can you give me a moment. I need to go and take some painkillers for my headache,' she said and spun on her heel and bolted from the room.

Kelsey made it to the foot of the stairs. Upstairs she could hear the boys and Mark laughing and milling around. Casting a frantic gaze around her glance fell on old grandad. Perfect she thought and in a swift movement she slipped the memory stick into the clock's secret compartment.

Satisfied Kelsey slowly made her way back into the kitchen. The detective arched her eyebrow. Before she could speak Kelsey said, 'Sorry about that, Rosie. I was feeling a bit woozy from the thumping in my head. The tablets will help.'

Kelsey felt bad about lying to her friend. But there were too many people in the room, and in the back of her mind was a voice telling her to keep the information safe and secret until the right time. To forestall any probing questions from the detective she picked up the bag again and lifted out a mobile phone. She stared at the words *Fearless* emblazoned on its white cover and held it up for everyone to see.

A screech came from across the room, '*You whore!*'

Kelsey released her hold on the satchel and took an involuntary step back. GG was stalking towards her with her fists raised. The veins in her neck stood out in anger. Charlie reached out and caught his sister just as she lunged. She wriggled ineffectively against his strong grip.

Bren and Eli burst into the room. The smiles left their faces.

'Mum,' said Bren, 'what's wrong?'

'Let me go,' GG screamed. 'She's the one...I'm gonna kill her.'

Bren turned to stare at Kelsey, his eyes widened in shock. He pushed his floppy fringe back from his face and opened his mouth to speak but GG screamed, nearly lifting the roof off the house. She fought hard to loosen Charlie's grip.

Kelsey dropped the phone and raced across the room towards the back door. She flung herself out into the night and raced down the path. The heavy rain soaked through her thin dress as she splashed her way barefoot through muddy puddles and headed towards the river.

What the hell had just happened?

Chapter Twenty-Nine

Charlie was stunned. GG's sudden meltdown had totally caught him by surprise. Kelsey's terrified look had him swooping on his sister and pulling her into a tight clench while his sluggish brain tried to work out what the hell was going on.

He whispered soothing words close to GG's ear, reminding her that letting the red haze win would only result in a whole world of hurt and regret. As he spoke he stroked the scar on the back of her neck. As a child, in a fit of rage, he had caused her an injury that had put her life at risk and left a permanent scar. He had never forgiven himself. That's why he worked so hard to keep his temper in check. The screaming stopped and GG began to pant.

He was startled when the kitchen door slammed. Gazing across the room he saw Gil's lip was hitched in a smirk of amusement. He seemed to be relishing the drama taking place, like it fed his soul. The look irritated Charlie.

'Gil, go on back to camp and have your dinner,' he said. 'Detective Bloom can chase you up later when things have calmed down here.'

A look of disappointment crossed Gil's face at being given his marching orders. He slipped his hands into his pockets and took his time to saunter out the door. Charlie shifted his gaze to Bren who was standing directly in front of his mother demanding to know what was going on.

'GG, calm down and tell us what's got you so steamed,' said Charlie.

GG pointed to the phone on the floor. 'That's Josh's phone.'

Remembering their conversation earlier, Charlie's stomach knotted and his heart began to ache. How did Kelsey come to have his brother-in-law's phone in her bag? Surely she wasn't the one having an affair with him? That would be too cruel for words.

'Yeah, it's dad's phone...so what,' said Bren scrunching his eyebrows together in a puzzled frown.

'Oh, you wouldn't understand, you're too young,' GG snapped at him and tried to shake herself from Charlie's grip.

'That's enough, mum,' retorted Bren in a deep strong voice that brooked no argument. 'I am so sick and tired of being shut out by you. I'm almost a full-grown man now and without dad here it is my job to look after you.' Bren reached forward and gently removed Charlie's arms from around his mother. He drew her into his own embrace and said, 'Now calm down and tell me what it is that is upsetting you so much.' GG clung to her son and began to sob. Bren stood patiently waiting for her to compose herself.

'Dad,' said Eli, his eyes bright with unshed tears. He was staring at the door that had recently closed behind Gil. 'Kelsey's gone, she's outside alone...and it's not safe.'

Charlie broke his golden rule and swore.

Rosie looked around startled by Eli's words. 'Shit, Bull. We need to get after her.'

Charlie was torn, the revelation that the woman he had fallen for might just be another Amelia hurt but he couldn't let anything happen to someone under his care. 'I need to make sure GG's fine first...'

'I've got her, Uncle Charlie...you go after Dad's brain's trust.'

'Brain's trust...,' said GG, lifting her tear-stained face from Bren's shoulder and hiccupping.

'Yes Mum...'

'You mean to say that was your father's foster sister?'

'Yes, Mum.'

'How can you be sure, we've never met her?'

'Dad pointed her out to me once.'

'Well why didn't you say you knew who she was?'

'I didn't know the mysterious desert nymph named Kelsey was dads BT. He always called her by her nickname...remember.' GG nodded and stared wide-eyed as her son continued. 'This is the first time I've laid eyes on her since we arrived...she was in her room all afternoon.'

'So if you've never met how do you know that our Kelsey is this brain trust?' Charlie asked at the same time as GG blabbed out, 'When did you meet her? Was I there?'

Bren sighed and chose to answer his mother first. 'No, you weren't. I guess its confession time. Dad organised a meeting with one of his client's – Chef Zac the head chef of the Sheraton, so I could get some pointers on what I needed to do to become a chef myself. He snuck me out of school for the day. We did it a couple of times this year, whenever he had appointments to see his restaurant clients. We didn't tell you because you woulda gone mad at us.'

'Were some of those places the Hyatt and Aviary?'

'Yeah, how'd you know? Oh, yeah right, dad would have said. He never could keep a secret from you. Anyway, Kelsey zoomed past us in the street one day and Dad told me who she was. He ran after her, they only spoke for a minute and she wrote something down for him. He was a bit distracted after that, like he got when he was planning one of his spy games.'

'But why has she got his phone?' said GG not yet quite ready to accept she had stuffed up.

'She was doing a job for him, and she doesn't have one of her own,' said Bren, stating the obvious.

Charlie felt a burden lift from his chest. He turned to Rosie and said, 'You and Mark go check the garage. If she's not there check the stables. I'll scout the surrounds and down by the river. We'll need Jimmy's help. He can mobilise the crew. Eli, go chase him up will you. Bren, if Kelsey comes back, keep her here and send up a flare.' Eli was already on his way out the screen door when Charlie called out, 'Oh and Eli, get Jimmy to send everyone out in pairs will ya.'

'Right, Dad,' said Eli. His pounding feet could be heard over the rain on the roof as he headed towards the married quarters where Jimmy and Naomi lived.

Charlie opened a cupboard and handed Mark a torch. He grabbed one for himself and rushed towards the door.

GG called out to him, 'Shit, Charlie. I'm so sorry for being such an idiot. Please find her safe.'

Chapter Thirty

Rosie snatched the torch from Mark's firm grasp and led the way. She set a harsh pace as they raced towards the vehicle shed. She was impressed that Bayden kept up. Yes, he was huffing and wheezing like he was in the throes of a full-blown asthma attack but he'd matched her loping stride and didn't falter. Rosie was angry and gave herself a mental dressing down. She should never have allowed Kelsey to rush away like that, but she had gotten so involved with the impressive meltdown Bull's sister had been having she'd taken her eye off the ball. And something to do with Gil had set off her spidey senses. Rosie got the impression he was playing a deep game and she intended to take a much closer look at him. Rosie was pretty confident she knew who she was hunting but she was just lacking that vital piece of evidence to confirm her suspicions. All would be good as long as the wrong person didn't know Kelsey was somewhere out here alone.

'I don't think we'll find her in the garage,' gasped Mark. 'Remember, she doesn't own a car or have a licence. I don't reckon she knows how to drive so I don't think a vehicle would be her first option.'

'You're probably right but we still have to check.'

Flipping on the light switch she scanned the garage. It was full of vehicles, but there was nothing to indicate a human presence.

Pointing left, Rosie said, 'Bayden you take that side. Check inside and underneath everything.'

'Yes boss,' panted her offsider.

She called softly, 'Kelsey, are you here? It's Rosie and Mark. It's okay to come out now. You're safe.' There was no reply. Not surprising thought Rosie. This would not be where I'd run to if I was scared, especially seeing the track leading up to the garage was unlit and the building seemed larger and more intimidating in the dark. Still not everyone thinks clearly when they're frightened, that's why so many people get themselves into dangerous situations.

Rosie flashed her light under a dark blue four-wheel drive. 'This is new, Bayden. I haven't seen this vehicle before.'

Mark glanced over, 'Must be the sister's.'

'Remind me to check when we get back to the house.'

'Sure boss.'

'How you going there, Bayden...find anything?'

'No...ah...maybe. I think there's an SUV missing.'

Rosie's heart gave a stutter. She straightened her back and hurried towards where Mark stood in a parking space occupied by a fresh clump of drying mud. She scanned the quiet shed, studying the remaining vehicles.

'Isn't this where one of the hands usually parks their private vehicle?'

'Yeah, boss. If I remember correctly, it was a silver cruiser.'

'Right...find out who owns it and where they've been tonight,' said Rosie. The silence around them spoke volumes. 'It's too quiet, she's not here, Bayden. Come on let's go check the stables.'

Jogging down the road heading towards the homestead, Rosie could see torch lights bobbing in the distance. A voice called out

Kelsey's name. It sounded like the station foreman, Jimmy. She altered her course and headed in that direction. As she approached a light veered off to the right and hurried towards the equipment shed.

She flashed her light towards the house and saw Jimmy crouched at the gate running his fingers along the damp ground.

'Hey Mac, got anything?'

He raised his head and squinted up at her.

'Detective,' he said as way of a greeting. 'I've got footprints heading towards the river.'

'Bull went that way'

'These aren't Bull's. Smallish, size seven, no shoes.'

A rifle cracked.

Everyone froze.

Chapter Thirty-One

Kelsey sat on a fallen tree. The bark was smooth and wet. She pulled her bare knees up to her chest and brushed away the mud clinging to her feet. A rustle under her arm made her realise she still had the bag with shoes clamped there. She opened the bag and dropped it on the ground while she pulled the white runners onto her feet. They fitted perfectly. Of course they did, they were hers – the ones she'd been wearing when she arrived at Mount Ibour Airport. She stared at the untied laces and sighed. The sound of the fast-running river began to soothe her frazzled nerves. She had no idea why Charlie's sister had been so angry with her. Kelsey was positive they had never met before. Bren on the other hand had evoked a strong resemblance to someone she loved and respected, her only friend in the whole world, her foster brother, Josh.

Memories came crashing in.

Kelsey had lived with Josh's family while she recovered from the injuries to her arm. He always treated her with respect and kindness and made her feel welcome. He'd even given her a funny nickname, BT. Short for brain's trust, because, he said, his most confidential secrets would be safer in her mind than on any old computer as she could never be hacked. As a joke she called him Lancelot because of his middle and last names. Lance Elliot. Josh had protected her from the school bullies who blighted her young life.

Mr and Mrs Elliot had been lovely too. They had tried so hard to keep her in their family, but the social services worker had ignored their pleas and sent her to a girl's home for the rest of her childhood.

After that Josh and Kelsey would see each other at school, but as Josh was four years older than her they didn't get to see each other very often. He left at the end of the next year to go to university. They'd touched base occasionally, but life moved on and over time they lost regular contact. Kelsey was away on a job overseas when he'd gotten married and again when he became a father, so she'd never had a chance to meet his family. They lost touch and then suddenly, there he was in the street asking her for her phone number so they could talk. And talk they had, catching up on all the missing years. Then had come the defining phone call – Josh really needed her help. A big fat tear rolled down her face. If Bren was his son, then according to Charlie, Josh Lance Elliot, her Lancelot, was dead.

Sighing she gathered the laces on her left shoe to tie them. A twig snapped and she leapt to her feet, her heart pounding in fright. She took a step backward towards the river almost tripping over her loose laces, held her breath and waited. A beam of light touched her face and she turned to run.

'Stop Kelsey, please don't run away. You shouldn't have taken off like that it's not safe,' said Charlie. His voice was harsh, he sounded angry.

Kelsey snorted, not safe! Was he for real? Hadn't he been in the same room as her when his precious sister had exploded in rage? She backed away a step then remembered him promising he would never hurt her. She decided to test that promise and to stand up for herself. Better now while there was room to run away.

'Well, it wasn't safe in the kitchen either.'

'Your reaction is understandable. Things seem to be getting out of hand around here.'

'I'm sorry, Charlie. I don't know what I've done to bring all this grief to your family. Please don't be angry with me, I couldn't stand for you to be angry too.'

The light moved closer. The soft wet leaves muffled Charlie's footsteps. For a big man he moved quietly.

'It's alright. There's just been a misunderstanding. GG is sorry she had that meltdown and scared you.'

Kelsey waited for a heartbeat, but he didn't explain, so she took the bull by the horns and asked, 'Is it because of Josh?'

'Josh? Well yes...tell me, how did you know him, do you re-member?'

'Yes, I remember. My memories are all starting to return.' She held her hand up to stop the light shining in her eyes.

'Sorry,' murmured Charlie, and switched the torch off. He moved closer.

She waited for him to join her at the river's edge. They stood side by side and stared out into the gloom and listened to the water.

When Charlie stirred she sighed and went on with her story. 'I lived with Josh and his parents for a year while I was recovering from my foster father's attack. Is he really dead?'

'Yes,' said Charlie, his grief was apparent in that one word. 'Didn't you know?'

'No. He asked me not to contact him because he didn't want anyone to know that we were working on a case. He told me it was necessary to keep me safe.'

'What case? What are you talking about?'

'I was doing a job for Josh. We had a system. He would ring me at work when no one was around and I would update him on the research I did on his behalf.'

'What was the job?' asked Charlie folding his arms across his chest.

'Last May, Josh rang me at work and asked to meet late that night in Queens Gardens. He gave me a flash drive which contained details of overseas bank accounts and business financial records. Josh asked me to do my whiz-bang stuff and check if there were any financial discrepancies. He also gave me a mobile phone to call me on. I was never to contact him. It needed to be that way for my own safety. It took me a couple of weeks as I could only work in the evenings and yes there was definitely something shonky going on. I told him I needed to see the real accounts and compare entries with paperwork to confirm the existence of an intricate syphoning system that had been built into the program. Josh said leave it with him and he'd organise something. Then one morning he rang and asked me to meet in Mount Ibour. He'd organised for me to go undercover as a book-keeper at Zentra Flats Station.'

'Why Slab Johnson's place?' asked Charlie turning sideways to get a better look at her face.

At that moment the soft rain stopped and the moon popped out from behind a cloud. A soft breeze ruffled his scruffy hair and she had the urge to run her fingers through the curls. Kelsey clasped her hands together resisting the urge, unsure of how their relationship stood. Charlie uncrossed his arms, reached down and took her hand. It was warm and comforting. She took heart and said, 'Last Christmas, while Josh and his family were here at Rivers Run, Mr Johnson rang him and asked if they could meet, evidently he was worried about the Zentra Flats finances. Had been for a while and as he knew Josh was an investigator for the tax department wanted some advice. Josh met and suggested an independent audit of the Station's books, so he could get a clear picture of what he was facing. Josh said he got a prickle of unease after their chat and he decided to do the rounds and have a chat with a couple of other graziers in the district. Most of them expressed the same sort of concerns about their economic situation.'

'Yeah, it's been a tough couple of years, what with the drought and the beef market being down...'

'And having what little income you have got coming in embezzled out from under you just makes it all the worse,' finished Kelsey.

'Embezzled?' said Charlie, his voice rose and echoed across the water.

'Yeah, embezzled. There's more I'm afraid, Charlie. I think there's something wrong with your accounts.'

Kelsey's statement was met with silence. She waited patiently for him to argue or even deny the possibility.

'It has to be that little weasel, Gil,' he growled. 'I've had a feeling something's been off for some time. If that bastard's cooked my books, I'll kill him.'

'Now I'm afraid this just won't do,' said an amused voice from behind Charlie's right shoulder. They both started and began to turn. 'No don't turn around.'

A rifle nozzle was shoved roughly behind Charlie's ear pushing his head forward. Kelsey froze and held her breath, praying that the finger on the trigger didn't twitch.

'What do you want?' asked Charlie, his voice cold and calm.

'How about we start with...oh everything! The station, the prestige and especially the royalties that will be coming in from the Zentra diamond mine.'

'And how do propose to achieve that?'

'Well now your sister's free to marry...'

'Over my dead body,' snarled Charlie.

'That wasn't the original plan...but okay.'

A woman's delighted laughter floated in on the air at the comment, startling Kelsey. Involuntarily her head moved as she tried to look behind her.

'Don't move!' said the gunman.

Kelsey froze. Charlie still had hold of her fingers. He squeezed them gently. Before she could return the gesture her arms were reefed behind her back.

'I think grazier Charlie Morgan and his new love interest are going to meet with a tragic accident.'

The gunman gave a vicious chuckle.

The fingers holding Kelsey's arms tightened and dug in. She tried hard not to react but a small yelp slipped from her lips and the hands got rougher.

'Here, Kitten, take these and tie him up.'

The strong fingers on Kelsey's arms let go and she received a hard shove in the centre of her back which forced her to her knees. Kelsey's hands shot forward and she managed to save herself from falling on her face.

'Anything to please you, lover,' purred a familiar voice.

Charlie slowly straightened his spine and turned around.

'I said, don't move,' Gil repeated, shoving the rifle against Kelsey's head.

Charlie froze.

Steve stepped into sight and ran her hand up Charlie's chest, tweaking the tuft of black hair that grew at the base of his throat. She gave a murmur of appreciation before stepping behind him. She reached around his waist and grabbed his wrists, rubbing her breast intimately against his back as she did so. Giving a sharp tug she pulled his arms back. Kelsey heard a cable tie zip and saw a slight twitch of Charlie's lip. Steve must have really secured his wrists tight. She prowled back into view and slung her arms around his neck and plastered her mouth over his. His back stiffened and he stared blankly ahead. She stepped back laughing.

'Really, Bull, you're just no fun.'

The rifle nozzle moved to a position under Kelsey's chin and pushed upward.

'Now you. Get up,' ordered Gil. Kelsey struggled to her feet. He stepped back moving the weapon to rest on his shoulder with the barrel pointing skyward and gave a self-satisfied chuckle. 'Ok, Kitten do the girl.' Charlie dropped his head and charged. Gil rapidly stepped back and flipped the butt of the rifle up. It smacked Charlie square in the forehead. He staggered backwards and fell into the river.

Chapter Thirty-Two

Kelsey watched in horror as Charlie lost his footing and tumbled down the sharp cut of river bank and landed flat on his back in the water. He didn't react, so he was either unconscious or dead.

Ignoring the danger to herself she sprang forward and dove in after him. The untied sneakers on her feet were dragged away by the fast moving water. As she surfaced from the depths she heard a sharp crack from the rifle followed by a yell.

'You bloody idiot Steve, you'll alert everyone and get us caught.'

The woman's vicious reply was indistinct because the strong current tugged Kelsey downstream. She struck out and swam with strong strokes towards where Charlie, his head barely above the surface, was rapidly sinking. With his hands tied behind his back, she knew Charlie wouldn't be able to swim and save himself. As she drew near he sank. Kelsey hastened her stroke and kept her gaze on the spot she'd last seen him. It only took moments to reach. Kelsey trod water, sucked in a huge lungful of air and duck dived into the water's inky depths. Cloudy water and darkness made visibility non-existent, so Kelsey waved her arms around in a frantic search. Her lungs began to burn and cry out for oxygen. She ignored them and swam deeper, repeating the arm waving procedure.

Why couldn't she find him?

The blood in her eardrums pounded, her chest threatened to suck in the cold Annie River in a desperate bid for oxygen. The need to breathe became vital. Kelsey lowered her legs to kick her way towards the surface and her foot bumped into something solid. She reached down and felt something soft almost silky, rippling with the current. Kelsey clutched a fistful of the threads and pulled as hard as she could. A bulk rose beside her. Taking a firmer grip she kicked hard and fast, hauling her find upwards towards the surface. As her face broke free from the water she gulped in a long shuddering breath. Her lungs screamed in relief and the burning sensation in her chest eased. She looked right. Charlie's inert form was beginning to sink again. Kelsey quickly reached over and cupped a hand under his chin and pulled him towards her, holding his mouth out of the water.

She trod water and checked his throat for a pulse. Her freezing fingers were so numb she couldn't really make out if there was a flutter of a heartbeat there or not. Panic and fear welled up from her gut bringing with it an overwhelming pain of loss. No, she couldn't give in to it, not yet. There has to be hope. Desperately, Kelsey peered around, trying to work out how to get them both to dry land. The shore line, a silhouette of tall trees, steep banks and silver moonlight, ghosted quickly past. The current was now pulling them rapidly downstream and she knew it would be too strong for her to swim against, especially while dragging Charlie's limp form.

She glanced over her left shoulder and saw they had nearly reached Annie Bridge. The centre span was weirdly shaped, almost as if a child had drawn criss-cross lines to represent the bridge. She squinted for a better look and almost laughed.

A scaffold decorated the outside of the bridge and Kelsey recalled
Eli mentioning Pod and Roscoe had erected the steel framework to
support the bridge while repairs were carried out. She turned her
body slightly so her hip supported Charlie and she hitched his face
further up out of the water to nestle on her shoulder. Using a side
stroke with her free hand and scissor kicking with her legs she angled
their trajectory to meet one of the fast approaching poles. The bridge
drew closer. Kelsey could feel her strength waning. The water was
cold. The chill seeped into her bones making her limbs ache. As the
current pushed her closer she held out her numb hand and tried to
grab a hold. Her fingers didn't get a good grip and the pole slipped
away. They spun and the river carried them under the bridge. She
kicked hard against the current and tried to line up with the next
pole. This was her last chance. If she missed they would be washed
downstream to who knows where. The post came up fast and she
concentrated on getting a good handhold. Her palm slapped the
metal and she clutched hard. This time her grip held. The pull of the
current jerked her shoulder in its socket as they came to a halt. The
water flowing past buffeted against her chest and splashed up into
her face and into her eyes. Kelsey anchored her leg around the post
and used it to draw them in close to the steel pole. Struggling against
the current Kelsey manoeuvred Charlie so he lay cradled against her
chest, his head propped up on her shoulder. She wrapped her left
leg around his torso and pinned him in place. With Charlie wedged
tight between herself and the pole, Kelsey worked her way around
so her back was to the current and clung to the pole like a limpet,
praying she had the strength to hang on until help could arrive.

Surely the gunshot had made someone in the homestead curious.
Kelsey peered down. Charlie's eyes were half open but seemed
glazed. A small trickle of blood ran down the centre of his forehead
and a large bruise had formed. She lowered her ear so it was close

to his mouth to listen for the sound of breathing. The gurgling and sucking noise of the river made it difficult and a large knot formed in her stomach. Kelsey gave him a gentle shake, 'Charlie...Charlie, come on speak to me.'

Charlie gave a small watery cough. She placed her lips over his for a moment. They were ice cold but moved in response to the kiss.

'Hang on buster, I don't dive into a cold river for just anyone you know, so don't go bugging out on me now,' she said, hoping to bring Charlie back to the surface of full consciousness. His lips flickered in a slight smile then his face went still.

Kelsey scanned the gloom, staring up at the bridge and sideways towards the bank. She tried to formulate a plan of escape. The situation was challenging as she was clutching an unconscious, muscle-bound, 100kg man with his hands fastened behind his back. She didn't have the physical strength to lift him out of the water.

'I'll get us out of here somehow,' she whispered.

Chapter Thirty-Three

'She's been here. This is the bag that had the shoes in it,' said Rosie bending down to examine the abandoned plastic bag lying next to a fallen tree trunk. She didn't touch it as it was evidence and she wasn't wearing gloves.

'There are scuff marks, here at the water's edge,' said Jimmy squatting down on his haunches to examine the disturbed ground by torchlight. 'Looks like one, no maybe two people have gone into the river.' He squinted closer at the marks before looking up. His face was creased with worry lines. 'This print here looks like the heel of Bull's boot. These others are smaller, a sneaker. With the current as strong as it is at the moment and the cold temperature of the water, their survival rate is not good. We need to find them – fast.'

Mark gave a loud grunt and with a folded handkerchief covering his hand, reached under a prickly bush. He gave a triumphant grin and held up a shell casing. 'Boss, does this look familiar.'

Rosie examined the shell casing clutched in his cloth covered fingers and nodded. Mark dug around in the large pocket on the leg of his cargo pants. With a triumphant grin he produced one of the many evidence bags he'd stored there. The bullet casing was very similar to the ones found at the site of the cattle slaughter. Rosie cursed under her breath. If only they had the bag of missing evidence. Damn it, luck was still being elusive.

A loud rustling echoed along the track they'd taken to get to the water's edge. Rosie's jujitsu training kicked in and she spun around to settle into a defensive stance. A low tree branch shook, showering them in moisture from the raindrops that had settled there in the last downpour. Eli stepped into the clearing and let the branch flip back into place. She relaxed and flashed her light on him. He cradled four battery-operated handheld spotlights.

'Everybody is out searching, Uncle Jimmy. Tangles, Pod and Mini have gone to scour the orchard. Roscoe and Darcy have taken one of the quad bikes and are checking the home paddock. Naomi has gone up to the homestead. She says she'll man the radio from there and keep an eye on Aunt GG. I saw Steve's car driving towards the highway when I went into the store to collect the spotlights. I'm not sure who's with her or if she's alone. I couldn't find Gil anywhere.'

'Goodo, thanks mate. Eli you're with me, we'll go downstream. We need to search the water and river bank. Detective, can you and Constable Bayden take a quick gander upstream? Check to see if our swimmers came out that way.' Rosie nodded at Jimmy's hurried request. It was important to cover as much ground as possible. 'Take care, detective there's footprints going that way that don't belong to Bull or Kelsey. Are you armed?' asked Jimmy.

Rosie's teeth flashed white with a smile that had once been described as feral. It had scared many a criminal into confessing. She patted her left hip where a leather holster was neatly strapped to her belt. 'Never leave home without it when there's a murderer on the prowl,' she said. 'You?'

Jimmy reached behind his back and drew out a long-barrelled pistol from the waistband of his jeans. He gave a cheeky grin. Rosie cocked her head and tried to hide an approving smile. She waved her forefinger at the competent and well-prepared foreman and said, 'Mac whatever you do, don't use it unless you have to. The paperwork's a bitch.'

His laughter rang out like a machine gun spraying bullets. He leant forward, gave Rosie a light buff on the shoulder before handing her one of the spotlights.

'Come on Eli, shake a leg. We need to find your dad pronto.'

Eli, teeth chattering in fright, shakily handed Mark a light and took off at a brisk gallop shining his torch along the water's edge and called out at the top of his voice, 'Dad, Kelsey.'

Jimmy turned to follow but Rosie laid a restraining hand on his arm.

'Mac if...no...when you find them alive, don't announce it on the radio.'

Jimmy's eyebrows meshed together in a puzzled frown.

'I'll explain later,' she said and spun around to follow the Annie River upstream.

'We need code...I know. If I find them I'll call for assistance from the Silver Dingo. If you find them announce yourself as Silver Dingo.'

Rosie glared at his retreating back. 'I hate that friggin' name.'

Chapter Thirty-Four

Kelsey's teeth clattered loudly and her limbs shook from the cold. It seemed like she'd been clinging to the damn pole for hours but in reality it was probably less than fifteen minutes. Still, that was long enough. She was more than ready to get out of the water. The clouds drifted away from the face of the moon and bright silver light spread its glory over the landscape providing enough luminosity for Kelsey to examine the scaffolding rising above her head. It looked solid and was well braced. The guys had drilled holes and secured the frame with bolts and clamps to the existing bridge structure to ensure stability. Nobody wanted to be standing or climbing on a wonky work platform over a fast moving river while they worked. If she'd been alone, Kelsey would have attempted to scale the scaffold but that was impossible with an unconscious Charlie cradled in her arms. She stared down at his face. It was marble white with the slightest dark tinge around the lips. His colouring worried her.

'Hey buster,' she said. 'It's time for you to wake up now. I need your help.'

A small moan escaped his lips. Well that was something. Kelsey tried again.

'Come on darling, wake up. I'm cold and want you to make me one of your wonderful coffees then carry me upstairs to your warm cosy bed.'

His lips moved but she couldn't hear the words so she put her ear against his lips to listen. He must have been dreaming because what he said didn't make sense.

'Can't...I'm in love with a desert nymph.'

She placed her lips on his forehead in a tender kiss before laying her cheek on his damp, black hair and stared out across the water.

A painful shudder racked her limbs as the cold sank deeper into her core. To distract herself she let her mind roam, recalling the nicer things that had been happening in her life of late – the delicious first kiss she'd shared with Charlie and the glow of passion and desire it had ignited within her. Her toes curled at the memory of the feelings it had evoked. What else? The warming moment Naomi had called her *Tidda*. The sense of belonging that had given her was wonderful. Kelsey had never really belonged anywhere before. And then there was Eli, with his bright chatter and easy acceptance of her as a friend. Sweet, talkative Eli, relating fun details of his family history, how great it was to live on a Kimberley cattle station and of all the creatures she was likely to encounter. She flicked through the list he'd reeled off – cattle and horses, a raft of native fauna he'd thought she'd like to draw, like brolgas, goannas, kangaroos and emus. She smiled as she remembered how long his list had been. Her mind scrolled thorough them and conjured up images of each one. One image came to mind and the smile left her face. She almost forgot to breathe as fear began to coarse through her veins. Creatures of the far north-west of Western Australia....oh bloody hell, they were in the Kimberley weren't they, and here she was in the waters of the Kimberley where there were friggin' *crocodiles*!

Her heart gave a mighty bang against her rig cage like it was trying to escape her chest. She lifted her head and scanned the surface of the water surrounding them. Something glinted to her left. It highlighted the ripples on the surface before moving away. She stared hard at the spot and it happened again.

Was that a crocodile or was someone flashing a light?

Uncertain she eyeballed the shore, frantically scanning the bank, praying someone was there. Suddenly, two bright domes of warm, yellow light appeared and bobbed along the walking track. One beam searched under the shrubs growing along the river's edge, another was being directed across the water. Every now and then the light was directed towards the middle of the river to slowly skim the surface. It had to have been this she'd seen not a dreaded reptile. Kelsey tried to cry out but all that emitted from her throat was a weak and insipid croak.

Not good.

She filled her lungs with air and did something she had only ever read about in books.

'Cooee.'

Her voice rang out and echoed across the water's surface, loud and solid. It seemed to reach the tree tops. The lights on the bank stopped moving and flashed in her direction. One skimmed across her face, moved away before returning to hold steady.

'Kelsey, its Mac. Hang on, love, I'm coming for you.'

She heard a pounding of feet on the bridge above and voices resounded clearly through the night. She stared up at a clatter on the scaffold above her head. Jimmy, his feet bare, was swiftly climbing along the metal struts with his torch looped around his neck by a cord. The light swayed from side to side with every movement. When he reached them he paused, hooked a leg around a rail and hung down holding out his hand.

'Take my hand, I'll pull you up.'

'I can't, Mac, I've got them wrapped around the pole so I don't lose Charlie.'

'Shit,' said Jimmy. He grabbed his torch and directed the beam to light up the bundle cradled to her chest. 'Bull you still alive, mate?'

Kelsey nodded vigorously, 'He was a couple of minutes ago.'

'Can you pass me his hand? Then you can climb up.'

'Can't...they're tied behind his back.'

Her comment was met with silence.

'Eli...' Jimmy yelled, scaring almost half a year's life from her with its volume. A light appeared on the bridge above. 'They are both here and *alive*. I need rope, harnesses and blankets. Fetch the rappelling gear in the zip line kit from the equipment shed, will ya.'

'Okay, Uncle Jimmy,' yelled Eli. 'Hold tight, I'll be quick.'

Jimmy reached down and with a rough calloused hand brushed the back of Kelsey's head in a gentle caress.

'How you doing there, *Tidda*?'

'I'm fine, Mac. Don't suppose you could turn the heating up on the jacuzzi could you? It's a tad cold.' Kelsey's teeth gave a loud rattle causing her words to come out in a jerky stutter.

'Nah sorry, forgot to pay the heating bill,' said Jimmy, making her chuckle. 'You hang tight, it's only for a little while longer. I promise to get you out as quick as I can.'

'I'll do my best, Mac but it's not easy.'

'I'm gonna make you a bit more secure by looping my trouser belt around your waist and tying you off to the post. I don't want you slipping away on me. While I'm doing that can you tell me why Bull's sulking and not talking to me?'

Kelsey stuttered out a quick explanation. 'The hit to his forehead made an awful crunch when the butt of the gun slammed into it. Charlie tumbled arse first into the river. I got to him as quick as I could, but he spent a long time under the water. He's been semi-conscious ever since and not everything he says makes sense. He's been babbling about desert nymphs.'

There was a flurry of activity above, halting her words. A vehicle screeched to a standstill. Three heads, the faces cast in shadow by the vehicle's headlights, leant over the edge of the railing and stared down at them.

'Sorry, love, I'm going to have to leave you for a moment. I need to go get hooked up then I'm coming for you both. I'll be quick, I promise,' said Jimmy. 'Will you still be here when I get back?'

She was feeling slightly more secure with Mac's belt holding them in place. 'Yeah, Mac, I don't have any pressing appointments at the moment – I'll wait,' she quipped.

Jimmy gave an amused chuckle. 'Good girl.' With a final warm caress to her cheek he clambered away, making the climb to the top look easy. The warmth of his hand on her face faded and even though hope bloomed in her chest she was fearful that something would go wrong. Could she hang on? The shakes were getting worse and she could no longer feel her hands or feet. Even as she thought it, her fingers slipped and the current pushed them forward. Her face smacked against the post, dazing her and the current caused them to spin around the pole. Thank God for the belt anchoring them, it stopped the river from snatching them away. Floundering against the fast-moving water she managed to get her numb fingers working and grasped the pole again. Unfortunately, now they were face on in the current, the buffeting and pulling against her shoulder joints was sapping the last of her strength.

'Please hurry, Mac. I'm not going to last much longer,' she sobbed.

There was a loud splash on her right. Kelsey screamed in fright and let go. A warm arm wrapped around her waist and drew her into a tight comforting embrace.

'Told you I'd be quick,' said Jimmy with a cheeky grin. She looked up into his dusty green eyes and called him a name. He roared with laughter and grabbed one of the two harnesses dangling at the end of a rope beside him. He fiddled around under the water, first feeding her legs through the strapping and then her arms. 'I'm going to take Bull from you. All you have to do is hold on to the rope as best you can. Eli, Rosie and Mark will do all the work and haul you up.'

Kelsey nodded. Jimmy did some sort of manoeuvre and suddenly her load disappeared and she was being held against his side with one of his arms around her waist.

'Ready?' he asked and let rip an ear-piercing whistle before she could answer him.

Her rope tightened and in a rush she rose out of the river. The water cascaded from her sodden clothing like a waterfall and rained down on the men below. Within seconds, hands so warm they were painful, pulled her over the lip of the bridge. She lay in a wet puddle on the bitumen surface trembling. From the corner of her eye she saw Mark and Eli drop the rope they'd used to haul her up and begin tugging on a second one. Rosie came running towards her from the vehicle and encased her in a thick dry blanket. Kelsey tried to sit up and draw the folds closer around herself but her body wouldn't co-operate. Rosie sat on the ground next to her and physically lifted her into her lap. She wrapped her arms and legs around Kelsey's body and rubbed her hands vigorously all over her limbs. The action caused a small flicker of warmth in her upper arms. It quickly became a tingle and began to spread to the rest of her body. It felt wonderful.

There was a loud plop and Charlie, wet and inert, was also on the bridge. Mark dropped the rope and started the body warming process that Rosie had used on Kelsey. Jimmy clambered over the railing and stood, water dripping everywhere, with his arm around Eli's shoulder watching intently. Mark rubbed vigorously and Charlie gave a groan. That was enough for Jimmy. He leant forward and said, 'Come on Bull get your lazy arse up.'

Kelsey's heart skipped a beat when Charlie croaked, 'Quit ya hollering, Mac.' His voice was weak and shaky but the words were clear. 'Where's Kelsey? She safe?'

'Yeah mate, she's safe. No thanks to you, I might add. She sure saved your sorry arse.'

'Where is she?'

'I'm here,' said Kelsey and crawled from the warmth of Rosie's embrace, over to the prone man. Charlie flung out an arm and wiggled his fingers. She put her hand in his and closed her fingers tight around his hand.

Eli sank to his knee and put his face on his father's chest. 'You okay dad?' he asked in a choked voice.

'Yeah mate. Bit cold is all.'

'Eli, get the vehicle fired up and heater on. Mark, give us a hand with Bull. He needs to get into the warmth. Rosie, you right to help Kelsey?' said Jimmy.

'Yeah Mac,' answered Rosie.

With the help of her friend, Kelsey staggered to her feet on rubbery legs and stumbled towards the vehicle. Sliding into the driver's seat she gratefully held her hands to the vents and grimaced through the pain as warm blood began forcing its way through her freezing limbs. Charlie sat next to her groaning in pleasure as he too began to warm up.

'Why's my bloody head hurt?' he growled.

'Because Gil belted you with a rifle butt,' murmured Kelsey.

'Bastard.'

Eli, jammed in close to his father in the passenger seat, stared at her goggle-eyed. 'No way. Why'd he do that?'

Before Kelsey could reply the door next to her flew open.

'Right,' said Rosie. 'Let's get you both up to the house. You need dry clothes and hot food.' She glanced over her shoulder and said, 'That includes you Mac. Whatever possessed you to jump off the bridge like that?'

Mac gave her a crooked smile and said, 'Kelsey was at the end of her tether...'

'Humph,' snorted Rosie.

'It was okay,' said Mark placing a gentle hand on her shoulder. 'Eli and I had a rope and harness on him.'

'And I'd have never let him go,' said Eli. 'He hasn't paid me my wages this week.'

Jimmy roared with laughter.

Chapter Thirty-Five

Rosie listened to Jimmy radio the crew, calling them into the home-stead kitchen. Everyone responded except for Steve and Gil.

'Try again, Mac. I want everyone in, so we can sort this mess out.'

Jimmy nodded. 'Young, Connors this is Big Mac, report!'

The radio remained silent.

'Nothing Dingo.'

'Don't friggin' call me that,' snarled Rosie at the grinning fore-man. 'Bayden, get on the blower. Call the station and get the sarge to put a rush on the background checks for Gil Connors and Steve Young, and get him to send someone out to keep an eye on the highway in case they've done a runner. Oh and Bayden, get a search warrant. Mac, I don't want anyone going into their rooms until I've had a chance to investigate. Put a bloody padlock on the door if you have to.'

She stomped out of the kitchen and into the lounge to stare at the couple snuggled in warm blankets and sipping from mugs of hot tomato soup. They sat side by side on the comfortable looking leather couch. Both had showered and were in dry clothes. GG sat next to Kelsey and held one of her hands. There was a peaceful look on her face that had been missing earlier in the day. Rosie studied Kelsey's face, the colour had returned and she was a healthy pink but Charlie still looked a bit pale. A large purple bruise had developed above his eyebrows. Maybe the paleness of his colour was highlighted because of his tanned skin but it worried her. Eli and Bren had settled their teenage butts side by side on the coffee table in front of the pair and were talking up a storm. The excitement of all the drama still fizzed in their bloodstream and they were analysing each event with boyish enthusiasm.

Naomi cuffed them both lovingly under the ear. 'Hush up you chattering butcherbirds.'

The boys paused for breath and Rosie took advantage.

'You sure you're okay, Bull? I can call in the flying doctor,' she said.

'No, no doctor. Swallowing a couple of litres of Annie River isn't gonna hurt me. What about you, Platypus – want a doctor?' asked Charlie. A crooked grin creased his right cheek and a very sexy dimple appeared. To Rosie's amusement, Kelsey blushed at the endearment while giving Charlie a puzzled look. 'They hang out in rivers under bridges,' he continued with an amused chuckle.

Kelsey gave a small smile and snuggled a bit deeper into her blanket. 'No, no doctor – it's nice just to be warm again.'

'No fair dad, I've already named Kelsey...'

'Nah cuz, Dad named her Brains Trust...' said Bren, shaking his head and brushing his floppy fringe away from his face.

'Brains Trust? You want to explain that one to us, Pus?' asked Charlie.

Rosie watched the joy leave Kelsey's face. She was about to intervene, give the woman time to decide whether to reveal her true abilities or not, but Kelsey forestalled her.

'Lancelot – sorry GG,' said Kelsey giving the woman next to her a timid glance, 'I mean Josh. He nicknamed me BT because I have what the specialist described as HSAM.' A puzzled expression passed over everyone's face. Kelsey straightened her spine and sat forward. She stared directly into Charlie's eyes. Rosie saw her take a deep breath before continuing with a rush, 'Highly Superior Auto-biographical Memory – a photographic memory. I can recall past events, images, numbers and dates in great detail – well usually I can. The old brain box has been a bit on the fritz lately. For example, I can tell you that I ate an apple for lunch on Saturday April 19th, 2014. It was the 109th day of the year of the Gregorian calendar and there were 256 days remaining until the end of the year. The time of my first bite was 1.04 and 32seconds.'

'Cool,' exclaimed both boys in a long drawn-out syllable. Their eyes were stretched wide and mouths formed into a circle.

Charlie began to roar with laughter. Rosie saw pain crease a rivet in the corner of Kelsey's eyes before she dropped her gaze to the mug clasped in her hand. Anger surged in her chest. Rosie had thought Bull was a better man than this – to laugh at this brilliant woman's gift was unkind.

'Bull,' she snarled.

'What?' said Charlie, tilting his head up to stare at her.

She nodded towards Kelsey. His gaze flicked to the woman who sat beside him. Still chuckling he reached forward and lifted her chin with the knuckle of his forefinger, so she had to look at him. 'I wasn't laughing at you sweetheart – it's the boys!'

'What about the boys?' Kelsey whispered.

'Their future is so cooked – they'll never get away with anything ever again.' And he roared with laughter at their united, 'Awe Dad, Uncle Charlie.'

Rosie watched satisfied, as the realisation of their easy acceptance sank into Kelsey. Her face began to glow. It shone with love and contentment. Rosie hated to intrude on the moment but she had two criminals to apprehend.

'Okay you lot stay here. I'm going to have a word with your crew. See if we can sort this mess out. Mark's organising a road block, if Steve and Gil have left the property, they won't get too far.'

'That's one unhealthy relationship,' murmured Charlie.

'Sure is. I've suspected for a while that there was something going on with those two, I mean full-time flirts ignoring each other like that – *please*.' She crossed her arms and rocked back on her heels.

'You didn't seem surprised when we told you who it was that attacked us,' said Kelsey.

'No – but to show their hand like that was a stupid move on their part. I've got a suspicion Steve knows something about the backpacker who went missing from Kelly Creek Roadhouse. She was very evasive about that whole trip to Broome.'

'What trip?'

'The one you and Eli took when you had the contract meeting with Downey Babcock Exploration.'

'How'd you know about that?'

'Steve told me.'

'How'd she know? I sent her home before Eli and I went to that meeting.'

'Well, she didn't go – I suspect her and Gil met up somewhere.'

'Nari,' said Kelsey, suddenly. 'Nari worked for Downey Babcock Exploration in their Broome office.'

'Did she now?' murmured Rosie, folding her arms and tilting her head to the right as she stared at Kelsey.

'Yeah, she mentioned it when we were chatting in the car from the airport. Nari told me she was on leave from her job as a contracts clerk at DBE and the reason she was collecting me from the airport was because Slab Johnson had asked her boyfriend, Gil, to do it but he was tied up at work. She hoped I didn't mind. We were to swing by his place and have a cup of tea and wait – he'd collect me from there and take me out to Zentra Flats Station. It confused me because I thought my arrival was a secret and Lancelot was going to take me to meet Mr Johnson.'

'But Josh was dead, had been for months,' said GG. 'How could he organise to meet you?'

'I didn't know. We had made the arrangements ages ago...late May...when he gave me his phone. He did that so nothing could be traced back to me. I was never to contact him, he always rang me. My working at Zentra Flats Station was supposed to be a secret.'

'Zentra Flats keeps coming up. Give me five minutes I think I need to give Hector 'Slab' Johnson a call and have a chat,' said Rosie dashing from the room into the study.

Her conversation with Slab, as he insisted Rosie call him, went on for ages.

'Well that was interesting,' she said, strolling back into the lounge, hands in pockets as she mulled over all that she learnt on the telephone. 'Slab Johnson reckons he didn't know you were coming.'

'I sent him an email with my flight details.'

'Believe it or not, Slab doesn't use a computer. He has a reliable admin clerk and book-keeper by the name of Gil Connors who takes care of all his admin stuff so he has less to worry about. He did admit to ringing Josh Elliot last Christmas with some concerns that Josh promised to look into. He forgot about it as it wasn't long after that Gil introduced him to Steve and they fell into a relationship. He couldn't believe his luck that she'd fall for an old codger like him but it seems she took a great deal of interest in him and his doings,' said Rosie shaking her head. 'Poor besotted man's going to be heartbroken when he finds out she was just spying on him.' She gave the boys a gentle shove to move them off the coffee table and took their seat for herself. She crossed her arms and legs and stared enquiringly into Kelsey's brilliant green eyes. 'Tell me what happened after Nari picked you up from Mount Ibour Airport.'

'It was really hot and I was sweating. Nari cranked up the air-conditioning and handed me an unopened bottle of water. We talked about Broome, how much she liked living there. My eyelids grew very heavy and I was struggling to stay awake. The next thing I remember was waking up in the cargo area of a four-wheel-drive. The vehicle was stationery. There was a bright pink sports bag and my satchel lying next to me. It was dark outside.' Kelsey stopped speaking, cast a glance at Naomi and the boys, flicked a look at Charlie before returning her gaze to Rosie.

'Keep going.' Rosie reached over to clasp one of Kelsey's knees and gave it a gentle squeeze of encouragement.

'I could hear a voice outside the vehicle. It was a woman. She said that this was a good place. She'd used it before. The back door was flung open. Gil was looking over his shoulder grinning. He didn't even look at me as he leant forward and tugged on the handle of the bag. It slid over the tailgate and fell to the ground with a thud. He dragged it over to a waiting Steve and I saw her in the torchlight begin to unzip it. Gil blocked my view as he returned to the car. He grabbed my ankles, one by one and pulled my shoes from my feet. He turned laughing and tossed them at Steve yelling, "Catch". Steve had this ghastly smile on her face.' Kelsey gave a small dry retch and took a hurried breath, 'She was stroking Nari's dead face and crooning, "Oh my pretty we had such fun – such a shame you missed most of it". That woman is sick. I wasn't going to wait around to see what they had in mind for me. I rolled out of the car, knocked Gil aside and began to run. Steve yelled and gave chase. She caught me and managed to get a hand around my throat. Her intention was obvious when she began to squeeze. I lifted my leg and did something I'd learnt when fending off my stepfather – I kicked her in the stomach. I took off running, managed five long strides and then nothing. The ground under me disappeared and I was falling. I landed hard on my back – just as the world was fading I saw Steve lit up by torchlight looking down the shaft at me. I think she wanted me to see her face as she laughed and said, "Mind the last step, it's a real killer". I blacked out.'

The ticking of the grandfather clock down the hall was the only noise in the room.

Eli rushed forward and flung his arms around Kelsey, nearly knocking Rosie from her perch on the table in his rush. A muffled voice came from his shoulder, 'It's alright, Champ. I'm safe, your Dad's safe, we're all safe. Detective Bloom is going to put a stop to all this. Then we can go back to our normal lives.'

Charlie leant over and whispered something to the hugging pair. Eli's grip eased and he said, 'I love you, Kelsey.'

Kelsey freed her hand from GG's and stroked the back of his head. 'And I love you too, Champ. Now do me a favour and go and look in the clock.'

Eli pulled back in surprise and dashed from the room, closely followed by Bren. Rosie stared at her in surprise.

'You need evidence, Rosie. I have a memory stick which lists embezzlement activities and overseas bank accounts and passwords that track back to Gil,' said Kelsey. She looked up at Charlie, 'With it we should be able to get everyone's money back.'

'Was the memory stick in your book?' asked Rosie. Kelsey nodded. 'I thought the painkiller ploy was a bit off.'

'I couldn't give it to you in front of Gil,' murmured Kelsey.

'Yeah, well I think he might have noticed and that was why he went looking for you at the river.'

The boys dashed back in the room clutching a small red object. Kelsey pointed to Rosie and Bren handed it over. Eli leant over the back of the couch and hugged Charlie and Kelsey.

Rosie placed her hands on her knees, pushed to her feet. 'Thank you Kelsey. It's good to have something tangible to hold Gil on. Now I can see things are about to get sloppy so I'm off to catch some criminals. Bull, keep your family in the house, where it's safe. I wouldn't put it past those two to double back. I'll let you know when I have them in custody.'

Naomi followed Rosie into the kitchen where the stock hands were milling around with mugs of hot drinks clasped in their hands, curiosity the main feature on their faces.

A young woman, her belly button stud exposed was talking with a short dark-haired girl in fancy cowboy boots. 'This is a nice room. I wonder what the rest of the house is like.'

'Didn't you have a sticky beak when you were up here the other day, Darcy?'

'You must be mistaken, Mimi. This is the first time I've been in the homestead.'

'Sit down you lot and stop cluttering up the room. The detective here wants a quick word with you all before you bugger off to your beds,' growled Naomi.

Everyone rushed to obey. Rosie gave an internal smirk. Naomi would make a great drill sergeant. She certainly had this lot under control.

When everyone had settled at the table Rosie took her time to study each face. Darcy with her dirty-blonde hair clipped into an untidy heap on the top of her head began to fidget under Rosie's intense scrutiny. She moved closer to the long-haired and scraggly bearded, Roscoe who was slouched in a chair beside her, as if seeking protection. Roscoe met her gaze with a steady one of his own. Patience etched small lines around his chocolate-brown eyes. Tangles sat on the other side of Darcy with his arms folded across his chest and ignored her gaze – he was conducting a study of his own. His bright eyes were narrow as they flitted from face to face. A chair scraped the floor as the man directly opposite him shuffled himself into a better position. He was thin and willowy, with a flared nose and ebony skin. So, this was Pod who spent a lot of time with cute little Mimi. I bet there's something going on between those two! As if to confirm the thought as it passed through Rosie's mind, Pod put his arm around the shoulders of the young, fit looking woman beside him and drew her in close to his side. She gave a timid smile and lowered her gaze to her lap. A blush touched her honey-coloured cheeks. Rosie looked up at Jimmy and Naomi who stood holding hands in front of the kitchen door and gave them a polite nod.

'Bayden, where's that file,' she yelled.

Everyone at the table jumped in fright. A small smile touched Jimmy's lips before he rearranged his face to mask the amusement. Mark stepped into the room, his polished boots shining and a bland, unfazed expression on his face. He handed her a manila folder.

Assured she had everyone's attention Rosie didn't pull any punches. She was in a rush and needed a few details confirmed.

'Does anyone know where Steve or Gil are?' Everyone shook their head. 'No...well, tonight Bull Morgan was attacked. He was knocked unconscious and pushed into Annie River.'

Rosie studied the faces around the table. The shock was real and unfeigned. It satisfied her.

Darcy sat forward, tears pouring down her cheeks. 'Is...is... is he okay?' she sobbed.

Rosie didn't answer her question, instead asking one of her own. 'When you were at the stables, Darcy, on the day Kelsey Delaney was attacked, did you see anyone?'

'Not really...'

'What does 'not really' mean?'

The girl took a shuddering breath. 'Well, I thought I saw God's gift rushing into Steve's room, but there was nothing unusual about that.'

'God's gift?' asked Rosie.

'Gil Connors. He thinks he's some sort of stud muffin and women should fall down with their legs open for him anytime he clicks his fingers. He gives me the creeps.' She gave a shudder and rubbed her hands up and down her forearms as though she was cold. 'Him and Steve are always sneaking away for a root. They're a good pair actually. She's kinda wired wrong as well.'

The men at the table stared at Darcy in amazement. Mimi just nodded her head in agreement.

'How do you know they were rooting,' asked Roscoe, his wild grey flecked eyebrows lifted so high on his forehead they almost melded with his hairline.

'Oh *please*, you could smell it on them whenever he was here,' snorted Darcy. 'At least Mimi and Pod take a swim afterwards.' Mimi's face turned bright red.

'Hmmm...,' said Rosie.

'Tell me, Darcy, why did you remove the battery from the smoke detector?' asked Jimmy.

Darcy's head swung around and she stuttered in fright at him, 'W...w...what?'

'Oh come on, *Bunji*,' said Naomi with a smirk at her husband. 'We all know Darcy has a huge crush on the boss. She was so jealous when he gave the detective a hand through the mud she almost turned green.'

'Well, we might forgive you the smoke detector, Darcy, but not the snake on Kelsey's bed. That's a whole different level of jealousy.'

'S...s...snake, what snake? I don't like snakes.'

'No, that's true,' said Mimi. 'Darcy squeals like a banshee if anything rustles in the bush. It gets very tiring.'

'When'd dis happen?' asked Pod.

'Poker night, we think,' said Jimmy.

'I saw Steve heading dis way carrying a small bag, when I stole away from da game for a smoke. Sorry, Love,' said Pod in an aside to Mimi. 'You tawt I'd stopped, but sometimes the urge just gets me. Anyway, I didn't tink it odd. Tawt she was heading for a bit of slap and tickle with the Bull.'

'Why?' asked Rosie.

'Day is engaged.'

'No they're not,' said Darcy in anger.

Pod raised his eyebrows and smirked. 'Jealous?'

'How is Bull?' asked Tangles, his face white and stress lines around his eyes. 'Is he okay?'

His question seemed to sober everyone. Rosie decided to ease the burden that Tangles was carrying. The poor lad had been through enough.

'Bull's a very lucky man – the young woman who walked out of the desert last week dived into the river and rescued him from drowning. She kept him safe until we could pull them out.' The tension around the table eased. Rosie ramped it up again. 'I need some straight answers from you lot. First, have any of you ever seen this woman?' She held the photo of Annalisa Wagner aloft so all could see. 'She went missing from Kelly Creek Roadhouse. You may have heard about it on the news. To jog your memories – Steve drove Bull and Eli to Broome to catch a plane to Perth.' The photo was passed around the table and everyone shook their heads.

'Tell me who was around and what was happening on the station that week?'

Pod sat forward and said, 'Mac and Naomi were away dat week. I 'member Cookie had a drinking binge. Darcy here, she on work experience, she cook us hamburger and vegemite sandwiches for tucker.' Laughter erupted in the group.

'And what's wrong with that?' asked Darcy, an embarrassed look on her face.

'No-ting,' said Pod. 'Just different is all. I act the foreman dat week. Steve, she drive Bull an young Eli to Broome. She s'pose to come straight back but was two days late. She ring, left a message so we no send a search party. Said she doin' job for Bull. It her turn to drive for the weekend pub run. I do dat instead but had to cut the weekend short. We only go for Friday night not all weekend as I couldn't leave da station un'tended.' Everyone began nodding as they remembered.

'That's right, the bowls club was running a carnival that Saturday arvo with five hundred bucks prize money. I was really looking forward to it, but then I had to pull out of my team. I was gutted because the buggers won,' drawled Roscoe. Everyone stared at the scrawny, untidy man in surprise. 'What? I love me bowls – it's a great game.'

Pod's lip tilted up in amusement. 'Dat Steve, she didn't get back until late arvo, Sunday.'

Roscoe nodded, 'Yeah, I remember. She was all flushed and excited and took off again not long after she got back. She rushed past me with a backpack in her hand. She was a bit jumpy when I asked where she was off to. She said she was heading into Mount Ibour for the night. I told her not to be late for work next morning.'

Pod looked at Jimmy standing across the room and said, 'Hope I did right lettin' her go like dat, Mac. She reckon Bull okay it.'

Jimmy nodded but remained silent.

'Probably going to shack up with God's gift for the night,' said Darcy, her nose wrinkling in distaste.

'What colour was the backpack?' asked Rosie.

'The usual, army green,' said Roscoe.

'Was there anything distinguishing about it?'

'Dist... what?' asked Pod.

'Distinguishing, like did it have bright buttons or badges or even a name sewn on it...'

'I didn't pay any attention,' replied Roscoe.

'What about you, Pod,' asked Rosie. 'Did you notice if she had the pack with her when she returned from Broome?'

'She carried sometink green, but I was more cross she was goin g'nst my aut'ority. You know what she's like Mac, acts as if she owns da place. I had to be careful 'cause if she marries Bull my job will be toast.'

Rosie decided to push on. Time was tight and the conversation was diverging.

'Anyone know this girl?'

Tangles closed his eyes momentarily as she held aloft Britt's image.

'That's your cousin isn't it, mate?' murmured Roscoe, taking the photo gently from Rosie's hand and eye-balling the image before passing it on to Darcy. His voice was deep and rumbled from his throat like boulders rolling down a hill.

Tangles nodded but said nothing.

'She's so beautiful. Is she back in town yet? Maybe we can all go out for a beer, next time we're in Mount Ibour,' said Darcy in a bright chirpy voice that was out of place to the events going on. Rosie began to suspect that not a lot went on between her ears, though she had been pretty perceptive about the relationship between Gil and Steve.

'She's dead,' said Rosie, bluntly. 'We found her remains and those of two other women in the well on Heartbreak Hill.' Darcy's mouth fell open and her eyes pooled with tears. Not waiting for her to succumb to another crying jag, Rosie continued, 'Does anyone remember ever seeing Britt in Mount Ibour? She arrived in June 2018 and was picked up by someone at the airport.'

'No, we've been over this heaps of times with Tangles,' said Mimi. 'We even took time out of our weekends in town to poke around for him, but came up with nothing.'

'Alright, does anyone recognise this necklace?' Rosie held up the photo of the gold cross.

Mimi's fingers rose to her throat. 'That looks like mine,' she whispered. 'Were did you find it?'

'In the very clean, rear compartment of the station's RAV4,' answered Rosie.

Mimi stared at Pod. He nodded like he was giving consent. Mimi took a deep breath and said, 'About a month ago, Pod and I got married...'

'Oh...'exclaimed Darcy clapping her hands in delight.

'But Pod's family don't approve of me, so we've kept it secret. For our wedding night we borrowed the RAV4 and spent the evening together at Red Rock watering hole. Pod cleaned it up real nice beforehand for us and we decked it out with the doona...'

'Okay I don't want the details, thanks,' said Rosie pleased that two questions had just been cleared up satisfactorily.

* * *

The phone in the study rang and Rosie sent Mark to answer it. When he returned he said it had been Sergeant George to let them know a road block was in place disguised as a random breath testing stop so as not to raise any suspicion. So far there had been no sign of Steve and Gil. She couldn't just sit around and wait so Rosie threw Bayden the keys to the police cruiser.

'Come on constable, we need to take a run along the highway.'

As the vehicle sped along the bitumen road, Rosie asked, 'Bayden, did anything the crew say jar with you? Or did everything match the social chitchat you've had with them?'

'It matched, boss. That Darcy's just a silly girl and I don't reckon she had anything to do with the attacks on Kelsey.'

'No, I have a fair idea who hit her. As for the snake that is something right up Steve's alley don't you think? Sneaky and vindictive.'

'Yeah,' said Mark.

Native wildlife scattered to the side of the road as the police cruiser, with its blue lights flashing, rushed along the highway. Rosie had to admit that Bayden was a good driver. She eyeballed the side of the road looking for signs of a vehicle.

'Something's going on up front, Boss.'

The darkness ahead was cut by the glow of lights. A four-wheel drive was parked at an odd angle on the highway. A large mound lay in the middle of the road. As they drew closer two people, highlighted in the vehicle's headlights, started wrestling over something. Before Rosie could tell Mark to take care he eased back on the accelerator. Their vehicle glided to a halt. As Rosie opened her door a gunshot rang out. She ducked behind her door, drew her weapon and shot a concerned gaze at Bayden to check he was okay. The constable was slumped low in his seat.

'You okay, Mark?'

'Yeah, Boss. I don't think the shot was aimed at us. I'm looking at the dash-cam monitor and there's someone on the ground in front of the crashed vehicle.'

'Well get on the radio and call for back up – and an ambulance,' said Rosie, and with her weapon drawn she stepped away from the vehicle yelling, 'Get on the ground with your hands behind your head.'

Chapter Thirty-Six

Rosie and Bayden guided the handcuffed prisoner to the interview room. Rosie flicked a switch on the panel outside the room to start the video and audio recording system before opening the door. It wasn't the most attractive room in the police station but it was functional and suited their needs. The room was sparsely furnished – a sturdy table and four hard-backed metal chairs were bolted to the cement floor. Video cameras and fluorescent lights adorned a bright white ceiling and a large clock ticked the minutes by on a wall that some colour challenged designer had painted duck-blue. A small white cupboard had been bolted to the wall above the table, its doors removed and replaced with a lockable, shatter-proof sliding glass panels that protected the voice and video recorder housed behind them from being tampered with by undisciplined guests. It was hot and stuffy, and this combined with the stale sweat left by a previous tenant tickled Rosie's nose and left an unpleasant taste in the back of her throat. Her shirt clung to the beads of sweat along her spine. She ignored the uncomfortable atmosphere and pointed to a chair on the far side of the table.

Bayden settled the prisoner onto the seat. The wall next to the prisoner's chair was chipped and scarred where the nervous fingernails of previous salubrious guests had picked away at the plaster and pulled tufts of sound proofing material through the holes.

Mark unfastened the handcuff from one of the prisoner's wrist and relatched it to a metal loop welded on the side of the chair. The prisoner now only had the full use of one hand. It paid to be cautious.

Sergeant George sauntered into the room. His polished black boots glowed in the harsh fluorescence thrown out by the ceiling lights. He handed Rosie a sheaf of papers, placed three disposable cups of water on the table, one in front of the prisoner and murmured, 'Sorry about the heat. The aircon's broken.'

She looked up at the wall mounted air-conditioner. It had an out-of-service tag sticky taped over the vent. She shrugged and slipped her half-moon glasses on to her nose and began to peruse the pages in her hand. It was the background check she'd asked for. Mark handed him a plastic wrapped rifle and the evidence bags containing spent shells and bullets they'd found hidden under the driver's seat of the crashed vehicle.

'Thanks Sarge,' she murmured. 'Can you get ballistics to do a check on these and compare them to the rifle.'

He nodded. The door snicked quietly closed behind him as he retreated into the police station's main work area.

'Read the prisoner their rights please, Constable Bayden,' Rosie said without looking up from the paperwork in her hand.

Mark's voice droned on in the background while Rosie absorbed the interesting information before her.

'I don't want a lawyer. I've done nothing wrong, it was an accident so let's just get this over with so I can go home.'

Rosie settled into a chair with Mark positioned on her left. She stared at the prisoner seated across the table from her and said, 'We are required by law to record all interviews. Everything on the video and audio recordings will be time and date stamped. Do you consent to us recording our talk today?' she asked.

'Yes, yes...get on with it.'

Rosie nodded to Mark. 'Present at today's interview,' he began, 'Detective Rosie Bloom and Constable Mark Bayden. For the recording will you please identify yourself.'

'Gil Connors.'

Rosie raised her eyebrows and said, 'Full name please sir.'

'Gilbert Moresque Connors.'

'Thank you. Now Gil,' she said, clasping her hands together on the table in front of her and giving him a small friendly smile, 'Can you please tell me what happened out on the road tonight.'

Gil gave his shackled wrist a wriggle and asked, 'Do I really need to be handcuffed for this?'

'I'm sorry Gil, its standard procedure I'm afraid. If you just answer my questions fully this shouldn't take long, then we can all get out of here.'

Gil tilted his golden head slightly to the side and gave a disarming smile. 'Okay, fair enough. Well, Steve Young and I were driving along the highway. We were out searching for the woman who went missing from Rivers Run.'

'You were a long way from the homestead. I wouldn't have thought a woman on foot could possibly have walked that far in the dark.'

'We didn't know she was on foot, we were just told to pair up and search.'

'Alright, sounds reasonable. So, who was driving and how did the RAV4 get wrecked?'

'Steve was driving – the car is her personal vehicle and it was very generous of her to use it for work. She may have been driving a touch too fast, but we were concerned for Kelsey's safety. I hear she's been through a lot lately. Anyway, we'd gone far enough and had just decided to turn back when a steer bolted out onto the road. Steve didn't have time to brake. She hit it – hard.'

Rosie nodded. The damage sustained by the four-wheel-drive matched what you'd expect to see from hitting a large animal at speed. The skid marks leading up to the impact told a different story. Someone had been fooling around, swerving and skidding from side to side while they drove.

'Why the rifle?'

'The bloody steer wasn't dead. It was making a hell of a racket, sickening it was. You can't leave an animal injured like that, so Steve got out her rifle and put it down.'

'Took three shots – that must have been one tough steer.'

'She wanted to make sure it was dead. Plus, I think she was a little angry about her car and pulled the trigger a couple of times.'

More than a little angry, thought Rosie, there was evidence that the rifle butt had been used as a club to bash the poor animal. Rosie just hoped that it was already dead at the time.

'What happened next?'

'Steve was checking out the damage to her vehicle when she slipped in the blood on the road. As she fell the rifle went off. She shot herself.'

Okay, thought Rosie, there was at least three blatant lies in his statement already. There was no indication that they were about to turn the vehicle back. In fact the skid marks on the road indicated either the driver was hot-dogging or that there was a tussle going on in the cab. And Steve did not slip in blood and shoot herself – Gil and Steve were grappling for the gun when it discharged. Well at least the police vehicle dash-cam had recorded that very clearly, so Rosie had evidence of Gil's involvement in the shooting.

Time to apply some pressure.

She glared over the top of her glasses at Gil and said, 'That's not what we saw when we drove up, was it constable.'

She flicked her glance sideways at her partner. He was shaking his head. She returned her glare to Gil and said, 'Tell Mr Connors what we witnessed constable.'

Mark said in a clear voice, 'It looked to us as if you were fighting for control of the rifle.'

Gil stared at Rosie and a touch of angry red colour flamed across his cheeks. 'I don't know what you think you saw but we weren't fighting. Steve was just a little out of control so I was taking the weapon from her hand when she slipped and it went off.'

Gil's version seemed to be a very loose interpretation of the facts. It was time to shake him up.

'You two are lovers aren't you?'

Gil nodded with a smirk.

To throw him off-stride Rosie said, 'Tell me what happened when you spoke with Bull Morgan on the banks of Annie River tonight?'

'I didn't. I was nowhere near the river.'

'Well, your footprints say otherwise.'

Beetling his eyebrows together Gil gave an excellent performance of looking puzzled. He used a fingertip to clear the frown on his brow, flashed an endearing smile and said, 'Those footprints are probably from when I was fishing this afternoon. I was down on the bank by the fallen tree.'

'Fishing with a rifle?' Rosie held up a hand to stop him and continued, 'We have the shell casing to prove it.'

'Well, there was a snake...'

'Just to be clear, Gil, you're saying – you did not go to the river tonight, did not see or speak with Charlie Morgan or Kelsey Delaney and that your footprints were made when you went fishing this afternoon.'

'Yeah, that's right detective. Why?'

'Bull Morgan and Kelsey Delaney were either pushed or fell into the river and a rifle was used to shoot at them as they were washed away in the current.'

A look of contrived concern settled on Gil's face. 'Oh my God – that's terrible. I need to leave, get back to Rivers Run. GG will need me. It's not that long ago she lost her husband, now her brother's dead – she's going to be devastated.'

'Why would Bull Morgan's sister need you?'

Gil's eyelids began to rapidly blink. 'We're getting married, after the socially acceptable grieving period for her husband is over of course. It's so sad she now has to cope with the loss of Bull.'

'I thought you'd be happy he was out of the way. That was the intent with the anonymous letter wasn't it? Get Charlie Morgan investigated, even locked away for the murder of his wife.' Gil smirked. 'So what does Steve think about you marrying, GG? I mean she's your lover, she might want to marry you herself.'

Gil laughed. 'Not going to happen. Can I go now? I need to go comfort Georgina over the terrible loss of her brother.'

'Oh, didn't I say, so sorry' said Rosie keeping her smirk hidden, 'Charlie Morgan isn't dead. He and Kelsey Delaney were pulled from the river at Annie Bridge. They had a very interesting story to tell.'

The smile left Gil's face and all colour left his face. Rosie poured on the pressure, hoping to get Gil riled and talking.

'Not the smartest move by you and Steve, exposing yourselves like that. Tell me, which one of you was driving the car that ran Josh Elliot down?'

'It wasn't a car.'

Rosie's eyebrow lifted slightly in surprise. Suddenly Gil became smug, his eyes shone with humour. 'You didn't know that, did you? Steve hired a motorbike. She said the helmets and leathers would be good disguises. I didn't know what she intended when we went for our bike ride.'

'What did you think she meant when she said helmets and leathers were a good disguise?'

Gil shrugged and stuck out his bottom lip before pulling it back in his mouth with his teeth.

'So how was Josh Elliot killed?'

'Steve whacked him with a baseball bat as we sped past on the motorbike. He didn't even see it coming – flew through the air and landed on the road. The wheels of the bike went over him.'

'Steve used a baseball bat and ran over a man all while steering a motorbike at top speed. You, of course had nothing to do with it. Come on Gil, that's a little far-fetched. I think I'll ask Steve for her version. I bet she'll be very interested to hear she's getting blamed for everything.'

'S-s-Steve? Where is she?'

'It's about time you showed some concern, after all Steve is your sister isn't she?'

'Half-sister – different fathers.' Gil squirmed in his seat and began muttering to himself. 'But she can't be alive – the gun was under her chin when it went off. I made sure of it.' He stared down at his cup of water, his face blank. Suddenly he began to laugh softly. 'As kids we were always close. Mum had an abusive boyfriend. They'd get drunk together and when she'd passed out he'd come looking for

Steve and me, to have a little fun he'd say. After the first couple of times we got smart and hid in the attic where he couldn't find us. We moved a mattress up there and then we started having our own fun. We enjoyed deceiving everyone over the years. Then Steve learnt she could use sex to get men talking, so we came up with a scheme to fleece them for as much as we could get. Old Slab Johnson is a perfect example. Boy does he love to talk, and so casual with his computer and banking passwords. I had no problem getting into his accounts. Stupid mug, fancy thinking that someone like Steve was really turned on by his ugly old mug or that he knew how to satisfy her. I was the only one who could do that.' Gil giggled. He finger combed his blond fringe back neatly on his head then dropped his hand to his lap.

'So, what changed?' asked Rosie, leaning forward and taking a sip from her water, washing the bile back down her throat. Mark's lip was twisted in disgust. Rosie tapped his ankle with the toe of her boot. He quickly glanced at her. She gave a slight shake of her head. He straightened his features to stare blankly at the warped man on the other side of the table.

'It was around about May this year, Slab started bragging about how he was getting Elliot to organise an auditor to come and look at his books. It took Steve all of two minutes to pump all the information we needed to know from his empty head.' Gil rocked his head from side to side. 'I couldn't allow an audit, now could I. I've got a very lucrative business going and when you're the book-keeper with clients who know diddly squat about spreadsheets you don't want anyone coming in and messing that up. Steve and I talked it over and we decided that if we got rid of Elliot the audit wouldn't happen. So in June we both went to Perth to take care of him.'

'Is that when you met Britt?' asked Rosie, laying Britt's photo face up on the table in front of him.

He stared at it. He gently stroked his finger down her cheek and said, 'No that was last year. Steve picked her up in a nightclub – literally. Britt tripped over Steve's out-thrust foot. Steve was always doing stuff like that, so she could pick up girls for us to share.' He continued to stare at the photo as he said, 'This is a nice shot, can I keep it?'

'No, Gil, you can't. It belongs to her family. Tell me why she had to die?'

'Because we were careless and let slip that we were from Mt Ibour. It wouldn't have mattered except Britt telephoned from Perth Airport, said she was flying to Mount Ibour for a while, maybe even long term if she could pick up some work. She wanted to know if we could continue our little *ménage à trois*. That was bad – I couldn't risk her telling anyone about Steve and me.'

Rosie was sickened by his words but kept her expression blank. She didn't want the well to dry up.

'So, tell me what happened.'

'I only know what Steve told me. I was away in Broome at the time working on something else. From what I can gather Steve rang Britt on her mobile and guided her to where she'd parked. She told Britt she'd hurt her ankle and couldn't walk. Once the girl was in the car she gave her a bottle of drugged water to knock her out. Then took her somewhere out in the bush and strangled her.'

'What happened to Britt's things, do you know?'

'She buried it.'

'Where?'

Gil gave a shrug but the small dimple at the side of his mouth told Rosie he was holding something back. She decided to come back to the question later.

'So tell me about Nari Quartermaine.'

'Who?' asked Gil. He turned sideways in his seat, hooked his elbow over the back of the chair and settled his spine against the wall. The position looked uncomfortable with his shackled arm tucked between his body and the table but he didn't seem to notice so intent was he on getting his story right.

'Nari Quartermaine – your girlfriend.'

'Oh, Nari. She's not my girlfriend, she's just a girl from Broome I was screwing. Why?'

'She's dead...'

'No,' said Gil, plastering a realistic look of shock on his face. 'H-how sad.'

Rosie placed the sketch of Nari next to the photo of Britt. '...but you knew that already. Constable, what was Mr Connors's response when you previously showed him this sketch?'

Mark made a show of flipping through his notebook. 'Gil Connors stared at the sketch and said, *Not my type mate – nah, don't know her,*' the constable said, reading the exact quote from the copious notes he'd taken throughout the course of the investigation.

Gil squirmed in his seat. His mouth opened and closed a few times. He seemed to be having trouble coming up with an excuse for not recognising the girl. Sweat beads formed large droplets on his forehead and ran down his temple and nose. He swiped at them with his shirt sleeve.

Rosie didn't give him anymore time. 'We know Nari worked as the contracts clerk for Downey Babcock Exploration. Did you cultivate a relationship with her in order to find out about the proposed mining agreement being negotiated with Charlie Morgan?'

'What mining agreement?'

'Come on Gil, a smart guy like you wouldn't let something as lucrative as a diamond mine lease slip past you,' said Rosie, laying on the charm.

Gil gave a self-satisfied smirk and said, 'Yeah, it's true, I knew all about it. Bull thinks he's so smart and secretive but I've had access to his email account for a long time now. I probably know more about this leasing business than he does.' Gil started chuckling to himself. 'That's how I found sweet little Nari. Her name was on the emails. She wasn't hard to track down and seduce. You women love to talk after sex, don't you...I just guided her and she kept me fully in the loop about everything going on.'

'So why was Nari in Mount Ibour? Surely she wasn't part of your plans?'

'Nah, the stupid cow had her knickers in a twist – she'd heard that DBE shares were skyrocketing and the Australian Securities & Investment Commission had received a tip-off that someone in the DBE contracts department was involved in insider trading. She was worried the things she'd been doing for me might not have been quite legal. So naïve, of course they weren't legal, but that was her problem, not mine – until she made it mine by taking time off from her job in Broome and showing up on my doorstep. She was crying and wanting to know if I'd talked to anyone about her.'

'And had you?'

'No – but I did buy a few shares.'

Rosie flipped through the paperwork in front of her and found the page she wanted. She placed her forefinger under a paragraph and said, 'More than a few – according to your financial records you have invested heavily in DBE stock and are set to make a major killing when the contract is announced. Do you know who tipped ASIC off about the insider trading?'

Gil shook his head.

'Josh Elliot. He and his auditor traced the stocks and shares back to you and the last phone call Josh made was to ASIC. They want to talk to you.'

Gil's face turned purple and the muscles in his neck bulged. 'Bastard, I should have hit him harder with that bat.'

Good, anger was making him careless with his words. 'So, you're admitting to your active involvement in the death of Josh Elliot.'

'Yes,' Gil giggled. 'I swung the bat – good shot don't you think. Steve turned the bike around and we ran over him.'

Rosie's gut churned. 'And Kelsey Delaney – was she going to be another one of your conquests?'

'Little miss auditor, good God no! She's too chaste for my tastes. Do you know she won't even flirt. No, turns out Elliot had already organised the book-keeping position with her as cover while she audited Slab Johnson's accounts. I needed to waylay her before she got her hands on his books and blabbed to him what I was doing. He would have been on the phone in about two seconds flat warning all my other clients.'

'Walk me through what happened.'

Gil seemed to mentally drift away. He straightened in his chair, rested his chin on his hand. A far-away smile played across his lips as he began to relive the incident.

In a sing-song voice he said, 'Dear sweet little Nari...so dumb she believed everything I told her. I had her convinced Kelsey was blackmailing me over our affair. So I used her.'

'I can't be seen at the airport, so you'll have to pick her up,' I explained as I pushed a hypodermic needle into the plastic screw-cap bottle. The colourless drug mixed with the water and disappeared. The small hole from the needle was invisible to the naked eye.

'Nari my sweet, I want you to give this to the woman you're picking up at the airport. Her name is Kelsey Delaney and she's due in on the afternoon flight.'

"I don't want to do this Gil. I don't want to hurt anyone."

'It won't hurt her, precious. But it is super duper important she drinks it because it's a truth serum. It may make her go to sleep for a while, but when she wakes up she'll tell us everything we need to know. Then I can find out where she's hidden the documents implicating you and I can destroy them. She told me she was coming after you and if you don't pay up she's going to send you to jail. I don't want that to happen, you're too important to me.'

Nari's teeth were chattering in fright so I pulled her into my arms and kissed her deeply. It seemed to relax her because she wrapped her arms tightly around my neck. It was cloying but I played along for a while before breaking away from the embrace.

'Right, I'm heading into the office – to establish my alibi. I'll be back at nine, alright?

I wanted to be home before Nari returned from the airport, but I lost track of time – playing online poker. I raced the car into the driveway and had to slam on my brakes. Red dust flew everywhere as I narrowly avoided ramming the rear of the silver RAV4 parked in my usual parking spot. Leaning nonchalantly against the front door was Steve.

She quirked her lip, held out an open stubby of beer to me and said, "Surprise."

'What the hell are you doing here?'

"What, can't a girl come visit?"

'I thought we agreed – not until all this was over.'

"Yeah, well I missed you..." she said, running a languorous long fingernail down my cheek. Steve always knew how to make me feel good. She moved closer and our eyes met. Gently I took the stubby from her hand and lifted it for a long slow sip without breaking eye contact.

"Gil?"

Nari stood uncertainly on the footpath outside the gate. Her car was idling behind her and the auditor was slumped in the passenger

*seat. I hadn't heard her pull up so engrossed had I been in Steve. It
threw me for a moment.*

*'Nari, d-darling you're early. I wasn't expecting you until at least
9:30.' I know I stammered. I was worried about how much she'd seen.*

*"Yeah, well the plane was early and Kelsey was first passenger off.
She only had hand luggage, so it took no time at all. Is this a bad time
for you?" she asked, crossing her arms and staring at Steve with a sour
expression on her pretty face.*

*'No my darling it's not. Come on in. This is Steve – my sister. She
has just arrived – a surprise visit."*

*"Oh." Nari seemed to relax because her arms fell to her sides and
she gave Steve a tentative smile.*

"Hi," she said.

*Throwing back her head Steve smiled in amusement then twirled
her fingers in a small wave at the girl before turning to go inside.*

*Over her shoulder she murmured to me, "Bring them in, Gil. We
can't do anything with the auditor until nightfall. Let's have a little
fun in the meantime."*

*Nari was petite and dark-haired. She wore a lightweight floral
frock that swirled seductively around her lean legs. Just Steve's type!
My heart sped up in excitement.*

*The three of us lay naked on the bed. My brain was a bit fuzzy. I
must have absorbed some of Nari's spiked beer. I stared over at her face.
She was no longer so pretty, her face had contorted a bit in death.*

*Steve gave me a self-satisfied smirk. "This little visit has certainly
been fun, but it's now time to get to work."*

*I propped myself up on an elbow, watching her rise and prowl
naked around the room. She was gorgeous.*

*'Did you have to kill her now,' I asked. 'We could have done it
later, when we do the other one.'*

"*Nah, I had a better orgasm this way. Not as good as when you did that German girl. God that was such fun – remember?*"

I smiled at her enthusiasm. 'It's always fun with you, Kitten.'

Rosie slid the photo of Annalisa Wagner across the table to join the other two. She didn't speak, not wanting to break the flow of words. Gil smiled when he saw Annalisa's face and stroked his fingers over her image.

'Ahh, Annalisa,' he purred. 'She fought so hard. Steve really enjoyed that.' Gil stopped speaking and seemed lost in his memories. 'My darling sister picked her up hitching at Kelly Creek and I had two days of fun with her before Steve took her away. She never did tell me where she put the body.' He frowned at the photo. 'Why are you showing me this? I wanted to talk about Nari – now where was I?'

As a prompt Rosie said, 'It's always fun with you, kitten...'

The sing-song recital continued.

Steve opened the wardrobe. The reek of dirty socks and sour shoes knocked her back a step making me laugh.

"*Geez Gil, you ever heard of air freshener?*"

I watched, aroused as her breasts swayed while she pulled the cleanest looking outfits from the pile on the cupboard floor.

She tossed a set of clothes over to me, smirked and said, "Get dressed, lover boy and find us something to put the girl in."

I pulled on the clothes, knelt at the foot of the bed and fished out a long, empty, pink sports bag. Together we rolled Nari into the bag and zipped it up. While Steve fossicked around in the jumble of discarded clothing on the floor looking for the car keys, I went to check on sleeping beauty. She was still out cold on the lounge.

Steve collected up Nari's handbag, dress and shoes, packed everything into a paper bag she found in the kitchen. I double checked the street was dark and deserted before we loaded both girls into the back of the car.

It took us an hour to drive out to Heartbreak Hill.

'So tell me what happened at the well. Why didn't you kill Kelsey?'

'The drug must have worn off. She came around just as we were preparing to drop Nari down the well. Bitch put up one hell of a fight and managed to somehow push me over. That got Steve all excited, another new game for her – hunt the victim. She gave chase, caught Kelsey and managed to get her hands around her throat. Somehow the bitch broke free and ran straight down the well. It was the funniest thing. We dumped Nari on top of her, buried their gear under the boab tree with the other girl's stuff and got out of there. Steve's lust was up as she'd been denied a kill, so we did a little target practice on Bull's cattle to appease her.'

'It must have been a real shock when you discovered Kelsey was alive and staying at Rivers Run.'

'Yeah, but what a scream – she's got no memory so she'll never be able to tell on us.' Gil burst into long drawn out laughter. Mark moved restlessly in his seat. Rosie reached over and put a restraining hand on the constable's arm to settle him. The laughter stopped and Gil said, 'I've finished here detective – can I talk to my sister now.'

'I'm sorry Gil, but she's dead. Don't you remember – you killed her.'

'Dead...oh that's right, she was screaming at me. I wanted to get to the airport – leave the country. We have millions stashed away in overseas bank accounts. But Steve had slipped over the edge, she wanted to go back to Rivers Run and kill everyone. I had to stop her. I made sure the barrel was under her chin...' he shook his head, 'Can I go now?'

'No Gil – you are now being charged with the murders of Josh Elliot, Nari Quartermaine, Britt Larsen, Annalisa Wagner and Steve Young. You will also be charged with the attempted murder of Kelsey Delaney and Charlie Morgan. There will also be charges of embezzlement, larceny and assault, but we will discuss them tomorrow. Take him to a cell, constable.'

Chapter Thirty-Seven

Rosie had just finished relating to Charlie and Kelsey everything she'd learnt from Gil and the fate of Steve Young when Mimi tentatively entered the kitchen. She wore tan shorts and a bright yellow tee-shirt with a daisy and the word love emblazoned in glitter across the front. Her knee-high low-heeled cowboy boots decorated with long leather thronged tassels made her short legs seem stumpier. Her black hair had recently been cut into a shoulder length bob with a blunt fringe. She looked cute and uncomfortable.

'Come on in, Mimi,' said Charlie

'Have I done something wrong, Bull?' she asked in a soft breathy voice.

'No mate, nothing wrong. I believe congratulations are in order. You and Pod hey? We hope you'll be very happy together.' Mimi's face blazed bright red.

'I'm sorry, Bull. We should have told you. I know how you feel about crew having relationships.'

'I'm not against crew members falling in love, Mimi. It's falling in lust and breaking up that causes the problems. Anyway, that's not the case here. I'll get some married quarters sorted out for you guys next week. Now, can I get you a cuppa?'

Mimi shook her head. 'No thanks, Bull.'

'Okay. Well, Detective Bloom here wants a quick word with you.'

Mimi's eyes resembled two large saucers as she turned to face the detective. Rosie held Mimi's necklace up to her. The girl relaxed. 'I just wanted to return this to you as it's not part of the investigation.'

'Thank you, detective. It was my mother's and I'd hate to lose it again,' Mimi said with a wistful smile on her lips. 'Is that it? Can I go now?'

'That's it,' said Rosie with an amused chuckle.

Mimi turned towards the door but halted when Charlie said, 'Oh, Mimi, Mrs Elliot got those cruise brochures that you wanted.' He pushed the pile towards her.

'Fantastic, please thank Mrs Elliot for me.' Mimi quickly flicked through the pile. She pulled out a thick, blue booklet with a river cruise ship on the front. 'I won't need this one. Pod and I've decided against going to Europe. The plane trip is too long. We'd rather catch a ship out of Perth or Brisbane.'

Charlie picked up the booklet of European rivers cruises and idly flipped through the pages. He stopped flipping to admire the glossy photo of a well-appointed cabin. An impossibly handsome couple stood sipping champagne on a balcony as they stared at a castle on a hill overlooking the Rhine River. The photo spoke of luxury and elegance. Charlie wondered if Kelsey would enjoy a cruise. He was about to turn the page when the tilt of the female model's head caught his eye. He took a closer look at her face and his heart nearly stopped. He must have let out a croak because all conversation in the room stopped. Everyone stared at him.

The dull ache that had been his constant companion for eight years eased.

'What's wrong?' demanded Rosie.

'Absolutely nothing,' he said, as he put his finger on the photo of the glamorous model and pushed the booklet towards her. Rosie grabbed the magazine and took a look at the photo. She lifted her puzzled gaze to his.

He placed his finger on the face of the female model, smiled and said, 'That, Detective Rosie Bloom, is my soon to be ex-wife, Amelia.' Charlie reached over and took Kelsey's hand in his. 'And now my lovely you and I can get on with our lives – together.'

Rosie smiled at the sparkle of love that shone in Kelsey's eyes.

K.A. Hudson was born in New South Wales. As a child her family moved around Australia, living and working in a variety of mining towns. She met her husband and they continued to follow the family tradition for many years. This has given her a wealth of experiences and characters to draw upon when crafting her novels.

Now retired and living in Perth, Western Australia, she is an avid reader and passionate about the written word.

For more information about K.A. Hudson please visit :

Arrowsmith Publishing: www.arrowsmithpublishing.com.au or https://kerriehudsonauthor.wixsite.com/website-1

www.ingramcontent.com/pod-product-compliance
Lightning Source LLC
Chambersburg PA
CBHW070054120726
47909CB00002B/389